STEPHANIE ALEXANDER

Mean Low Water

Mean Low Water
Red Adept Publishing, LLC
104 Bugenfield Court
Garner, NC 27529
https://RedAdeptPublishing.com/

Cover Art by Streetlight Graphics[1]

1. http://StreetlightGraphics.com

To my husband, Dr. Jeffrey Cluver

THE TIDE RISES, THE tide falls,
The twilight darkens, the curlew calls;
Along the sea-sands damp and brown
The traveler hastens toward the town,
And the tide rises, the tide falls.

—Henry Wadsworth Longfellow, "The Tide Rises, the Tide Falls"

MIDWAY UPON THE JOURNEY of our life, I found myself within a dark forest, for the straightforward pathway had been lost.

—Dante Alighieri, *Inferno*

MY OLD FRIEND, STOP a moment and think...
Your nostalgia has created a nonexistent country,
with laws alien to earth and man.

—George Seferis, "The Return of the Exile"

Prologue
Ginny, 1995

The classroom doorway frames Lisa Lightstone into an unsmiling portrait, like one of the snooty queens who glare up at us from our tenth-grade history textbooks. New kids are rarer than an albino alligator at Ashepoo High School, yet this unfamiliar girl stands there looking like a living, breathing Raphael painting in a flannel shirt and knockoff Doc Martens. Everyone else is oogly-googly about her looks, but my fascination goes beyond her pretty face. As soon as I lay eyes on her, something comes over me.

That in itself isn't out of the ordinary, because *something* comes over me pretty often. I know stuff for no reason—familiarity without explanation. My kind of déjà vu isn't limited to the distant past but stretches in all directions like a flood tide—the last century, the last month, the last hour; tomorrow, next Christmas, and fifty years from now.

Get this—sooner or later, whether past or present, it always reveals some truth.

During my childhood, my strange talent flummoxed my mother, but we did our best to understand it. Mama decided the future and the past were rivers on their way to bigger water, like the Ashepoo, the Combahee, and the Edisto flowing through the ACE Basin and dumping into the Saint Helena Sound. In the sound, that dark water churns until it's no longer part of one river or another.

Time rolls from all directions toward its own sea. When the past, present, and future blend into one shifting body of water, the currents are fast and unpredictable. Mama says I ride those currents. I'm a navigator, and my visions are readings on time's compass.

On this October afternoon, a few weeks into sophomore year, Lisa Lightstone makes my compass whirl. My brain sends electric shocks to every hair on my head. I *see* something, but I also *hear* it, like words on paper recited in my head. I've never found a better way to describe my readings.

> *Ginny and Lisa share something neither girl shares with anyone else. Ginny knows it as sure as she knows the smattering of freckles on her own nose.*

"Hell, yes," I whisper.

Lo and behold, the seat beside me in the back is empty. Lisa darts between the rows of desks like Cinderella running from the prince as her ball gown turns into rags. She sinks into the vacant chair and looks down at a hole in her jeans.

"Lisa just moved to Asheburg from West Columbia." Our teacher, Ms. Mullins, watches us through Coke-bottle glasses like Velma's from *Scooby-Doo*. "Let's make her feel welcome!"

I wonder why Lisa and her mom would plop their butts down in this Podunk town an hour south of Charleston when they could go another fifty miles and be in a real city.

"Lisa's mother is a new shift supervisor at the Walmart." Ms. Mullins gives a big ol' smile. "Next time y'all go shopping, say hello to Ms. Lightstone."

Lisa blushes as Ms. Mullins talks, like it's embarrassing that her mom works at Walmart. As if the Walmart isn't one of the most important places in Asheburg.

The Burg is within shouting distance of Chucktown, so we got the Lowcountry essentials. Oak trees dressed up in Spanish moss like old ladies wearing shawls on hot days. We got pastel houses with wide front porches, friendly folks who drink gallons of sweet tea, and antiques shops on Magnolia Street. Plantations and hunting lodges abound. We're smack in the middle of the ACE Basin, the expanse of picturesque marsh created by the lazy zigzagging of the Ashepoo, Combahee, and Edisto Rivers. As we learned in seventh-grade science, the ACE Basin is a refuge for every Southern critter imaginable. Gators, snakes, river otters, deer, feral hogs, armadillos, birds of every shape and size, and the nerviest mosquitos known to man. Asheburg smells like fishy mud, jasmine, and smoked barbeque from Joe Green's Famous Roadside Pig Stand.

But under all that Southern charm is a deep-fried helping of country reality. Look here at the dirt roads, single-wide trailers, free-roaming chickens, collapsing sheds hunkered back in the woods, and fields full of those magic mushrooms that make you trip balls. Every Sunday, our preachers remind their congregations that we're all destined for hell. We have one McDonald's, one Taco Bell, one Wendy's, a Piggly Wiggly, and two gas stations. Honestly, the Walmart is the center of the universe in Asheburg. No shame in working there.

Someone needs to help Lisa chill out, so I whisper, "Don't sweat it."

She looks at me like we're in French class and I'm speaking German. Her huge eyes have thick black lashes that don't need mascara. "Huh?"

"We all got problems."

Well, not *all* of us. My best friends are the swanky kids in town, and my boyfriend, Makepeace Smith, lives on a plantation on the South Edisto River. His father is the richest lawyer in Colleton County. As for me, Mama always says one more DUI from my father will put us on the state's tab.

"Something to say to the class, Ginny?" Ms. Mullins asks.

"No, ma'am."

Lisa watches me with eyes that are every color a human eyeball can be—green and brown and gray and gold all mixed together. Her right one twitches, and goose bumps race down my arms.

I want to drag her out of the classroom, but that will go over like a lead balloon with Ms. Mullins. My genius-level test scores and my failure to live up to them already drive her crazy. Kidnapping the new girl won't get me any extra credit. As usual, my grades are crap, so I need the points. I'll wait for a better opportunity to ask Lisa if her hair is doing the running man on her head.

Excitement makes me extra jittery, and my butt already has natural chair repellent. Mama believes other people like me must exist, but Asheburg is such a little bitty town. I'm about the only redhead, so I'm surely the only navigator. My whole life, it's been only me, Virginia Emily Blankenship—the lonely teenage psychic or amateur prophet or whatever the hell I am, though I like Mama's version. A navigator is someone on an adventure. I always want adventure, even though I live in the sticks.

Ms. Mullins carries on with our unit on Henry VIII and the rest of the Tudors. I actually like hearing about H-Eight and all his wives—so much drama—but Lisa is more interesting. We stare each other down, Lisa with her straight dark-brown hair hanging down her back like draperies in a funeral parlor, and me with my strawberry-blond waves. She's tall, and I'm short. I'm pale, and she's sort of swarthy. Back in the day, they called Anne Boleyn swarthy, and Lisa is the same—like she's got a tan all year long. Her nose is arched. Mine is a stub. She's got those kaleidoscope eyes. Mine are pale blue. Two white girls couldn't look more different, yet the universe has told me we have something in common.

"Anne Boleyn had many enemies," Ms. Mullins says. "Why?"

Mama says Ms. Mullins is one of them feminazis, but she's cool for a teacher. I agree with her about a lot of stuff, especially when she hints about men being a total pain in the ass for all of human history. I don't usually say anything productive, but I raise my hand.

"A lot of people hated Anne because she was uppity," I say. "She was damn smart and damn feisty. She said what she thought and didn't give a *damn* what anyone else thought about it."

"Language, Ginny, but you're on the right track. While Henry liked Miss Anne's spunk before they got married, it wore on his nerves once she was his wife."

"Sounds like my mama and daddy," says my best friend, Rollo, who is a total hoot. "But if Daddy chops off her head, we'll all starve. Daddy can't even microwave a frozen burrito."

Everyone laughs, but Ms. Mullins is about sick of us—me with my *damn this* and *damn that* and skinny-ass Rollo Blanchard with his too-long white-blond hair and his big fat mouth.

"Morbid. Would your parents approve, Mr. Blanchard?"

"No, ma'am." He winks at me, and when she turns around, he mimes chopping off my head.

"Who were some of Anne's enemies?" Ms. Mullins asks.

To my surprise, New Girl Lisa raises her hand. "There was Mary Tudor, Henry's first daughter."

"Very good! Anne didn't give Henry the son he wanted, and Mary was a threat to Anne—"

"She is my death," Lisa says. "And I am hers."

"Pardon?"

"'She is my death, and I am hers.' Anne said that about Mary."

"Now *that* shit is morbid," Rollo whispers.

Everyone cuts up again.

"*Language*, Rollo!" Ms. Mullins says, but she cares more about us participating for once than she does about cussing. "History is often morbid, y'all. You're right, Lisa. Anne did say that."

Lisa blushes as if surprised by her mouth, but to me, her words are smoke—more potent than the weed I inhale with the boys in

Rollo's field at night, as mesmerizing as gray fumes over the campfires. Filled with tantalizing hints of things to come. Any glimpse into the future excites me. I crave it the way a bee craves nectar or a dog drools over a juicy bone. Even when it frightens me, I want more of the future, like my dad reaching for another liquor shot when he knows he shouldn't because he'll be driving.

Lisa Lightstone's words tickle my supernatural funny bone. Whether they came from her or they're a hidden message from whatever made me this way, I can't say. But I can't *wait* to talk to her.

Chapter 1
LeeLee, 2015

I try not to think about Makepeace Smith. In the curriculum of my life, he's Ancient History. Thirteen years have passed since I last laid eyes on him, and two decades have slipped by since I first fell in love with him. Peace is on my mind anyway because my husband, George Clayton Moretz, Jr., Esquire, keeps sending me links to waterfront lots.

I sit at my desk in my law office on State Street in downtown Charleston and scroll through Clay's texts. When I need a break, I stare out the window. Past the uneven cobblestones of Chalmers Street, the steeple of St. Philip's Church pierces the springtime sky like the good Lord flipping the bird at the devil. I pop blueberries into my mouth and pray to the patron saint of long-time spouses—whoever she may be. I say *she* because that much-called-upon saint must be a woman.

Clay's descriptions of the links are all variations on a theme.

One acre, 9 feet MLW

.75 acre, 6 feet MLW

Almost two acres, 15 feet MLW!!

Clay is obsessed with buying a plot of waterfront land, where we'll someday build our ultimate Lowcountry-lifestyle dream house. He considers only properties with a minimum five-foot mean low water, meaning at low tide, the depth is at least five feet. Without true deep water access, we couldn't tie up a decent-sized boat at the dock.

He wants the real deal, even if it means building a dock long enough for an NFL quarterback to practice passes. The main dock at Peace's family plantation, Saltmarsh, is so long, I have to squint to see the big house from the boat lift. It juts into the South Edisto River like an exclamation point on pilings. In addition to the main dock, the Smiths have a short one, and that was where the mean low water got us into boating trouble as teenagers. At high tide, we used to tie up at the short dock and save ourselves the hassle of hauling our boat supplies down the long dock. At low tide, however, a veritable bog surrounds the short dock, nothing but pluff mud—the viscous black marsh muck that sucks the shoes right off my feet—and razor-sharp oyster shells.

The fishy scent of pluff mud dominates all my memories of Saltmarsh. *Au de Pluff Mud* isn't pleasing like the perfumes of pine trees, flowers, or rain, but I love it anyway. It's the smell of home and freedom and first love.

For years after Peace left town and Asheburg and Saltmarsh faded into my past, one sniff of pluff mud awakened the strange powers only my old friend Ginny Blankenship knew about. When we were teenagers, she used to call it *navigating*, but that never sat quite right with me. Like so many other things in life, Ginny and I understood our abilities differently. She always thought of it as a gift. To me, it's a curse.

No matter how much I love the scent of pluff mud, I learned long ago to ignore it, lest I live my life in a haze of erratic, time-bending readings. Still, thoughts of tides and pluff mud always take me back to Saltmarsh. Saltmarsh makes me think of Peace. That simple and that complicated.

I open Clay's latest message about a lot on John's Island, not far from Kiawah. Our rush-hour commutes will go from five minutes to over an hour if we live that far from town, but Clay has a bee buzzin' in his boxer shorts. My framed photo of Ruth Bader Ginsburg joins me in an exasperated sigh. A couple of years ago, Clay was equally obsessed with moving downtown, into Charleston's fabled historic district. We just moved into our house on Council Street a year ago. We're two thirtysomething lawyers living in a quirky house on a peaceful street a block off South Battery with our three young sons. I feel like we've made it big, but Clay always wants more, more, more.

Clay means well, but lately, we aren't reading the same chapter, let alone on the same page. As a wannabe novelist who has never completed a book, I have zero literary street cred. Regardless, I always relate life to stories. While Ginny used to think of herself as a *navigator*, I've always considered myself a *storyteller*.

Everyone has a narrator in their head, but mine speaks loud and clear about strange things beyond my memories, ruminations, and day-to-day activities. My head contains my story but also bits and pieces of other people's, stories of time long past and time that hasn't happened yet.

Ginny had her way of understanding it back then. I have mine. Who can say who's right or wrong about something that shouldn't even be?

In my internalized collection of personal fairy tales, "The Tale of Clay and LeeLee" began as a great journey in which we created a magnum opus of American family life. Instead, after falling in love during law school and spending thirteen years together, we're wandering through unexpected plot holes and disappointing character arcs. Clay thinks a lovely view and a boat at the dock will solve everything. Or perhaps he simply wants to move farther from town to hide from his mistakes.

General spousal malaise morphs into true despondency, so I refocus on that which carries its own challenges but feels under my control. I set down my phone and seize my computer mouse like a life ring. With a wiggle of my wrist, my dueling computer monitors blaze to life.

As a family court attorney, I've been working on a pro bono custody action for a client of My Sister's House, the local domestic violence shelter. I probably take on too many nonpaying clients, but given my haphazard childhood and the emotionally draining atmosphere of high-asset domestic litigation, those victories are worth it.

Britt, the firm's perky blond paralegal who keeps the place running and the window boxes in bloom, pokes her head into my office. "LeeLee, a guy is here to see you."

"A client?" My cursor hovers over an email from the shelter's caseworker.

"No. He says he knows you personally."

"Hmm. Did he give his name?"

Britt leans into the office and lowers her voice. "Something weird. Not sure I heard him right."

"I have a few friends with those kinds of names. Don't we all around here?"

"This was unusual even for Charleston. Something like... Prince?"

"Don't know a Prince."

"Prince Smith?"

My stomach flip-flops. "Peace Smith?"

"That it? Tall guy with dark hair?" Her voice becomes a conspiratorial whisper. "Really freakin' good-looking?"

"Yes." My pulse hammers in my ears. "Yes, to it all."

"Do you want to meet him in the conference room?"

"Give me a minute, okay? I'll... ah. Yeah. The conference room. I'll be right out."

Britt gives me a thumbs-up and closes the door.

My hands shake as I sip from the water bottle I keep on my desk. My phone dings. I swipe across a text from Clay. *Did you get my message about JI lot?*

With my past blasting into my professional life like a high-velocity skeet target, I have to relegate Clay's obsession to the back burner. I set down my phone again, stand, and check my reflection in the mirror across from my desk. I run a brush through my dark hair. I'm thirty-five, but miraculously, given the stress of the past year, I have no gray yet. Startled greenish eyes look back at me.

Maybe it's someone else. Do I know a Pete Smith? *Pete* sounds like *Peace*. That must be it. Someone named Pete Smith. A referral from another client. Believing it isn't him is a relief. No one has heard a peep from Peace and Ginny in so long. Our friends half-jokingly speculate they're living in Costa Rica in a hippie commune.

There's no way Makepeace Bryant Smith, Jr., is in my conference room, like I used to find him in the Ashepoo High School parking lot or on our apartment's back porch in college—waiting for me. Or Ginny. Or both of us.

A quick whisk of a lint roller over my dark-green dress—part of my routine before meeting with any client. I grab a legal pad and a pen and open my office door.

Nope. It's *not* Peace. But just in case, I pause to put on some lip gloss.

LESS THAN A MINUTE later, I sit across the conference table from Peace Smith. I imagine my trembling, glossy lower lip glistening in the beam of sunlight that bounces off the polished mahogany.

I didn't say anything as I settled into my chair, and Peace was mute too. Perhaps he read my name on the business cards in the waiting room—*Lisa "LeeLee" Lightstone Moretz, Esquire*—and thought it was someone else named Lisa Lightstone upon whom he'd bestowed a nickname that stuck for twenty years. Another woman who had passed the bar exam and married into the legal dynasty of the Columbia Moretz family while he'd traipsed around the southeast, doing drugs and wasting his tremendous potential.

We stare at each other across the no-man's-land of the conference table. I know how the past thirteen years have changed me—the post-baby curves I fight into mature yet still-pleasing submission, the forehead lines I treat with organic moisturizers and occasional Botox, and my nose that seems to get a little bigger with each passing year.

Peace's hair is that frustrating salt-and-pepper color that works for men yet sends most women hauling ass to the nearest salon for highlights. He's lost weight since his beer-guzzling college football player days. Thinness lends a sharper chisel to a jawline that always seemed carved from marble. He's almost too thin, which reminds me of the alcohol-soaked and drug-fueled reasons he left town in the first place. His eyes are bigger than ever, dark azure melting into sky blue around his pupils like crushed hydrangea petals. Like a proper grown-up South Carolina boy, he wears a pair of beat-up brown boots, khakis, and a blue-checkered button-down shirt.

When he finally opens his mouth, I steel myself against his voice. A hint of wry amusement always hid under the rumble when he whispered in my ear as we lay wrapped around each other in my twin bed. Despite the gray hair, his voice remains the same. I remind myself I'm married, even if my husband forgot for a while.

"You look good, Lee. But that's no surprise." Peace glances around at the shining conference room. "None of this is surprising. You were always going to make things happen."

"Darlene Donnelly's name is on the door. I'm the associate, not the principal. Now, why are you here?"

"Right to it, huh? I must look like shit, myself."

I switch to deposition mode. "Answer the question, please."

He tips his chin at me. "Now *that* is a complicated question, Counselor. Do you mean why am I here right this moment? Or why am I here in general?"

"You know what—forget why you're here. Where've you *been*, Peace?" I check the time on the antique cuckoo clock on the wall. "I have a conference call in an hour, then I'm going home to my kids. So get started."

"I've been everywhere. Florida. Myrtle Beach. Ended up in Boone, North Carolina. The... you know. My *issues*."

"Booze? Drugs?" My eyes narrow. "You better not have drugs in this office."

"I don't! I've been clean for well over a year."

"That's great. It took you over a year to come home? Does anyone else know you're here? Jessalyn or Palmer? The rest of the boys?"

"I'm staying with Tommy," he says. "Been there for about a month. Rollo knows since he and Tommy hang out regularly. My brother, Drew, and Ginny's mom know."

"You've been in town a *month*, and you haven't talked to—"

"Just listen, okay? Let's go back to why I'm here right now."

I give him permission to continue by sitting back in my chair and tapping my pen against my legal pad.

"My dad is sick," he says. "Did Jess tell you? She must have heard from someone in our family. Her mom. My brother. One of our other hundred-odd cousins."

"She mentioned it via text a couple of months ago, but I live downtown. Palmer lives in Mount Pleasant, and Jess is back in Asheburg. I have three kids. Palmer has *five*, and Jess has a baby. We haven't seen each other in forever." I shrug. "But anyway, yeah. I was sorry to hear it. Melanoma, right?"

"Cancer took Mom. Now it's taking Dad too." Unlike most small-town South Carolinians, who talk about our mamas and even cling to our daddies, Peace takes a more formal approach with his parents. "Remember how Ginny predicted they'd both die of incurable cancer?"

He mentions Ginny's prophetic power as if it's no big deal—like bringing up a mildly annoying habit or an old T-shirt she always wore.

"Uh. Yeah," I say. "I think so."

"But she didn't know when. Or how."

My pen starts tap-tap-tapping again. Whenever our friends chat about Ginny's abilities, I get nervous. I never embraced my oddities like she did. Peace still doesn't know Ginny and I are two peas in a supernatural pod, and I have zero reason to own up to it now.

I've spent my whole life working to calm the storm inside me. Even if I fall face-first into a vat of pluff mud, I rarely have readings anymore. Ginny always took the opposite approach and kept trying to get herself struck by lightning. One reason I'm a practicing attorney, while Ginny shot off the rails long ago like the Little Engine That Couldn't Keep Her Shit Together.

"I could never bring myself to tell either of my parents," he says. "Why scare them if she didn't know details? But now I feel guilty. If I told him to go to the dermatologist—"

"Old Peace wouldn't wear sunscreen on the boat while deep-sea fishing. Sunscreen is for pansies, remember?"

Peace chuckles. "Oh yeah. He has a long list of sissy behaviors."

"How long does he have?"

"A couple of months. I didn't come back for so long because I couldn't face him after how I let him down. But now I need to mend the fence before the Four Horsemen of the Apocalypse bust through it. And I want to help Drew manage things. He's been dealing with Dad and Saltmarsh on his own. I wasn't ready to see *everyone*, but thanks to the Asheburg grapevine, Cheryl heard I'm back. She's been blowing me up, looking for information about Ginny."

"Ginny is Cheryl's only child. Of course she wants information."

"I wish I could give it to her, but I don't have any."

"Ginny's not here with you?"

"No. We broke up about two years ago."

"So where is she now?"

"I really don't know. She left me for another guy when we were living in Myrtle, but it had been bad between us for a long time. We were both using. And you know how Ginny is."

I nod, though Ginny Blankenship always sort of defied explanation, from her unruly charm to her otherworldly readings to her inhuman tolerance for hard liquor.

"She got worse," he says. "Especially the readings. Everything was a vision, like the drugs were clouding up that part of her mind. She mixed up dreams with reality. She thought I cheated on her and everyone stole from her and people were following her."

"Maybe schizophrenia?"

"Anyone who doesn't understand the truth of Ginny's readings would think that. The last few years were one long nightmare. One night, she attacked me. Went crazy like a rabid cat, scratching and spitting. She packed a bag, and she was gone."

"Did you look for her?" I ask. "Or go to the police? Call her mom?"

"No. I should have, but I was so messed up myself. I moved to North Carolina soon after. Ended up in Boone. It's a great town. The mountains were good for my soul. I got sober up there." He leans on his elbows and rubs his eyes. "Sounds terrible, but it was easier without Ginny and her hoodoo clouding my thinking."

Peace's association of Ginny's power with dark magic justifies my anxiety about discussing the supernatural.

I return the conversation to the real world. "Did you tell all this to Cheryl?"

"Yeah, but she doesn't believe me." He rubs his eyes again, hard. When he opens them, they're bloodshot. "She's... pissed."

"She *should* be, since you didn't tell her that her daughter was missing."

"It's more than that. She thinks I had something to do with it."

"With what?"

"With Ginny vanishing. She even accused me of..."

"Of hurting her?"

He nods miserably.

"Good lord, Peace. It's not out of the realm of the reasonable. Most women who die violently are killed by their intimate partners—"

"Shit, Lee. You think I'd do something like that? You *know* me. Better than anyone."

He takes my hand across the table, and my pulse picks up of its own accord, like a three-stroke engine after a hard tug.

"No. I don't." I stand. "You should go."

He gets up and walks around the table. I back away. Then something happens that's more confusing than a peek into the future and more disturbing than a glimpse of the past.

Please believe me, Lee. That matters to me more than anything. You have to believe me.

The most dreaded kind of reading. The ones I fear anyone discovering. Who wants to interact with someone who unintentionally reads their very thoughts? I hold up both hands, as if I can block Peace's thoughts with my upraised palms.

Dumbass, you're freaking her out... Stop it. Calm down. Stop it.

"Stop it!" I yelp.

He flinches as if I've punched him in the stomach, but at least his thoughts go silent. Any more, and I might jump out the window behind me and land in Britt's flower boxes.

"I'm sorry," I say. "It's just a lot—"

"No, LeeLee. Hell, *I'm* sorry. I'm sorry I even came here."

I retreat into one of my old defense mechanisms against the readings. I picture my childhood self with my hands over my ears. Little LeeLee sings "The ABC Song" over Peace's thoughts. *Ayebeecee... jaykayelemenopee... doubluexwye... zee.*

"You being here is so out of the blue... I think I'm in shock." Despite—or maybe because of—the weird situation, I giggle. I touch the old light switch on the wall behind me. "*Zzzzzt.*"

He smiles. "There's the sound I love. Listen, I don't have the right to ask you for a damn thing. But Cheryl is threatening to go to the cops. And sue me. And all kinds of other stuff I don't understand."

The legal ramifications distract me from my psychic worries. "I'm no criminal defense attorney. Still, while she can go to the police, she has no *proof* anything bad happened to Ginny. I can't see the cops doing anything more than asking you perfunctory questions. I'm not a civil litigation attorney, either, but if she's talking about a wrongful death suit, it's the same logic. Not much of a case when Ginny is probably basking on a beach beside the Gulf of Mexico right now, telling people's fortunes and downing Fireball shots."

He exhales. "Thank you. I needed to hear that from someone with a clue."

"I don't have much of a clue beyond criminal law and torts from law school. But I think you're okay, legally."

"I truly am sorry I came here. Just... Tommy means well, but he's always swum on the surface, you know?"

"Yeah. He can't stand anything rocking his center-console fishing boat."

"He can barely handle his own drama with his ex-wife and kids. And Rollo—"

My affectionate chuckle cuts him off. "Can't be serious for five minutes, bless his heart."

"Y'all never gave Rollo enough credit. He's been cool about everything in his way."

"If you're trying to stay sober, should you hang out with them? From what I've heard, they're both regulars on the bar scene. And they smoke more weed than Cheech and Chong."

"I don't go to the bars with them. They don't smoke around me. I found a good AA meeting on Sullivan's Island. At least the boys are supportive. My brother is pissed I'm home, and he's got his own family." He holds up his phone. "Seems like *everyone* has been busy making beautiful families. I googled all of y'all. Stalked you on Facebook too."

"What? Good Lord. I didn't know you were on there."

"I only lurk. I'm too embarrassed by how I turned out to have a real account. You're obviously busy with your family too. But I needed to talk to someone who knows me, even if she thinks she doesn't."

"I'm not sure what to say." It's the truth.

"Don't say anything right now. Except you believe I didn't hurt Ginny. I'm not that kind of person."

I think of the sweet, gentle young man he was. I watched him slip down a slide into a hell of his own making, greased by disappointment, sadness, and a craving for painkillers and hard liquor. "I believe you. I know you're not."

"Thanks. Now I got one thing going for me." He flops into his chair. "Ginny's mom won't back off without a fight, and my brother is determined to make things harder between me and Dad. I tell you, Lee. If Ginny was here, she'd predict this shit will get a lot more complicated before it gets easier."

Chapter 2
Ginny, 1995

A week after she appeared in my history class, I invite Lisa Lightstone to my house after school. I've sort of been stalking her. I offered to help her find her classroom when she appeared lost in the hallway. I sat beside her in the library and asked questions about the book she was reading, *Carrie* by Stephen King. Creeped me out when she told me what it was about—friendless high-school girl gets revenge on the cool kids—but I still asked her to sit with us at lunch.

My best friends, Palmer and Jessalyn, were unsure at first because our tradition was to sit with our boyfriends—Palmer with Tommy, Jess with Landon, and me with Peace. They questioned the wisdom of inviting the pretty new girl to sit with us, as all the boys were curious about her. An attractive new person hasn't shown up at our school since Tommy moved to Asheburg from Walterboro in the fifth grade.

I reminded them that Rollo always sat with us, too, so Lisa wouldn't be a seventh wheel. Then I appealed to their sense of sisterly compassion for the lonely newcomer. Palmer is a total sap, so she talked Jess into it. Funnily enough, Jess liked Lisa right away. Lisa's sort of shy, but she's funny as shit when she does say something. Those two bonded over their snappy comebacks.

Home is about five miles outside of Asheburg, in an unincorporated community called Burnt Mill, or just *the Mill*. Cornfields and sod farms used to surround my house, but real estate bigwigs like

Rollo's dad realized people want the deep water land. The only water around my house comes from kids in the neighboring trailers making homemade Slip 'N Slides out of old shower curtains, so no one is hankering to buy it.

Peace has been driving me to school since he got his license at the end of last year. The drive takes him around his ass to get to his elbow—Saltmarsh is only a few miles from Ashepoo High School—but when a girl's boyfriend drives, he can't let her ride the bus. When we pile in to his pickup truck, I think about offering Lisa the passenger seat, since she's so much taller than I am, but girlfriends don't sit in the back, so she sits behind me in the truck's cramped cab. Since I'm nice, I scoot my seat forward until my knees hit the dashboard.

Peace pulls out of the school parking lot. "You okay back there, Lisa?"

She smiles at us with her knees near her chin. "Sure. I'm good."

"You look like a pretzel," I say.

"Slap some mustard on me, and that's about right."

Peace and I laugh, and she blushes. That girl can blush with the best of them.

"You sure you're ready to meet Miss Cheryl and Mr. Burt?" Peace asks.

"Are they scary?" she asks.

"Ha. Not scary. A little..." Peace pokes my thigh. "What would you call them, G-Love?"

"My parents? I call them wackos." I grin at Lisa over my shoulder. "My mama is crazy in the best way. Daddy, now... he's another story. But it will only be about half past three when we get to the house. Hopefully, he hasn't started drinking yet."

Peace has seen my father's drinking for himself. He takes my hand and squeezes.

"My daddy was a drinker too," Lisa says. "He ran off when I was five. From what my mama says, he did us a favor."

"How'd y'all end up in Asheburg?" Peace asks.

"Mama always wanted to be close to the ocean."

"You should come with us to my family's place at Edisto Beach."

"It's great," I say. "They don't even card anyone at the bars."

"Y'all have a beach house, like, *thirty minutes* away?" She sounds oddly perplexed.

Peace and I look at each other.

"Yeah," he says. "A lot of people in town do."

"I still think about the beach being someplace hours away where you go for vacation."

"Not around here," I say. "Sometimes, we go after school."

"How... cool," she whispers in awe.

Having grown up surrounded by salty water and sand my whole life, I've never thought about it. "I guess. Sounds like a dream come true for your mother."

"Yeah. She also—" The smile is gone. "She needed to get away from someone. My stepfather. Sort of. They weren't married. He wasn't very... nice. And he was getting meaner."

"Say no more," I say. "I hear you. We can't all have perfect families like the Smiths of Saltmarsh. Peace's daddy—we call him Old Peace but never to his face—can't decide if he wants our Young Peace to be an NFL quarterback or a Supreme Court justice."

Peace snorts. "He'll choose both if he can. I'd rather do something with my hands."

"You already do." I blow him a kiss and wiggle my eyebrows.

Lisa blushes again, like she might combust.

"Damn, Gin," Peace says. "Too much information. You gotta ease Lisa in."

"He means his woodworking stuff," I say. "He's real talented."

"Dad won't go for his son being some artsy-fartsy weirdo. So if my choices are football and law school, football is more likely than law school."

"He's just modest. Peace is a total nerd at heart. And the football recruiters are already calling."

"That's great," Lisa says.

"We'll see." Peace shrugs.

We drive in silence for a while, except for Peace's hip-hop mixtape. Peace mutters the words under his breath as it cycles through Cypress Hill's greatest hits. I glance in the rearview mirror. Lisa's staring at him. I keep watching until she notices me. She gives me a close-mouthed smile and looks out the window.

I don't blame her for staring at Peace. Everyone does. I'm used to it. We've been dating since the eighth grade, but we go back even farther. He gave me flowers for Valentine's Day when we were ten and asked me to be his girlfriend. I said yes then broke up with him two days later. Then Rollo was my boyfriend for a whole month in seventh grade, a Combahee Middle School record, then I broke up with him too.

The boys still tease Peace about how Rollo stole his girl for a month, but that's how it is in a small town. Everyone who isn't related dates at some point. Peace's parents would rather he date Palmer—my best friend who also happens to be my cousin—since she represents the respectable side of the Blankenship family. To Peace's mama, Lucille Monroe Smith, I'm like a stray cat she fed too many times. Now she can't get rid of me.

We drive down Magnolia Street, the main drag in town. We pass antiques shops and Old Peace's law office. Then Sweetie Pie's, the bakery where my mom works, the Marshside Diner, and the ACE of Spades, the local bar—cleverly named after the ACE Basin—where, unfortunately, everyone knows our families and we can't get served.

"Tommy Dukes and Rollo Blanchard live down that way," I say as we pass the corner of Magnolia and Monroe Streets.

The Burg's little historic district is Rhett Butler central. Double-decker porches, circular driveways with sprinkling fountains, and overhanging oak branches splayed like witches' fingers.

"They live on Camellia Street. All the streets are flowers or family names. Dukes Street, Monroe Street." I point at Peace. "Makepeace Street."

"I noticed the flowers," Lisa says. "I'm on Carnation."

"Right." It makes sense, given her mom's job at Walmart.

The town planners chose the regal flowers for the rich people's streets—Camellia, Jasmine, Azalea. On Carnation Street, the houses are a lot smaller and the neighbors rougher, but Carnation isn't as bad as Dandelion.

"Where do Jess and Palmer live?" Lisa asks.

"Past the town dock and the Proper Park."

"The Proper Park?"

"Yeah," Peace says. "Supposedly, a bunch of moms organized a petition like forty years ago for the town to set up a *proper park*. It stuck."

"Jess and Palmer and Landon Walters, too, they live in Combahee Estates," I say. "Near the yacht club, where we had to do cotillion last year. Such a pain in the ass."

"That all sounds nice." Lisa chews on her pinky nail, as if she's starting to understand how Asheburg works. While Camellia Street might be a few blocks from Carnation Street, with Combahee Estates only another mile down the road, a world of distance exists between her new rental house and my friends' places.

Peace turns off Magnolia onto Dukes Street. We pass Redemption Corner, where the First Baptist, First Methodist, First Presbyterian, and St. Mark's Episcopal Churches have an ongoing redbrick versus white clapboard standoff over which church is the prettiest and which congregation is the holiest. Once we pass the parking lot of St. Mark's, I roll down the window.

"Enough insane in the membrane." I pop out the mixtape and slide Janis Joplin into the CD player. "Let's get back to the classics."

"Whatever you say, Gin." Peace turns onto the state road that leads to Burnt Mill. "But don't blow out my speakers."

Janis starts in about Bobby McGee, and I join her. People are always shocked when such a big voice comes out of a small person like me. I rock out to Janis with my body swaying and my voice matching hers pitch for pitch, vibrato for scratchy vibrato. Peace grins, and Lisa's mouth hangs open.

I stick my head out the window. "*Hey, hey, heeeeeey!*" I call out to Bobby as if he lives in one of the trailers along the state road.

A few dogs bark, and Peace and Lisa laugh.

"Wow, Ginny," Lisa says. "Your voice is—just wow."

"Thanks, girlie."

"If I'm going into the NFL," Peace says, "Ginny will be a famous singer."

My scalp starts tingling, as if my hair has gotten too tight for my skull. My nose twitches, but no sneeze builds up behind it. That familiar, darkly knowing feeling falls over me. Like a flashback from a dream I haven't had yet.

> *Janice Joplin died at twenty-seven. Janis and Hendrix and Jim Morrison. Kurt Cobain, gone last year. Another woman with a sultry voice and black hair she wears in a bouffant will make her mark and die at that cursed age too.*

"I'll live past twenty-seven," I say. "But who knows what will happen beyond that?"

Peace pokes me, twice this time. "Hey. Gin. What are you talking about?"

I shake my head, and the reading fades. Lisa and I make mirror eye contact again.

I lean into the fresh air and inhale. "Nothing. Talking to myself."

"Don't scare LeeLee back there. You keep forgetting she just met you."

"LeeLee," I say. "I like it. Anyone call you that, Leee-sa Liiiight-stone?"

She smiles. "Nope. I hate my name. *Lisa Ann Lightstone.* Lisa is so boring. Then you add Lightstone, and it sounds like a soap opera star."

"Or worse." I mime a strip tease with my thrift-store Pearl Jam T-shirt, and Lisa and I crack up.

"Exactly! My mama claims to love Jesus, but she gave me a stripper name!"

"LeeLee it is, then," Peace says as we turn onto my dirt driveway.

Our little one-story house sits in the woods a hundred yards back from the state road. When we pull up, I get out, and Peace walks around to the passenger side to adjust the seat so Lisa can squeeze past it.

He offers her a hand. "Let me assist you, Miss LeeLee."

Lisa takes his hand and steps down to the ground. My girl is *tall.*

I have to look up at her. "Welcome to my humble home."

She smiles as she looks the place over. Probably because my house is more Carnation Street than Combahee Estates.

A shrill voice calls from behind us, "Here comes trouble!" My mama, Cheryl, walks out the front door. She's tiny and skinny, and though her face is worn from years of overnight shifts at Sweetie Pie's, she's still the prettiest mom in town.

I hope I look like her when I'm thirty-six. If I make it that far. I shake my head against that weird thought. I'm not keen on my powers of prophecy dropping hints about my death. That would be enough to drive anyone insane in the brain, for real.

"You must be Lisa," my mama says. "I'm Cheryl, sweetheart."

She insists on all my friends calling her plain old Cheryl. Not Mrs. Blankenship. Not even *Miss* Cheryl, like Peace politely said in the truck. Just her given name. Sort of scandalous around these parts. Half the time, I think of her as Cheryl myself.

"It's LeeLee," Peace says. "She's got a new Asheburg name."

"I like it! You want to come in for something to eat, Peace? Burt actually made it to work today, so it's quiet enough inside."

Every week, my daddy gets so drunk he misses a few days of work at Blankenship Electric, Incorporated. My grandpa started BEI, and Palmer's dad, my uncle Jack, keeps Daddy on as a part-time office manager out of pity for us. Believe me, no one trusts my father with any live wiring.

"No, ma'am," Peace says. "I gotta get home and study for a chemistry test."

"Mr. Smarty Pants. Hopefully, you'll rub off on Ginny."

"LeeLee is a brain too," I say. "I can tell from her answers in history class."

"Oh, gosh. Thanks, but I'm not all that—"

"Don't be shy, sweetheart." Cheryl cuts Lisa off—no, *LeeLee*—I'm already starting to think of her as LeeLee—and wags a finger at her. "If you're a scholar, you shout it from the rooftops. I hope you rub off on my Gin too."

"I don't need school, Mama. Not with my lungs. I shout in my own way."

"That you do." My mother runs a hand over my hair as Peace gets in his truck and backs down the driveway. "Y'all come in. Ginny's told me about you, LeeLee."

"Really?" LeeLee asks. "We just met."

"That may be true, but we already know the most important thing." She walks toward the house. "And that, *ladies*, is what we're going to discuss. Over some snooder-dooders."

CHERYL'S SNICKERDOODLES are legendary. Two such nonsense words together are already a mouthful, and with divine inspiration, my confused toddler's tongue dubbed those blobs of heaven-sent deliciousness *snooder-dooders*. Now it's their official name. Their little sign in the case at Sweetie Pie's says Cheryl's Famous Snooder-Dooders. Everyone in Asheburg knows about snooder-dooders.

LeeLee sits at our kitchen table.

My mother offers her signature cookies and calls them by their God-given name. "Have some snooder-dooders, sweetheart." Cheryl, the goddess of baked goods, stands beside our old yellow fridge with a blue platter in her hands. The hand-painted sign on the fruits-and-veggies wallpaper behind her reminds us this is Cheryl's Kitchen, run by Cheryl's Rules.

"Ma'am?" LeeLee looks alarmed until Cheryl removes the tinfoil from the plate. The smell of warm cinnamon fills the kitchen. My new friend beams and takes two.

"My mama hates baking," she says. "Chips Ahoy! are her idea of cookies."

"Sacrilege," Cheryl says. "Chips Ahoy! will never sully my kitchen. You'll chip a tooth on those things."

"These are yummy. What do I taste under the cinnamon? It's—"

"Lemon," I say. "Mama's had me in this kitchen, covered from my ears to my butt in flour and sugar, since I could walk. I can teach you how to make them."

"That would be fun. Thanks for being so... so nice to me." She sips the sweet tea Cheryl poured for her. "Coming to a new school has been super scary."

"I'd be totally freaked out. I've known all my friends forever. Palmer and I are related."

"On their dad's side," Cheryl says. "I'm from the Upstate. Pickens County. Towny girl who met a Clemson student while working at the Bi-Lo bakery. Fell madly in love."

"Then she got pregnant. Daddy failed out of Clemson from drinking so much. So here we are, back in the Burg."

"Do you have any brothers and sisters?" LeeLee asks.

"Nope," Cheryl says. "One Ginny is more than enough."

"Ha ha, Mama," I say with zero annoyance. I know I'm a handful.

"Everyone in Asheburg has been nice so far."

"Give it time. You're a Southerner." Cheryl wags a finger at her. "You know how we smile to your face while holding an anvil over your head."

"Our friends aren't like that," I say. "At least, not with people we *like*."

"Y'all haven't liked anyone outside your little posse for years. Last person y'all let in was Tommy—only because Palmer had a crush on him. But you'll be the latest addition to the group, LeeLee. Ginny knew right away."

"I'm not, like, complaining," LeeLee says, "but I don't see what's so special about me that you went out of your way."

Cheryl and I exchange glances.

"You want to explain, or me?" Cheryl asks.

"You go on," I say. "I'll get spazzed out talking about it."

Cheryl turns to LeeLee and stares into her face. Her intense gaze meanders between LeeLee's two eyes and her mouth. "When Ginny saw you, she *knew* y'all would be friends. Ginny often *knows* things, if you get my drift."

I can barely hold back my spazzing. "You know things, too, right, LeeLee? Things no one else knows?"

"What do you mean?" LeeLee looks like she might abandon her snooder-dooders and run out of the kitchen, Cheryl's rules be damned.

"You *know* what I mean, girl!" I say to encourage her to stick around. "You're a navigator too!"

"A what?"

"Ginny. You wanted me to explain, so let me do it before you confuse the poor girl." Cheryl leans toward LeeLee. "You and Ginny. Y'all have a gift from the other world."

As they talk, another reading comes on. This time, it's not the future bugging me—it's the past. The past is usually easier to understand, but it's often painful. As if whatever doles out the readings prefers to show me the shittiest memories. If the future is a dream, the past can be a nightmare. I close my eyes and start talking.

> "LeeLee is five years old, and she's outside playing at a neighbor's house. She knows her daddy is beating on her mama. He's pushed Mama around before but never struck her in the face. Mama's crying. Bleeding. She hurts so bad, but the fear is the worst part. LeeLee is afraid, but she walks straight home. Mama is in the bathroom, taking a shower, and Daddy is at the kitchen table, smoking a cigarette. LeeLee says to him, 'I know what you did to Mama's face, and I'll kill you if you hurt her again.' Daddy says, 'Lisa, don't you dare sass me, and how'd you know that?' LeeLee is having none of it, though she's so scared, she feels like Daddy's cigarette has smoked up the whole house and she can't draw breath. She says, in a voice much more grown up than the mouth it's coming out of, 'God shows me things no one else can see, and he'll show me how to kill you.' Daddy leaves that night, and he's gone for good."

I press my fingers against my temples. Such a long, intense reading might bring on a headache.

"Oh, good lord," LeeLee says as my eyes open. Like a hooked bass, she gawks at me with her mouth hanging open.

"Did she speak true?" Cheryl asks.

LeeLee nods.

"Now don't be afraid. That's what we're here to talk about—"

"You know anyone else like us?" I scoot my chair closer to her.

"No," she whispers.

"Me neither! This is *so* great!"

"Ginny, you're spazzin'. Give her some space—"

I grab LeeLee's shoulder and shake her. "I can't *believe* we found each other! Isn't it amazing?"

"Uhhh... sure." Then she faints.

Chapter 3
LeeLee, 2015

After Peace leaves, I hide in my office. Phone calls and emails drown out my scattered thoughts and Britt's gossipy curiosity. I sneak past her desk as the bells of St. Michael's Church strike five and pull into our driveway on Council Street a few minutes later. Council is only a block long. The houses are sedate by the standards of nearby storied thoroughfares like Tradd and Legare Streets. Our house is near the corner of Tradd and Council. It's a Charleston single, built in the 1870s. Double-decker piazzas overlook a postage-stamp yard behind a white picket fence. The brick carriage house is billed as a garage nowadays, but it's not big enough for our vehicles. My Volvo SUV fits on the cracked driveway, but Clay's GMC Sierra is relegated to street parking.

The house itself has planked-wood siding painted pale pink. It tilts like a layered cake without enough icing to hold it in place. Inside is a small foyer then a parade of four rooms—office, family room, dining room, and the little kitchen with its ancient Formica countertops, yellow-plaid wallpaper, and lime-green linoleum. Upstairs, the master bedroom opens to the piazza, and there are four more small bedrooms. It desperately needs a renovation—one 1970s full bathroom for five people—but I love it anyway.

The front door opens right onto the sidewalk. With no front yard, I make the most of the flower boxes. Britt came over after work one day with her two green thumbs and helped me out. On this late

April day, my petunias peek over the edge of the boxes like baby birds that aren't quite brave enough to fly. They'll leave the nest soon if I remember to water them.

My three boys are in the kitchen, having a snack with Kylie, the cute blond College of Charleston student who picks them up from school and runs them around to their activities for me. I sneak in, change into mom gear of running shorts and a 2008 Cooper River Bridge Run T-shirt, and clop down the stairs in my flip-flops.

"Thanks, Kylie," I say as I walk into the kitchen.

"Mama!" My youngest son, Malachy, jumps down from his chair. The other two are hot on his heels.

"Hey, buddies!" I kneel, and the three of them almost knock me over with their greeting. "I missed y'all today!"

Kylie is halfway out the door. "Got to get to yoga." She smiles. "Y'all be good for Mama!"

"You better get going while the gettin's good," I say. "Spin class this morning about killed me. I might run off to yoga myself for a full-body stretch."

"Don't know how you get up so early."

"I either go before this crew rises and shines, or I don't go at all."

She closes the door behind her, and happy chaos ensues. I can't think about Peace's visit with my kids running around, jumping on me, demanding my attention, and of course, fighting. With three boys, someone is always fighting with someone.

We also do a lot of giggling, and I work on first-grade math homework with my oldest, George Clayton Moretz III, known as Trey. I monitor his times tables while five-year-old Bowman and not-quite-three-year-old Malachy watch TV. After a rowdy, splashy bath routine, we climb onto Trey's bed for a bedtime story.

"What do y'all want to read tonight?" I ask.

Trey's big greenish eyes look up at me from under his dark, curly hair. "Can you tell us a story instead, Mama?"

Bowman chimes in. "Yeah! One of the funny ones you make up." Bowman has my dark hair, too, but his is straight, his eyes dark blue. Malachy—named after the cherubic younger brother in my favorite book, *Angela's Ashes*—is a blue-eyed towhead, like his father was as a child.

"Mama-tale!" Malachy says around his thumb.

"Let's see..." I gently remove Malachy's finger from his mouth. "Mal, you pick an animal. Bowman, you pick a... vehicle. Something that goes *vroooom*. And, Trey, you pick a... superpower!"

I regale them with a story about a giraffe with X-ray fire vision that drives a fire truck—a "fertuck" in Malachy speak. The boys dissolve into shrill giggles when Super Giraffe stretches his *looooong* neck and looks into the bank's top floor with his X-ray vision. Therein he discovers the dastardly bank robbers. He burns their sneaky butts with his laser eyeballs then drives them to the hospital in his fertuck.

I kiss Trey's forehead then walk Bowman and Mal to their rooms and tuck them in. Someone will inevitably ask for water, so I sit on the floor in the hallway. The front door creaks open, and Clay comes up the stairs in his suit. He blows me a kiss before sneaking into each of the boys' rooms to whisper good nights.

"Hey, baby," he says as he enters the hallway. "Sorry I'm so late. Long day. Trial prep is exhausting."

"Hey yourself." I stand and follow him into the bedroom. "One of the benefits of family court. A lot of settlements and only a few trials."

"True, but less drama in construction litigation. My clients aren't heartbroken and trying to kill each other." He removes his jacket and tie and tosses them over the chair across from the bed. I find myself comparing him to Peace. Both men are over six feet tall and still have good hair, though Clay's is light brown and he has a short beard. He has pale-blue eyes like his youngest son. Lighter than Peace's deep blue. While Peace has thinned out, long work hours and fatherhood have caught up with Clay. He hits the gym when he can, but no one has seen his six-pack abs in about eight years.

I promptly quash my petty assessment. None of us are twentysomething anymore. I certainly don't want anyone comparing me to my dear friend Palmer, with her mommy-makeover tummy tuck and her boob job.

Clay walks across the room and puts his arms around me. I hesitate before returning his embrace. Since I found out about his adultery last winter, hesitation is my automatic reaction whenever he touches me. I remind myself that I decided to forgive him. We're supposed to be moving forward. I slide my arms around his waist and squeeze.

"You smell nice," he says.

"You must love the smell of chicken nuggets."

He kisses my neck. "Did you get a chance to look at any of the lots?"

"No, sorry. I had a crazy day too."

"What happened?" Since we started marriage therapy, Clay has made a point to ask me about my work.

"Just prepping for a temporary hearing in a case for My Sister's House."

He squeezes tighter. "Your philanthropic nature has always turned me on."

"Okay, silly." I kiss his scratchy cheek and step away. "I also had a weird blast from the past show up at the office. My old friend Peace Smith."

He stiffens. Peace and Ginny had already lit off for Florida by the time I met Clay, but he's seen photos in my old albums. He knows we have a history.

"Weird," he says. "I thought he was a drug addict in Texas or something."

"Nope. Florida for a while. Then Myrtle Beach. Then up in the North Carolina mountains in Boone. Now he's back."

"What did he want?"

I give him a truncated version of the reason for Peace's visit.

"Interesting." Clay strips down to his boxers. He dons a pair of SpongeBob SquarePants pajamas the boys gave him last Christmas. "He shows up when his father is about to die and leave an extensive estate, right? Old Peace Smith was one of the best civil litigators in the state in his day. My dad went up against him in federal court a hundred times. They're two pecans in the same pie. Both overbearing assholes."

"Come on, now. They're not *that* bad—"

Clay raises an eyebrow.

"Fine. You're right," I say. "They're both the legal version of Foghorn Leghorn, and neither of them was father of the year."

"So me and your buddy got something in common, but I'm not in danger of being written out of the will. I *think*. That convo about gay marriage at Easter dinner may have been the last straw with George Senior."

"I guess y'all do have something in common." A weird thought. Even weirder that I've never considered it. "Yes, Peace's dad has a lot of money. Then there's the family farm. It's just Peace and his brother, Drew. Drew is a dentist in Asheburg."

"Looks like Peace came back to get on Daddy's good side before the cash is doled out."

Hadn't thought of *that*, either, but my hackles automatically rise, like they used to when my mother warned me that Peace might have *a li'l bit of a problem*. "He wants to mend fences. He and his dad were close back in the day. Well—as close as you can be to someone like his dad. Old Peace thought Peace would follow in his footsteps."

"But he followed Jim Beam and Mr. OxyContin instead."

"Clay, that's not fair. Peace has a legitimate addiction. He's been clean for a while. I'm proud of him."

His smile is more patronizing than humorous. "Even though your best friend's mother, who was like a second mother to you, thinks he killed your friend?"

"He did *not* kill her." If I were a cat, my tail would be a puffed-up feather duster.

"People do crazy shit when they're strung out. You of all people know that, given what you see in court."

"Peace wouldn't swat a fly on his own birthday cake. If anything, Ginny ran all over him. Besides, Ginny is the toughest person I know. She's the *definition* of a survivor. She's out there somewhere. Hopefully, she's sober too. If not, she needs my help. They both need help."

"Whoa. Hold up. Are you getting involved in some weird down-home Asheburg drama?"

"I-I-I don't *know*." I sputter like a candle standing up to a powerful extinguishing breath. "I've had no chance to think about Peace showing up. I had a long workday too. Then I got home and had to deal with the kids by myself."

"I said I'm sorry. I *had* to work late." The bed frame groans when he plops onto the edge of the mattress. It's heard these work-life-balance arguments before.

"That's not what I—"

"I don't want you inviting this stuff into our lives, Lee. Some *reformed crackhead* shows up on your doorstep, you don't invite him in. Not when you have *three kids*."

His sanctimonious tone makes me want to scream, and I break out the big guns. "Hello—you invited your drama into our lives. Need I remind you about your friend *Christina* emailing me last winter?"

"Here we go *again*." He stands, and the bed frame lets out a metallic sigh of relief. "I said it a million times, but I'll say it again.

It was one week at the bar conference. I was lonely and drinking too much. We hadn't had sex in three months—"

"Now here *you* go again."

"I told Christina I regretted it after the conference. She was mad, but I had no idea she'd take it so far. And it's not like you busted me. I confessed to you *before* she even sent the emails—"

"Only because I knew something was up with you."

"How?" He turns in a circle, as if the answer hangs on the wall between the artsy black-and-white photo of the Angel Oak and our framed wedding invitation. "I still don't get it."

The day Clay returned from that damn conference, a reading had come on, though I hadn't had one in months. Sometimes, my internal narrator feeds me only feelings or words, but it was one of the brutal ones—an actual scene like something out of a dream. I heard Clay's truck pull up in front of the house. I walked down the hallway to greet him, but when I blinked, the blink lasted too long.

> *Clay sits in his truck at the end of Council Street, listening to their wedding song, "Into the Mystic" by Van Morrison. Tears stream down his face. Guilt soaks into his blue polo shirt like vinegar in a wound. It takes all his willpower to start his truck, drive down the street to their house, park, and step onto the sidewalk. He opens the front door, and it squeals on its hinges as if in horror at what he's done.*

When he walked past the creaky door, I knew he'd sat at the end of Council Street for an hour, grieving over something terrible. He delivered an overtly cheerful greeting, but his purported happiness didn't touch his puffy eyes. His face belonged to two people—bottom half a grinning jester, top half a somber funeral goer—the comedy and tragedy masks personified.

I had the misfortune to read a few of his thoughts too.

LeeLee... the boys... sorry... ruined my life... What the hell was I thinking?

I confronted him as we lay in bed that night, and the truth came tumbling out. He'd slept with another attorney—a woman named Christina Somebody—during the annual South Carolina Bar Association conference. Nothing had been the same since.

Despite our years together, when it comes to my supernatural abilities, Clay is no more in the know than anyone else in my life.

"I just *knew*," I say. "Women can tell these things."

"The point is, I *told* you," he says. "I came clean. I had no idea she would contact you. It's the biggest regret of my life. What does that have to do with you getting involved with your ex-boyfriend's potential murder case?"

"It's not a potential murder case, Clay. Good Lord! Peace came to me because he's freaked out. Ginny and Peace are my friends." I make up my mind as I talk. "Ginny was my best friend for years, no matter what happened between us or what problems she has. I *absolutely* should try to find her—for both their sakes."

"No, Lee. I don't like it."

I glare at him. "I don't give a shit whether you like it or not."

And that's why Clay sleeps on the sofa that night.

BY SOME HAPPY MIRACLE, the next morning, opposing counsel agrees to my proposed temporary consent order, thus saving me from the stress of appearing in court for a contested hearing. Her client will be under strict alcohol consumption restraints pending review by a guardian *ad litem*—an independent investigator who represents the children's best interests.

Relieved, I turn my attention to our typical marital litigation. Our client claims her estranged husband is an alcoholic. She wants sole custody of their kids. He, in turn, claims *she* is the one with the drinking problem. And so it goes with so many of our cases. With Peace's reemergence, I suddenly have too many alcoholics in my life, though everyone has a different threshold for what qualifies as a true drinking problem. From my observations, half the adults in Charleston are alcoholics.

The Lowcountry is a happy place. People here enjoy life to the fullest. How can we not, when we're surrounded by so much beauty? Beautiful landscapes, architecture, and weather. Even unusually beautiful people. Every occasion is a reason to party, and every locale is an appropriate venue. Drink until the myriad of bars shut down. Imbibe on the beach and on the boat. Golf-course beers. Concert beers. Mimosas at brunch after church. Girls'-night-out wine and boys'-hunting-weekend whiskey. Take shots on a damn porch, and everyone needs to mind their business about it, thank you very much.

People who fight some deep-seated internal ugliness—a dysfunctional childhood, a tendency toward addiction, even general melancholy over a bunch of first-world problems—require significant self-control not to lose themselves in the thrill of a never-ending good time.

So much boozing might seem out of character in a state that regularly attempts to write the Bible into its laws, but as Ginny's mama used to say after another torrid Asheburg marriage scandal, the more they pray, the more they stray. With everyone on a perpetual whirlwind of alcohol-fueled socializing, married people encounter endless opportunities to get themselves into trouble. We see all kinds in my office, from newlyweds who throw in the towel after less than a year to geriatrics who've been married for decades. Even the folks who simply drift apart usually have a cheating or boozing complaint.

Hell, if Clay and I ever separate, I'll sing the same song, "Your Cheating Heart." But I don't hold with blaming everything on one person. I've seen too many divorces.

Lately, I've been asking myself a question that makes me squirm but must eventually be addressed. What have I done to contribute to the marital quagmire we find ourselves stuck in? It took two to row our family boat into dangerously shallow waters.

Our client's anxious email gives me an excuse to further delay my response to that quandary. Her panic over her ex-husband's latest threatening text messages requires a soothing response. I type, hit Send, and walk into my boss's office to get my next marching orders.

Darlene Donnelly doesn't pussyfoot around, as she's prone to tell everyone from her clients to opposing counsel to the bartenders at the local pubs. She's somewhere in her mid-sixties, and she's a family court legend. She grew up downtown, flew through law school at the University of South Carolina, when only a handful of women were in her class, and returned to Charleston to set up her practice. She married, had two kids, and divorced her own philandering husband.

Some older, chauvinistic male attorneys refer to Darlene—with her bleached-blond hair, her red lipstick, and her penchant for brightly colored, slightly too-tight suits—as a battle-ax. She doesn't care. Neither do I. I adore her.

"Hey," I say. "We settled the Russell case, for now. You need anything at the moment?"

"Nice job, Mama," Darlene says, but she barely looks up from her computer. "With your bleeding heart, I'll lose you to the Department of Social Services someday. Will you compile case law on alimony reductions? Potential new client coming in for a consult. Need to freshen up on how *broke* he needs to be to get off the hook."

"Sure. No problem."

"I heard you had a visitor yesterday. A handsome stranger."

"Not a stranger. An old friend."

"Sounds like *tee—rouble*."

"Nah. But he needs some help."

"If he's got a baby mama coming after him for child support, we don't work for free unless it's for My Sister's House."

"Nothing like that. He doesn't have kids."

"That he knows about." Darlene wags her eyebrows at me.

"Do you know a good private investigator up in Myrtle Beach? He was here about a mutual old friend who took off. I want to put out some feelers for her."

"I'll have Britt send the names."

I thank her and return to my desk. I open my emails. The usual hysterical rants from clients, passive-aggressive messages from other lawyers, and updates from the South Carolina Bar Association and the state supreme court.

One email address jumps out at me, LoveGinnyB525@gmail.com.

The subject line: *Ginny.*

I click on the message. Palmer, Jess, and I are the recipients. My heartbeat speeds up with every word I read.

Sorry if this message surprised you, but I had to get your attention.

Your friend Ginny is dead. Will you help me bring her killer to justice?

He's back in Charleston and trying to get money off his dying father. Mister Nice Guy, right? Wrong. He wanted to be rid of Ginny, and he killed her. I'm not going to let him get rich after what he did.

Please reply if you want to help me expose the truth. I have more information.

For Ginny's memory.

Justice for Ginny.

I reread the message three times. Frantically, I try to make sense of it or identify the person who wrote it, but nothing in the text is familiar. Just that address, with a reference to Ginny's birthday, May 25. Otherwise, anyone could have written it.

I pick up my phone. Seven text messages from Palmer and Jess await my reply. Long blue bubbles of frantic typing from my two best friends. Gorgeous blond former pageant queen Palmer. Short, dark-haired, adorably freckle-faced Jessalyn. A pang of missing them strikes me like an emotional gong.

I send my message.

Me: *Y'all, we can't text about this. We need to meet up.*

Jess: *Okay. When? I'm shaking I'm so freaked out.*

Palmer: *Same. What the hell! Omg. I'm about to cry.*

Me: *Can y'all make tomorrow work? I know it's last minute.*

Jess: *This is an emergency. I'm there.*

Palmer: *Same, but I'm volunteering at the kids' school tomorrow. Can we meet for evening drinks?*

Jess: *I get off work at 5, and I'll drive into town.*

Me: *I'll ask my nanny to stay late. Salty Mike's at 5:45.*

Palmer: *Yup.*

Jess: *Yes. Can't believe it's taken an email claiming Ginny is dead for us to schedule happy hour.*

Chapter 4
Ginny, 1995

No one has ever fainted in our kitchen before, but my mama knows what to do. We hold a plate of warm snooder-dooders under LeeLee's nose. The smell wakes her right up. I help her to the sofa and sit beside her. Cheryl gets her some ice for the lump on her head.

"I'm so embarrassed, y'all." As usual, LeeLee's face is red under her swarthiness.

"Not a word about it," Cheryl says.

"Sorry I spazzed," I say. "I waited my whole life to meet someone else like me."

"You *really* knew when you saw me?"

"Yeah. Did you feel anything? A reading?"

"Maybe, I—" She frowns. "You call them *readings* too?"

"Yes! They're readings on a compass!" I clap like a toddler with a new toy. "Mama, how crazy LeeLee calls them the same thing—"

"I don't know anything about a *compass*. I call them readings because a voice in my head tells me stories. I can hear them and sort of *see* them too." LeeLee covers her face with her hands. "I can't believe I said that. It sounds nuts."

"No, it doesn't! It *totally* makes sense to me." I give her a brief explanation of how Mama and I explain it. Navigation, compasses, rivers of time, and whatnot. "So I'm a navigator."

"I..." She swallows. "I think of myself as a storyteller."

"When it comes to psychic powers," Cheryl says, "to each her own."

I talk around a mouthful of snooder-dooder. "So, did your brain light up like a Fourth of July sparkler when you saw me?"

"I felt something. But I pushed it away."

I swallow and cough. I wave my hands, and Cheryl hands me my sweet tea. Once my snooder-dooder goes down the right pipe, I say, "You did what?"

"I, like, shut it down."

"Why would you do that?"

"I don't like it. I worry about seeing something bad coming for someone I love. And the past... it's usually awful." She shivers.

"The past can be rough. Look at my reading of you just now! But it's clearer than the future."

"I hate seeing the future," LeeLee says. "You know how things make sense in your dreams but you can't explain them?"

"Yes. Talking about a dream can't do it justice. I have to fill in the blanks, even if it's not quite right."

"Prophecies are often confusing until they happen," Cheryl says. "But people who know Ginny understand the truth in what she sees."

"Don't mean to be rude, ma'am, but I can't imagine telling people about this stuff. My own mama doesn't know about it. What if I see her *die*?" More shivering, and her hands clench into fists. "What can I do? Should I try to stop it? *Can* I stop it if I want to?"

"So you *never* talk about it?" I ask. "How can you be a storyteller if you don't tell your stories?"

"Hush, Ginny," Cheryl says. "*That's* rude."

"It's okay," LeeLee says. "Maybe you're right. But I can't help it. I don't like it *at all*."

"I think it's amazing, even when it's sort of scary. When a reading comes on, it's like that feeling right before I jump off the trestle bridge into the river." I tap one of her clenched fists. "But you... you sensed something from me, but you stopped it on purpose?"

"Yes. I've practiced my whole life. In my younger days, I saw too much. Sometimes, it came out of nowhere, but sometimes, it happened when I touched something—a book, a necklace, a tree. Once I picked up a pineapple at the grocery store. Suddenly, I was watching a farmworker in Hawaii accidentally cut off his finger."

"Words can trigger it for me too."

"Same!" Her mouth turns up at the corners, an acknowledgment that having someone else understand is, indeed, cool. "Smells are the worst. One sniff of some random scent can set me off."

"Music does that to me!" I squeeze Cheryl's hand. "Can you believe it, Mama? Finally, someone *gets* it."

"She gets it more than we do if she's got some control over it. Maybe y'all can help each other," Cheryl says. "LeeLee can help you understand when to quiet down—"

"But I don't *want* to quiet down."

Cheryl ignores me, like she did when I was little and demanded a third snooder-dooder. "And you can help LeeLee get more comfortable with it all. After all, honey, you got to live with it."

LeeLee's lip trembles, and a few tears plop over her crazy-long eyelashes. Cheryl retrieves a box of tissues from the kitchen table.

"Sometimes, I wonder if I'm legitimately crazy," LeeLee says. "Like destined for the nuthouse. Especially when the readings show me someone's thoughts—"

"Say what now?" I ask.

"Thoughts. Other people's thoughts."

Cheryl freezes. Her arm hangs suspended with the tissue hanging like a truce flag. One of my eyebrows creeps up my forehead.

LeeLee takes the tissue and dabs her eyes. "Don't you know other people's thoughts sometimes, Ginny?"

"I... I don't think so," I say. "I can tell what people were thinking in the memories I read."

"No. This is different. It's not the past or the future. It's straight from someone else's head in that moment."

"Do you know what we're thinking now?" Cheryl asks.

"Oh, no, ma'am. I don't read thoughts all the time. Only bits and pieces here and there. A few words. Sometimes a whole sentence."

"Wow. What brings *that* on?" I ask, fascinated.

"Sometimes, it happens when someone is really upset or really happy, but sometimes, it's just Ms. Mullins thinking about taking her dog out to pee when she gets home from work."

"Jeez. That's cool." Jealousy taints my compliment. I assumed our powers would be the same, but LeeLee can do something I can't. "Never happened to me."

"I hope it doesn't freak y'all out," LeeLee says. "*Please* don't tell anyone. I swear, I try not to read thoughts. I don't want y'all to think I'm loony—"

"You can't freak us out!" I say. She seems so earnest I forget my jealousy. "You're not loony, LeeLee. You're *special*. It's a gift. You got to think of it that way, or you'll legit go crazy."

"I recognized Ginny's *specialness* years ago," Cheryl says. "Age four, she predicted her father's first drunk driving arrest—"

"I told Mama to get Daddy out of the metal box he was stuck in," I say. "An hour later, Daddy called from the police station."

"Then there was the time she predicted Jess would break her ankle at her championship softball game."

"I told her, but, like, what could she do? She couldn't let her team down."

"Your *friends* know?" LeeLee asks.

"Yeah. Peace knows," I say. "Jess and Palmer. And Rollo. I talk to them about it. Tommy and Lands are more about good times, you know? Tommy's head might explode if he thinks about anything other than his next meal or Carolina football. But they know."

"Don't tell Jess or Palmer about me, okay? They might not want two psychics hanging around."

"Navigators. Or storytellers, like you call us," I say. "'Psychic' is so, like, cheesy. Makes me think of that creepy woman in *Poltergeist*."

LeeLee smiles through her tears. "*Carol Ann... Carol Ann...*"

"Right. We are *not* like that weird-ass lady. I won't say anything to anyone. That's up to you to tell."

"How do y'all know about this stuff?" LeeLee wipes her nose.

"We're learning as we go," Cheryl says. "But it's made me interested in all the magical things out in the world. There's more to life than what we see every day. Some people can cast curses, see spirits—"

"No way," LeeLee says. "I don't believe in ghosts."

"You of all people should believe in just about anything," I say.

"There must be some rules."

"Oh, there are all manner of rules," Cheryl says. "But they might be different for each person with a gift. Look at you, reading thoughts and whatnot."

"Right," I say. "I'm still figuring out those damn rules. What about you? You figured it all out?"

"Good lord, no." LeeLee laughs and exhales, and some of the tension finally drains from her shoulders. "I've lived with this as long as I can remember. All I know is I should keep it to myself."

"Now you don't have to!"

"Thank you. I'm so happy I met y'all. But now I have so many *more* questions. Like what else *is* out there? Who else is like us? And how can there be rules if they're different for different people?"

Cheryl pats her knee. "You should be a lawyer, sweetheart, with that kind of thinking."

LEELEE CALLS HER MOTHER and asks if she can spend the night at my house. Her mama, Donna, asks to speak to Cheryl. Cheryl charms her with her goofy chattering, like she charms everyone. Mama Donna drives out to our house to drop off some clothes and a toothbrush for LeeLee. Such a nice lady, tall like LeeLee but blond and pale. She looks exhausted from life but happy LeeLee is making friends.

It's fixing to be a clear October evening. We all drive out to Rollo's land—his father's land, technically—a few hundred acres of piney woods crisscrossed by dirt roads. We'll build a fire in our usual clearing, half a mile back from the state road, drink Milwaukee's Best beer, smoke cigarettes and weed, and tell stories. Some of us will sneak off to make out. A typical Friday night in Asheburg.

By nine o'clock, me, Jess, Palmer, and LeeLee sit on a log beside the fire with beers in hand. Peace's boom box sits on his truck's open tailgate. As a bunch of Southern white kids from the boonies, we have no dog in the East Coast–West Coast fight. His favorite rap mixtape crisscrosses the country. Wu-Tang to Dre. Biggie to 2Pac.

Given the unusually chilly weather, LeeLee has on a dark-green coat and cute pink mittens. None of us Asheburg girls have any decent cold-weather gear. Jess and I wear hunting jackets we borrowed from Peace and Lands, but Palmer's prissiness doesn't do musty camouflage. She has on a crop top under her flannel shirt, a red ski hat with a huge pom-pom, and a pair of her dad's work gloves.

"Palm, with that poufy hat and those big-ass gloves, you look like a clown," I say.

"Whatever," Palmer says. "Y'all look like deer-stand bag ladies. Not you, LeeLee. You *totally* look cute. But if you haven't learned yet, Jess and Ginny are the biggest camo clowns in town."

"Pennywise," LeeLee says.

"Who?" Jess asks.

"Pennywise the Clown. The monster in one of my favorite books. He lives in the storm drains and eats kids. But he's not always a creepy-ass clown. Before he kills you, he turns into whatever you're most afraid of."

"Great," Jess says. "I'll never be able to walk past a storm drain again. The clown will be lurking in there. When I lock eyes with him, he'll transform into Palmer after she hasn't shaved her legs in a week."

I start laughing. "Or her pits."

"Oh, hell no, y'all. So gross," Palmer said.

"I can see it now." Jess stands and struts around the fire in her giant camo coat. "I'm minding my damn business, walking down the street. Then Palmer's werewolf ass jumps out the drain and puts me in a headlock." She puts her hands around her own throat and gags. Her eyes bug out.

I can barely talk around my cackling, and Palmer starts laughing too. LeeLee watches, as if waiting for Palmer to get pissed off. She grins as she realizes Palmer couldn't care less about being the butt of the joke. It will be my turn, or Jess's, next time, maybe LeeLee's if she sticks around long enough.

Peace walks out of the darkness into the firelight. Tommy, Lands, and Rollo follow him. Those boys are a rainbow of hair colors. From Peace's black to Lands's brownish, Tommy's regular blond to Rollo's towhead. Peace is the tallest, followed by Tommy and Landon, who are so close they sometimes seem like the same person. They wear each other's clothes. They always have the same haircut, like maybe their heads are interchangeable. Rollo is the shortest and the skinniest, but with his white-blond hair, catlike green eyes, and pale eyelashes, he's the most *interesting* looking. They have the dreamy look that comes from good weed. I smelled them toking up out in the darkness.

"What are you ladies laughing at?" Peace's eyes are bloodshot.

"LeeLee told us about a monster who hides in the drains, changes into your biggest fear, and then eats you," I say.

"Damn. Tommy, what's your biggest fear?"

Tommy sits on the log beside Palmer and puts an arm around her. He brushes his shaggy hair out of his eyes. "Daddy longlegs, man. So creepy. How did God make a bug that's just legs?"

"They're not just legs, Tommy," Jess says with a classic Jessalyn Conway eye roll. "They got *bodies*."

"That little dot in the middle is *not* a body—"

"What about you, Gin?" Peace asks me. "What's your greatest fear?"

"Guess. You should know."

"If I guess wrong, I'm in trouble."

"But if you guess right, you'll get a special reward."

The boys wolf whistle, and Peace grins. He rubs his chin as he paces before the fire. "Hmmm. You don't like chickens."

"True. I hate an ornery chicken. Our neighbors' rooster—"

"But truth be told, I think your biggest fear would be losing your voice." Peace kneels and holds his hands before the fire. "Or maybe being trapped in a dream by yourself."

No one says anything, as if we're all shocked Peace called out my greatest fears in front of everyone.

Kind of ticks me off, even as I love him more for knowing me so well. I chuckle to break the silence. "Guess I have to come up with a sweet reward."

Peace turns to the rest of us. "Ginny was honest. What about everyone else? What's your biggest fear?" He pulls a little bottle of bourbon from his pocket, Evan Williams Green Label, rotgut in a bottle. "Confessions and a shot of Evil Evan. You already talked, Gin, so you get the first shot." He hands me the bottle. "Who's next?"

Like in a movie, the crickets are suddenly too loud. The fire pops and snaps, and no one says anything.

Finally, LeeLee clears her throat. "Heights. I'm terrified of heights. Couldn't climb up to the top of the jungle gym as a kid."

Peace claps, and I pass over Evil Evan. LeeLee takes a swig and winces. She might be afraid of heights, but she's just as afraid of everyone finding out about her power. I wonder what she feels like with everyone thinking about their fears. If someone gets worked up enough, maybe she'll hear some thoughts.

Peace turns to Jess. "How about you, cousin?"

"My girl isn't afraid of anything," Lands says.

"I am." Jess shivers. "Maggots. So gross. In the summer, when they're on the trash cans... squirming around..."

"Ew, stop," Palmer says. "Give her the booze so she shuts up."

We go around the circle. Palmer admits to being afraid of a tree falling on her house during a thunderstorm and crushing her in her bed. Tommy sticks with his daddy longlegs because he isn't thoughtful enough to have any legit fears. Lands is afraid of his dog dying.

"I'm afraid I'll never get over Ginny breaking up with me in seventh grade." Rollo grins and pops a Tootsie Roll into his mouth, an obsession that changed his nickname from Ricky to Rollo in the third grade.

"Ha ha," I say. "Be serious for once in your life."

"I'll try. Wait—I know. I'm—what's it called? Afraid of tight spaces. Catastrophic?"

"Claustrophobic, asshole," Peace says.

"Okay, *Webster's Dictionary*. What about you?"

Peace's bloodshot eyes follow the dancing flames as he ponders. "If I'm being honest, disappointing everyone, my parents, coaches, you losers."

"Awww, damn, buddy," Lands says. "My opinion means that much to you?"

Tommy claps. "So touching, man. So touching."

"Whatever!" Rollo says. "Just P. trying to be the good guy. You don't give a shit what we think."

"He's serious," LeeLee says loudly enough to make the boys shut up. She has a tic under her right eye.

I bet she read something—one of Peace's memories, or his thoughts. It's weird to think of another girl knowing what's in his head.

"That's what he's afraid of." LeeLee fidgets on the log. "Y'all know him better than me, but I think he means it."

"Thanks, LeeLee," Peace says.

"Enough with all this deep-thinking bullshit." Rollo removes a bag of weed from his pocket. "We built this fire so we can get stoned and stare into it silently, right?"

"I plan on giggling my ass off," Jess says, "then going to Wendy's for ninety-nine-cent chicken nuggets."

Everyone happily rattles on about this and that—who sells the best weed in the Burg, whether Wendy's or Taco Bell has better munchie food, when Lands's parents will be out of town so he can throw another keg party. It runs together for me, since I've heard the conversations a million times.

I elbow LeeLee. "Thanks for livening up the convo with your killer-clown story."

"It popped into my head, so I said it."

"Yeah. I know all about things popping into your head, or you know, *my* head. But now I know about your head too."

"*Please* don't tell anyone," she whispers. "I shouldn't have said anything about Peace being serious. But I read... he thought... 'Nothing is ever enough for Dad.'"

"That sounds about right." I look fondly at Peace across the fire.

He and Landon are imitating the Ashepoo High football coaches with *Beavis and Butt-Head* impressions. Rollo laughs so hard, he tips over backward in his rusty beach chair.

"You read anything else?" I ask.

"No. I started humming in my head. *La-la-la-la-la.* And I pictured myself when I was, like, five, with my hands over my ears. It's something I… do… to drown it out. I bet it sounds immature."

"Sounds like a good strategy to me. I'll keep it in mind."

"I know you don't think I should, but—"

"All good, girlie. Old habits die hard. We'll get you loosened up." I elbow her again.

"Or maybe I'll get you to *tighten* up." She elbows me back.

"You can try." I slide my arm through hers. "No matter what happens, I won't say anything. It's in the vault. Our vault. The touched-by-the-Lord storyteller-navigator vault only you and me can access."

She smiles. "The Ark of the GD Covenant."

I hold up my beer. Our cans clink together. "Amen to that, girl. Amen to that."

Chapter 5

LeeLee, 2015

In Charleston, venues come and go, but a few storied bars absorb the city's preservationist spirit and become part of its fabric. Salty Mike's Deck Bar is almost as abiding as the oak trees along the Battery. All four Asheburg girls attended the College of Charleston, though Ginny dropped out of C of C after a year. She stayed in our apartment on Bull Street while waiting tables, and we spent four years canvassing downtown haunts. A Citadel cadet bought me my first vodka tonic—in a plastic cup—at Salty Mike's. Any underlying taste of lime still reminds me of summer.

Inside, it's a typical dive, with low ceilings and concrete floors, a rambling bar bedecked in Christmas lights, and decrepit pool tables. The outdoor deck bar, however, makes up for the interior's lack of ambience. It hunkers beside a swath of marsh overlooking the mouth of the Ashley River, the bustling Charleston City Marina, and the modern arch of the James Island Connector. Umbrella-shaded tables dot the deck like haphazardly placed checkers. Like most waterfront Charleston dining spots, it smells like pluff mud and boat fuel.

I shade my eyes when I step from the dim interior into the bright sunlight cascading over the deck. Palmer sits at a table close to the water. She wears white jeans and a pale-blue top that emphasizes her light eyes. Her perfectly wavy blond hair hangs past her shoulders and pleasingly frames her surgically enhanced cleavage. She's reading a book, but she looks up as I approach as if she has BFF radar.

"Lee! Honey." She stands, and we hug. "You look gorgeous."

"Just thinking the same about you. Sorry I'm late. On the phone with a client."

"No worries. Jess is still stuck in traffic. Your hair is so long!"

I remove the hair tie from my wrist and wrestle my hair into a ponytail. "It's out of control. I can't find one skinny minute to get a trim. I'm a giant split end."

"I wish mine would grow like that, but I color it too much. It's as fried as my grandma's chicken." She holds up her book.

The woman on the cover faces away from the potential reader. The faceless figures on Palmer's books often wear powdered wigs or trim 1940s pencil skirts. Today's lady is of the contemporary, beachy-hat variety. She stands on a wide front porch and looks out over a garden. The blue ocean slumbers in the distance. I imagine she sips coffee from a Live, Laugh, Love mug.

"You need to borrow this," Palmer says. "It's Clara Ann Morris's latest. So good."

"I haven't read her last five books."

"Girl, you used to read all the time! Now you can't find time for a haircut or the written word."

"Three kids, a house, and a job."

"You at least written something yourself?"

My as-yet-unwritten novels fascinate Palmer. She plans to host my book release parties at her Mount Pleasant mansion. She probably has the party favors, appetizers, and a signature drink lined up. I love her for it, even if she sometimes exasperates me.

"No time to read means no time to write."

"But writing is your calling! That short story you published in college literally made me cry. I want to have a complete Lisa Lightstone Moretz literary experience."

"You crack me up. You asked me for my annotations for every book we read in AP English. Now, you're in four book clubs."

"I'm doing my kind of reading these days. None of that call-me-Ishmael BS. Besides, I need a hobby that keeps me thinking. The mom life, you know?"

"You manage five kids, school, sports, dance, social lives. That takes a full-time coordinator. Your brain never stops."

She leans toward me. "You could write something like that. You're surrounded by inspiration. I bet Clara Ann and company are sitting in their estates on Kiawah and the Isle of Palms, dreaming up stories between book signings."

"It's not that simple, Palm."

"You're busy, right, but you can't let that stop you! You're a natural storyteller."

As soon as she says it, my ears start ringing.

Ginny and her mama stand in "Cheryl's Kitchen." Cheryl is teaching Ginny her coconut cake recipe. LeeLee Lightstone just left after their first sleepover.

"She calls herself a storyteller, Mama," Ginny says. "But she's afraid to tell any stories. It's not right."

"Didn't you start a novel?"

Palmer hadn't stopped talking while I'd inadvertently looked in on Ginny and Cheryl back in 1995. "Sorry, what? Oh, yeah. A few unfinished manuscripts languish on my computer."

"I want to read them!"

"Believe me, you don't. They're not ready to see the light of day. True inspiration would have moved me past chapter five before I shelved them. I can't find a story compelling enough to write it."

"When you do—"

"Hey, y'all." Jess about plows into the table in her nursing scrubs with a giant purse over one shoulder, a water bottle in one hand, and her phone and keys in the other. A messy bun perches on her head like a chocolate doughnut, and her face is red under her freckles. "What a day. Half the kids in Charleston broke bones this week. You add West Ashley traffic, and I'm about to fall over."

"MUSC is lucky to have you," I say.

Jess works as a nurse in one of the medical university's pediatric clinics west of the Ashley River.

"We'll see. The drive is killing me. I'm contemplating Ashepoo Medical Center. It's three miles from my house." She dumps her stuff on the chair beside her and orders a Corona Light from the server.

We're all too freaked out to jump right into the Ginny dilemma, so we take a few minutes to catch up on our regular lives. They know about Clay's indiscretions and how we've decided to work it out.

I have no other real update, so I change the subject to their problems. "How's Dean?" I ask Palmer.

"Same as always. Works sixty hours a week and plays golf the rest of the time. As long as his back can handle it. When it's acting up, he sits on the couch and watches the golf channel." Palmer married her husband, Dean—a wealthy real estate developer eighteen years older than us—when we were twenty-two. She had five kids in ten years. She woke up one day to the unsettling revelation that her emotionally unavailable husband was about to join AARP and she had spent the past decade being pregnant, raising kids, decorating her house, and getting plastic surgery.

She had an affair with our old friend Tommy after his wife left him. Palmer almost divorced Dean, but she ultimately stayed in her marriage, either because of her kids or because of money fears. Or both.

Dean still doesn't know about the affair, since after a lot of soul-searching, she had decided not to tell him. She had learned her lesson, and the affair was over. So she didn't see the point.

I sense Jess's disappointment in her, but when it comes to friendships like ours—the ones that last for decades—disappointment is inevitable.

Not surprising that Jess has trouble hiding her emotions, since she's possibly the most opinionated person I've ever met. She takes zero shit from anyone. Jess and Landon dated through high school and into college until she broke up with him for getting hammered at her family reunion and embarrassing her. She dumped him on the spot and didn't speak to him for about eight years.

Out of the blue, as we approached thirty, she casually informed Palm and me they were dating again. Two years later, they got married and bought a house down the street from their parents in Combahee Estates, but one dark smudge marred their picture-perfect Asheburg life—infertility. After years of trying, they now have a beautiful one-year-old daughter.

"I'm going back for round two of IVF," Jess says. "Landon doesn't want to go through it again, but Mia won't be an only child if I can help it. We have one kid, and he spends most of his free time fishing. I'll manage. How much harder can two kids be?"

This time, I sense Palmer's judgment of Jess, and I agree with her. If Jess plans to strong-arm Landon into spending thousands of dollars on IVF while telling herself two children will not be much harder, she's sort of delusional.

Again, we've been friends for a million years. I'm sure I annoy them. It comes with the territory and doesn't mean we love each other any less.

"Y'all." I finish my second beer. "A thousand-pound gorilla is on this patio."

"More like a cute, redheaded, hundred-pound monkey," Jess says. "Named Virginia Emily."

"That email about gave me a heart attack. Whoever wrote it is talking about Peace, right?" Palmer says. "I texted Tommy, and he admitted that Peace is staying with him."

I nod. "Yeah. He's back."

Jess scowls. "So this person is saying that Ginny is... dead. Like, dead-dead? And *Peace* killed her?"

Palmer sips her wine. "Good grief, Jess. What other kind of dead is there? Half-dead? Ten percent dead?"

"Ginny isn't any kind of dead. She's just... Ginny. She got a wild hair and skipped out. Finally cut off Peace like she's cut off everyone else."

"I think so too," Palmer says. "She ran off somewhere."

"I'm as hopeful as y'all that she's okay somewhere," I say. "But Peace told me she fell down a deep booze-and-drugs rabbit hole before she vanished. Something awful *could have* happened."

"Even if it did, *Peace* didn't kill her," Jess says.

"Agreed," Palmer says. "That man lives up to his damn name. He's the only Asheburg boy who never got into a McDonald's-parking-lot fight."

"So, who wrote that email?" Jess asks. "Should we reply?"

"LeeLee should reply," Palmer says. "She's the lawyer. It's, like, more official. Plus she's got that way with words."

"Okay. I'll reply. But we all agree that Peace didn't do anything to her, right?"

Jess sighs. "I've known Peace my whole life. He's been a train wreck for years, but if he hurt Ginny Blankenship, I'll eat this beer can."

"If we want to clear his name," I say, "we need to figure out who's out to get him."

"What we *need* to do is find Ginny, since she's missing," Jess says.

"Yeah, Lee," Palmer said. "Ginny is in more trouble than Peace."

Their disapproval rolls over me this time, and I deserve it.

"Of course," I say, appropriately abashed. "Ginny is our number one priority. I already asked Darlene to recommend a PI in Myrtle to look for her."

"I'll pay for it," Palmer says. "Throw money at this problem like I do with everything else. We should talk to Drew. He's the only one who's had contact with Peace over the past decade."

"Drew is far from my favorite cousin, but he's still family. I'll talk to him," Jess says. "I'll track down Cheryl too. I can stop by Sweetie Pie's and try to catch her."

"Didn't she buy the bakery with Burt's life insurance money?" I ask.

"Yeah," Palmer says. "But she's been off since Uncle Burt died in that car accident. Between losing him and losing Ginny, she lost herself too."

"Employees are mostly running Sweetie Pie's," Jess says. "She hides out at her house in the Mill with her cats."

"I should call her," I say. "She must be in a terrible place."

"We all should. But we should do a lot of things, right? Like maybe Ginny should've come home for her own father's funeral. Anyway, I'll find a way to talk to Cheryl. Find out when she last talked to Ginny."

"What about Peace?" Palmer asks. "Should we question him?"

"Peace gave me his number," I say. "I'll handle him."

Palmer's perfectly arched eyebrows try to move, but her Botox holds them in place. "You and Clay are like my daddy's bourbon. On the rocks."

"You don't need the temptation," Jess adds.

"Y'all, I'm *married*," I say.

"So am I," Palm says. "I fell into Tommy's arms."

"Just promise me you won't keep anything from Clay," Jess says.

"Clay knows he's back."

Jess crosses her arms. "How did he take it?"

"Uh, okay. I guess." Now, that's a big fat lie. Clay hasn't sent texts about deep water lots all day—or any texts at all.

Palmer rests one arm on the back of her chair and looks toward the harbor. "We need someone like Ginny, who sees the future and the past and whatever happens in between."

"Ha, right," Jess says. "Too bad we don't have a Ginny to find our Ginny."

I squirm, as if they'll suddenly figure out my secret after twenty years. "There's only one Ginny."

"Now *that's* the gospel truth," Palmer says.

Gospel truth, indeed. We might share a talent, but Ginny is one of a kind.

OUR MARITAL PROBLEMS are great for Clay's billable hours. He works even later than usual that night, like he did after the cheating came to light. I push through the evening on autopilot. Homework, kick the soccer ball in the yard, dinner, baths, stories, tuck in. No great victories, but no meltdowns, either—from the kids or me. A pleasant parenting Groundhog Day.

Once the kids are asleep, I wander into the office. Plantation shutters cover the windows so lost tourists can't see into our house. I open the shutters and crack the windows. The flowers in the boxes are perking up. The scent of potting soil floats into the room.

I sit at my desk and open my computer, but an old college photo album catches my eye—from the days when we took our photos on disposable cameras and developed them at camera shops. I haven't assembled albums in years. Clay and I frame the best photos and rely on technology to store the rest. I remove the album from the bookshelf and start flipping through the crackly pages.

So many simple shots of everyday life. The girls in the dorm room or on the porch of our apartment. We were simultaneously thinner and had fuller cheeks. As the years went by, our eyebrows got skinnier and our eyeshadow got sparklier. My hair color never changed, but Palmer's got darker, and Jess went through a chunky-blond-highlights phase.

Photos from fraternity parties and twenty-first-birthday bar hopping. Pics of the Asheburg boys' visits and our Gamecock football weekend visits to them in Columbia. Their apartment outside the Five Points nightlife district smelled like beer-soaked carpet. The fridge contained nothing but alcohol, ketchup, and leftover hot wings. The single shower drain inevitably clogged. We girls always came armed with Drano when we stayed with them.

We religiously documented the events that South Carolinians, great traditionalists that we are, look forward to every year. If anyone actually saw a horse at the Carolina Cup steeplechase in Camden, we considered the day a failure. The girls wore wide-brimmed hats, and the boys sported bow ties. Jess wore the same black straw number every year. Ginny and I borrowed hats from Palmer, who had a whole mess of them lying around. As if they were her everyday necessities, like pearl earrings or cotton underwear.

St. Patrick's Day in Savannah, one of the biggest celebrations in the country, is when River Street shuts down and a hundred thousand questionably Irish revelers descend upon that storied city. Freshman year—or maybe sophomore year—we didn't book a hotel room in time, so we slept in Tommy's Bronco. I woke up to Jess asleep on the cooler in the back of the truck.

New Year's Eve celebrations are only identifiable by the ridiculous glasses we wore: 1999, 2000, 2001. Nothing from 2002. By then, Jess and Landon were on their eight-year hiatus, Peace and I had broken up, and Ginny was driving us batshit crazy with her antics.

I pause on a photo of Peace and me bundled in warm clothes at his fraternity's annual Beta Alpha Epsilon Mountain Weekend. He stands behind me with his arms around my waist. I beam at the camera like the Archangel Gabriel himself holds me up. Another from his BAE formal. His classic black tux complements his dark hair and eyebrows.

"That green dress," I whisper. My favorite color and strapless with a fierce slit up the side. I bought my first pair of four-inch heels for the occasion. My feet ached, and I was almost as tall as Peace, but I felt like I was attending the Oscars.

The sight of Peace's fingers on my waist makes me tingle in places that have nothing to do with my readings—that is, until the tingle spreads to my head.

I can't stand to relive some memory from those days, so I bite my lip until the pain overrides the tingle. I shut the album, stick it on the shelf, and open my laptop.

Once I'm certain no reading will torment me, I text the private investigator in Myrtle Beach, a former Philadelphia cop named Lou Marciano. He promises extensive connections with the local homeless shelters, law enforcement, and the food and beverage industry. Even small-time drug dealers. As he put it, *I knows them. They knows me. If she's still round these parts, I'll find her. And get yous any other information they got. Tell Darlene that Big Lou says Heya.* Since she's paying his fees, I include Palmer on the text chain. She sends me a message after our last exchange.

Palmer: *You sure we didn't hire Tony Soprano to find Ginny? Maybe he's in the witness protection program.*

Me: *Darlene says he's the best up there. He's licensed. He's not allowed to do anything, like, illegal.*

Palmer: *How reassuring.*

Me: *Come on. Who better to track Ginny than a former mafioso posing as a former cop posing as a PI? She'd love the drama.*

With the PI lined up, I turn to the most basic level of sleuthing. I google Virginia Blankenship.

I find her old address in Asheburg and our apartment in Charleston. Two addresses in Florida. The website FindMe.com notes several public records under her name, so I pay for a one-month premium subscription to read several citations in Bay County, Florida, home to Panama City; and Horry County, South Carolina, home to Myrtle Beach.

Biker capitals of the world. Peace and Ginny could really pick 'em. Still, they're saltwater people at heart. Maybe they tried to hold onto something from home.

In 2002, the year they left Charleston, Ginny burst onto the criminal scene with disorderly conduct and public-drunkenness charges then a DUI and a shoplifting charge. Public drunkenness appears again in Myrtle Beach. A three-year-old DUI in Myrtle rounds out the charges.

A search for Makepeace Smith turns up page after page from Old Peace's illustrious fifty-year legal career but nothing about Young Peace beyond a *Charleston Post & Courier* article from 1997, the year he signed a letter of intent to play football for the University of South Carolina.

FindMe.com reveals three DUIs for Peace. One in Florida, one in Myrtle, and a last one in Watauga County, North Carolina. Maybe the last incident made him get sober. Third time's a charm, after all.

I open Facebook and type in both their names. The only Ginny Blankenship is a sixty-year-old woman from Omaha, Nebraska. No Makepeace Smith. Old Peace wouldn't use social media, and Young Peace only lurked.

As I scroll, I come upon a post from the previous fall that mentions his name. The poster, a pretty, dark-haired woman named Meredith Preston, lives in Boone. She grins, waving at whoever took the photo. Behind her, the autumn Blue Ridge Mountains glow like freshly polished brass.

Ten months ago, I finally changed my life! Thank you to God, my friends, the recovery community, and my darling Makepeace Smith. We got this, baby!

I click on her profile. Most of her posts are private, but I find a pre-AA photo at a Boone brewery. Meredith and Peace each have a beer in one hand and a shot in the other. Peace rests the hand wrapped around his beer on Meredith's knee. Even after all these years, the sight of him touching another woman makes me slightly ill.

Would I have felt this way before I discovered Clay's adultery? What about five or ten years ago, when I still believed Clay and I were soulmates?

I don't know. Maybe I never stopped being in love with Peace. When I loved Clay with what I thought was my whole heart, maybe a photo of Peace Smith with another woman could still nauseate me. Subconsciously, I was probably glad when Peace left Charleston. I never had to see him move on with Ginny or anyone else.

The front door opens, and Clay steps inside. I shut my laptop.

He pauses when he sees me and sets his briefcase on the floor. "Hey."

"Hey. You have a good day?"

"Eh. Just okay. The judge—"

My tears come on like an unexpected flash flood. I cover my face with my hands.

Clay's work shoes clack across the hardwood floors. He kneels in front of me. "Lee, baby." He grabs my fingers.

I turn away from him.

He doesn't give up. He gently forces my hands away from my face. "Honey. I'm so sorry."

"For what?" I ask through my sniffling.

"Whatever is making you sad."

That makes me cry harder, but it also makes me question why I'm crying at all. Because my marriage is falling apart? Peace? Ginny? Looking at old photos? Being exhausted from parenting three kids? My job, which exposes me to the absolute worst in people every day? PMS? All of the above?

Clay pulls me onto the floor and wraps his arms around me. I sob into his shoulder like someone has died. He leans against the refinished antique desk, beside a pile of Star Wars action figures.

When I finally dry out, he whispers, "Can you ever truly forgive me?"

"I want to. But it's so much harder than I thought it would be."

"What can I do?"

"You apologized and listened to me cry and answered all my questions. You gave me all your passwords. You blocked that woman on everything." For the first time, I allow myself to be brutally honest. "I don't know if there's anything more you can do."

"So that's it, huh?" His voice cracks. "Do you want a divorce?"

I sit up and wrap my arms around my knees. "I don't know what I want. I love you. But something has changed, and I don't know how to change it back."

He blinks, but a tear sneaks out. "Maybe we need to take a break. But I don't know how to do that. You're the family court attorney."

"Maybe the FROG again? For a little while." We have the South of Broad version of a Furnished Room Over the Garage, a finished space over the carriage house that serves as our guest room. It has a shower and a kitchenette. He slept in the FROG for a couple of days when I first found out about the cheating then again for a week when Christina contacted me.

Clay swipes at his wet cheek. "If that's what you want."

"Just for a while. I need some time to think."

"Yeah. Sure. I told you I'll do whatever you want me to do." He kisses my cheek and stands. "I'll go upstairs and put some stuff in a bag—so I don't come into the bedroom."

"You can if you need to," I say from the floor.

"No. Last time, I slept in the FROG, but everything else felt weirdly normal. If we're going to do this, we need to do it."

"Okay. Whatever you think."

"No, Lee. It's whatever you think." He stops on the stairs. "I want to see the boys. Work makes it hard enough to find time with them. I won't hide in the FROG all weekend."

"Of course not. Maybe... maybe I can stay with Palmer this weekend."

"Cool." He starts up the stairs then stops again. "Have you talked to Peace since he came to your office?"

"Not much. A few texts. I told him that Palmer, Jess, and I want to find Ginny."

He sighs. "Right."

The sound of his shoes clomping on the steps grates on my nerves. When he walks out the door, I'll be able to exhale. In the FROG, he'll be too far away for me to read his thoughts. Distance will protect me from his sadness and guilt and anger. Whether he has a right to be angry at me or not, he is. He wants forgiveness. He did everything humanly possible to help me forgive. I'm still sending him into backyard exile.

He walks into each of the boys' rooms then comes downstairs in his SpongeBob pants. He doesn't say good night as he opens the back door.

I pick up my phone and read a text from Peace.

Peace: *Hey. Thanks for helping me. I can't tell you how much it means to me.*

Me: *I'm trying to help Ginny.*

Peace: *I know. But you're helping me, too, even if you're not trying.*

Me: *I have to go to sleep. I'm so terribly tired. I'll let you know what the PI says.*

Peace: *You okay?*

Me: *Honestly, not really.*

Peace: *Do you want to get together and talk?*

Right or wrong, there's only one answer. *Yes.*

Chapter 6
Ginny, 1996

By the end of sophomore year, I've almost forgotten LeeLee's real name. It seems like she's been in Asheburg, in my mama's kitchen, at our lunch table, in the back seat of Peace's truck forever. Still, some things she couldn't learn over the winter. She lost fifteen summers to the hot wastelands of West Columbia, and now, I'm determined to show her how we do summer in the Lowcountry. That means taking the boat to Boot Island on the first Saturday after school lets out.

I borrow my mom's car and pick her up at Mama Donna's cracker box house on Carnation Street. We meet Peace, Rollo, Tommy, and Landon at the dock behind the yacht club in Combahee Estates. They already have the boat in the water, so LeeLee misses them racing around like the Four Stooges getting it off the trailer. Jess has a softball tournament, and Palmer has pageant rehearsal, so it's just LeeLee; the boys; Rollo's boat, *Reel Nasty*; and me.

As we walk onto the dock, LeeLee says, "Rollo has his own boat?"

"They all do," I reply. "Rich Asheburg boys get pickup trucks for Christmas and a boat for their sixteenth birthdays, or whichever comes first."

"That's crazy. I won't get a *car* till I can buy my own. Until then, I'm borrowing Donna's '88 Camry."

"Since we arrived in style in Cheryl's '89 Civic, we're in the same boat."

"Or *not* in one."

"We got plenty to choose from between these fools. But Rollo's is the nicest. The rest of them got hand-me-downs when their fathers upgraded."

"Ladies!" Peace waves his beer can in our direction. He takes our hands and helps us step aboard *Reel Nasty*, a center console Contender with two shiny black two-hundred-fifty-horsepower outboard engines. I stash my beach bag in the storage compartment on the bow. Then I open the cooler and rummage through the ice for a couple of beers. My hand about freezes off, and the ice cubes scratch my palms, but since it comes with the anticipation of a good buzz, I don't mind.

"So, Boot Island," LeeLee says to no one in particular. "Am I supposed to ask what boots have to do with this island?"

"It's basically a glorified sandbar," Landon says. "In the middle of Saint Helena Sound. Nothing lives out there but birds, snakes, and some damn raccoons whose great-great-grandparents must have been great swimmers."

"Boot comes from the shape of it," Peace says. "Though the foot part of the boot eroded, like, a hundred years ago."

"It's more like Peg Leg Island these days," Tommy says. "Rollo's family has owned it for... well, forever."

"How does someone own an island in the middle of the sound?" LeeLee asks.

"Some Blanchard went out there before the Civil War and *decided* he owned it," I say. "Like planting the flag on the moon."

"It's well-known in the Burg that the Blanchards have always been pushy assholes," Landon says. "But don't tell anyone I said that."

Rollo flips Landon's visor off his head with an affectionate swat. "Don't insult my forefathers. I'll hang you off the side of this boat like a bumper."

Peace pokes LeeLee's arm. "The Blanchards have a cabin out there. It's as basic as they come—no running water, just a generator for power."

"No shitter," Tommy says. "But it's heaven, man. Heaven."

"*Dude* heaven," I say.

"When we go out there after fishing, it's perfect," Peace says. "We go all *Lord of the Flies*, and no one bothers us."

"Y'all sit down," Rollo says. "I'm gunning it."

I yank my cover-up over my head, tie it to the console, and tug LeeLee toward the bow. We sit on the bench seat. The motors go from a hum to a roar, as if Rollo is riding a tiger and has kicked it with spurs.

At ten in the morning, the Ashepoo River is still flat and shiny. I watch the bed-pillow clouds through my sunglasses. A pelican flies alongside us for a while with its wide wings skimming inches above the water.

"Show-off!" I yell.

I swear that bird winks at me before dropping into the water to swallow his fishy breakfast.

LeeLee gleefully points out a family of surfacing dolphins. I've seen so many dolphins, I'm not fussed up about them anymore, but her enthusiasm reminds me of how cool it all is.

The sun blasts my skin but not in a sticky late-summer way. June heat will bake us slowly. In August, we'll steam up like a bunch of briny oysters. The air blasting past my face is a mixture of oxygen, water beads, and boat fuel. Even in a Koozie, my beer warms, but I don't care. We have a full cooler, a fast boat, and a beautiful day.

The CD player blasts "Closer to Home" by Grand Funk Railroad. Rollo is our captain, *yeah, yeah, yeah, yeah*, and he isn't letting anyone forget it. City people would pooh-pooh our parents for letting sixteen-year-olds tear across the river, but Rollo knows these waters like he knows the intersection of Magnolia and Monroe Streets. Our boys can follow the channel in their sleep. No sandbars can hide from them. The currents are in their bloodstreams.

Slow going in the no-wake zones gives LeeLee a chance to admire the houses along the river. Long docks reach over the marsh and stop short in covered pier heads. Metal lifts raise boats from the water as easily as my mama's spatula scoops snooder-dooders off well-greased cookie sheets.

"I'd love to have a dock someday. Are those dogs out there?" LeeLee points at the still canine forms on some of the docks.

"No, girlie. Those are coyote statues. They keep the gulls and pelicans from landing on the docks."

"Pelican poop is no joke," Landon says.

We pass the mouth of the Ashepoo, and the *Reel Nasty* starts growling again. The shoreline behind us becomes a dark line along the horizon.

I point out the new shoreline ahead. "That's Boot. We'll pull around to the north side. Shallow water around here. Boats get stranded sometimes. Only one channel leads in."

"Not many people know about the channel," Landon says. "Between that and Rollo's dad's No Trespassing signs, no one ever comes out here. It's our private island. Not exactly the Bahamas, but it works."

"It more than works for me," LeeLee says. "So cool, y'all."

Landon and I smile at each other like LeeLee is our child on her first Walt Disney World trip.

Even in the channel, at low tide, we can't get close. Rollo has Peace throw out the anchor about thirty feet from the line of pluff mud. A skinny beach sits behind the mud, but we usually walk across the dune and past the Blanchards' cabin to the beach on the south side, where the bottom is sandy.

"I'll carry y'all," Peace says as Rollo pulls a few pairs of waders from the storage compartment under the console.

"My hero! LeeLee, Peace always carries us, since he's the tallest—and the strongest." I whisper in his ear, "And the hottest."

Peace kisses me. "You're the hottie, G-Love."

Rollo kills the engine, and Peace eases into the water. He looks ridiculous yet adorable, waist-deep in the water in his bathing suit and waders. I follow him down the ladder and climb onto his back. He starts toward the shore.

"Don't drop me," I say.

"When have I ever dropped you?"

"There's a first time for every—"

He stumbles, and I scream, but he laughs. "Kidding!"

I bite his ear. "You jerk."

"Am I a jerk?"

"Peace Smith, you're the opposite of a jerk, and you know it." I rest my head on his sweaty shoulder. I like the feel of my bikini-clad boobs rubbing against his back. I peer down his stomach for any signs he's enjoying it, too, but I don't get past his rock-hard abs.

Peace gets me to dry land and goes back for LeeLee. I happily stretch my arms over my head and take in the familiar landmarks around me. Rotting, oyster-covered dock pilings march out into the water. An ancient metal boat with a basketball-sized hole in the side hunkers in the marsh grass like a passed-out drunk. One of Rollo's relatives painted Good Times across the side in red block letters.

"Good times, y'all!" I say as Landon and Tommy join me on the sand with a cooler strung between them. They high-five me then take off their waders and put on the flip-flops they stuck in their pockets. Peace disappears behind the boat and reappears with LeeLee on his back.

Her long, tanned legs dangle in the water. She wraps them around Peace's waist so she doesn't lose her flip-flops. She keeps looking at the water around her like a shark might jump up and bite her ass. She and Peace don't talk, except for her repeatedly telling him she's sorry for something or another and him smiling and shaking his head. Her dark hair escapes its ponytail and flies in his eyes. He laughs and spits it out, and she apologizes again.

It dawns on me that LeeLee's boobs are now rubbing against his back. Hers are bigger than mine. My eyes automatically flip to his crotch to see if *she* is getting a reaction out of him. It doesn't seem like it, thank goodness. If Peace gets a hard-on, a baggy bathing suit won't hide it.

LeeLee laces her hands over his chest, and her face is beside his neck.

They seem to be taking a *long-ass* time.

I exhale, hard. I've been holding my breath like a ridiculous, insecure ninny. Peace and I have been on lockdown for two years. I never worry about him wanting anyone else. If I fussed about such things, I wouldn't have invited LeeLee into our group. She's become one of my best friends. I *love* her. I grin and wave. "Y'all come on!"

Peace bounces LeeLee to get a better grip on her thighs. She winces. He isn't close enough to shore, but without warning, she jumps off his back and hop-skips across the rest of the pluff mud until she stands beside me with her feet covered in brown goo. She's made it through the last few feet of mud without losing her shoes or cutting her leg open on an oyster shell, but the force of her escape has shoved Peace into the muck well past his knees.

She turns toward the water with her hand over her heart. "Oh, good Lord. Oh my *gosh*."

Peace stands in the mud like an abandoned dock piling. Tommy and Landon drop the cooler and start laughing, Tommy bursting out with his raucous *a-ha-a-ha-a-ha*. Landon doesn't make any noise when he laughs. He looks like he's in pain, and tears stream down his face. He clutches his stomach like he's going to puke. The gulls circling our cooler twitter.

Rollo calls from the boat behind Peace. "Ayo, P., you stuck? We gonna have to wait till the tide comes in to get you out!"

"I'm *so* sorry," LeeLee says. "Ginny, I'm sorry."

Peace throws up his hands. "That's what I get for being a nice guy."

Peace and I join Tommy, Landon, and the seagulls with the laughing.

I pat LeeLee's shoulder. "Don't worry about it. We've had bigger problems."

Rollo joins us on the sand in his waders. "Yeah, LeeLee. Don't sweat it. Better a stranded Peace than a stranded boat."

"But how will he get out?" she asks.

I've never seen anyone look so mortified.

Tommy and Landon put on their waders again. They trudge through the pluff mud to Peace. Rollo follows them. All four boys cuss and hoot as they pull and tug on him.

LeeLee swipes at her eyes behind her sunglasses.

"Girlie," I say. "Are you crying?"

"I'm embarrassed. I have zero seafaring skills." She sniffs. "I... got scared, and I jumped. No wonder I can't think of myself as a navigator."

"Don't beat yourself up about Peace. That boy has pluff mud in his veins. About your navigating... I still plan to get you to loosen up and embrace it."

"I don't know *how* to loosen up."

A yelp of accomplishment, and Peace's legs are usable again. The guys slog onto the shoreline.

"I'm sorry, Peace," LeeLee says.

He smiles. "Seriously, Lee. No worries. It makes for a great story."

"This might be our first LeeLee story," Tommy says. "'The Time LeeLee Stranded Peace in the Pluff Mud up to His Butt Crack.'"

Despite herself, LeeLee giggles. "Good Lord. Can I get a damn beer?"

"You're singing my song," I say. "Let's head to the real beach, and if we're lucky, we'll come up with some new stories."

IT'S ONE OF A HUNDRED afternoons we've spent cutting up and getting high in these waters. Getting high means drinking beer and, for everyone except LeeLee, smoking weed. The best high comes from laughing our asses off and having no parents hovering around us.

LeeLee gets tipsy and insists everyone put on sunscreen. She hunts me down in the shallows and about tackles me trying to slather me up. "Damn you, Ginny!" She chases my nose with her thumb. "You're worse than the five-year-olds at the YMCA camp I worked at in Columbia."

"You're gonna make me all splotchy!" I reach into the water, grab a handful of sand, and smoosh it on her stomach.

Her mouth falls open in mock outrage. "Now you're gonna pay. SPF fifty-five for you!"

By the time she finishes, white streaks cover me. I look like a red-headed zebra, but I won't die of skin cancer. The boys are more co-operative. She wipes down Rollo, Landon, and Tommy's backs, then she hands me the bottle to attend to Peace.

He grumbles as I work the lotion into his shoulders. "I'm gonna be all sticky."

"Mama LeeLee insists," I say. "LeeLee, you wanna pee in the woods?"

"Can't y'all pee in the water?" he asks.

"I told her I'd wait half an hour for my sunscreen to dry."

"You *are* a mama's girl, whether it's Cheryl or LeeLee giving you instructions."

I pinch his butt and walk toward the dune. LeeLee meets me where the sand turns into a pine-needle-covered path. We keep going until the woods provide cover. LeeLee crouches behind one tree, and I crouch behind another. I smack a mosquito that lands on my arm.

"Is that the cabin?" LeeLee asks.

I look up past a sticker bush. "Yeah. That's it."

The cabin's whitewashed wood blends in with the trees and bushes around it. A box on ten-foot stilts, it sits in a clearing behind a brick firepit. A window sits on each side of the cube and two more near the roofline to let air into the loft above the kitchen and sitting room. The steep staircase leads to a little porch.

"Pretty cool. Is it up on stilts so it doesn't flood?" LeeLee asks.

"I think so."

The cabin *is* cool. Fishing memorabilia cover the walls. Some of the men in the faded photos are long dead. Every few years, Rollo and his dad bring out new cot mattresses, cushions, and blankets to replace the stuff that rots out. Plaid curtains hang in the windows, and canned goods slowly expire on the shelves above the gas stove. The Lowcountry version of Grizzly Adams's cottage.

I like the cabin, but I don't *love* it the way the boys do. They would spend the entire summer out here if they could. Daytime visits are enough for me. Palmetto bugs—giant flying cockroaches that should be South Carolina's official state mascot—live in the cracks and crevices, and it smells like fish guts and mildew. Peeing in the woods is all good now and then, but if it's necessary, it loses its charm.

Besides, the last time I entered the cabin, something went haywire with my internal compass. I felt a reading coming on, but then it stopped, leaving me with that uncomfortable feeling of a sneeze that ends mid-achoo. Suddenly, the cabin was too small. It was, as Rollo might have said, catastrophically claustrophobic.

"Can we go inside?" LeeLee asks.

I never figured out if that stilted reading was trying to show me the past or the future. Given the cabin's long history, I bet it was the past. I have no interest in seeing one of Rollo's long-gone relatives commit some terrible sin. I haven't gone into the cabin since. "Not unless Rollo turns on the generator and the AC unit. It'll be eight hundred degrees inside."

"Then no thanks." She stands. "It's hot enough out here."

"So we need another cold beer." I stand too. I swat at a cloud of no-see-ums, biting gnats that give the palmetto bugs and skeeters a run for their money in the competition for most annoying Low-country insects. "Ugh. Damn bugs. Gas on it, girl, before we get eaten alive."

We link arms and run back to the beach. Our sunscreen dries, and we have no need to pee in the woods again. The boys keep watchful eyes on the boat. The tide comes in, so Rollo moves it closer to shore. They take turns walking across the dune to mess with the anchor. The cooler empties out as our shadows stretch behind us.

We lounge on beach towels in the sand. Tommy dozes off. Landon stares into space and hums to himself. Peace and Rollo sit at the water's edge and talk about dude stuff. Boys have entire conversations about hunting, fishing, and football. Blah. Blah. Blah. It's so much more interesting to talk about people and, like, life in general.

I work my shoulder blades farther into the sand then turn toward LeeLee and shade my eyes. "You had any good readings lately?"

Her nose points at the clouds above us. "Good?"

"Interesting."

"Not really. You?"

"Nah. A lot of the past," I say. "Some guy in the Piggly Wiggly, watching his dad beat up on his mom."

"Ugh. Why do so many men out there do that kind of stuff?"

"If your daddy hadn't run off, maybe you could have asked him."

"I hate him. I wouldn't ask him to step inside if he was gonna be struck by lightning." She faces me. "I'd like to help women escape men like him someday."

"Is that, like, an actual job?"

"Maybe. I want to go to law school. Those women must need lawyers."

"Maybe being a storyteller will help you as a lawyer. Your readings can reveal if people are guilty!"

"But I can't control it," she says. "Not like that. That's what I hate most about it—no control."

"That's what I *love* about it." I reach toward the sky, as if to grab a cloud and pull it down. "It's like a surprise every time. It's exciting."

"It's weird we think about it so differently."

I grin, and my arms flop back onto the towel. "You and me are a prime example of *opposites attract*."

She smiles back and takes my hand. "I guess we are."

"That means we're the best of all things." I sit up and point at Peace. "Me and P. are the same. He's so chill, and I'm—well—I'm me."

"Y'all are a great couple." She sits up too. "You're awesome, Ginny. Thank you so much for everything you've done for me."

"Are you crying again? Jess would not approve. I haven't seen her cry since we were six and she fell backward off a swing at the Proper Park."

She shrugs and bites her lower lip.

"Lee. Girlie." I drape an arm over her shoulders. "We're *meant* to be friends. You were *meant* to move to the Burg. And it's not only about our powers. It's about us."

"I'm so glad I moved here. I can't believe I'm sitting on a beach, in the middle of the sound, in this beautiful place, like something I'd dream up in a book. But it's more than all this prettiness. It's that I'm here... with my best friends."

"We are your best friends. And you're ours." I rest my head on her shoulder. "And that's how it will be."

"Always."

"Yup. Always."

Chapter 7

LeeLee, 2015

The day after unceremoniously deporting Clay to the FROG—and agreeing via text to meet Peace Smith for lunch—I spend a good portion of my morning staring into my office computer screen. I want to find out who wrote the alarming email and—if LoveGinnyB525 actually knows anything—get some insight into Ginny's location. I type and delete and type some more. Once my effort satisfies me, I reread what I've written.

Hello,

As one would expect, this email caught Jessalyn, Palmer, and me off guard and alarmed us. As Ginny's oldest friends—and, in Palmer's case, her first cousin—we have always been concerned for her health and well-being. She chose to exclude us, as well as her other friends and family, from her life for many years due to her ongoing struggles with alcohol and drug addiction.

As far as we know, Ginny last lived in Myrtle Beach, South Carolina. Given the upsetting nature of your email, we are trying to locate her in that area and/or find out where she may have gone when she left Horry County. We deeply hope what you wrote about her possible passing is false. However, we would welcome any information you can provide about Ginny and anyone involved in her disappearance.

Thank you,

Lisa Lightstone Moretz, Palmer Blankenship Grossman, and Jessalyn Conway Walters

I cc Jess and Palmer and hit Send, then I write a message in our group chat.

Me: *The chicken has flown the coop.*

Jess: *I read it. Sounded good to me.*

Palmer: *Ginny had no patience for chickens.*

Jess: *She was known to kick a cranky rooster.*

I snigger and type out another message. *What was the name of that rooster that lived at the trailer next door to Cheryl's house?*

Jess: *Omg. The Claw Daddy!*

Palmer: *HAHAHA the Claw Daddy was a beast, bless his heart!*

Me: *Only Ginny could put the fear of God in the Claw Daddy.*

Jess: *RIP C.D. I hope you ended up in Mrs. Green's Crock-Pot.*

Me: *Omg I'm dying. Love y'all. More soon.*

Jess: *Xoxo!*

Palmer: *Love y'all too.*

Revelation—it's damn hard to concentrate on work when lunch with your first love is on the afternoon agenda. At a quarter to noon, I ask Britt to take messages, and I drive to Taco Boy, a restaurant on Huger Street with unusually ample parking. The outdoor patio bustles with busy waitstaff, sweaty tourists, networking professionals, and college students. Slobbery dogs lunge out from under tables to catch falling bits of fajita chicken. Peace sits at a table with a fizzy Coke and a bowl of chips and salsa.

"Hey." I slide into the chair across from him.

"Hey, you." He smiles.

The server approaches our table.

Before I ask for anything, Peace says, "Get a beer if you want. I don't mind."

"Nah. I have to go back to work. A water, please."

"How are the kids?" Peace asks.

"They're great, thanks."

"Remind me of their names?"

I don't think he ever knew their names, so it isn't really reminding him, but I oblige. Names and ages lead to descriptions of their personalities and looks. "I'm rambling. It must be boring to hear someone blab about their kids when you don't have any."

"No, I like to hear about them. I always wanted kids, but it wasn't meant to be."

"You're a guy. You're only thirty-five. There's still time."

"I don't see that happening. But you struck it big. Three boys! It's funny to think of you living with all dudes. You were never a one-of-the-guys type."

"I love having boys. Of course, I'd love to have a girl too. Clay and I thought about a fourth, but then—" I stop. "Anyway, I have my three guys."

"You still have time too," he says.

The server reappears, takes our order, and hustles to the next table.

Once she's gone, I switch to a less awkward but more complicated subject. "I replied to that weird email."

"Let me know if you get a response. I wasn't sure if I should bring this up... but my... uh, my ex-girlfriend got a similar message from the same email."

I pretend I know nothing about any girlfriends other than Ginny and me. "Oh. Who's that?"

"Her name's Meredith. She lives up in Boone."

"What happened?"

"She's a nice person, but it didn't work out. She texted me a screenshot." He holds up his phone.

I take it and read another email from LoveGinnyB525@gmail.com.

Hi Meredith,

Your ex-boyfriend is a murderer. He killed his girlfriend he knew his whole life. Ginny Blankenship. You probably escaped the same fate.

Rest in Peace, Ginny.

If he comes back, don't let him in.

"What a nice pun," I say. "Was she upset?"

"She's a little freaked out. *You* sounded freaked out last night—if someone can sound freaked out over a text."

"Clay cheated on me last year." I hadn't planned to say anything, but there it is. "I'm thinking about leaving him."

Peace blinks like I sneezed on him. "Wow. Not what I expected. I imagined y'all had a perfect life. Two successful Charleston lawyers. South of Broad lifestyle. Three adorable children. Y'all got a labradoodle yet?"

"Ha ha, no. I can barely handle work and kids, much less a dog. Probably one reason my marriage is falling apart."

"What do you mean?" He leans on his elbows and tilts his head.

He looks so genuinely sympathetic and interested, I start yammering away.

"I see this dynamic every day at work. A couple has a bunch of kids close together. Boom, boom, boom. Both parents work demanding jobs. Or maybe one works long hours and the other stays home up to their eyeballs in laundry and Goldfish crackers. Anyway, they forget they're married. They're *Mommy* or *Daddy*, not *honey* or *baby*. They resent each other. Fights. Silent treatment. Keeping score. The sex... I mean, you know..."

"I know what sex is, Lee." He speaks from across the table, but his thoughts float to the forefront of my mind. *Don't you remember?*

Yes, I remember. Good Lord. Of course I do. Before Peace, I knew nothing but high-school make-out sessions and a couple of fumbling romps with fraternity guys when I got sick of being a virgin. After Peace, there was little I didn't know about sex.

My face flames, and the rest of me starts heating up too. I stand. "I gotta go to the bathroom."

"Whoa. Don't run off." He holds up his hands. "No more sex talk."

I settle back into my chair. We're grown adults, damn it. Nothing but a conversation between old friends. I grip my knife as if to stab the tension between us. "*That* part of our life was nonexistent. The point is, LeeLee Moretz, family court attorney, should have known better than to let it get so bad. So Clay strayed, a one-time thing. He owned up to it. I told him we'd get through it, and we've been going to therapy. Still, I don't know if I can get over it... but we have three kids, and... we have *three kids*."

"I can't say I understand, obviously, but I do *get* it. Can I help in any way?"

"You sound like Clay."

"That's because we both care about you and want you to be happy."

That exchange has more layers than a pile of pulled-pork nachos. Luckily, the server drops off our food, and sizzling beef saves me from trying to find an appropriate response.

"How's your mom?" Peace waves away the smoke rising from his steak fajitas.

That simple, polite question reminds me of how long he's been gone. "Mama Donna passed away." I pick up one of my chicken tacos. "Brain aneurysm the year after I graduated from law school."

"Shit. I had no idea." He shakes his head. "There's so much I don't know."

"She went quickly. Never knew what happened. Fell over in her backyard in the Burg."

I leave out my excruciating guilt over the fact that her neighbor found her the next morning, not me. I was working long hours at my first law clerk position. Clay and I were madly in love. We had our exciting new careers, and our apartment on King Street in vibrant, exciting downtown Charleston. Mama begged me to move back to

Asheburg, but Clay had no interest in moving to a tiny town where Old Peace Smith's firm had dominated the legal landscape for forty years. Besides, any notions I had of raising a family in Asheburg had Peace entwined like a sweetgrass basket weave. Living there without him would have suffocated me.

My mother eventually stopped asking, and I believe she understood why we wanted to live in Charleston, but she still died alone.

I change the subject. "How's Tommy doing?"

"It's hard. He and his ex-wife are always at each other's throats. He only sees his kids every other weekend. But he's the VP of Dukes's Marine. His dad still goes into the office, but Tommy really runs the show. I'm working for Dukes's too. Docks. Boat lifts. Seawalls. I've been collecting wood from job sites. People always talk about reclaimed barn wood, but reclaimed dock wood is equally cool. Got a whole stash in Tommy's garage."

"That's great. You built anything?"

"I'm still tinkering. I haven't messed with woodworking in years. For a long time, my hands weren't steady enough. But I'm excited to see what I come up with."

"Me too." I love the idea of Peace finally pursuing his creative talents. Ideally, Old Peace doesn't pour proverbial gasoline on his woodpile. "What about Rollo?"

"Rollo is Rollo." He smiles. "You know he still lives in the Burg. He's supposedly a real estate agent working for his dad, but he has a hell of a lot of spare time. He's a free spirit."

"Free spirit?" I repeat with a laugh. "Oh, *Rollo*. He's Peter Pan in the Lowcountry Neverland. Never grow up. Never settle down. He dated this nice girl from Walterboro for, like, six years. We all thought they'd get married, but *nope*. In the end, he couldn't commit."

"Lands is the only one of the boys with a normal life. Tommy tried and failed. Me and Rollo never made it that far." He points at me. "You girls kept it together for all of us. Though it sounds like Palmer has her own issues, given the drama between her and Tom."

"Ginny didn't exactly keep it together. As far as Palm and Tommy, that's their story to tell."

"Ginny has always been a loose cannon. That's what we all love about her." He chews thoughtfully. "Speaking of stories, you written your masterpiece yet?"

"Good lord. Palmer just asked me the same thing. What's up with y'all, all up in my literary business?"

"It was always your dream." He mimes flicking a lighter. "Somebody's got to light a creative fire under your ass."

"With everything going on in my life right now, that's less than zero on my priority list. Besides, I told Palmer. I don't know what to write."

"You live in Charleston. Can't you dream up some moonlight-and-magnolias mystery?"

"Ha. More like mom life and mimosas. My only mystery is what to do about my existentially disgruntled educated-white-woman problems. Aside from Ginny, of course."

"Ginny is more than enough to occupy anyone's mind. Believe me, I know."

We finish eating, and Peace insists on getting the check.

"You don't have to do that, silly," I say. "You're working part-time for Tommy's dad."

"And you're a lawyer. But I haven't bought you a meal since Waffle House in college. Give me my moment."

I laugh and agree. We walk into the gravel parking lot. Peace has a beat-up gray F-150 with North Carolina tags.

"Gotta get that changed back to South Carolina," he says as we pass his truck on the way to my Volvo.

"You're really here to stay?"

He gently punches my arm. "If the Palmetto State will have me."

"We never wanted you to go in the first place."

I push him back, and he bumps his hip against mine. It's like we're eighteen again, testing the waters that have churned between us for so long. His hand slides down my arm. I can almost hear his heartbeat. My ears start ringing, and his thoughts flicker in my mind like excited newborn fireflies that have just discovered they can glow.

Man, being with her feels so good. This is what it's supposed to be like...

Those scattered thoughts encompass all his emotions. His giddy happiness and hopefulness and the kind of longing I've tried fruitlessly to describe in my failed attempts at novel writing—longing that defies words or description and can only be felt.

For a moment, I'm back in my teenage-girl body. Energy surges through my limbs. At thirty-five, with three kids and a mortgage, I never experience such vital electricity anymore. I blink, and the Peace in front of me has salt-and-pepper hair. He wears a crisp white polo shirt, not an old Ashepoo High School football T-shirt. Our hands intertwine, and our fingers lace together. I lean against my car. His face is inches from mine. The wind picks up, and a strand of my hair blows across his cheek like I've slapped him.

I shouldn't do this to her. He steps away from me. "Sorry," he mumbles.

"No. Peace. It's okay. We haven't seen each other in so long, and we're both in a weird place." I don't want to cry, so I say, "I'll go. Thanks for talking to me."

"Anytime."

I get into my car and crank the engine. He backs toward his truck and raises his hand. He drives away and puts a safe distance between us, so I can't read his thoughts, but I can't go anywhere yet. I might drive off the road—emotional DUI.

Two days ago, Peace Smith was an old fantasy. Someone who rustled in my memory on long drives or walks on the beach. Or the boat, during quiet stretches at the end of the day, when the kids fell asleep in towel-wrapped bundles around me. The busy Intracoastal Waterway became the quiet stillness of the South Edisto River, and I was a teenager in love with my youth and all my friends but especially with Peace. Not a mom in love with her kids and questioning whether she still loved her husband.

Peace rematerialized in my life like an exotic bird that should be extinct—the fantasy coming home to roost on the unstable branches of my life. Like Ginny drop-kicking the Claw Daddy, I should give him the boot. In so many ways, Ginny was always tougher than me.

Chapter 8
Ginny, 1999

LeeLee and Jess flew through our freshman year at the College of Charleston with straight *A*'s. LeeLee has a full scholarship. She has to keep her grades up, but she would have anyway. Jess is too stubborn to make anything less than *A*'s and always has been. Palmer's grades are only so-so, but she's been having plenty of success with dudes. She drives all the C of C and Citadel boys crazy with her hotness.

As for me, by the middle of spring semester, I'm on academic probation. My uncle Jack, Palmer's dad, pulled strings to get me into C of C, and my high SAT scores made up for my terrible high school grades. Uncle Jack said my grandfather would have wanted me to go to college even if my loser daddy failed out, so he even paid my tuition. I felt guilty about academic probation but not guilty enough to study or make it to class.

Peace, T-Dog, and Lands all go to the University of South Carolina up in Columbia. Tommy and Landon are with me in the land of academic probation. Peace, who should be in LeeLee and Jess brainiac land, is in Palmer country with mediocre grades and a rock-star social life. From what Tommy and Landon have told me, Peace went from a mullet in a small pond to a world-class marlin in the middle of the ocean. I always knew our little Asheburg bubble couldn't contain Peace's charisma and good looks forever.

That's why I broke up with him last fall. I refused to let him descend upon the unsuspecting sorority chicks of Columbia as the hot new football quarterback with me as his hick high-school girlfriend waiting in the wings to be dumped on my ass.

Only Rollo stuck around Asheburg after high school graduation and took a couple of classes at Lowcountry Tech. He knows his dad will give him a job doing something. Mr. Blanchard owns Blanchard Realty plus a bunch of rental houses and a few gas stations. Whether it's as a real estate agent or the manager of a BP, Rollo will always have a job and a house. No wonder he's always so chill and happy. Why worry about falling out of a burning building with Daddy's giant net underneath him?

So, now it's a few days after the end of the spring semester and our freshman year, and I'm back in the Burg at my mama's. Ro picks me up in the souped-up black Chevy Silverado his parents bought him for graduation. We drive toward town to meet up with Chad Dooley, one of the Burg's amateur dealers. Rollo buys from a couple of those dudes, but he's been giving Chad most of his business since he started hooking up with Chad's skanky-hot younger sister.

Rollo starts yakking about his latest schemes to get extra cash. "Forget weed." He chomps on a Tootsie Roll. "The jam-band market is hot—the Dave Matthews lovers, Widespread Panic and Phish fans—and they want shrooms, Gin."

"What's that got to do with you?" I take a drag off the joint he hands me.

He points over his shoulder. "Look in the trash bag behind you."

"You got a body in there?"

"No, jackass. Just look."

I turn in my seat with my head buzzing. I gag when a muddy, musty smell pours out of the bag. Mushrooms in various stages of drying fill it.

"Where'd you get all this shit?" I ask.

"Exactly right. Shit. You know my grandpa's cow pastures—"

"Oh, hell *no*, Ro. You did not go out into the cow fields and pick mushrooms out of the piles of manure."

He grins. "Hell yes, I did. This is my third bag."

"Does PopPop know?"

"Nope. I tiptoe around the cowpies in the moonlight." His grin widens. "I'm the Robin Hood of cow shit."

My laughter is a snort. "Your dad will lose his mind if he finds out! President of Blanchard Realty, whose son is a shroom dealer."

"Dad doesn't know shit—ha ha—about the mushroom market." He takes the joint from me. "Tommy's gonna sell 'em up in Columbia this fall. Gonna give him a cut."

"Y'all are crazy." I lean back against the headrest.

"You want in? I need a Charleston... ah, saleswoman."

"Can you imagine if I tell LeeLee I'm selling shrooms out of our apartment?"

"Guess you're right." He snuffs the joint on a damp paper towel then sticks it into a plastic bag.

He hands it to me, and I stash it in the glove box.

"So," he says, "y'all moving out the dorm?"

I nod. "We found a three-bedroom on Bull Street. We'll put up a wall and make a fourth bedroom. Jess and Palmer get the real bedrooms, and LeeLee and I get the makeshift one. We'll pay less in rent, since our parents don't foot the bill."

"My shrooms could pay your rent and then some."

"It's tempting, but nope. LeeLee would seriously lose it. She can't have anything on her record when she applies to law school. Not even a minor alcohol possession." I giggle. "She climbed out a bathroom window at the Sigma Alpha house when the cops showed up and landed on a fire-ant hill."

We turn from one state road onto another. "Y'all gonna have nothing but a bunch of plywood between you?"

"Yeah. Why not?"

His eyes flick in my direction then back to the road. "You *know* why."

"Uh... no, I don't."

"You really don't know?" Something in his voice is ominous, as if he *wants* me to know so he doesn't have to say it.

"Just spit it out," I say.

"LeeLee and Peace."

I'm not prepared for those two names to be connected the way everyone used to say *Ginny-and-Peace*. I wince as if he's dropped hot ashes on my bare arm. "What about LeeLee and Peace?"

"Hold on." He pulls off to the shoulder, into the entrance to a dirt road. He puts the truck in park. "Ginny."

"What, Rollo?" I stare at the signs stuck to a utility pole in front of us. Purebred Lab Puppies. We Haul Junk Cars. Jesus Is Lord. All the small-town necessities.

"You must know," he says. "Come *on*, Gin."

"I swear to God, Richard Blanchard, if you don't talk straight, I will cut your ass, push you out of this truck, and drive off into the sunset with your damn bag of shrooms."

"Something's going on with LeeLee and Peace."

There it is again, like *LeeLee-and-Peace* is one person. "They're friends. We're *all* friends."

"If they're just friends, I'll eat that whole bag of shrooms myself. I may die, but I'll die right." He looks me dead in the eye. "Everyone came home this past week. Have you seen Peace?"

I shake my head. "Haven't seen him since Landon's party when we were all home for Easter."

"You didn't notice anything then?"

"I avoided him. We're *broken up*."

"I saw him and Lee coming out from behind Lands's shed like raccoons creeping out from behind a garbage can."

I cling to an irrational rationale. "They were probably smoking a bowl."

"Please." He cocks one eyebrow at me. "LeeLee never smokes. The rest of the night, they were shooting eyes at each other over the firepit."

"Why didn't you say anything then?"

"I didn't see them, like, *kissing* or anything... but look. Peace got home on Wednesday, and his parents went out of town Friday morning. Me and Tommy wanted to come over and smoke on the dock. He pushed us off. Claimed to be tired. Peace—tired on a Friday night. Yeah, right. We drove out to Saltmarsh Saturday morning to wake and bake and give him shit, pulled into the drive, and LeeLee's mom's car was sitting in the driveway."

Cold realization soaks me. "She didn't go to the movies in Charleston with the girls Friday either. We talked about seeing *Wedding Crashers* for weeks, but she said she had PMS."

"Ha ha, Peace Make-Out Syndrome."

I shove him. "Screw you, Rollo." If only I had LeeLee's mind-reading talent. Might've heard what they were thinking at the Easter party or LeeLee's thoughts in our dorm room. At least my inferior supernatural powers could have shown me *something* in the last two months. I wouldn't be sitting here feeling naïve and stupid.

Rollo doesn't seem to notice the shove. "Hey. Come here."

He pulls me toward him, and despite my determination to keep it together, a few tears track down my face.

"You know in your heart you and Peace aren't right," he says. "You're too much for him. LeeLee is more his speed."

I sit up and sniff. "Sure. You're *totally* right. He and LeeLee are perfect together. They can *be perfect* together, go to law school, work for Old Peace's firm on Magnolia Street, live at Saltmarsh. She'll fit right in with the Smiths. Me and LeeLee might both be poor, but she's better at faking it than I am."

"We love you for who you are, Ginny."

"If I'm so great, why would Peace be with LeeLee..." I suck in a harsh breath. "And not me?"

"Peace does love you. Y'all dated for five years. That doesn't mean you're supposed to be with him forever." He wags a finger at me. "You knew that yourself. You broke up with him, remember?"

No way am I telling Rollo I broke up with Peace so he couldn't break up with me first. I figured he would move on, at least for a while, but with a sorority girl in Columbia—a Tri-Delta or a Kappa Delta or an Alpha Delta Gamma Mu Mu—not with my best friend.

I smile instead. "Yeah. I *did* break up with *him*."

"In his defense, he had a hard year. Football was a total bust after his knee injury. He couldn't even practice with the team and spent the whole year doing physical therapy."

"And pledging a fraternity. He partied his ass off."

Peace, Tommy, and Lands joined Beta Alpha Epsilon, one of the biggest and oldest fraternities at Carolina. Peace's father and grandfather had been members. "It wasn't all tough times."

"Point is, I bet he's falling back on LeeLee as, like, a comfort thing. It won't last."

I ask myself why she comforted him, not me. I will my supernatural powers to tell me something, but as usual, when I call upon them, they're silent.

"I'll tell you what would comfort me right now. Some more weed." I point down the road. "Let's go."

Five minutes later, we pull into the driveway of the Dooleys' double-wide. Chad sits on the front porch in baggy jeans and a white wifebeater tank top—a misplaced rapper in a country white boy's body. As we get out of the car, his sister, Reesie, bounces down the stairs in her too-big jeans with her belly button ring showing below her crop top. She's a bony little thing with a bad bleach job but pretty enough for Rollo.

"Heeeey-yeee, y'all," Reesie says.

"Hey." I smile, though I still feel like crying.

"Hey, Rollo," Chad says. "Ginny B. Good to see you, girl."

He's a couple of years older than us, shortish and skinny-ish with close-cropped dark hair. He reminds me of a creepy guy in one of my favorite movies, *Dazed and Confused*—the one who likes high-school girls because he keeps getting older and they stay the same age.

All small towns have a Chad Dooley, who peaked in high school, lives in his mama's house, and makes a living as a petty drug dealer. Still, he's cute in a roughneck way. His jawline could cut glass. And he has the best stuff between here and Walterboro.

I peek up at him from under my eyelashes. One of the only benefits of being short myself. If I turn just so, my eyes can lure a man in like a cat mesmerizing a mouse. "Hey yourself. What're y'all up to?"

"Shit, as usual," Chad says. "Can I get *you* the usual, Rollo?"

"Yeah," Rollo says. "But I want to talk to you about those mushrooms—"

"Hell yeah. I'll sell those bitches so fast your head will spin like you're trippin' yourself—as long as I know they're good."

"'Course they're *good*," Rollo says as if Chad disrespected Pop-Pop's cows.

"Well... my mama ain't home. She's left for her overnight shift." Chad's mother is a janitor at Ashepoo Medical Center.

"My mother works overnights at the bakery too," I say. "The people want their bread products early in the morning."

"Yeah, life's a bitch when you rely on muffins and toilet bowl cleaner." Chad grins.

Luckily, he was blessed with straight teeth, since Ms. Dooley couldn't afford braces. As for Reesie, her two front teeth are longish. She eyes Rollo like an eager bunny looking at a carrot.

Chad tips his chin in the direction of the double-wide. "You'd think with all that workin', we'd have a real house instead of this dump."

"Shut up, Chad," Reesie says. "It ain't like you're paying rent."

"All I know is I'm not living in a house on wheels forever. I'm getting me something with a damn foundation someday."

"Impressive life goals," I say.

"I don't know if you mean that or not." Chad's Timberland work boots carry him closer. He hitches his jeans up over his nonexistent butt.

"That's the point."

"I like a girl who keeps me guessing." Chad purses his thin lips. "What I's saying is Mama's at work, so we got plenty of time to *chill*. If y'all ain't in a hurry, we could sample some of Rollo's fungus right now. I won't sell skunky shit to my people. I got a reputation, you know."

"You *sure* do," I say.

He drapes an arm over my shoulders. "Now what *exactly* you getting at, Sweet Ginny?"

"Use those brain cells you got left to figure it out." I push his arm away. "And don't touch me unless I ask you to. I'll cut your ass."

"Rude." Chad winks. "Your Mill is showing."

"Ro, I'm down," I say. "We got shit else to do."

"Why not?" Rollo winks at me too. "If our other friends are busy..."

"What a bunch of damn winkin' fools." I point at Rollo's truck. "Get those mushrooms before I change my mind." I walk toward the trailer's front door.

Reesie follows me. "I'm so glad y'all are staying," she says as we walk up the steps. "I wanted to get to know y'all better forever. Even before me and Rollo started... you know... *hanging out*. He's so cool. Has he said anything about me?"

"Uh... we don't talk much about that kind of stuff." I give her a tight-lipped smile. In reality, Rollo and I spend most of our time talking about exactly that kind of stuff. Poor girl's acting like our friends are movie stars or something.

She doesn't know some of us are heartbroken and lost, like everyone else in our town—except LeeLee. She's never lost. LeeLee always knows where she's going. So even as part of me starts to hate her, I envy her as much as this poor trailer park girl with buckteeth envies me.

A WEEK AFTER ROLLO and I have tripped our faces off in Chad Dooley's bedroom with the black light's purple glow making us look like vampires and Pink Floyd playing on Dooley's giant stereo, Peace invites everyone out to his house on Edisto for the weekend. Jess wants me to drive out there with her and Palmer and LeeLee, but I go with Rollo instead. He invites Reesie and Chad Dooley. Chad brings a bottle of Goldschläger in the truck, and we cut up like a bunch of fools on the familiar drive from Asheburg to Edisto Beach.

I've been kind of down all week, but the Dawho River Bridge lifts my spirits as we drive onto Edisto Island. I wasted hours of my childhood in my parents' car waiting for boats to pass under the old drawbridge. The new bridge isn't *that* new anymore, but that open road through the sky still gives me a thrill. I roll down the window, and the early-summer wind blows away my sadness.

The Lowcountry has many beaches, but for Asheburg people, Edisto Beach is *the* beach—where family cottages perch on spindly stilts to avoid flooding and our clever forefathers added a few extra feet of clearance to fit a boat on a trailer under the house. Cracked asphalt streets become dirt roads for no obvious reason, as if the town ran out of cement and shrugged. It has sulfur-scented well water, hard-packed gray sand, and an ocean that heats up into a salty bathtub by late June. The bars are the same ones our parents snuck into as teenagers, and the restaurants are still where couples dance the shag to beach music between the tables.

If Edisto Beach ever changes beyond the modern convenience of the new bridge, I'll finally take the Bible seriously—a sign of the end times.

We're sauced up by the time Rollo's truck pulls into an empty spot on the Smiths' lawn. The three-story yellow house towers over the main beachfront drive, Palmetto Boulevard. The sign on the front says, "The Defense Rests, Asheburg, South Carolina." Porches wrap around each level like screened-in scarves. True to its name, the Defense Rests has more bedrooms than a cheap motel. From the rooftop deck, a person can watch the sun rise over the Atlantic Ocean and set over the Saint Helena Sound.

Rollo offered us mushrooms on the ride out here, but I said *hell no*. The nasty soup Chad made out of those things wasn't worth the freaky experience. Trippin' made me feel anxious. I prefer weed making me super-chill and booze making me dance, not mushrooms making me question whether my cheeks are attached to my skull.

Everyone else is already there when we arrive at the Defense Rests. I feel not the least bit restful. I'm in rare form. I bounce around the house like I have pogo-stick legs, yell out names and add some vibrato for shits and giggles, give out hugs like they're contagious. I even hug Peace, though it's been ten months since we've touched each other.

He flinches when I throw my arms around him, but if I want a dramatic reaction, he won't give it to me. "Hey, Gin. All good with you?" he asks in his mellow Peace way, as if we hadn't lost our virginity to each other.

"Always, P." I grin up at him.

LeeLee watches our reunion. Now that I know, it's *so obvious*. I was a fool for not sensing the tension between LeeLee and Peace over Easter weekend.

"How's the family?" I ask him.

"My parents are up at Duke Medical Center for the week. Second opinion about Mom's breast cancer."

"Oh no. That's terrible—"

Before I finish my thought, Rollo yells for me to join him on the back porch for a smoke.

"I'm coming, Ro! What do the doctors say about—"

But Peace has already retreated to the keg. I head for Rollo, all the while grinning like the Cheshire cat. I hold my imaginary hands over my imaginary ears, like LeeLee does when she wants to block out readings. I hope it works in reverse too. I refuse to give her the pleasure of overhearing my thoughts.

We order a bunch of pizzas, and before anyone claims a cheese-and-beer coma, I suggest an evening at Dockside Bar and Grill on Big Bay Creek. We split up between the Smiths' three golf carts. I go with Rollo and the Dooleys. Jess and Lands sit behind LeeLee and Peace. Palmer and Tommy take the last cart. Palmer scoots close to him. I predict a hookup tonight, even if Palm and Tom's relationship didn't survive the hundred miles between Columbia and Charleston. I had assumed Peace and I would have our own passionate reunion this summer. As the saying goes, assumptions make an ass out of you and me. Or just me.

We pull up to a clunky cinderblock building along Big Bay Creek, and I blast through the door. I rapid-fire blink until my eyes adjust to Dockside's welcoming smoke-filled dimness, the red pool tables and warped paneling, the flashing neon beer signs from Anheuser-Busch to Zima, the slick wooden bar with its edges worn down by happy people leaning against it. The band, three thirtysomething dudes who call themselves the Crab Pot Trio, wolf whistle.

The singer shouts, "There she is! Miss Ginny B! Get up here, girl. We've been waiting for you to show up!"

I make a beeline to the stage. For the next hour, my sister songstresses give me a safe space to pour out my emotions about Peace and LeeLee. Martina McBride inspires me to declare that today is the day of reckoning. I channel my inner Stevie Nicks and scream at Peace to go his own way. The Wilson Sisters help me admit that I never really cared until I met him. Bless those fierce women. Their words let me get it all out and still be a badass.

Peace was right that night by the fire. If I ever lose my voice, I'll shrivel up and die. At least I still have that, even if my other greatest fear has come home to roost. I'm trapped in a terrible dream where Peace chooses LeeLee and I'm alone.

By the time the band takes a break, I'm pouring sweat and I've lost all my people in the throng of sandy, salty boozers who crowd the place like a school of mullet.

Chad Dooley steps into my path as I make my way to the bar. "I heard you could sing, but that was some wild shit right there."

"Thanks. Where's everybody else?" I swab my damp neck with a few cocktail napkins, and the bartender hands me a Rolling Rock. I'm unusually sober—no chance to drink while performing, and I sweated out my earlier beers.

"Rollo went back to the house with my sister and Palmer and Tommy. Jess and Landon are out back."

"What about Peace and LeeLee?"

"Haven't seen 'em."

I walk through the crowd and cross a short dock over the marsh. Chad follows me onto the restaurant's covered pierhead. Jess and Lands stand under a dangling lightbulb. Bugs zoom around the lamp as if trapped inside a cartoon thought bubble. I tap Jess's shoulder.

She jumps. "Shit, Gin. You scared me."

"What are y'all canoodling about? *Canoodle*, don't you love that word? LeeLee taught it to me. Where *is* LeeLee, anyway?"

"Not sure," Jess says.

Lands drapes his arm around my shoulders. "They were here, but they—"

"*They?* I only asked about LeeLee."

He tries to backpedal. "Not *they*. Her. Uh. We. I—"

"That her?" Chad points at a shadowy female figure walking up the plank from the boat docks.

Peace's dad rents a boat slip down there. His fishing boat, *It Depends*, spends the warm months sandwiched between the creaky shrimp boats. Old Peace claims that "it depends" is a lawyer's answer for everything. When we were kids, he threw that response at us whenever we asked him a question. When I called Saltmarsh and asked if I could speak to his son, Old Peace would say, "It *depends*, Ginny!" and har-dee-har-har at his own old joke.

That old joke seems like an appropriate answer for how I feel. Do I want to scream at LeeLee and punch Peace? I suppose *it depends*.

"Yup. My girl," I say. "Leeeeeee!"

LeeLee slows when she sees me and blushes in the lamplight. "Hey."

"Let's get a beer," Lands says.

"Great idea." Jess tugs on Chad's arm. "*Dude.* Come on."

Chad's eyes dart between me and LeeLee. He whispers to Lands, "Ahhh. I get it. Catfight."

"Shut up, man," Lands says as the three of them disappear inside.

"*Sooooooo*," I say. "Now *where is* Peace?"

"He's on the boat."

"You been down there with him this whole time?"

"No. We listened to you sing a few songs. You were great." She shifts on her feet.

The bugs keep up their frenzied circling above our heads, a gathering storm of agitation.

Sweat rolls down my back. "Wouldn't it be great," I say, "if one of us had a reading right now, so we could see how this will turn out?"

"Most likely, that would be you. You know I don't have them very much anymore."

"That's because you're a grade-A wuss."

She flinches. "It takes more strength than you know to drown it out."

"Whatever. You got this amazing talent, and you're too scared to use it. You call yourself a story*teller*. What a bunch of bullshit."

"It's not like there are *laws* about what I'm supposed to do with it." She crosses her arms over her chest. "Cheryl said the rules are different for everyone. Besides, you *really* want to fight about who is the *superior psychic* right now? Bigger fish are bubbling away in our deep fryer. Rollo told me y'all talked. I wish he let me speak to you first."

"I'm *glad* he told me. You've been living with me for two months..." I point at her, and my accusatory finger shakes. "And didn't say one... *damn*... thing!"

It's official. For the first time in the history of our friendship, I'm *furious* with LeeLee. The emotional fireworks between us might spark a reading. She knows pretty much everything about me, but I don't want her to know anything else—not my past, not my future, definitely not my thoughts. I try to reel in my anger, but that fish keeps yanking on the line.

"I didn't say anything because *nothing happened* until this past week," she says.

"Don't lie to me. Rollo *saw y'all* on Easter."

"We *talked* on Easter, about how we felt. Nothing *happened*."

"Sure. *Riiight.*"

"You expect me to *ruin* my friendship with you for a drunk make-out session?"

"Who says you're ruining our friendship? Who says I give a shit what you and Peace are doing? Do I care at all?" I snigger. "Well, now, LeeLee. *It depends.*"

"Ginny. Stop twisting everything—"

"You should have told me, whether I give a shit or not."

Her arms flop to her sides. "Peace and I didn't want to upset you over nothing. We needed to make sure we both want this before telling you."

"Rollo said you were at his house last weekend." I take a deep breath. "Did you sleep with him?"

She stares at me. That's my answer.

"Huh! *Okay.* Clearly, y'all want it."

LeeLee grasps my hands. "Ginny." Her voice cracks. "I thought maybe you'd know anyway—"

I shake her off. "Hello? You know we can't count on our readings to show us anything concrete. What a total cop-out."

"But you read things all the time. You *try* to read."

"I don't have a crystal ball to tell you whether you should sleep with him."

"I'm not just *sleeping* with him. I—I'm in love with him. And he's in love with me."

I feel as if she's smacked me upside the head with her empty Miller Lite bottle. "How long has this been going on?"

"We never talked about it before Easter."

"But how long has it been *going on*?"

"I can't speak for him." She sucks in a breath then spits out the words. "But I've felt this way for a long time."

"*Right.* I get it."

"I wouldn't have *done* anything about it. Not ever!" Something in her voice is desperate, as if she assumes I won't believe her. "But you broke up with him almost a year ago, Ginny! You didn't seem fussed about it then, and you never even talk about him anymore. I thought you didn't want him."

"You're right! I did break up with him. *I* was the one who ended it."

"So are you saying it's okay for us to be together?"

She sounds relieved, but I'm not letting her off that easy. "Y'all want my blessing? I'm not y'all's mama."

"You're my *best friend*." The desperation is back. "You were my first friend when I moved to the Burg. You made everyone else take me in. You and I share a secret I've never shared with anyone else—"

"Not Peace?"

"No! I haven't told him. I only told you and your crazy-ass mama. I love her, and I love you." Tears track down her blotchy face like raindrops on a stained-glass window. "If you don't want me to be with Peace, I won't be with him."

I want to shake her, but she's still *my* best friend. I take her hand this time, and out of the blue, a reading comes on.

> *On a rainy spring night, LeeLee lies in her dorm room bed, wrestling with her feelings for Peace and her loyalty to Ginny. She has to get up for her early-morning honors microeconomics class, but rest eludes her. She stays quiet because Ginny is asleep in the bunk above her. Knowing her friend is so close, sleeping soundly with her unbroken heart, makes it worse. LeeLee bites the inside of her cheek until pain mixes with confused tears, but she doesn't sob. She doesn't wake Ginny. She last looks at the clock at four in the morning before she silently cries herself to sleep.*

LeeLee wants to do the right thing. She always does, which is more than I can say for myself.

So I hug her. "No. LeeLee. You be with him if that's what y'all want."

"Do you hate me?"

"No. How can I hate the keeper of the vault?" I rest my forehead on her shoulder, since she's so damn tall. A thought hovers behind my forehead like a balloon. *It's weird as shit... but I don't hate you.*

LeeLee exhales and squeezes me. "I know it's weird as shit—"

"Are you spying into my head?"

"No! I can't spy on anyone. You can't *spy* without meaning to."

"I wish *I* could spy into people's heads. Then, I would have known you were in love with Peace months ago, and I wouldn't feel like such an idiot."

"I'm serious, Gin. I'll walk back down that ramp and tell him it's over—"

"No, you won't. But *I'm* going down there for a few minutes. I got some things I want to say to him."

She looks panicked, and I remember she has reason to be threatened by me. I'm the one who broke *his* heart.

Then she gives me a watery smile. "Of course. I'll find Jess and Lands."

"They're inside with Chad Dooley."

"Good Lord. Why is he here again?"

"He's not so bad."

"I... I'm glad we talked." She looks at me with those big rainbow eyeballs I remember from her first day in Ms. Mullins's class. "Are we okay?"

"Yeah. Sure." I'm *not* sure, but what else can you say in that situation? "I'll be back up in a few."

She nods and walks inside.

On the way to the boat dock, I pass the little outdoor bar. I have a ten in my pocket. "How many shots can I get with this?"

"Of what?" the bartender asks.

"Whatever is cheap and you have plenty of."

He takes my ten and pours me six shots of clear liquor. "An extra one, for the pretty girl with a big voice."

"Thanks." I down three of the shots myself.

"Wow. You got an iron liver *and* iron lungs?"

"*It depends.*" I walk toward the boat ramp with the three remaining shots balanced in my hands.

PEACE TURNS AROUND when I step onto the boat, but his welcoming smile flattens into a bland straight line when he recognizes me. "What's up, Gin?"

I hand him a shot. He holds onto it, like he thinks I might poison him.

"Not much, P. I had a nice conversation with LeeLee."

"Great. What'd y'all talk about?" His voice is as wishy-washy as his expression, as if he's making small talk with an acquaintance at the Piggly Wiggly.

"Oh, this and that. She did mention y'all conducted a long-distance love affair behind my back. And let's not forget y'all screwed last weekend. Where? In your bedroom? One of the guest rooms? The game room? The pool table is so romantic. Oh, duh! I bet it was the dock! The smell of pluff mud is so sexy at low tide—"

"Stop it, Ginny." He sounds like he's silencing a yappy bird dog in a duck blind.

I smile. "I'm *teasing* you. I'm happy for y'all."

"I find that hard to believe."

"Give me a break. *I* broke up with *you* almost a year ago. You slept with other people in Columbia. I slept with other people in Charleston." That's an exaggeration. I slept with one guy at his fraternity house, but that clumsy experience only made me miss Peace. "It's been over between us for a long time."

Peace sniffs and rubs his nose, but he doesn't contradict me. "It was a hard year for me—the knee injury, Mom getting worse. Would have been nice for you to call."

"I didn't think you wanted to hear from me."

"I did. For a long time." He downs his shot. "But when you didn't call, or even ask how I was over the holidays, I realized breaking up was the right thing."

I fight to keep my voice steady. I don't want to give off LeeLee's desperation vibes. "You didn't reach out to me either."

"Did you expect me to chase you?"

Yes, I think. *That's* exactly *what I hoped you'd do.* A very different response comes out of my mouth. "I bet LeeLee was more compassionate than me."

"Yeah. She was. She is."

Those frantic thoughts keep coming. *I was scared you would leave me, you would find someone else your sick mama would love, who wasn't prone to scaring you with vague premonitions about the deaths of your family members. I couldn't stand it, so I had to leave you first. Don't you get it?*

Too bad he can't *read* my thoughts, because I'll never be able to *say* any of that. It will live in my head, making perfect sense but never spoken aloud.

"Y'all make a good couple," I say as my thoughts keep hammering away. *LeeLee-and-Peace, Peace-and-LeeLee.* "Have you... have you always wanted her?"

"No." He sighs. "Maybe. I don't know. We've always had potential, but I would never cheat on you."

"I'm glad I made it easier for you."

"I can't tell if you're being serious or sarcastic."

"Neither can I. Curse of my life."

It has to be past midnight, and Edisto is a sleepy town. The restaurant behind us and flickering porch lights across the marsh provide the only visibility. One by one, the porch lights snuff out, as if smothered by passing clouds. The lights on the dock go dark.

Pure blackness embraces me. My hair stands on end. My mouth starts running of its own accord, and I jump blindly into the abyss of the unexplainable future.

> "LeeLee is Ginny's death, and Ginny is hers. Peace is the moon, pushing and pulling the tides of their lives. How strong his gravity is remains to be seen, but Ginny is not afraid. We cannot be reborn unless we die."

"What the hell was that?" Peace takes my arm. "One of your readings?"

I press my fingers into my temples. "Yes. I—"

"What the hell does it *mean*? You, me, LeeLee? People dying?"

"LeeLee quoted Anne the first day we met—in Ms. Mullins's history class—and it's always stuck with me. But that was... what's it called? Metaphorical. Mary and Anne didn't *actually* kill each other—"

"Marianne who?"

"Not *Marianne*. Mary *and* Anne—"

"Forget it. Can we stop talking about death, please?"

I try to reassure him. "I'm not supposed to be afraid. That's positive, right?"

"Damn it, Ginny. It's one thing to tell me my cat will get hit by a car, or tell Tommy he'll fail algebra. But you can't tell people their parents will die. You can't put it on me that I *might* do something that *might* mess up all our lives someday. I can't take it. I never could. Thank God my girlfriend isn't having psychic visions anymore." He hurls his empty shot cup, but it's so light, it floats toward the trash bag.

I almost tell him LeeLee is like me—*ha ha on you, Makepeace Smith*. But I remember our vault. I keep my mouth shut.

"Hey, y'all," someone says from over my shoulder. It's Chad Dooley. "I came down to smoke. Couldn't help but hear y'all arguing. Figured you might want something to chill things out." He holds up a pipe.

"Bring it on," Peace says.

Chad steps onto the boat. He lights the bowl and passes it to me. "Y'all having a lover's quarrel?"

"No." Peace and I reply at the same time.

"Just clearing up some things," I say. "Peace and LeeLee are dating now. I'm happy for them." I take a hit from the bowl and hold it in for a few seconds before exhaling then give the bowl to Chad. The sickly sweet weed smell envelops me like a worn, comforting blanket.

"I watched all of y'all over the years," Chad says. "I wondered how y'all could be so up each other's asses but not have any drama."

"We had drama," Peace says. "Ginny broke up with Rollo in seventh grade."

I chime in. "Once, Tommy punched Lands in the face when they were drunk because Lands told him he had small feet."

"Totally offended Tommy's manhood," Peace says.

My snickers turn into flat-out cackles as I try to spill the story. "Then Peace... then Peace had to—"

"I jumped in to break it up. Landon's old coon dog thought I attacked him, so the dog bit me square on the ass. I couldn't sit for a week." He hobbles around the boat and clutches his behind.

"That was the most loyal, senile dog in Colleton County." I wipe my eyes.

"Rest in Peace, Moonshine, you old fleabag," Peace says.

My laughter trails off as Chad takes a hit and passes the bowl to Peace. Small waves smack against the boat's hull, as if the creek keeps chuckling over our story.

"Good stuff, man." Peace exhales and coughs.

The smell is strong now, even for the likes of us.

Chad grips the bowl between his thumb and forefinger. He holds it away from himself like a dead mouse. "I got some other good stuff if y'all are down."

"No more shrooms for me," I say.

"Better than shrooms. I don't usually do giveaways, but let's call it a—what did my grandma say when she took a present to someone to say thank you?"

"A hostess gift?" I suggest.

"Right. A host gift for letting us stay at your sweet house, Peace."

"It's got a real foundation and everything," I say.

"Nice one, Ginny." Chad removes a sandwich bag filled with green pills from his pocket. He gives Peace a pill then offers me one. "For the clever little lady too. I'm feeling generous."

"What is it?" I ask Chad, but Peace replies first.

"OxyContin. Doctor prescribed me these over the winter for my knee."

"What a high, right?" Chad grins. "And it's legal. What more do you want?"

Peace holds that little green circle before his eyes. "Yup." It disappears into his mouth.

I jiggle the pill in my palm. One side says OC. The other side, 80. I try to swallow it, but it sticks in my throat. I wash it down with a gulp of beer.

"Y'all want to head to the bar?" Chad asks.

"I'm going back to the house." Peace looks past me—for LeeLee, probably.

She might think we had a last quickie on the boat. My head is starting to swim, and I can't say it doesn't cross my mind.

Chad steps onto the dock and starts walking up the ramp.

Peace takes my arm. "Don't fall."

"I won't. I'm glad we talked," I say, though it's about as anticlimactic as Peace chucking the shot cup into the trash bag.

"I'm glad we talked too."

"Sorry about the reading. I really don't know what it means."

"I know you can't control them. It's not like you *want* to have them."

"Right," I say.

Peace knows so much less about me and LeeLee than he thinks.

"Maybe it doesn't mean anything."

"Sure. I was upset, and... my subconscious puked up weird memories from high school." Simpler to think that than ponder how Peace might be the literal kiss of death for me and LeeLee.

"I'm sorry I bit your head off," he says. "It was kinda dramatic, though—in a very Ginny way."

"What other way is there for me?"

We catch up to Chad, and Peace picks up the pace.

"See y'all," Peace says.

He leaves Chad to hold me up. Not the most comforting thought, but Peace is a man on a mission. Just Chad and me, so I lean on him.

"You told me I can't touch you unless you ask," he says.

"I'm asking."

"Then, I got you." Chad puts an arm around my shoulders. He pats his pocket, where he stored his bag of pain-killing peas. "I got whatever you need."

Chapter 9

LeeLee, 2015

Retired mobster or not, Big Lou Marciano wasn't exaggerating when he claimed to know people who knew people. He sends me his first email report within four days of hiring him. I message Jess and Palmer.

Me: *Y'all, check your emails. Incoming PI report.*

Jess: *Damn, that was fast. How do they find this stuff?*

Me: *Anyone can walk into a bar and ask a question. You gotta have the balls and the street cred to do it.*

Palmer: *Or maybe he left a horse head in someone's bed.*

Me: *Don't ask, don't tell.*

I reread the report before I send it to them.

Report for Ms. Lisa Moretz
Subject: Virginia Blankenship
Client Information Only/Not for Official Use

I found the following information about Virginia "Ginny" Blankenship in addition to the attached criminal record.

First record of Ginny in the Myrtle Beach area is a public drunkenness charge in 2008. Ginny was a server at Mama Moo's Bar and Grille in approximately 2008–2009. She also performed live music with various acts. Multiple sources reported Ginny as a talented singer who was erratic. She often called out of work due to what coworkers and other musicians described as excessive drinking and smoking marijuana. At the time, she was dating Makepeace Smith. Mr. Smith also worked as a bartender at Mama Moo's. Coworkers described Mr. Smith as having alcohol and drug problems.

Ginny was a server at the Beach Hut for about nine months before being fired for getting into a verbal altercation with a patron. While Mr. Smith did not work at this establishment, coworkers knew him as her "boyfriend" and stated he sometimes visited her at work.

Ginny and Mr. Smith participated in several Narcotics Anonymous meetings at Oceanside Presbyterian Church in approximately 2010, but the consensus among other members of this meeting (speaking on the condition of anonymity, as NA rules forbid discussing meetings) was that Mr. Smith made Ginny attend with him. They did not maintain more than a week of sobriety.

Between 2008 and 2013, Ginny and Mr. Smith lived in several rental apartments between Myrtle Beach and Garden City. They stayed at the Sleepy Time Inn, presumably during times when they didn't have an apartment. They also spent multiple stints at a local homeless shelter between the years 2010 and 2013. Helping Hands House, Inc., is a privately run 503(c) nonprofit organization specializing in assisting addicts in securing services while providing overnight shelter.

Mr. Smith last stayed at Helping Hands in early June 2013, while Ginny continued to stay at HH sporadically for several weeks after he left the facility. At that time, the staff noted an unknown male stayed in her room on multiple occasions. As this was against policy, staff asked Ginny to leave the facility. She did not return. I could find no record of her whereabouts after June 2013.

Because of Ms. Moretz's concerns about Mr. Smith's potential involvement in Ginny's disappearance, I did preliminary research into his own employment and criminal record (see attached criminal history).

Mr. Smith was employed more regularly than Ginny, but he, too, cycled through employment as a bartender, working at no less than six establishments in the Myrtle Beach area between 2008 and 2013, in-

cluding MacDaddy's, a local gentleman's club. Coworkers knew him to be a heavy drinker and "pill popper." MacDaddy's eventually fired Mr. Smith because Ginny regularly showed up at the club, accused him of cheating on her, and harassed the dancers, other staff, and patrons.

Mr. Smith occasionally worked on charter deep-sea fishing boats through Grand Strand Adventures (GSA). The owner was not aware of Mr. Smith doing drugs while working for him, but sometimes, he called Mr. Smith in for a shift and got no reply for a week. When he did work, however, GSA found him knowledgeable about the water, fishing, and boating, and he was good with clients.

According to a contact who is familiar with such activity, Mr. Smith was a regular customer who purchased marijuana, cocaine, and illegal oxycodone and Adderall. To his knowledge, neither Mr. Smith nor Ginny used heroin or methamphetamines.

The last record of Mr. Smith in Horry County is a speeding ticket in August 2013. He then relocated to Boone, North Carolina. I searched records for him there and found his final DUI in December 2013.

I will report any further findings. Thank you for letting me help you with your investigation.

Lou Marciano, Private Investigator

I hit Send then wait for my text messages to start lighting up.

Jess: *Two words. Unidentified male.*

Palmer: *Did y'all feel SO SAD reading this? I cannot believe our old friends lived like that for so long. Why didn't they reach out to us?*

Jess: *It's really sad but also makes sense. I bet Peace had too much pride to ask for help and Ginny was flat-out off her rocker.*

Me: *I agree it's terribly sad, but let's focus on the unnamed male Ginny was shacking up with. I'll tell Big Lou he's priority numero uno. Otherwise, we know Peace's story lines up. He said they broke up about two years ago. He last stayed with her at that shelter in June 2013. She's involved with another man around the same time. Then Peace moved to Boone later that summer.*

Palmer: *That doesn't let him off the hook. Last known contact with her in June. He was in Myrtle until August.*

Jess: *It almost looks bad. She goes missing, and he leaves town soon after?*

Me: *Maybe she wasn't missing yet. Maybe no one knew where she was.*

Jess: *Lee, that's like the same thing!*

Palmer intervenes with text diplomacy before Jess and I can get our bicker on. *Any reply from LoveGinnyB?*

Me: *Nothing yet. BTW, I have to get out of my house this weekend. Clay is in the FROG again.*

Jess: *Oh snap. Why now?*

Me: *Too much to text. Palm, can I stay with you?*

Palmer: *Ugh. Dean's parents are in town this weekend.*

Jess: *Come out to Asheburg and stay with us. We can stalk Cousin Drew for information and get some boiled peanuts at the Peanut Shack.*

Me: *The Nut Sack? Say no more.*

Palmer: *Eww, that old Rollo joke still grosses me out. Stop it!*

Jess: *Love you Prissy Palm *smiley face**

Me: *Love y'all both. Jess, I'll be at your house by like 7. Good?*

Jess: *Lands can get Mia to bed. I'll have foamy keg beer and shots of Jägermeister waiting.*

Me: *Ha ha. Then you better be prepared to drink alone.*

Jess: *Girl, you know the deal. If you're finally back, we're taking it waaaaaay back.*

"SO, YOU'RE GOING TO Jess's this weekend?" Clay asks.

We stand on our first-floor piazza, watching the boys run around the yard. My weekend bag hangs on my shoulder, and my car keys are at the ready. I need to make a quick getaway before tears attempt a jailbreak from my eyeballs.

Clay sips his Friday-evening beer. "The whole gang getting back together?"

"No. Only me and Jess—and Lands taking care of their baby. Peace won't be there, if that's what you're asking."

He shrugs and sets the beer on the window ledge. "We're heading to Wadmalaw tomorrow to hang out with my parents. We might stay the night."

Clay's parents recently retired from Columbia to Wadmalaw Island, somewhere between Edisto Island and Charleston. Their house on Bohicket Creek is a waterfront paradise. As Clay loves to remind me, his parents have twelve-foot mean low water.

"Where did you tell them I'm going this weekend?" I ask.

"I said we're having some problems and you need some space. They asked me to come out so they can help with the kids."

My mouth hangs open. As far as I know, Clay's parents are unaware of our issues. "You told George and Elsie without consulting me?"

"They're *my parents*, LeeLee. I told them we haven't been getting along, so you decided to stay with some old friends."

"Good Lord, Clay. That makes it seem like everything is my choice—"

"It *is* your choice—"

"And *my* fault!"

"I never said that. I acknowledged that I'm the bad guy, didn't I? And I didn't give them any details."

"They're going to ask for details eventually," I say. "Do you plan to tell them the truth?"

"I don't know what I'll tell them. I should have talked to them before everything blew up." He gives an annoyingly nonchalant shrug. "My parents have been married for forty-five years. My three sisters are all married. Not one divorce. They must be doing something right."

Harsh words spill out of me like water forced through a colander. "George is a *patriarchal dinosaur*, and Elsie has been dependent on him her entire adult life. You've said so yourself a *million* times. Bringing your parents into *our* problems is *not* the solution."

"So what *is* the solution, Lee? What we're doing clearly isn't helping. *Hey, Gelsie!* We're having marital problems." We always lovingly refer to his parents as *Gelsie*, our geriatric version of Bennifer or Brangelina. Familiarity makes his sarcastic tone sting worse. He cups his hands over his mouth and yells across the yard. "News flash! Marriage is hard!"

"What's hard, Daddy?" Trey stops pulling his brothers around in their wagon and looks up at us.

"Nothing, buddy," Clay says. "Just being goofy."

"Will you stop?" I hiss. "I *do not* want you airing our dirty laundry to your parents—"

"Please stop telling me what to do with my family, LeeLee. *You're* the one who potentially wants a divorce. If we split up, I'll need my family's support. Plus I'd rather not blindside them. My mother will be heartbroken. Mama Donna would be heartbroken, too, if she were still with us."

His words knock the fight out of me. "That's... that's just... *mean*, Clay."

"I can't say anything right. Why don't you go? This conversation isn't getting any better."

"Right. Y'all have fun this weekend."

He exhales, as if he's held in his goodbye all day. "We will. You too."

I turn away from him to say goodbye to the boys, but his frustration and anger wash over me and about knock me off the steps. His thoughts ricochet through my head.

If I find out she's staying with Peace Smith, I'm going straight to Clark.

Clark is Clark Middleton, a compatriot of my boss, Darlene, and the most feared family court attorney in town.

Annoyance makes me careless with my words. "Clark won't represent you. I've worked on dozens of cases with him. He knows me too well. You better call one of your daddy's friends in Columbia."

Clay's eyes widen. "I don't know what you're talking about."

"And I'm *not* staying with Peace!"

"Go ahead, stay with Peace! Go back to your *druggie college boyfriend* and live the life you dreamed of in 2001! See how it works out for you!" He whistles, and the boys stop their bickering. "Y'all, say goodbye to Mama. Then come on in. We're ordering pizza."

"Peeeet-zzaaaaa!" Bowman runs to me and throws his arms around my legs. "Have fun, Mama!"

I kneel to hug him. "You, too, little man. Love you. I'll call you tomorrow, okay?"

"Yup." He runs up the stairs and into the house.

Trey lugs Malachy out of the wagon. I walk across the yard and scoop up my littlest guy. I lean down with Mal resting on one hip and kiss the top of Trey's head. "Love you, buddy. Help your dad, okay?"

"Yes, ma'am," Trey says. "Mal, want a piggyback?"

"Yes! Pumeedown, Mama." Malachy squirms in my arms.

I set him on his big brother's back and kiss his cheeks. He bounces in place.

"Malachy. Careful," Clay says from the porch. "You'll hurt Trey's back."

"I got it, Dad," Trey says. "Oink! Oink!"

I kiss Mal's cheek, but Trey's porker routine enthralls him, so he pays my departure little mind. Trey and Malachy disappear into the house, and I flee to the safety of my car. Clay still stands on the piazza as I put the car in reverse. He watches me back into the street. It seems silly, given our altercation, but I wave. He waves back then goes inside.

I drive down Council Street and turn left onto Tradd. I'm leaving home behind, yet I'm heading toward home.

Chapter 10
Ginny, 1999–2000

The inaugural summer of LeeLee and Peace passes blessedly quickly, in part thanks to Rollo's constant supply of good weed. Before I know it, it's August, and we're all about to head back to college for the fall semester. Everyone except Ro-Ro, King of the Burg. On the last Saturday before classes start, His Highness wheels the *Reel Nasty* off the trailer for a final boat day blowout.

This boat has always seemed big to me, but as we motor away from the marina, I think the tension among everyone might have shrunk the hull. Palmer and Tommy are deciding whether or not to try long-distance for a second time. Landon and Jess have been arguing because she's about done with his sloppy drinking.

"He's sauced within an hour of leaving church and acting the fool," Jess said to me as we drove to the Combahee Estates boat launch. "There's a time and a place, and it's not at Me-Mere and Pe-Paw's dining table for Sunday lunch."

I try my damnedest to hide it, but LeeLee and Peace still weird me out. At least they don't rub it in my face. He lifts her into the boat with his hands on her waist. She subtly touches his arm whenever he leans past her to get into the cooler. She slathers sunscreen on his back, and he doesn't complain. He once chided me for being a mama's girl, but Mama LeeLee sure has him under her thumb these days.

Last week, I asked Palmer about LeeLee and Peace when we strolled the mall in Charleston looking for new school clothes. We'd been avoiding the topic for months, but she looked me straight in the eyes.

"I'm not gonna sugarcoat it, Gin," she said. "They're madly in love. Peace is so relaxed and content it's like watching a spoiled cat snooze in a sunbeam. LeeLee glows like a firefly when he touches her. He touches her a lot when you're not around."

There I had it. I might as well get used to it. On this last Saturday before we move into our apartment on Bull Street, I'm determined to be myself and have a good time.

I sit with Rollo in the captain's chair in the heavy August heat. We need gills to breathe in this kind of humidity. The temperature makes the ice-filled cooler look like a welcoming feather bed. While the rest of us sweat out our romantic angst, Rollo has zero reason to be disgruntled, since he never dates anyone for more than a couple of weeks.

He chews on a Tootsie Roll and presses Play on the CD changer. Grand Funk Railroad starts in with "Closer to Home." Since we turned eighteen, he's started acquiring tattoos at a rate that alarms his upstanding Baptist parents. He has a new one on his forearm. A clipper ship with swirly cursive writing underneath that says, "O Captain! My Captain!" The only poem Rollo has ever read from beginning to end.

We cut through the glassy water for a few minutes. No one says much. Everyone needs a few beers to loosen up.

Rollo gives me the side-eye from behind his glasses. "You okay, Gin?"

"Pssht. Of course, oh, Captain, my Captain. Why wouldn't I be?"

"P. and Lee."

"I'm so over that." I backpedal. "Wasn't ever really *under* it, if you know what I mean."

"It's okay if you care."

"I don't." I smile. "I'm heading back to Charleston in a couple of days. Four thousand Citadel boys better watch out—the C of C fraternities too."

"Be careful, seriously. A lot of the guys at C of C and the Citadel are assholes. You don't know those dudes like you know the boys from town."

"I know I'm spoiled. Growing up with a bunch of gentlemen like y'all. I'll be careful, Ro. Where we heading?"

"Up the river instead of out into the sound. Some bridge jumping to leap into the new school year."

We exit the no-wake zone, and Rollo picks up the pace. The river narrows and deepens as it slithers inland like an agitated water moccasin. Houses huddle at the edge of the woods behind wide stretches of soggy, living shag carpet. Only a few docks reach across that big marsh. No one but the richest richies can afford to build such long docks. They cost more than my whole house and the land it sits on.

Reel Nasty leans into a sharp curve, and the trestle bridge appears. The last train crossed the bridge, like, fifty years ago, but there's no reason to knock it down. Grass and weeds grow in its cracks and crevices, and a full-grown tree has sprouted in the middle of the span like a stubborn cowlick. The tide is going out, so Rollo wants to anchor on the far side of the bridge. Stripes of light shine through the trestles as we pass under them. A family of mourning doves coos its disapproval of our invasion.

Rollo points the bow into the retreating tide, and Landon throws the anchor. It seems to run forever before it catches. The boat floats back a few feet and stops. I home in on a dead tree in the marsh. It doesn't move, so we're good and stuck.

"The current is rippin', y'all," Rollo says, "but it will take you right to the ladder."

"See you bitches on the other side." Tommy dives in, swims across the river, and scales the ladder. He walks along the trestles, a bare-chested circus performer on an iron tightrope. He stops in the middle of the bridge and faces away from us. The dark water waits twenty feet below him.

"If he moons us, I will cut his ass before he can pull up his shorts," Palmer says.

Tommy spares us the sight of his white butt below his tanned shoulders. He does a backflip and lands feet first, like a country Olympian.

"Nice!" Landon yells as Tommy pops to the surface and shakes out his hair.

"I expected a double flip," Peace says. "Or at least a twist."

"Let's see what you got, asshole," Tommy says.

Peace dives into the water, and for the next thirty minutes, we take turns jumping. Everyone except LeeLee and me. She never jumps because heights terrify her, and I have a plan brewing.

I sidle up beside her. "You want to jump?"

"You know the answer. I want to, but I won't."

"Come on, Lee. It's the last day of summer, in the last summer of the *damn century*! Jump. I'll go with you."

She watches Palmer and Jess link hands and leap, screaming, into the water. They emerge laughing and trying to yank their bikinis into place.

"My suit cut my butt in half!" Jess yells.

To my surprise, LeeLee removes her sunglasses. She hands them to Peace.

"You sure you wanna jump?" he asks her.

"Yeah. It's about time."

"You don't have to."

"Stop babying her, Peace." I dive into the water. This time of year, it's like leaping into a pitcher of tea after the ice has melted in the sun.

I surface and spit out a mouthful of brackish water then turn back to the boat just in time to see Peace kiss LeeLee before she dives. I spit again to get rid of the nasty taste the sight leaves in my mouth.

We swim to the bridge, climb the ladder, and step onto the trestles. The metal bits will burn our bare feet, so we stand on the wooden slats. LeeLee clings to the pilings.

"We gotta walk to the middle," I say. "Can't jump here. Too close to the marsh."

"Okay," she says, but her face pales under her tan.

"Give me your hand," I say.

She lets go and takes my hand. Her clenching fingers dig into mine.

"You got this, LeeLee!" Palmer yells from the boat.

I look down. All six of our friends gaze up at us like they're watching a lunar eclipse. Peace crosses his arms over his bare chest. His sunglasses hide some of his expression, but he sure isn't smiling.

I walk slowly toward the center of the bridge and tug LeeLee along with me. "Don't look down."

"I can't help it. I see the water through the slats and... oh, good Lord."

"It's okay. Come on. Almost there."

She freezes again and closes her eyes. "Shit, shit, shit."

"You okay, Lee?" Landon calls up to us.

"She's fine!" I say.

"I can't, Ginny," LeeLee says.

"Yes, you can." I entice her a few more feet toward the middle. "Look. We can jump now."

She peers down at the water. "No. I can't."

"Don't be silly, girl. It's a lot easier to jump than to climb back down."

"I *can't*, Gin. I have to turn around."

"LeeLee, get a grip!" I snap. All this drama when she just needs to freakin' jump.

A splash below us. I look down at Peace swimming toward the bridge. Either to climb up and bring her down, or climb up and jump with her. Either way, it's so *annoying*. She's *my* friend. My scaredy-cat friend. If anyone gets her to jump, I will.

"Hold on, Lee," he says.

She takes a deep breath. "I think I'm okay, P. Give me a second." She squeezes my fingers enough to cut off my circulation.

"Just jump, LeeLee," I say. "We all do it. It's not a big deal, damn."

"I'm trying... I—" She looks down again. "No. I can't. Peace!"

"I'll be right there," he says.

Peace coming to the rescue and LeeLee being a damsel in distress is too much for me. She's such a *wuss*, whether about jumping off bridges or having readings. Someone needs to get her to toughen up.

You're such a chickenshit, LeeLee! I'm with you. Just jump, damn it!

Her eyes widen, and I know she read my thoughts, but I don't care. I grip her fingers myself and jump.

I drag her along with me through the hot air. We're still holding hands when we hit the water, but the force of impact drives us apart.

For a few seconds, I don't know where she is. I open my eyes as I shift my bikini top back into place. The salt stings, and I can't see her in the shifting liquid darkness. I kick to the surface. She isn't there. My heart about stops. A splash, and she surfaces. She coughs and grabs her bathing suit. I swim to her and hold her arm as she sputters and treads water.

"You okay?" I'm so relieved to see her, I forget how much she pissed me off.

"Yeah, I—"

"I'm sorry. You're not a chickenshit."

"You knew I read that?"

"I figured from the look on your face. It was a loud thought."

She wipes her eyes. "I am kind of a chickenshit."

"No. That was awful of me to think about you."

Peace swims up beside us and spins her around. He pushes her hair out of her face. "You okay?"

LeeLee nods. "It wasn't so bad once I got into the air."

Peace looks at me over her shoulder. For the first time ever, he truly seems pissed at me. "That was *bullshit*, Gin."

"It's *okay*. I wouldn't have done it on my own. Now I have." LeeLee grins up at our friends in the boat. "Maybe I'll do it again!"

I'm not sure if she's genuine or trying to protect me. Once they see her smiling face, everyone starts cheering for her rather than glowering at me.

I smile, too, though I still feel bad. "See, P.? Every bird needs a little push out of the nest."

"Let's get back in the boat. Didn't Cheryl send us some snooder-dooders?" LeeLee looks between me and Peace like a parent trying to manage squabbling siblings by offering them a bribe.

"Yeah, she did." I swim toward the boat ladder beside the engine. "*Whoooo, LeeLee!* You did it, girl!"

"Let's do a shot to celebrate!" Rollo removes a bottle of Evil Evan from the cooler.

I get into the boat, and Landon hands me a towel. Peace and LeeLee stay in the water behind the boat. He puts his arms around her, as if to keep her afloat. She wraps hers around his neck and kisses him.

It's not pleasant to watch, but that's what I get for being an asshole. Then again, LeeLee always said she *wanted* to jump. If I hadn't been an asshole, she may never have done it. If Peace got to her first, she would have climbed down in defeat. At least now she made the leap, and maybe she won't be scared to jump next time.

I have a thought as Rollo hands me a shot. *Who is the hero, and who is the asshole?* Sometimes it's hard to tell.

US GIRLS LIVE TOGETHER, but we don't see much of each other these days. It's sophomore year, and I took the spring Y2K semester off. I work most nights at the Silver Dollar Bar on King Street. I'm up late, and I sleep later. Jess and Palmer are on the parental tabs, so they spend the afternoons studying or cutting up on the back porch of our Bull Street apartment. LeeLee is double majoring in prelaw and sociology, and she has a job in the College of Charleston's student center. She also spends weekends in Columbia, visiting her boyfriend. Who, of course, happens to be my ex-boyfriend.

LeeLee and Peace have been dating for almost a year, so I'm used to Peace being around our place sometimes. When he comes to Charleston, I pick up extra shifts. I barely see him, which is how I like it. Jess and Palmer ask me all the time if I'm okay with Peace-and-LeeLee. I always say yeah, sure. No need to mention how my skin feels too tight when I see them together.

Our apartment is one of six units in an antebellum mansion, and the gardens were paved over to make a decent parking lot by Charleston standards. Since LeeLee and I don't have cars, Peace takes our extra spot when he visits.

His truck is still there when I bike into our parking lot that Sunday afternoon in March. To reduce LeeLee's chances of reading my thoughts, I do my damnedest to squash my feelings as I walk up the rickety iron staircase into the apartment. Best to be emotional mayonnaise—bland and colorless.

When my best friend is sleeping with my first love, flavorless feelings are easier said than done. She not only has Peace, she had to one-up me in the psychic department with her mind-reading. But it might not always be like that. Sometimes, when we sit on the porch, listening to Palmer and Jess complain about Tommy and Landon, I focus on the inside of LeeLee's head. No words have come through yet, but I'm convinced *something* is happening behind her college superwoman routine.

Of course, I might have imagined confusion and frustration underneath LeeLee's laughter and wisecracks. Maybe hiding my feelings and grasping for hers is loosening my screws. My head will split open like a watermelon falling out the back of a truck and striking hot tarmac, and I'll finally go truly crazy.

By the time I cross the apartment's threshold, my mood is more Hellmann's than hot sauce. Our apartment takes up the house's grand old ballroom. We live under cathedral ceilings, alongside several fancy marble fireplaces that don't work. A walled-in piazza contains the kitchen, bathrooms, and Jess's and Palmer's bedrooms. LeeLee's and my shared bedroom—complete with drywall barrier—is divided from the rest of the apartment by a heavy sliding door.

My reflection in the living room's cloudy antique floor-to-ceiling wall mirror shows a smiling chick with reddish hair in a Silver Dollar T-shirt and jeans. She doesn't look one bit jealous or annoyed. All emotional condiments are under control.

LeeLee and Peace sit on the sofa while Palmer's Blink-182 CD plays on the stereo. She's drinking a Coke, and he has a beer. A bag of weed and a pipe occupy the table, and LeeLee has lit a flowery candle to cover the smell. Peace likes to smoke a bowl before he gets on the road. That means he'll leave soon, thank goodness.

"Hey, y'all," I say as cheerfully as I can.

"Hey, Gin," they say at the same time, in the awkward way our conversations always start.

"How was work?" LeeLee asks.

"March Madness day shift means legit madness, but at least I got off early. Can I get a hit?"

"Sure." Peace packs the bowl for me.

I take a long drag then hand it to him. He starts to inhale himself, but LeeLee clears her throat.

"You have to drive," she says.

"Right. Okay." He returns the pipe to me.

He'll light up again as soon as he gets in the car. He's appeasing her, but he used to appease me, too, in different ways. They don't call him Peace for nothing. I giggle.

"What's funny?" LeeLee asks.

"Nothing. I already smoked at work. Yours went straight to my head, Peace. That's prime stuff."

"Thanks," he says.

I giggle again. What a goofy response, as if he grew the weed himself, like Jack and the Weed Beanstalk. Then again, the whole scene is goofy. It always is among the three of us.

"Are you sure you can drive?" LeeLee asks him. "You could stay the night."

"I can't. I gotta get to my early class. I'm already failing. But I'm fine. I promise."

"What about your knee?"

"It's not bad yet, but it will be if I don't take a pain pill before I get on the road."

Peace's knee injury from the previous year hasn't improved much, then another bad tackle sidelined him again during August training. He didn't play this past season either.

"At least you'll get a little buzz for your trouble," I say. "You going to suit up for spring training?"

"Nope," he says. "I'm out."

"Next season too? That sucks." I take another drag from the bowl.

"No. I mean I'm *out*. Like, forever."

I cough. "Like, forever-forever?"

"Yup. My football career is over. I can have surgery, but I'll never play at the highest level."

I can't imagine a world where he doesn't play football. "What about your scholarship?"

"Gone too." He reaches across the table for the bowl. "Good thing my parents have money, right?"

"You're pretty chill about it."

"Nothing to be done," he says.

I look at LeeLee, and she raises one eyebrow. Peace won't show us how he feels about his career-ending injury—no more than I'll reveal my true feelings about their romance or let LeeLee read my thoughts like a trashy tabloid magazine.

"Will you have the surgery anyway?" I ask. "You should if it will make your knee better."

"Exactly, Gin. That's what I've been telling him."

"Nope," he says. "I can handle the pain with medication—"

"That's not a long-term solution!" LeeLee says.

"And it might improve on its own."

"I'm not, like, a knee surgeon," I say, "but that seems far-fetched."

"*Thank you!*" LeeLee and I are temporarily on the same team again.

"I'll get it done someday if it doesn't get better," he says. "I can't mess with it right now. My parents have enough on their plates."

"How's your mom?" I ask.

When Miss Lucy had a successful mastectomy, I hoped I had misinterpreted my reading about her impending doom. Then the cancer came back with a vengeance and spread into her lymph nodes.

"Not good," he says. "As you predicted, cancer will take her out."

"How awful." I lean across the coffee table and touch his knee.

He shifts away, as if I might leave a scorch mark on his Gamecock football sweats. An instinctive and instantaneous withdrawal, like a fish darting into deeper water when an osprey's shadow passes overhead. LeeLee must be pleased. I would be if he were still my boyfriend.

I sit back against the cushions. "I wish I could have given you more specifics about what would happen to her."

"It wouldn't have made a difference. She caught it early, and she's still going to die."

LeeLee takes his hand. She squeezes, and he squeezes back. He wipes at his eyes. Such heavy sadness hangs over him. I can't even feel jealous he accepted LeeLee's comfort while rejecting mine.

I have to keep talking. "How's your dad? Drew?"

"I feel sorry for Drew. With me in Columbia, Drew takes all of Dad's heat. He's a decent running back, but he won't play college ball. All Dad's plans for another Smith in the Gamecocks Hall of Fame blew up with my knee. But if Dad focuses on being mad at me for messing up his great white hope and getting shitty grades to boot, he doesn't have to be sad about Mom—or disappointed by Drew. I officially took over as the disappointing son."

"You are *not* a disappointment! It's not your fault you got injured," LeeLee says. "And your grades will come up. You're just having a hard time."

Peace doesn't acknowledge her attempt to pump him up. "Drew is only sixteen, and he's watching Mom waste away and listening to Dad's nonstop BS. I need to spend more weekends in Asheburg. We were talking about that when you came in."

"Chad Dooley is still the hookup back home," I say. "Not just weed. He's got a guy who gets oxy from a pharmacist in Barnwell. If you, like, run out."

"I'll keep that in mind," he says.

"You have a prescription," LeeLee says. "You don't need any more."

Peace looks at his watch. "I gotta get going, y'all."

"I'm afraid you'll fall asleep and get in a wreck," LeeLee says. "The beers. The weed. Now an oxy."

"You worry too much, honey." He stands. "Good to see you, Gin."

"You too," I say. "I'm so sorry about the football stuff. Tell your parents hi for me."

"I will. Thanks for the tip about Dooley." Peace gives me a genuine smile, and I smile back. I understand something about him that LeeLee doesn't. He'll be perfectly fine driving to Columbia. I know because I've driven thousands of miles with him.

Peace retrieves his bag from LeeLee's room then takes her hand and pulls her up from the sofa. His fingers lace through hers. I walk into the kitchen to mess with some dishes. I don't need to see them holding hands.

Lee follows him outside. They reappear in the window over the sink. She leans against his truck. Peace is surely reassuring her that he can drive. He makes her laugh, and she ruffles his hair. When he pulls her close, I draw the curtains. I want to hold onto the warmth I saw in his eyes. Watching them kiss will snuff it out.

Chapter 11

LeeLee, 2015

Since my mother's death, I don't have much reason to go back to Asheburg. I feel a little sick to my stomach as I drive through town to Jess's house. My brain resists adjusting to the changes. Even long-abandoned structures serve a purpose in my memory. Small towns track time by collapsing roofs and broken windows.

An expansive new Refuel gas station lords over the intersection where River Road becomes Dukes Street. Jersey Mike's Subs has joined the town's short list of fast-food options. New Jersey's bready infiltration of their deep-fried town must have scandalized Old Peace and his compatriots. Rollo's dad bought the sod farm across from Ashepoo High—mascot Al E. Gator, 1998 and 2003 state football champions—and built two boxy brownish apartment buildings that look like giant rabbit hutches.

On Magnolia Street, a farm-to-table restaurant, FEED, has replaced Dukes's Feed and Farm Supply. Combahee Coffee churns out brews a few doors down. The old-time eateries are holding on—the ACE of Spades, Marshside Diner, and Sweetie Pie's. The antiques shops continue to sell a mix of treasures and junk, depending on one's definition. Old Peace's law firm, Smith, Smith & Smith, LLP, still occupies the historic Asheburg Inn across from the town hall and the Proper Park. During college, I imagined marriage might add me to the storied list of Smiths who practiced law in that building.

I figured I would stay here, in this town I loved, along the rivers I loved, with people who taught me how to love.

A revelation comes over me as I instinctively slow while passing the tiny Asheburg Police Department. Convenience hasn't been keeping me away from Asheburg. Change pushed me away and not just the new buildings and businesses. Many friends answered the call of the big city, like I did. I lost my mother to a burst blood vessel in her brain. Cheryl was sucked into a vortex of grief over her daughter and her good-for-little husband. And of course, my sweet Peace and my true soul sister, Ginny, were both stolen by addiction's merciless dictatorship. For years, I've simply preferred the version of Asheburg that exists timelessly in my memory.

At the four-way stop sign at Redemption Corner, where the churches are as abiding as the Bible verses their preachers argue over, I linger to decide whether I should drive past Mama Donna's old rental on Carnation Street. I wanted so badly to escape that humble place, even as it sheltered me through my early heartbreaks—the Sunday evenings in college when I fled Charleston for the comfort of my mother and Carnation Street after nursing Peace through another weekend bender, my white hands clutching the ragged steering wheel of my first car. Sara McLaughlin's plaintive longing and Alanis Morrissette's unfiltered anger provided the soundtrack to my turn-of-the-millennium confusion and angst, while Tori Amos's eclectic poetry somehow captured my emotions even when I wasn't sure I understood her metaphors.

I intended to buy the Carnation Street house for Mama Donna when I had the money, but she didn't live long enough. As buyers snatched up waterfront property around the Burg and real estate prices crept up, Clay sometimes lamented the lost investment. Clay's fear that we'll be priced out of waterfront property adds urgency to his current obsession, but given the state of our relationship, maybe waterfront lots are a moot point.

Some things change. Some things stay the same. Some things never happen at all.

MY EMOTIONALLY FRAGILE state can't handle a cruise past Mama Donna's house, so I make a left at Redemption Corner. I drive two miles to the entrance of Combahee Estates and turn onto Marlin Avenue. I pass one piscine thoroughfare after another as I head toward the river—Flounder Lane, Sea Bass Drive, Tuna Street, and my personal favorite, Mullet Terrace. My adult eyes shrink the neighborhood's one-level ranches and 1970s split-levels that seemed grand to a teenager who lived in a Carnation Street shoebox. Lands and Jess live on Cobia Court, in a ranch with a wraparound porch. Their wide lot backs up to the marsh. Lands works for his dad's insurance firm. They're living the Asheburg dream.

For all Jess's banter about keg beer and Jägermeister, we do the acceptable mom thing and have a couple of glasses of white wine. We sit in rocking chairs on her front porch while Lands manages their daughter Mia's bedtime routine.

After her bath, Lands brings her outside in her quilted sleep sack. "Say good night to Mama and Miss LeeLee," he says.

Mia holds out her pudgy arms. Jess stands and kisses her daughter's rosy cheek. I reach up and shake one of her little feet.

"Night night, Mia," I say. "She looks so much like you, Lands."

Mia gives me a drooly smile and hides her face on Landon's shoulder. He runs a hand over his head. He's been shaving his noggin since his receding hairline got the better of him. With his big brown eyes, dark, dramatic eyebrows, and stupidly long eyelashes, he's the rare man who can pull off a completely shorn head without looking like Mr. Potato Head or a neo-Nazi.

"Because she doesn't have any hair?" he asks.

"No! Look at those eyes and those lashes," I say. "Like a baby deer."

"I think she's her mama's spitting image and, hence, is *gorgeous*."

"Flattery will get you everywhere, darlin'." Jess pokes his butt.

"I hope so, so don't stay up too late." He kisses the top of his wife's head and disappears inside the house.

Their domestic bliss warms my heart. "Y'all are always so cute."

"*Always?* Hardly. You know we've had our moments over the last twenty-some years. But I do love his goofy ass." Her affectionate smile collapses into a glower. "Hopefully, I can convince him to give up some sperm soon."

"He seems ready to go once the baby is asleep—"

"No. For the IVF. He's still dragging his feet. Meanwhile, I hear my biological clock tickin' like Big Ben." She sips her wine. "You want to talk about what's going on with Clay?"

"Not really. It's been going on for a year. Same dog doo, different day."

"But it sounds like it's coming to a head."

"Maybe. We'll see." I tuck my feet under me as she refreshes my drink. "You see Cheryl yet?"

"No. Been busy, but I'm probably hemming and hawing. It will be hard to see her." She screws up her face and theatrically wipes her dry eyes. "Especially if she starts bawling about Ginny. You know how well I handle tears."

"You don't." I throw a balled-up cocktail napkin at her, and it bounces off her head. "So, where do you think Ginny is right now?"

"Girl, I don't know. I pray she's off somewhere driving another man crazy and singing in bars. Or maybe she's found Jesus and gotten sober. But all this talking about her lately has made me miss her."

"Me too. I feel terrible saying this, but when she first left town, it was like we got a reprieve. She'd gotten so unpredictable."

"She was more anchor than buoy those last few years," Jess says wisely. "Remember when she made you jump off that bridge?"

"How could I forget? I was simultaneously pissed at her and glad she made me do it." A common conundrum with Ginny.

Jess and I are on the same page.

"That's Ginny," she says. "She'll twist your brain into a tight knot, but there's never a dull moment."

"We got so caught up in our own lives after she and Peace left," I say. "It was too easy to forget her. I'm embarrassed to say that too."

"Maybe enough time has passed that we can remember how she was before things got bad."

"I can't imagine how bad it got all those years she and Peace lived together."

"He was the only one who could put up with her." She chuckles. "Half the time, she wasn't even very nice to him. I never really got it. Don't get me wrong. Ginny was beautiful when we were young—those blue eyes and her hair like the sunset growing out of her head. Whew."

"She always reminded me of Tinker Bell," I say. "Like... shimmery. A fairy with too much pixie dust."

"Yeah. I was about to ask why Peace put up with her. But she had her magic."

"All y'all did. When I met y'all, I thought you were the coolest people in the world."

"By Asheburg standards, we probably were."

I shake my head. "It was more than that. Each of you brought something special. Landon was more low-key than the other boys, but they knew they needed him. He was the rudder rerouting the rest of them when they got too crazy. You and Palmer and Ginny... I'd never met girls like y'all, who laughed so hard and were so damn tough and were gorgeous to boot."

"You're making me blush," Jess says, but her voice purrs with real pleasure at the compliment.

"I'm serious. Plus y'all loved each other so much. I never knew people could be so close. I wasn't close to anyone but my mama until I moved to the Burg."

"When you put it that way, we were pretty badass." Jess smiles. "Ginny recognized the badass in you too. You were like Lands—keeping us girls in line."

"Was I boring?"

She snorts a laugh. "Girl, no."

"You don't have to blow sunshine up my ass."

Another snort. "When have I ever blown sunshine up anyone's ass? LeeLee, we wouldn't have scooped you up if you were *boring*. We already lived in a boring town. We only suffered fools who livened things up."

"We were a bunch of fools, for sure. Roaming around town with your daddy chasing us in his Cadillac."

"But he never caught us." She points at me. "You were strategic to our escape more than once—like you knew where he was going before he did."

"Just luck." On more than one occasion, I warned Rollo or Peace or whoever was driving to avoid the McDonald's or the Taco Bell. Readings showed me Albert Conway in his car in a dark parking lot, eating McNuggets or chalupas, reading his Bible, and watching out for rebellious teenagers. "Not many places in the Burg for Big Al to ambush us." I hope my shrug is genuinely nonchalant.

"You were exactly what we needed to complete our..." She counts on her fingers. "Octagon."

"I'll always be grateful to Ginny for embracing me."

"So we gotta embrace her now," Jess says. "From afar if we have to. We gotta find her."

"We will. I'm sure we will."

"It's good to have you here." She reaches over and pats my arm. "Just feels right."

"I'm going to come home more often."

"Famous last words."

"I'm serious." Years ago, Ginny yanked me off a bridge. Now, even in her absence, she's making me face my fear again. I will no longer let ambiguous disappointment and unaddressed grief keep me from coming home. "I love this kooky little town."

"Don't we all?" She props her tiny bare feet on the table and rock-rock-rocks. "Asheburg is like the people who live in it—far from perfect, but no place else feels so much like home."

PEACE CALLS AS I CHANGE into my nightshirt in Jess and Landon's guest room. It strikes me that his contact information has no photo attached to it. Only his name, Makepeace Smith. It seems impersonal, like a phone call from the electric company. All the important people in my life smile at me when the phone rings.

"Hey," I answer.

"Hey, you. How are things in the Walters household this evening?"

"All good. Lands played superdad and got the baby down while Jess and I had a glass of wine."

"Only a glass?"

"Maybe two. Everything okay with you?"

"Yeah, yeah. Of course. Just checking in. Figured a weekend away from your kids when things are rough at home might be hard."

"I cried most of the way here, so that's an accurate assumption." Despite that sad reality, his empathy soothes me like heat emanating from the firepit out at Rollo's dad's land. I lean into the phone, as if to get closer to the source of that warmth. "How's your Friday night going?"

"Oh, you know..." he says. "Went to an AA meeting. Now I'm having a fun party by myself eating cereal straight out the box and watching old episodes of *The Sopranos*."

"Speaking of mobsters, our man Big Lou Marciano came through with Ginny info. Everyone he spoke with validated her volatility and her addictions, but the most important tidbit came up toward the end of his report. Apparently, a random guy stayed at a shelter with her in 2013. You thought she was seeing someone else. Do you think that's the same person?"

"Maybe." Static in the phone from his harsh exhalation. "I wasn't *sure* she was seeing anyone. I sensed it. She stopped coming back to Helping Hands, stayed out all night."

"The Ginny I knew loved all-nighters, but she was also loyal. Maybe she wasn't cheating and this guy came along after. Regardless, whoever he is, he's the only clue we have so far. Do you remember a name?"

"Can I think about it? That time in my life is kind of a blur."

"Sure. Let me know if anything comes to you."

"We gotta find her. Cheryl will not get off my ass."

His lack of compassion for Ginny irks me, but before I say anything, he corrects himself.

"That was a dickhead thing to say," he says. "We gotta find her because she needs to be found. Sorry. I'm stressed out about Dad. It makes me itch for a drink. Or a pill. Both."

"She's the priority. But... you are too." I can't imagine the strength of will it takes to resist that itch. "You've come so far. We can't let this derail you."

"I got AA." A pause, as if to collect his nerve, then he forges ahead. "And I got you, Lee. You were always determined to keep me on the right path. I wish I listened to you fifteen years ago. Everything could have been so different."

I don't know how to reply, so I don't.

His voice fills the sixty miles of space between us. "Another dickhead thing to say. I don't want to make things more complicated for you."

"It's already complicated, P." My voice shakes. "Everything is so... *damn*... complicated..."

"You're crying, aren't you?"

"Trying not to."

Of course he can tell. He's heard me cry over the phone many times—when we first professed our feelings for one another and guilt over Ginny's reaction racked me, and later on, when I begged him to lay off the pills or call a cab instead of driving. Those conversations always ended with me smiling.

"I wish I could give you a hug," he says.

"That would be a disaster, since I want that more than anything. Oh Lord." I wipe my eyes. "You always made me feel like everything would turn out okay."

"Ridiculous, since I was so screwed up."

"You weren't always." Words spill out of me like the retreating tide, things I've wanted to say for years but never had the chance. "A part of you wasn't lost yet. I would have put all my eggs in that basket, even with the holes in it, if you'd at least *tried* to quit. I wanted to tell you that back then, but instead, I pushed you away. I thought I was tough, like Jess when she broke up with Landon. But that's not me. Even now, I know a lot about the law, but I'm not great at laying it down in my personal life."

"You told me you wouldn't be with me if I was using. With everything you had at risk, it was the right thing to do."

"Maybe if I asked you to stay... if I were more supportive—"

"Stop now, Lee." His tone is still kind but unusually firm. "I made my choices. They're not your fault, if that's what you're saying."

"I don't know what I'm saying. I still can't believe I'm talking to you."

"I'm *here*. I'm *back*. You can talk to me *anytime* you want."

That truth is too much for me. "I should go. I've said way too much already."

"You haven't done anything wrong."

"It *feels* like I have."

"Clay cheated on you, didn't he? You're *talking* to an old friend."

"I'll try to think of it that way. For now."

"You're steering this buggy, Lisa Lightstone." Humor creeps back into his voice. "I know the Piggly Wiggly parking lot is full of SUVs and you're a long way from the cart return."

I laugh despite my tears. "I'll have to remember that metaphor for the novel I may or may not write someday."

"I'm saying I know you got a lot on the line. I'll follow your lead. Okay?"

There. He said it without actually saying it. *Something* is happening between us, and it probably has been since I sat down across from him at the conference table. Something that could ruin my life. Or maybe fix it. It surely can't do both.

"Okay." I say it again to convince myself. "Yes. Okay."

"Now, what are you and Jess doing for the rest of your fun-filled weekend in Asheburg?"

"Well..." I sit on the edge of the bed.

We planned to go out to Saltmarsh to talk to his brother, Drew. I feel guilty for not telling him, but we agreed to keep the details of our sleuthing between the girls. "I have a bunch of work to do, so I'll take advantage of a quiet Saturday. Then dinner at FEED with Landon and Jess, the new restaurant on Magnolia. Sunday morning, Jess wants to drag me to First Methodist with the whole Walters and Conway crew."

"Good luck. Pastor Tomlinson will have plenty of updates about the impending moral apocalypse."

"I'm having my own moral apocalypse, thanks. Maybe..." This time, my exhalation causes static on the line. "Maybe I'll call you on the drive home Sunday."

"If you want to, I'd like that."

My head rests on the phone again, like it's his shoulder. "Good night, Peace."

"Good night, Lee. Sweet dreams."

The call ends, and I lower the phone. I have several notifications. I swipe over a text from Clay. His response to my question about the boys and bedtime.

Clay: *Decided to stay at Wadmalaw. Everything went fine. Everyone is asleep.*

Me: *Okay, great. Give them an extra kiss for me. And tell Gelsie thanks for helping out.*

Clay: *Will do.*

Me: *Good night.*

Clay: *Night.*

I plug in my phone and curl up under the covers. I just said good night to the two men who had the greatest impact on my life. The first "good night" was genuine and heartfelt. The second—the "good night" to the father of my children—felt cold and formal.

Peace doesn't think I've done anything wrong, but I'm not so sure. Clay had sex with someone he barely knew and didn't care about. I'm longing to pour my heart out to my first love, who clearly still means a great deal to me. Which is worse? And can I claim some kind of free pass, since Clay cheated?

Those questions have multiple answers. They all seem simultaneously reasonable and correct—and terribly wrong. I follow the truth in my head like a hunting dog chasing its cropped tail. I'll never reach it. I spin around until I lose my emotional equilibrium. Dizziness overcomes me, and I fall asleep.

I dream I'm slogging through pluff mud at low tide. Ginny is in front of me, but mist covers the marsh. Warm water condensed when it hit cold air, or maybe it's vice versa.

Ginny wants to tell me something, but I can't reach her. My legs are too heavy. The mud is too thick. No matter how I tell myself to run, run, run, I can only plod. Rivulets of water wash over the mud. The tide is coming in, and I'm far from shore. I have to abandon Ginny and turn toward dry ground, though she'll be swallowed by the incoming tide. If I can't make my legs move, I'll drown too.

Suddenly, as is the way with dreams, the water rises past my shoulders. If the tide has reached me, it has long since consumed Ginny. I abandoned her. She's truly lost, forever.

I awake with a start and stare into the unfamiliar darkness. I picture my dorm room at the College of Charleston. The blackness in front of me is the dark metal frame of Ginny's bunk above mine. She must be safely sleeping above me. Soon, she'll roll over, and the bed frame will creak like an old man's knees. I blink, and the darkness retreats.

A baby fusses, and Jess whisper-yells, "Mama's coming, babycakes."

I'm at Jess and Landon's house. Ginny is still missing. Other young women are sleeping in our old dorm bunk beds. And out in the marsh, the tide continues its endless cycle of in and out, advance and retreat, exposure and concealment.

Chapter 12
Ginny, 2002

Peace and I wait for Chad Dooley on the rickety porch of Chad's mama's trailer. Peace wants to score some oxy. I'm hoping for some decent weed. Since Chad and I are sort of dating, I suppose I'm also waiting for his company.

May of 2002 should have marked the end of my senior year in college—graduation parties, new jobs, big plans. Instead, I've been back in Asheburg for over a month. I couldn't live with LeeLee, Palmer, and Jess for one more day. I love them—of course I do—but we were under those cathedral ceilings together for almost three years, plus freshman year as suitemates in the dorm. Four years too long. They've gotten so... damn... *annoying*. I could not take it, so I left Charleston and moved back in with my parents. I would rather deal with my dad's drinking than my supposed best friends judging every damn thing I do.

Peace is back in the Burg, too, but he returned to Saltmarsh last fall. He made it through three years of college, as opposed to my one, but he eventually dropped out too. He told everyone he came home because of his mother's illness, but she passed away around Christmastime, and he never returned to Columbia. According to Jess and the cousin grapevine, Peace failed out, and his father is beside himself. At least my disastrous attempt at higher education didn't surprise my parents.

Neither of us could cut it in college. So here we are, on a lovely May morning, with our asses on Chad Dooley's porch. Peace is smoking a cigarette, a universal smell for me—my parents' house, bars, frat parties, Rollo's land, the front porch of the Bull Street apartment, the cab of Peace's pickup truck, the hunting jackets he used to lend me on cold days.

"You talked to the other girls yet?" he asks me.

"Nope," I say. "They're still pissed."

"You left them with a pile of bills, unpaid rent, and a few holes punched in the walls."

"You forgot the cops coming to the apartment." I cross one leg over the other, and my bare foot bounces. "Thankfully, I took my goods with me. They'll get over holes in the walls. They wouldn't forget going to jail if I left my weed in the bathroom."

"They're moving out soon, right?"

"Yeah. At the end of the month, after graduation. Movin' out and movin' on."

"Who knew we'd end up like this, huh?" he asks. "Four years after *high school* graduation, and we're still in the Burg."

"You have reasons to be screwed up. Your life fell apart—career-ending injury, your mom dying." I give him the side-eye. "LeeLee dumping you after two blissful, romantic years."

He doesn't bite. "My dad thinks I should have kept it together."

"Well, what's my excuse?" He starts to reply, but I cut him off. "Forget it. I don't want to know the answer."

"Remember when LeeLee and I started dating, and you had that weird reading on the boat? About us all being, like, *interconnected.* Was it a bunch of BS, like you said that night? Or am I still going to ruin our lives?"

Irritation bubbles in my stomach, like I've shotgunned an extra-fizzy Coca-Cola. I feel that way all the time lately, and it comes out of nowhere. I brought up Peace and LeeLee's two-and-a-half-year lovefest, but when *he* mentions her, my head feels like it will explode—pure fury, beyond LeeLee, Palmer, and Jess giving me the silent treatment for weeks. That's saying something since I seriously contemplated driving to Charleston and throwing rocks through the apartment windows.

I grit my teeth. "You were pissed at me for telling you about it. Now you want an explanation?"

"Relax, Gin. It was, like, a rhetorical question." He taps his cigarette against the dry-rotted porch. "I've made too many bad decisions to tell which ones may or may not have been part of your reading. Besides, who cares at this point? We're all going our separate ways, and it's about time."

My annoyance cools at the idea of him and LeeLee going separate ways, given that I'm still sitting right beside him.

My foot bounces harder. I want a cigarette—or a drink. *Something.* Maybe a pill. I have an oxy prescription, from the same doctor who prescribes my Ritalin and Valium. Dr. Burke, Asheburg's family doctor for, like, the past thirty years, will prescribe anything if the patient has the right complaint.

I got Ritalin because I couldn't concentrate, so I failed out of college. Valium because I was anxious about money and I couldn't sleep. All true, though I can't concentrate because I smoke too much weed and have money problems because I got fired from my job at the Silver Dollar. Not nearly as much money tending bar at the ACE of Spades on Magnolia Street.

Doc Burke prescribed oxy because I told him I hurt my back falling off my bike and it still bothers me. The bike crashes were legit because I fell off a couple of times while riding back to Bull Street after a late shift at the Dollar. The lingering-pain story holds no truth, since I was drunk enough to bounce off the concrete. Fortunately, Doc Burke doesn't ask many questions.

None of my special potions truly scratches my constant itch, but at least I have more readings when I'm high or drunk. Readings are their own kind of high. I've added my supernatural power to my list of recreational drugs.

Peace puffs away on his cigarette. "Had any other glimpses into the future lately?"

"Can I get a cig?" I ask.

He hands me one and clicks his lighter.

As the smoke fills my lungs, I relax some. "Nothing too interesting. Palmer will be the first one of us to get married. Like, soon. Maybe this year."

"You think she'll marry that old dude?"

"Getting married and having a passel of babies has always been her top priority. If she's not willing to wait for Tommy to get his shit together, she'll have to marry an older guy who's ready for that."

"That sounds like common sense." He shrugs. "Nothing supernatural."

"Think whatever you want to think." I have no interest in arguing with Peace, or anyone, about my readings. Take them or leave them, I always say. I'm almost twenty-two years old. My lifelong friends should understand me by now. My need to *make* them understand has worn thin over the years. Like my patience with Lee, Palm, and Jess and their tolerance of me.

At least I never have to explain anything to LeeLee. She doesn't demand more of an explanation than the universe provides me. Despite my annoyance about LeeLee being part of our conversation, I bring her up again. "You seen LeeLee recently?"

His jaw clenches, as if he expects me to add a snide comment. When I just sit there smoking my borrowed cigarette, he says, "No. You know we've been broken up since August. She gave me some pity time when my mom died, but for the past few months, she hasn't wanted much to do with me. She's probably moved on."

I detect a hint of a question, as if I might know something. "Don't ask me. From what I can tell, LeeLee has been working, studying, and taking the LSAT."

"Jess told me she got into law school at USC. So she's moving to Columbia?"

"Yup. That's our LeeLee. She got a scholarship."

"Good for her." He rests his elbows on his knees. His cigarette droops, and ashes plop onto the porch. "What about you? I haven't seen you since you've been home. How are things going?"

"I'm okay. I guess."

His deep-blue eyes rake me from my bare toes to the top of my head. "You look kind of thin."

I raise my chin and look right back at him. "That supposed to be a compliment?"

"Ha ha. You don't need my compliments. You know how pretty you are, Ginny. Not that you shouldn't. I always wondered why a pretty woman is supposed to think she's ugly. If I have a daughter, and some man tells her she's pretty, I want her to say, 'Thanks, I know.'"

"People will think she's conceited. But better for a woman to be conceited than a pushover."

"I'd want her to be tough, like all of y'all. You. Jess and Palmer." He clears his throat. "And LeeLee."

"You find some nice girl to marry, and we'll be your daughter's tough, hot aunts."

"Who knows when I'll get married, or if I'll get married?" He pauses, as if his comment might spark a reading in me, but my powers are silent.

"Sorry, nothing," I say.

"Worth a try. I usually don't play with that shit, but I'm having a quarter-life crisis."

"A what?"

"A quarter-life crisis. The earlier version of a midlife crisis. I'm looking for some psychic guidance so I don't make any more nutty decisions." He smiles, and it's beautiful, despite the disturbing statement that follows. "Like how Dad screwed his paralegal for years and confessed to my mother on her deathbed. That was the biggest midlife-crisis wacko decision in Asheburg history."

"Isn't that when he bought the big boat? What's it called?"

"The *Caseload*, another midlife-crisis purchase."

"The *Caseload* is sweet, but I loved *It Depends*."

"Stop by Saltmarsh, and Dad will give you a nice condescending lecture about your life that includes a lot of *it depends*." He pokes my arm, like he used to as we drove around the Burg in his Marlboro-smelling truck. "But you're doing okay? Really?"

I don't know if his questions—and that casual poke—are annoying or endearing. "Why do you keep asking?"

"Because I *care*, Ginny."

Chad pulls into the driveway. He slams the door of his beat-up Camaro and walks up the porch steps. "What a damn day—issues with my supplier, people sniffing around, if you know what I mean. Hey, baby." He leans down and kisses me square on the mouth. Maybe he wants to mark his territory.

He opens the front door and calls over his shoulder. "Come inside, Peace. I don't want to flash shit around in my yard."

I start to get up, too, but Chad points at me. "Stay out here, Ginny."

"I'm getting a beer—"

"Stay outside! Damn."

Chad disappears into the house. Peace frowns but follows him.

Chad comes outside again a few minutes later. He whacks the top off a bottle of Natural Light and hands it to me. "How long you been sitting outside with him?"

"Uh... maybe thirty minutes. Why?"

Chad clenches his teeth, and that oddly chiseled jawline of his sharpens like a fish fillet knife. "I don't like it."

"Huh? You asked me to come over this afternoon. You told Peace to meet you to get some pills. We got here at the same time."

"I told you to come this evening."

"No." I shake my head in genuine confusion. "You didn't, remember? You said—"

He grabs my arm. "Don't argue with me. You think I want to drive up to my house and see my girl sitting on my porch with her exboyfriend?"

"Since when am I your girl?" I wrench my elbow from his grip. "We haven't talked about it."

"I keep you supplied with what you need. You stay at my house, sleep in my bed. We have sex. What else is there to talk about?"

Genuine astonishment replaces confusion. "You *redneck asshole*! Don't you *dare* talk to me like that—"

Goddamn mouthy bitch!

I gasp. Chad didn't say a word, but his thoughts encircle me, like surround sound or a sputtering neon beer sign.

He knocks the beer out of my hand. It strikes the ground and shatters. Beer splatters up my legs. Bits of glass cover my bare toes. Chad stomps into the house. His thoughts were rude and mean, but the experience excites me more than the content upsets me. I can't *wait* to tell LeeLee.

Then I remember we aren't speaking.

Inside the trailer, the fridge door squeals then slams. Chad and Peace appear in the doorway.

"You're a good customer, Peace," Chad says. "But you need to stay away from Ginny."

"*Excuse* me, dude?" It's Peace's turn to be astonished by Chad's nerve. "Ginny and I have been friends since—"

"You heard me. You get going out of here. Let me know when you need something else." Chad disappears into the trailer again.

Peace walks out the door. "What the *hell* was that about?" He takes in the glass on the porch, my wet legs, and the lone tear that has snuck out of my right eye. "Gin? What the—"

"It's nothing."

His nostrils flare. "Oh, *hell* no. Did he—"

"It's *fine*, Peace."

"Bull*shit*. I'm going back in there and giving him what for. Bad enough he was so rude to you, but... he gets *rough* with you? No *way* I'm putting up with that."

I'm suddenly angrier at Peace than at Chad. If Chad roughs me up—if I'm with Chad in the first place—it's because Peace let me go almost four years ago, without a fight. He moved on to my best friend, who he probably still loves.

"Don't. *Do not.* I don't need you going in there and pissing him off more. He just got upset seeing us together."

"So he pitches a fit like some middle school kid and puts his hands on you? That's beyond screwed up, Ginny." He shakes his head. "Why are you *with* him?"

"I'm not. Or... maybe I am. Why do you care?"

"Because I *do*. Why would you ask me that?"

"I don't need you runnin' in there, playing the hero. I don't *need* you at all."

He raises his hands, as if to smack my hurtful words back in my face. "You got this, *obviously*. You always do, right?"

He walks down the stairs. His knee has not miraculously healed itself, and he still limps. He gets into his truck, cranks the engine, and pops something into his mouth. A pill he got from Chad.

Part of me wants to yell an apology and beg him to take me with him, but my pride will have none of that. Instead, I turn around and step over the bits of glass on the porch. Inside, I replace my beer and decide to sweet-talk Chad into being generous with those pills. Given my unexpected look into his unpleasant brain, maybe whatever concoction I throw back will inflate my expanding mind. At the very least, it will numb the pain.

THE ANGLE OF THE JUNE sun tells me noon has passed, and I've been sitting on Cheryl and Burt's front porch for hours. Mama is slinging snooder-dooders at Sweetie Pie's. Daddy is making a rare, timely appearance at BEI. For once, he isn't the one sitting around our house, tanked out of his mind.

Squirrels casually pick through old acorns in the grass below the porch, as if I rise early every day and converse with them in my pajamas, a handle of vodka at my feet. I'm always down for a heart-to-heart with Mother Nature, but this morning, I'm communing with the supernatural—or *trying* to, anyway.

Despite my exhaustion after yesterday's double shift at the ACE of Spades, Cheryl's early-morning kitchen rustling woke me before dawn. I pulled my pillow over my head, but my bladder reminded me of the last two beers I drank before I left work. I hustled into the bathroom, did my business, washed my hands, and tossed back several Dixie cup shots of water. My puffy-eyed reflection in the mirror urged me to go straight back to bed. I looked ridden hard and put away wet. As I vowed to never again fall asleep without removing my mascara, the pink-and-purple-striped bathroom wallpaper congealed into the murky gray of the floor-to-ceiling mirrors of my old Charleston apartment.

Like Alice and her looking glass, I peered through the mirrors into a different world. LeeLee stood in her bedroom amid a stack of cardboard boxes. Peace sat on the edge of her bed, watching her fold clothes and toss others into a Goodwill bag.

It had to be the recent past, since the girls just moved out of our old apartment. LeeLee is heading to Columbia for law school. Palmer and Jess moved into an apartment in Mount Pleasant. Jess has an RN job, and Palm works in property management for her new boyfriend's company. They all have plans. I have none, but neither does Peace.

After witnessing Chad Dooley's asshole performance a few weeks ago, Peace decided he wanted to keep an eye on me. Once we hung out a few times, he easily convinced me to ditch Dooley. With our old chemistry percolating like we're sitting on a Bunsen burner, the passionate reunion I predicted after freshman year finally seems inevitable.

Until the damn otherworld shows me that he went back to LeeLee, yet again. Or did he? I squinted into the bathroom mirror.

> *LeeLee wants Peace to quit. Quit it all—booze, weed, and definitely the pills. Peace thinks she's overreacting. He loves her. He wants to be with her. She loves him, too, but she's got too much at stake to drop a lit match on her haystack of hopes and dreams.*

Unlike the cheap, flimsy glass in my parents' bathroom, the antique mirror in Charleston was thick and dense. I could not understand the conversation, but words came through here and there. *Cut back. You said that before. Trust me. Give me a chance.* Then, a clearer sentence. *I've always cared about her.*

Peace said "her," not "you." Who was "her"? I leaned over the cracked porcelain sink until my forehead banged against cold glass. I couldn't make heads or tails of anything I observed. I was no navigator, cutting paths through the waves of time—just a storyteller who could only listen to the narrator inside my head.

If Peace won't quit, LeeLee won't let him in again, no matter how her heart is screaming at her to do so. In desperation, LeeLee throws down the gauntlet. Ginny is the gauntlet.

Then the reading ended. Just my face in the bathroom mirror again. Pink-and-purple-striped wallpaper behind me. Had I been asleep? No. *No.* It wasn't a dream. It was a reading, for sure—a reading in which Peace asked LeeLee to take him back, and she asked him to get sober. What had happened, and how did my name play into it?

I didn't go back to bed. I went straight to the porch with my vodka. Inebriated Ginny was more likely to become Navigator Ginny. I drank myself into a stupor trying to step back into the space between those damn mirrors. I got tore up from the floor up, all by my lonesome, but I don't get so much as a psychic squeak.

When LeeLee's car turns into our driveway, I think I'm having a breakthrough. It must be a reading. She has no reason to be at my house. We haven't spoken in almost two months, but it wasn't much better before I made the decision to get the hell out of that apartment. LeeLee and Palm and Jess kept whispering among themselves then shutting up when I came into the room.

They've gotten so uptight, always watching me and judging me. They're the ones who have changed, not me. I am who I am. Always have been. Always will be.

LeeLee saved for two years to buy a silver '96 Chevy Cavalier. Bass vibrates through the car's thin walls and my rib cage, proving it's not a reading. It's her, in the flesh. The thump-thump-thump of an Eminem song shuts off when she kills the engine. LeeLee claims to be all about girl power, but she loves Eminem, the man who writes songs about killing his wife. So *annoying*.

She gets out of her car and approaches me like I'm a rabbit in an open field and might dart off. Despite the June heat, I pull my blanket tighter around my shoulders.

"Hey, Gin," LeeLee says. "You okay?"

I smile at her. "Why does *everyone* keep asking me that?"

"You're on the porch in your pajamas wrapped up in a blanket in the hundred-degree heat."

"Just enjoying a fine summer day in Burnt Mill." A line of sweat drips down my cheek.

She looks at the front door behind me. "Is Cheryl here? I'm staying with my mom for a couple of days then—"

"Then you're heading to Columbia for law school."

Her greenish eyes meet mine again. "Uh, yeah. I move into my new apartment on Monday."

"Classes starting?"

"Summer internship."

"Oooh. Fancy."

"I wanted to say goodbye to Cheryl—"

"Not to me?"

"To you too. But I don't know if you want to talk to me." She shifts on her feet. She's wearing flip-flops, and dust coats her perfectly painted burgundy toenails. "You seem... preoccupied."

She's right here in front of me. I might as well ask about the reading so my vodka and I can retreat into the air-conditioning. "Why were you and Peace talking about me in your room when you were packing?"

"You *saw* that?" She takes two steps back.

"When was it?" I ask.

"Last Friday. Right before we all moved out."

"So are y'all back together?"

"No." She approaches again, slowly. She shades her forehead with one hand, as if I might see through her eyes and into her brain.

"But it seemed like he wants to get back together."

"Supposedly. But he won't get sober. So I told him no—" Her hands go to her hips. "But wait—I can't believe you were spying on me!"

"Whatever!" I say. "You're the one who said it's not spying unless you mean to do it. And you listen in on people's freaking thoughts."

"Don't go there with me. You never *tried* to shut it down. I'm the one who cares about people's privacy."

"Don't you give me your Miss Perfect bullshit." I bat my eyelashes at her. "*LeeLee Lightstone*, off to save the world at law school! While I sit here drunk as a coot on my parents' porch. You're the heroine. I'm the loser."

"You don't have to be a loser—"

"Ha!" I fling the blanket off my shoulders. "You think I'm a loser!"

"No—that's not what I meant. You're as smart as I am. Maybe smarter. Your SATs—"

"Jesus *pleasus*, LeeLee. Test scores aren't everything."

"You know what I mean. You used to memorize entire GD *Encyclopedia Britannica*s. You just didn't want to get your ass out of bed and go to class!"

"Now I'm *lazy* too." My shrill laughter sounds batshit crazy even to my ears. "Thanks, BFF!"

"You—Ginny—you—" LeeLee looks like she might rip her hair out if I don't shut up. "I don't know if you want us to feel sorry for you or if you hate us for it!"

"Maybe you should have asked me instead of shutting me out."

"We've all been trying to get through to you for years! You're always drunk. You're high on pills most of the time." She moves closer, until her flip-flops touch the bottom porch step. "What is the *matter* with you?"

"Nothing is the matter with me. I'm good—*so good* that my powers are getting stronger all the time. I even read someone's thoughts recently."

"What? *Who?*" She backs up again, like we're dancing a weird waltz.

"Don't worry. It wasn't Peace, thinking about making sweet love to me—"

"Stop, Ginny. Please stop." Her fists clench at her sides.

"It was Chad... actually... calling me a mouthy bitch." I snigger. It's too funny. I've spent years trying to read thoughts. My first big success is Chad freakin' Dooley insulting me.

"Stay away from him. He's bad news. And you need to be careful messing around with our powers. Reading thoughts all the time is awful. When I was a little girl—"

"Don't put your damn issues on me," I say. "I *want* to figure this all out, to see how far I can go."

"It's some bizarre thrill for you." She scowls at me like I'm a full-on psychopath. "Always has been. You're addicted to the readings as much as you are to booze and pills. It's messed up, Ginny."

"Of course. You're a better person than me, always have been."

"Why do you say things like that?"

"Because life sucks when your best friend is *perfect* and you're a disaster!"

"I'm not perfect," she says. "I'm a chickenshit. You said so yourself—"

"I told you I didn't mean that—"

"You're the one who is brave and daring and doesn't give a shit about what anyone thinks. *You're* the navigator. I'm just a storyteller who never actually tells any stories!"

I ignore the anguish in her voice and go in for the kill. "So stop hiding behind perfect grades and perfect behavior and your perfectly planned life and tell them!"

"Forget this. I'm leaving. I wanted to say goodbye—"

I stand, and the blanket pools at my feet. "I loved you, LeeLee. At first, it was because we understood each other, but then, it was because of who you were."

"I loved you too—"

"Then why did you steal Peace?" I ask, as if we're two sisters arguing over a favorite pair of jeans.

"I didn't *steal* him. You broke up with him!"

"I wouldn't have if I knew he'd go running to you!" I've been waiting for the chance to say this for three years. It's not a guilt trip. It's a full-on shame-cation. "I was the one who introduced you to him—to everyone. You're part of *us* because of *me*."

"Thank you, Ginny." LeeLee fights my guilt fire with blazing gratitude. "Thank you for recognizing my powers and for confiding in me and for keeping my secret. I'll always be grateful to you for introducing me to Jess and Palmer and accepting me into your little circle. Thank you for introducing me to Peace. You might not believe me, but you're not the only one whose heart he's broken."

"He *wants* to be with you!" I say, exasperated.

"I can't be with him when he's like this." Her hands are back on her hips, and her chin juts in my direction. "You want to know what we said about you, right?"

"Of course I want to know what kind of shit my two friends are talking behind my back."

Now it's her turn to laugh. "Could you be *any more* paranoid? We weren't talking shit about you. I asked him if he still had feelings for you, and he said you were his first love and—"

"He'll always have feelings for me." So *I* was "her."

"Exactly. So I told him y'all should be together."

My mouth falls open. "You did not."

"Yes, I did."

"What did he say?"

"He said he didn't know what to do. But he didn't say no." She presses her fingers into her eyes, as if to keep tears behind her eyelids. "He told me he wants to be with me, but he won't stop drinking and popping pills, and he didn't say he *doesn't* want to be with you. So that's all I need to know."

"He's so messed up, you can't be with him, so you're passing him off to me?"

She shakes her head. "No, Ginny... it's not like that. I don't know why you and Peace do this to yourselves. None of us do. Only y'all understand what you're going through. So maybe you two can figure it out together. Help each other."

"You really feel that way? It's not some big joke?"

"I'd be lying if I told you my dream wasn't for Peace to get sober and everything to work out between us. Telling him no was about the hardest thing I've ever done, but if y'all can help each other, so be it. I just want y'all to get better."

LeeLee broke her own heart to potentially save me and Peace. No one has ever done anything like that for me. No one has ever loved me so much.

"I have nothing else to say," she says. "If you ever want to talk, call me."

"About our powers?"

"About anything. Like we used to. It started out being all about our powers, but it wasn't always that way."

"LeeLee—" I want to mention my reading about Peace and the moon and gravity, but I decide it will only confuse her—and me. Aching sadness overwhelms me. So strong I figure she'll hear me if I speak up in my head. *I love you, Lee.*

"I love you, too, Gin." She gets into her clunky car and drives away.

Chapter 13
LeeLee, 2015

I don't sleep well after that strange dream, and Baby Mia wakes with the sun. I lay in Jess's guest room bed, listening to her happy family bustle about their Saturday-morning routine. I check my phone. No good-morning message from Clay, so I send one myself. *Morning. Please give the boys hugs and kisses for me. I miss them.* I wait a few minutes, but Clay doesn't reply, so I get up, get in the shower, and get dressed for another day of meandering down memory lane.

Memory lane is a half-mile gravel driveway, a passageway to the past that starts with a weathered iron sign emblazoned with stark-white letters that say Saltmarsh. Jess's crossover SUV is no lifted off-road vehicle, so we bounce down the rutted path toward Peace's childhood home in a cloud of dust. I squint through the brownish air.

If the sign has man-made longevity, the oak trees lining the road have the superior permanence of nature. I detect no changes in them since I first bumped along this glorified bike path in Peace's truck twenty years ago. They're too old and complex for the likes of me to recognize new growth or shed limbs. My whole life is a blip on their arboreal radar.

The trees seem to lean into one another. Their leaves whisper about me. *She's back, that Jezebel who didn't help our boy when he was at his most vulnerable—our beautiful boy who climbed our trunks and hung birdhouses in our branches. She pushed him further down his sad path. How dare she return to this place, the cradle of his childhood that would have been his legacy if she only stood by him?*

The rattle of pebbles against the undercarriage mocks me. *Selfish, selfish, selfish.*

We pass the ruins of the antebellum house. Local lore says the Union Army burned the place down, but Old Peace told me that's BS. It went up in flames when some hapless Smith ancestor installed malfunctioning gas lanterns. Despite the ruins' small footprint, everyone refers to the old house as a mansion. What constitutes a mansion has changed in the past hundred and fifty years.

The new, L-shaped house, circa 1930-something, isn't a mansion in the style of today's suburban monstrosities, but it puts the ruins to shame. The recently repainted white brick throws off a glare, and the shutters are a shiny Charleston green, but the boxy hedges need trimming, and the flower beds are equally forlorn. When we were teenagers, a pineapple fountain stood in the center of the circular driveway, but Old Peace replaced the fruit of hospitality with a voluptuous mermaid. Peace's mama surely rolled over in her grave at the tackiness.

A Mercedes SUV sits in the drive. The license plate reads SMILEDOC.

Jess parks beside the Mercedes. "That's Drew's ride. He said to come around back."

We get out of the car and walk through the breezeway between the garage and the house. The view opens up before us like a fairy-tale book. Manicured lawn melts into jagged marsh grass. The mighty wooden main dock spans to the gray-green river beyond it. The pierhead at the end of the short dock is where Peace and I first kissed, when his parents were at Duke Medical Center and I told my friends I couldn't see a movie because I had PMS.

Miss Lucy's wrought-iron furniture still sits beside the pool, but Drew has replaced her red cushions with yellow stripes. The crystal pool water and the searing blue sky reflect off one another. The seagulls are as argumentative as ever, and the air smells like the estate's namesake—salt and marsh.

My ears start ringing, but through herculean effort, I shut down an oncoming reading. It's enough to remember, to reimagine, like a normal person caught in the throes of nostalgia. I refuse to open myself up to a reading of some long-gone pool party, boat day, or evening beside the firepit with Peace's arm around me. God forbid the cruel narrator in my head take me back to the early days, when I stared at him through the flames with longing filling my chest.

"You look like you saw a ghost," Jess says.

"I'm seeing a whole battalion of ghosts. An army of haints, banshees, and poltergeists, all fixing to haunt my ass." I hold onto the mental image of the child Lisa—before she was LeeLee—with her dark pigtails and her knobby knees and her hands over her ears.

Drew Smith sits on the brick porch at a white wicker table with a pile of papers spread before him. Bills, invoices, a couple of old legal files. A can of Coke serves as a paperweight. He doesn't look much like Peace, who favors his father. Drew has the rounded features of the Monroe side of the family, handsome but not in the classic conquering-hero mold of his older brother. He looks up with a hint of annoyance, as if our timely arrival at the meeting he suggested bothers him. "Hey, y'all. Is it that time already?"

Jess sits in the chair beside him. "That it is, cousin. You remember LeeLee."

Drew closes his laptop and shuffles papers as I settle into a chair. "How could I forget my big brother's gorgeous girlfriend? His second gorgeous girlfriend. Ginny was the original. He was always a ladies' man. Who knows how many came along after y'all?"

"Right," I say.

Drew Smith graduated from Clemson and attended dental school at the Medical University of South Carolina in Charleston.

When Doc Lynwood retired, he bought High Tide Dental. These days, he has a lock on all the teeth in town. He's living the Asheburg dream life, like Lands and Jess. Still, even at thirtysomething, with a doctorate degree, he can't pass up the chance to dig at Peace.

"How's that molar treating you?" he asks Jess. "Crown all good?"

"Yup," she replies. "How are Ashley and the kids?"

"They're great. I got one in kindergarten, one in two-year-old preschool, and one finally sleeping through the night."

"From my experience, the third kid puts you over the edge," I say. "If you have three, you might as well have six."

"I'm just glad Ashley stopped teaching after our oldest was born," Drew says. "Between my practice and Dad and Saltmarsh, I couldn't manage if she had to work, too, especially since I'm doing it all without help from my brother."

"Peace told me he wants to help more."

"He doesn't know what's been going on. He'll be more of a pain in my ass than a help."

It makes no sense to complain about Peace not helping while also preventing him from helping, but it isn't my place to get that far up in their family business.

Drew goes on. "I've managed the farm for years. It was all too much for Dad—losing Mom, Peace disappearing, then two years of fighting cancer—and Peace shows up at the bitter end. He can talk all he wants about sobriety and making amends and whatnot. The truth is, he wants money."

I open my mouth to defend him, but Jess interjects. "None of us have talked to Peace in years. Y'all were in touch sometimes, right?"

"Barely. Years would pass without a peep from him, but I had an email address. I emailed him when we got Dad's diagnosis. Didn't hear back for six months. Then it was a bunch of crap about him getting his life together. Dad's been so bad off, I sent another message a couple of months ago, and that's when he decided to come home.

I didn't tell Dad when I heard from him. Still haven't told Dad he's back in town."

"That's not your decision to make," Jess says.

"You watch your father waste away to nothing and tell me if you want to add to his pain. Dad can't handle it if Peace breezes in with his AA reconciliation bullshit then flakes out again."

"I see why you're angry with him," I say. "But Jess explained we're here to talk about Ginny, right? She's missing, and we received some strange emails about it."

"Yeah. Jess told me about the emails and Ginny."

"So what do you think?"

"It's obvious." Drew slurps his Coke, as if wetting his throat before giving a speech. "Peace is trying to make amends with Dad. Miss Cheryl is on the warpath against him. She came by for a cleaning, and I had to listen to her rant for twenty minutes before I got a look in her mouth. She's convinced Peace did something terrible to Ginny, and she's telling anyone who will listen. So he's trying to distract from his guilt by making up some crazy shit. How easy is it to make a fake email?"

"Why would he blame himself for murder?" Jess asks.

"Who better to blame than himself? Then it *really* looks like someone is trying to frame him." Drew taps his temple, the picture of smugness.

"Did Peace say anything to you about Ginny when y'all communicated about your dad's illness?" I ask.

"Nope. I assumed they were still together. Then, when he got to Charleston, he called and said they broke up a few years ago and she's been MIA since."

"Did he say why they broke up?"

"Something about another guy."

"Who was the guy?" Jess asks.

He shrugs. "Some guy they bought drugs from, got high with."

So Peace *does* know who it is. "Did he give a name?"

"Not that I remember."

"What do you think happened to Ginny after they broke up?"

"It's terrible, but she's probably dead." Despite that supposedly horrific statement, he sounds blasé. "Especially if Peace was pissed about the cheating and went after her."

"That doesn't sound much like the Peace I know," I say.

"What do you know about him, LeeLee? He's a good-for-nothing druggie whose girlfriend of twenty years was screwing his dealer. Who knows what he might do while flying the oxy banner?" Drew snorts. "Besides, he was never as nice as everyone thought he was. *No one* is that nice."

I sit back in my chair. "So you honestly believe—"

Drew's phone rings. "It's MUSC with test results. I gotta take this." He stands and walks into the yard.

Jess and I look at each other.

"So Drew is in Camp Cheryl," she says. "He thinks Peace hurt Ginny too. Should we entertain the possibility?"

I try to be rational. "Peace showing up when his dad is dying is kind of shitty, whether he's looking for gold around Old Peace's gravestone or not. And he should have called Cheryl about Ginny. But we don't know what it's like to live with the humiliation of how his life turned out. Old Peace put so much pressure on him, like a hot iron on a wrinkled shirt."

"'My oldest boy—by God, there's a sharp splinter off the old oak tree.'" Jess does a fair impression of her uncle Peace.

"He wanted Peace to be exactly like him—*demanded* it—football star, legal star, perfect family man. On the surface, anyway. The whole county knew Old Peace screwed around on Miss Lucy." I peek through the window into the kitchen. Old Peace is bedbound somewhere inside, hobbled by pain medication, but I still expect him to blast through the doorway in his seersucker suit and bowtie.

"Remember how mad Old Peace was about P.'s injury, as if it were his fault? And how he acted when Peace went to him about the drugs—"

"Old Peace told him to get his shit together and 'just quit it, boy.' As if anyone would be an addict if it were that easy."

"At the bonfire the first night I hung out with y'all, we all talked about our greatest fears. His was disappointing his father."

"You're right." She winces. "I feel shitty even thinking about it."

"Don't. I examine every angle in every case I work on. The angles that are *not* indicative of the outcome my client wants are just as important. We have to think about it. Still, I do not believe Peace hurt Ginny."

"I agree," Jess says. "Drew talks a lot of shit, but let's face it. He's always resented Peace. When we were kids at family holidays, Peace treated Drew way better than the rest of us treated our younger siblings. He stood up for him, included him in all our games. But Drew was still a whiny ass. Now he's talking about how 'no one is that nice' when he's not nice at all."

"One thing bugs me, though," I say. "Peace didn't seem to remember who Ginny was cheating with in Myrtle. But he remembered enough to tell Drew it was one of their dealers."

"That is weird—"

"I have to go." Drew walks back onto the porch. "Ashley's at our daughter's soccer game, and the baby's melting down. Just what I need. All this damn paperwork, and Dad's nurses should be here. What the *hell* am I paying them for?"

As if on cue, an older woman pokes her head out the back door. "Dr. Smith? We're here to bathe Mr. Smith."

"Get on with it." He waves, and she disappears into the house.

"Were the test results bad?" Jess asks.

"He's got stage four melanoma. All the test results are bad." Drew checks his phone and shuffles his papers into a pile. "Ashley's blowing me up. I cannot believe I have to deal with this crap on my day off."

"Thanks for meeting with us," Jess says.

Drew shoves his sunglasses on his face. "No problem. I'm sure Peace told y'all I'm an asshole—"

Jess's thoughts float across the table. *You're showing us you're an asshole.*

"But I'm telling you, I've lived in his shadow my whole life. He's not what my father thought he was, so he's probably not what y'all think he is either."

TOMMY AND PALMER LIVE in Mount Pleasant, Charleston's premier suburb, where Clay and I lived for years before we moved downtown. Families flock to Mount P for some of the only good public schools in the area, a perk that kept Clay and me in Mount Pleasant until his parents offered to foot the bill for private school. Clay still drools over the waterfront properties in the historic Old Village, close to the Ravenel Bridge, but even he acknowledges that, barring a lottery win, we can't touch those places with a ten-foot pole.

Many of Mount P's cute-yet-cookie-cutter subdivisions and high-end apartment communities are built on heirs' property purchased from African American families who lived on it for generations, only to be sadly forced out of their communities by the value of their own land. The town has a wholly self-sufficient party scene, from the bars lining Shem Creek to the town's proximity to the beaches on Sullivan's Island and the Isle of Palms. A significant population of hard-partying singles mixes in with the family fun.

Despite its New South Utopia vibes, local attorneys know Mount Pleasant is a breeding ground for DUIs, clandestine drug use, and family court drama. Our old friend Tommy has plenty of drama, but fortunately, he hasn't gotten a DUI. Apparently, he sticks to smoking weed when Rollo comes to town from the Burg. Given the temptations of Tommy's lifestyle and the proximity to Shem Creek, etc., I urged Peace to get his own place, but he assured me Tommy and Rollo were a source of support, not temptation.

As I drive over the Ravenel Bridge into Mount Pleasant after my weekend with Jess, I'm more concerned by Peace's convenient forgetfulness than his living situation. His inability to recall the name of Ginny's mystery man was obviously an obfuscation. Despite my usual distaste for such psychological voyeurism, I wish he fudged the truth in person instead of over the phone. I might have gained an advantage through a peek into his thoughts.

Peace waits for me on the front porch of Tommy's post-divorce rental off Chuck Dawley Boulevard. He smiles as I get out of my car, but the stern expression on my face makes his stiffen. "You look like someone died."

"That's a shitty simile." I sit beside him on Tommy's wicker sofa. "Who was Ginny cheating with? You told me you didn't know, but Jess and I spoke to Drew. He said it was someone y'all got high with."

"Y'all spoke with Drew. Interesting." Peace rests his elbows on his knees. "I assume he didn't have much positive to say about me."

"No. He didn't. He seems very angry and resentful."

"He has plenty of reason to be angry and resentful. I'm trying to make amends with him, too, but I'm getting tired of him standing between me and Dad."

I sense an imminent standoff between the Brothers Smith. Something tickles the back of my mind. Just how angry and resentful is Drew? Angry enough to blast out a few vengeful, anonymous emails?

"Dad could die any day. If Drew doesn't tell him I'm back soon," Peace says, "I'm just gonna go out to Saltmarsh."

"I know you're frustrated with Drew. I'm sorry we didn't tell you we planned to talk to him, but now I *need* the guy's name so I can give it to the PI."

Peace's eyes follow a sparrow hopping around on the overgrown shrubbery. I try to open myself up to his emotions and potentially read something useful, but I don't know how. For the first time in my life, it strikes me as dumb that I never tried to take advantage of this ability.

I don't hear his thoughts when he speaks, just his plain old voice. "Chad Dooley."

The name registers, but it also doesn't. "I'm sorry, who? Chad Dooley from Asheburg?"

"The man, the myth, the legend."

"Why didn't you tell me?"

"I swear I planned to, but it's embarrassing. Associating with the hometown dealer is the definition of peaking in high school."

The name Chad Dooley exists in a college-era void for me. "I haven't heard anything about him in years."

"Neither had I until I ran into him in Myrtle. We'd been living there for a few years. One random day, in the middle of the week, Chad damn Dooley came strolling into the club where I worked."

"The strip club."

He blushes, but he nods. "Yeah. Chad had been living in Myrtle for a while himself. He was still... you know... doing his thing. He could get us what we needed. I didn't like him much. Never did. But we occasionally hung out with him and his girlfriend."

"And Ginny cheated on *you* with *him*?" A bizarre notion, like adding cayenne pepper to cake batter.

"He could get her what she wanted, whenever she wanted it," Peace says. "They had a history. Probably easy for her to fall back into it when she and I were fighting all the time."

"You let her go back to him? He was borderline abusive back in the day."

"I told you she got worse. Being with her was like living in a psych ward, but she was still Ginny. She could make a Chinese take-out menu written in French make sense. Half the time, I didn't know if she was crazy or I was. You think I could stop her from doing anything?"

"So she ran off with him, then—"

"I got a couple of ranting text messages from her, but that was it. I didn't reply." He closes his eyes, as if to hide from terrible memories. "I didn't handle it the right way, but at the time, I was just grateful to be out from under the pressure of living with her."

I sigh. "Totally different situations, but I kind of felt that way when Clay started staying in the FROG."

His eyes open. "Anything new with y'all?"

"I don't know. I need to get home and find out. I should get going."

I start to stand, but he grabs my arm.

"Hey, wait. I'm sorry I didn't tell you about Chad. I want us to be completely honest with one another. No more hesitation, I promise."

"I understand." I sink back onto the sofa.

Peace withholding information about Chad Dooley is frustrating, yet I've kept the biggest secret of my life from him for twenty years. I've kept it from my husband, from my mother. Have I ever been truly honest with anyone other than Ginny? I pick at a hole in the sofa cushion.

He covers my hand with his. "Is this okay?"

I nod, and he pulls my hand into his lap. His fingers wind through mine. My head rests on his shoulder. I feel more peaceful than I have in months.

I love you, LeeLee. I've always loved you.

His thoughts are needles aimed at my fragile bubble of tranquility, equal parts exhilarating and terrifying. "Whoa," I say. "Okay—"

"Did I do something wrong?"

"No. But..." I sit up and remove my fingers from his grip. "I really have to go. I'll ask the PI to start looking for Dooley. Hopefully, he has more information."

"Thank you."

"Thank Palmer." I stand. "She's paying for it."

"I will. But thank you—for understanding, for being here."

He takes my hand again and kisses it like we're Guinevere and Lancelot. I cup his cheek in my palm then lean down and kiss the top of his head. His hair smells clean, and it's soft under my lips.

"When can I see you again?" he asks.

"Soon." I turn and walk down the steps.

His happiness and his thoughts follow me for a few feet then trail off. *I still love you. I love... love...*

My thoughts echo his. *And I still love you, Peace.* It's an admission to myself as much as an unheard proclamation to him. As much as I want to find Ginny, I also want to do this for Peace—so he'll be free of suspicion, so sometime soon, we might both be free.

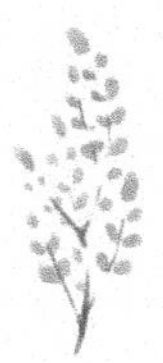

Chapter 14
Ginny, 2008

Peace and I left Chucktown in the summer of 2002, and six years later, we're still in Florida. Unfortunately, the Sunshine State no longer works for me. For the past few months, I've felt like I'm under a blanket that smothers my energy, my sense of humor, my desire to sing or perform. I don't even want to leave our apartment. I haven't had a reading in weeks—my longest dry spell *ever*.

My first reading of Chad Dooley's spiteful, nasty thoughts ushered in an awakening of all my psychic senses. Ms. Mullins, the feminazi queen of the Ashepoo High School history department, might have called it the golden age of navigation. Then, out of nowhere, came this supernatural allergic reaction. Everything is stopped up or swollen to the point of hives. My brain itches constantly. The addiction counselor I saw after my last public intoxication charge would disagree with me, but I've decided Panama City is to blame.

I've been leaning on Peace to move, but he doesn't like change. It took all my powers of persuasion to convince him to leave Charleston. Back then, we needed a fresh start, to get away from our families and friends and their frustration with us. One friend was front and center in my mind. For obvious reasons, I wanted to put space between Peace and LeeLee. We settled on Panama City Beach—plenty of bars where I could sing and wait tables and Peace could sling drinks. He can get extra work on fishing charters, and rent is cheap.

The Florida panhandle has traces of our Southern coastal roots, but let's face it, PC is no Charleston. As much as I miss the beauty of the Lowcountry and crave a fresh start, I'm not ready to go home either. I've been puzzling over moving destinations, but we aren't going anywhere if I can't drag Peace onboard my ship of not-quite-broken dreams.

On a balmy Tuesday night, I give my tingly scalp a good scratch and walk onto our efficiency apartment's balcony. We live on the second floor of a tumbledown beach bungalow. The shag carpet has faded to gray, except for a few blue and green splotches lingering under the furniture like algae blooms. Dingy windows give the impression we live inside a rain cloud, and the kitchen appliances are older than we are. The balcony is the only nice thing about it. If we position our plastic chairs just right, the ocean is visible between the neighboring buildings. Our neighbors—tattooed bikers, burned-out hippies, washed-up spring-break holdouts—don't care what we smoke out here. If we light up a joint, they come out of the woodwork in the spirit of community toking. It takes a village to get high.

Peace stands on the balcony. In one hand, he holds a monogrammed flask, MBS, Jr. His father gave it to him ten years ago at our high school graduation. He holds a lit cigarette in his other hand and watches our sliver of ocean. His pinky taps against the balcony railing.

Our supplier doesn't have any oxy, and his prescription ran out two days ago. He has almost a week before he can get a legit refill. In the meantime, he'll drink and chain-smoke and harass people at work for coke. My craving for pills isn't as bad as his. I gave him my last few, and I have to wait longer for my refill. That's love, I guess.

He stiffens when I touch his back. I know how he feels. Every muscle in his body is irritable, but if he allows it, my touch will help. Some of the tension drains out of him as I knead his shoulders.

"You thought any more about moving?" I ask.

"Yeah. It feels like a lot."

"Are you happy here?"

"Meh. But at least our hookups are established and I'm working." He tips back his flask, grimaces, and taps his cigarette on the railing.

He's too thin, but so am I. At least his hair is still black and his tattoos are all hidden. He hasn't made the mistake of bleaching his hair or tattooing his neck when he was soused, like I did. My tattoo is a bird—not an interesting bird, like a parrot or a flamingo, just a bird in flight to nowhere, trapped against my jugular.

"We can find hookups and bars and fishing boats somewhere else," I say.

"You don't want to go back to Charleston."

"Nope. Do you?"

He pauses, like he might disagree with me, but then he says, "No. Where, then?"

I throw out the first place that pops into my head. "Savannah?"

"Cheaper than Charleston but not PC cheap. We can barely keep up the rent here."

"That's my fault, right?"

"I didn't say that. I know you're trying."

"I am, P. I swear. My mouth runs away with me." I beam. "You've always loved that about me, right?"

"Yeah, but I don't poke the bear when it's peacefully hibernating. The stress of moving might wake up Miss Grizzly and send her on a rampage. Things are always harder when you're on a psychic bender. That's when you get fired, when you get DUIs."

I lean on the railing. "When I'm a bitch."

"Of course not. But... we *do* get along better when your mind is... clearer."

Irritation simmers below my skin, as if he's turned up the heat of my bloodstream, but I have to stay positive. If the grizzly starts grunting and growling, Peace will lie down on this porch, curl into a ball to protect his innards, and refuse to go anywhere.

Peace stares at that slip of ocean like he's pressed Pause on a memory. He's so sad these days. He doesn't know it yet, but he needs a change of scenery himself. Love surges through me for this patient, thoughtful man who is still amazed by my singing, though he's heard my rendition of "Me and Bobby McGee" a thousand times. Annoyance doesn't stand a chance against all that love.

"Thank you for putting up with me," I say. "I know I don't say it enough."

"You put up with me too." He pokes my arm. "I've had my grizzly-bear moments lately."

"I've always thought of you as more alligator than bear."

"The likes of us learned early to avoid taunting gators." Another poke, almost a tickle. "You gonna start prodding me now?"

I squirm, but his playfulness is a relief. "The change of scenery will be good for bears and gators alike."

He kisses the top of my head. "You sure you can handle it?"

"Totally sure. Things will be better somewhere else. I know it."

"Have you had a reading about it?"

I almost lie, but that wouldn't be fair. "No. But I believe it like a normal, non-psychic person."

"Any ideas other than Savannah?"

"Let's call Lester and see if he has any blow. Maybe that will inspire us."

Peace rubs my back. "We owe him money."

"Yeah. But he likes me."

"Everyone likes you." He kisses me.

I've been kissing him for approximately fourteen years, minus the blip of the LeeLee-and-Peace era. We're flat broke and anxious for a fix, but he still turns me on.

My hands wander below his belt. "I like you best," I whisper.

"You only like me?"

"Funny man. You know I love you."

"I love you, too, crazy ass." As always, he immediately responds to my roaming fingers, but his other cravings overpower it. "It's worth a try with Lester. I'll call him."

"'Kay. Will you get me some wine? We have a box of Franzia in the fridge."

"Of course, my lady." He calls over his shoulder as he walks into the apartment, "Maybe we can get a little wild tonight. Lately, I've been too sedate."

"That's my man! See, the idea of moving is already firing you up."

The potential relief of a line of coke is the likelier source of his improved mood, but I won't look a gift drug dealer in the mouth. I grab a cigarette from the pack he left on the plastic chair. As I light up, my scalp starts tingling—in the right way, the good way, the *best* way. That quiver is as welcome as the nicotine I suck into my lungs.

> *A pier and a Ferris wheel. Way too many pancake houses and a wide white beach. Harley-Davidsons revving up and down the strip. A band playing "I Love Beach Music" by the Embers. Mama Moo's Bar and Grille is hiring. Ginny walks in, all smiles, with her years of waitressing experience and her pretty voice, and they hire her on the spot.*

Myrtle Beach—the Grand Strand.

I walk into the apartment. Peace's back is to me, but his thoughts are front and center. *Need a hit... Gonna have fun tonight... Need a hit...*

"We'll find you a hit," I say. "And we'll definitely have fun tonight."

When he turns, the playfulness is gone, and he's scowling. "What else did you hear?"

Peace isn't crazy about me reading his thoughts, so we've made a pact. I always tell him when it happens. "Nothing. Let me call Lester. He's more likely to do us a favor if I sweet-talk him."

"You *sure* you didn't hear anything else?"

"Why? You thinking about something you shouldn't be?" It strikes me that he's thinking about LeeLee. No reading, just a jealousy jam with a thrumming suspicion beat. "Some*one*, maybe?"

"No, damn." He removes a plastic wineglass from the cupboard. "You know it's weird when you hear me thinking. Don't get mad about it."

"I'm not," I say, but I am. I'm trying to get him a hit and plan our future, and he's thinking about his old girlfriend. I just *know* it. I bite the inside of my cheek until I taste blood and will my powers to prove me right by sending me a reading.

Nothing happens. Just Peace, running cheap chardonnay into the cup for me.

I shake my head, and the icky feeling subsides. I should probably pay more attention to my whiplashing emotions—I'm no shrink, but something seems off—but I have more important things on my mind. Namely, Ferris wheels and pancake houses and a return to the Palmetto State. It isn't home, but it will be better than Panama City.

"All good." I walk to the counter, and he hands me my wine. "We won't let a little reading ruin our night. We have a reason to celebrate."

"What reason is that?" he asks.

"I know where we're moving."

Chapter 15
LeeLee, 2015

I was in Asheburg for two days—a long time for me to be separated from my family and the household I run—but Clay barely says hello when I walk into our house. The boys had finished an early dinner. They cling to me like barnacles and shout about their weekend at Gelsie's house on Wadmalaw. Boat cruises, dock jumping, pool swimming, feeding Grammy's goats, homemade ice cream, and lawn mower rides with Granddad—just hearing their litany of adventures tires me. I predict their rowdy enthusiasm will be short-lived. True to form, they're near comatose in the bathtub and unusually compliant at bedtime.

After doling out good night kisses, I return to the kitchen to tidy up, but Clay already washed the dishes and retreated to the FROG. Peace's unspoken declaration of love hits me like an Ambien when I take my weary rear end to bed. I pass right out.

I wake early the next morning and tiptoe into Malachy's room. My earliest riser still snoozes with his stuffed elephant in a headlock under one arm. I left my toiletry bag in my car, but I'm not ready to don a bra. I cross my arms over my chest, my phone in one hand and my car keys in the other, and sneak outside in a T-shirt and pajama shorts.

Clay is already out there in a suit beside his truck.

"Morning. You're heading in early," I say.

He looks up from his phone. "Hey. I have a deposition today. Need to do some more prep. A lot is landing on me right now with Susan out on maternity leave."

"Right. That's hard." I unlock my car, retrieve my toiletry bag, and slam the door.

I try to balance bag, keys, and phone while maintaining my modesty, but it's pointless to hide my bralessness from the man I've lived with for years. Perhaps my boobs aren't as enticing as they once were, because Clay pays them no mind.

"Susan's got it worse than I do," he says. "She's trying to work from home and take care of newborn twins."

"When does she come back?"

"Two weeks. She should be able to take more time, but her family can't afford to lose months of her income. We were lucky we could absorb a hit after each baby, and Darlene is flexible, unlike the dinosaurs at Moretz & Tucker. If I ever become president of the United States, I'll go all Scandinavia on the American workplace."

I smile. "You going to fight for fatherhood leave too?" For a good ol' boy, Clay holds surprisingly egalitarian viewpoints. I've always admired that about him.

"Hell yeah. We had it better than just about everyone, and it was still *so* hard. Even these days, raising three kids is no stroll in the park." Before I can agree with him, he abruptly ventures into unexpected territory. "It will be harder when we're divorced. We'll both be single parents half the time."

"Wait, what?" There's too much to unpack in that statement, so I drop the proverbial suitcase. "*When* we're divorced—and what do you mean *half* the time?"

He puts his briefcase in his truck. "I'll want fifty-fifty time with the boys."

I fall back on mom logic. "How would you manage with your hours? The morning routine, schoolwork, activities? What if someone gets sick?"

"I guess I'll nanny up."

"I figured you'd only want every other weekend."

"You figured wrong."

As hard as single parenting would be, the idea of being without my kids for a week at a time doesn't sit well with me. "We haven't gotten that far yet, have we?"

"No. But I'm trying to prepare myself for the inevitable."

"I thought we were taking a breather—"

"This is more serious than a breather," he says. "I can tell you don't feel the same."

Sadness, guilt. Sadness, guilt. *I tried Lee. I would have tried anything.*

"Clay, I still don't—"

"I know Peace Smith coming back into your life hasn't made anything easier, but I'm not mad anymore. Maybe he showed up to force us to *deal* with this shit. You never want to address anything head-on—"

"That's not true."

"But it is, LeeLee. You've always held something back from me."

I open my mouth to keep protesting, but he holds up one hand.

"This is kind of warped," he says, "but I think that's one reason I fell in love with you. Other women were always trying to get me to open up and talk about my feelings. With you, I was the one digging. It was enticing, you know? I wanted to get inside your beautiful, brilliant mind. But I could never enter without your express permission. I was a vampire floating outside your window, and you never invited me in."

I can't even argue with such poetic vulnerability. "I'm... sorry."

"Don't be. You're right. We couldn't keep on like we were, with me begging to be forgiven and you smiling reassurance when you want nothing to do with me." He walks toward me and takes my hand—the same hand Peace held last night. "If it took a blast from your past for you to admit it wasn't working for you, so be it. I created the first rift last year."

"It sounds like you're saying I created a rift years ago."

"Just figure out what you want, okay?" He squeezes and lets go. "I've been trying. I'll always regret what happened at the bar conference. But we both have to be honest about what we need. And I'm tired of climbing your emotional walls."

I picture him as an invading Viking trying to storm a medieval castle. Me on the wall, defending the battlements. Endlessly knocking down his ladder just as he reaches the top.

"I'm serious," he says. "Do what you have to do, Lee. I can't go on like this any more than you can, so I'm thinking about logistics."

"I don't know *what* I want," I say, even as my brain demands I get into my car, drive to Tommy's, and curl up in safety beside Peace. There, the biggest complication is a potential murder mystery, which somehow feels less daunting than divorce litigation.

"Just keep me in the loop. Not much more I can say." Clay gets into his truck and heads to work.

I turn back toward our house. Clay had stuck his foot into the logistical door and wedged it open. All the co-parenting conundrums come waltzing through—custody, decision-making authority, visitation schedules, being a single parent most of the time versus going days without seeing my kids, holidays, health insurance, the damn house. Who would keep it, or would we have to sell?

An insistent ding, and I realize I'm still gripping my phone. I hungrily swipe over a text from Peace. With the appearance of his name, I don't have to think about the reverberating ramifications of my hypothetical choices. I don't have to analyze Clay's comments about me keeping him at an arm's length and what that might mean about my contribution to the collapse of my marriage. I can't dwell on the rightness or wrongness of the free pass Clay may or may not have given me.

Peace still loves me, and I still love him, and that's temporarily my most pressing concern.

Peace: *Morning! I hope your day is starting out great.*

Me: *Not exactly, but hey, it's only 6:30 a.m.*

Peace: *I hate to hear that. Can I help?*

Me: *No, but thank you. I'm heading to the office soon. I'll text the PI about Chad Dooley when I drop the boys at school. Hopefully, we'll have some information in the next few days.*

I type out another short message. *I miss you.* I stare at the screen as if those three little words are a secret code then hit Send.

He replies immediately. *I miss you too. When can we get together?*

Me: *Clay will have the boys Wednesday night, which means I'm in the FROG.*

Peace: *Tommy, Rollo, and I planned to go out to dinner Wednesday for my eighteen-month sobriety anniversary. I'm meeting them after my AA meeting. You want to join us? It'll be like old times.*

Me: *I would love that.*

Peace: *Good. They'll be glad to see you.*

Me: *Okay. Text me the details when you figure them out. Talk later *smiley face**

Peace: *Yes. Definitely.*

Clay told me to do what I need to do. I don't know if this is it, but there's only one way to find out.

BY THE TIME I SIT DOWN beside Peace at Saltwater Cowboys on Shem Creek, Tommy and Rollo are each on their third beer. They have a table on the outside deck overlooking the creek, where spicy barbeque fumes mix with the lingering scent of an afternoon rain shower. The sunset is fixing to be a lovely one, as it always is after a spring rain. The dawdling clouds are cotton balls dragged across an artist's palette—red, orange, pink, purple.

Rain hasn't stopped the Wednesday-evening party at Saltwater Cowboys, the most festive restaurant in Mount Pleasant. A few exuberant women answer the DJ's call as he spins dance tunes beside the crowded deck bar. Hulking wooden shrimp boats rest quietly in their slips, but a navy of smaller vessels jockeys for position in the skinny creek. Shaggy-haired teenage dockhands throw lines and tie boats in lines like fiberglass sardines. People laugh and chatter as they disembark and meander between the restaurants. Charleston has emerged from winter hibernation, and the enthusiasm is contagious.

Peace has a Coke, but I order a Mich Ultra at his insistence. He doesn't want anyone to think of him as a buzzkill, even if his own buzz is deceased. Neither Peace's sobriety nor my intrusion into their boys' night slows Tommy or Rollo. They keep right on reminiscing about one of their many fishing trips to Boot Island.

"That was the year Ro-Ro tried to make popcorn on the fire and the pot exploded. Sounded like a machine gun on D-Day." Tommy puffs out his cheeks then repeatedly smacks the air out of them.

Rollo peers out from under his YETI baseball cap. White-blond hair sticks out around the hat's edges. He has a dark tan from year-round fishing. The lines of his older tattoos have smeared like diluted watercolor paintings. "It might not have been popcorn. Maybe it was dynamite."

"Maybe you're an idiot," Tommy says.

"Listen, LeeLee. You gotta hear this." Rollo turns to me, his new captive audience. "Peace was straight passed out by the fire, snoring, man, chainsawing logs, drooling like Landon's old hound dog."

"Point made, Ro," Peace says as I laugh.

"Then the explosion hit—" Rollo jumps to his feet like a tipsy scarecrow in jeans and flip-flops. He almost knocks over his beer, and he startles the girls at the table behind us.

"Rollo, what the hell? Calm down," Peace says, but he laughs too. "Sorry, y'all." He smiles at the disgruntled girls, and their annoyed scowls turn into blushing grins.

Rollo sits. "Peace jumped up and ran into the dark night like the devil with sunrise hot on his heels."

"I won't deny it," Peace says. "Smelled like my mama's hairdryer blowing a fuse."

"Are y'all going to Boot this fall?" I ask. "With Peace back, it would be like old times."

"We haven't been in a few years," Tommy says. "Rollo let the cabin fall into disrepair. Such a travesty."

"I'll make the repairs eventually," Rollo says. "But believe me, no one wants to go out there these days. Mother Nature has taken over."

"We could help you fix it up," Peace says.

"Maybe sometime. I'm too busy right now."

"Doing what, Ro?" Tommy asks. "You spend three days a week on the boat and another three hunting whatever is in season. That leaves one day for work, church, and spending time with your mama."

"I'm not staying out there until I set up one of them compost toilets."

Tommy scowls. "When'd you get so old you can't take a crap in the woods?"

"Damn, boys," Peace says. "Let's not tell fishing stories and talk about porta-johns with LeeLee here."

"We got plenty of other stories." I stick my beer into a complimentary Koozie.

"That we do." Tommy brushes his curly honey-colored hair off his forehead. He's as cute as ever, with his bright-hazel eyes, dimpled chin, and boy-next-door good looks. "But let's toast the real reason we're here. Congrats to you, my man, for being sober for eighteen months. You're an oak tree standing strong against the winds of temptation."

"Squirrely as hell." Rollo unwraps one of his omnipresent Tootsie Rolls.

"Thanks, y'all," Peace says. "I'll tell you this, if you ever start licking the bottom of the barrel—"

"Gross, P.," I say.

"No use sugarcoating it. I was way beyond scraping. I was stuck headfirst in that barrel. You hit rock bottom like that, and you'll find willpower you never knew you had."

"Forget rock bottom," Tommy says. "I already hit *boulder* bottom. Dealing with April's drama and her trying to keep the kids from me..."

Tommy keeps talking, but I glean more than his spoken words. *LeeLee can help me. She's an expert at this shit.*

Oh boy. I've been in this position before. I came for happy hour, but instead, I'll be offering free legal advice.

"And she says the kids don't want to see me. But if that's true, it's because she's talking shit about me to them... and she's got her asshole boyfriend around them all the time..."

I declined to represent Tommy in his divorce because I sensed impending disaster. Tommy is famously bullheaded, while his ex-wife is notoriously high-maintenance and self-centered. When she moved on with their son's baseball coach as soon as the ink dried on their settlement agreement, Tommy went ballistic. Over two years later, they're still at each other's throats. I pity his attorney, the ineffective commanding officer in the hundred years' war of the Dukes.

For the next thirty minutes, I save him a couple hundred bucks in attorney's fees by listening to him grouse over his ex's plot to turn his children against him. I advise him to speak to his lawyer about six times before Peace comes to my rescue.

"You want to talk about seawalls, Tom?" he asks.

"Huh? Hell no."

"LeeLee doesn't want to talk shop either."

"It's okay," I say. "But seriously, I don't know the details of your case—the history, your attorney's strategies, what's in your court order—so I'm speculating."

"Isn't speculation your whole job?" Rollo asks. "Remember what Old Peace used to say—"

"It depends," Tommy and Peace say at the same time.

"It's true, that's a lawyer's answer to basically anything," I say.

"Y'all speculated any more about Ginny?" Tommy asks. "Landon filled me in on that weird email and Palmer hiring a PI and—"

"Hey, y'all." Rollo looks at his phone. "I've been trying to meet up with this chick from Tinder, and she's at Tavern and Table." He elbows Tommy. "You want to come? She's with friends."

"Man, I don't know."

"You gotta get back in the saddle," Rollo says. "You can't sit around waiting on Palmer to get divorced."

Tommy's face reddens.

"Harsh, dude," Peace says.

Tommy drains his beer. "No. He's right. I'll go. But hold on. I want to hear what's happening with Ginny—"

Rollo stands. "I don't, man. It's too sad." He drops a fifty-dollar bill in the basket of condiments, walks around the table, and kisses my cheek. He shakes Peace's hand. "I'm gonna hit the head. I'll meet you outside, Tom."

"There's not much to say," I tell Tommy. "We're still looking for information."

"It's crazy to think of a world without Ginny. Even if she's been out of our lives forever. Sorry, P. I know it's fresher for you—or something."

"It is, but we all love her."

"Rollo can't even talk about it. We all love her, yeah. But I think Rollo *really* loved her."

"You think so?" I ask. "Rollo and Ginny always seemed like brother and sister, and Rollo had so many girls around. I can't believe he survived the nineties without getting an STD."

Peace grins. "Maybe he kept his diseases on the down-low. You know what they used to say about Heather Lewis—"

"Herpes Heather? *Riiiiight.*" Tommy subtly points at his crotch. "Maybe ol' Rollo got the pox after all."

"Y'all, stop it. So *gross*," I say.

"Sorry, Lee." Tommy gets up from his chair. "I've been on my own too long. I forgot how to be a gentleman. Now that I'm living with this caveman, I'm regressing even more." He adds his cash to Rollo's. "You saw Palm recently, right?"

"Yeah. Me and Palm and Jess got together to talk about Ginny."

"How's she doing?" *Does she miss me like I miss her? Does she talk about me?*

I can't answer his unspoken questions. It isn't my place to elucidate Palmer's feelings, nor do I want to reveal that I know he's wondering about them. "She's hanging in there."

"Tell her I said hello," Tommy says. "Haven't talked to her since she texted me, reaming me for not telling her Peace was back. But she told me we shouldn't talk and—I'll shut up. You don't want to be my therapist any more than you want to be my free lawyer."

"I gotta run to the bathroom." I stand, just for an excuse to hug Tommy.

He stiffens when I put my arms around him, but then he squeezes me back.

"Thanks, Lee," he whispers.

"Love you, T-Dog."

"Love y'all too. Enjoy this pretty evening."

He walks through the crowd. I sit down again.

"I thought you had to go to the bathroom," Peace says.

"False alarm. Pregnancy does a number on your insides. My bladder hasn't been right since."

"Damn." He chuckles.

"Too much information. Sorry."

"No, no. I learn something new every day." The breeze picks up, and he tucks a few stray strands of my hair behind my ear.

Heat flows from his fingers to my cheeks, so I turn down the fire by transferring my gaze to a family of dolphins in the water below us. I track their irregular surfacing, like haphazard chess moves across the creek.

Beautiful... beautiful... beautiful...

His silent incantation lures me away from the dolphins and their underwater labyrinth. "What are you looking at, silly?" I ask.

"You know what."

Since I read his thoughts, I know exactly what, but I ask, "Do I?"

"Thinking about how beautiful you are. Always have been. I can still picture you in the cab of my truck the first time I drove you and Ginny to her house."

"I kept staring at you. I felt bad about it, of course. You were Ginny's boyfriend."

"I was staring at you, too, and I felt just as bad. I fought my feelings for you for a long time," he says. "It's strange because I truly loved Ginny. She broke my heart when she dumped me before we left for college. But at the same time, I was falling for you."

"Love is complicated at any age, but the older I get, the more convoluted it feels. Everything is more complicated—feelings, people, the world, life in general. I'm less sure about it all."

"When we're young, everything is right or wrong, just or unjust, black or white. Our hair goes gray for a reason as we get older."

I touch his hair. "You don't have much gray."

"I'm a late bloomer, and I still got a lot to learn. What about you? That hair a dye job?"

"You shouldn't ask a lady such things. But if you must know, no. My father was part Choctaw. At least, that's what our family lore says. Our hair holds color, even if my mindset is going gray."

"I didn't know that. You never talked about your father."

"What's to say? He beat up my mom and ran out on us. All he gave me was a good hair gene." I tap my nose. "And this nose, from the photos I've seen."

"I always loved your nose."

"Since I hate it, a nose compliment is the way to my heart."

"I'd like to find my way back there." He leans toward me, and the nose in question comes dangerously close to his cheek.

"You want to leave?" I ask softly.

"Do you?"

I nod. He gets the check.

WE GO BACK TO TOMMY'S rental house. Peace offers me a beer, but I refuse. I feel drunk after one and a half Mich Ultras, under the influence of fierce attraction, intoxicated by desire. Within minutes, we're on the sofa, making out like teenagers who've purposely missed curfew—minus any adolescent clumsiness. We're grown adults. We learned a lot from each other back in the day and a lot since.

"I've been waiting about fifteen years to kiss you," he says as we come up for air.

"Was it worth the wait?"

He grins as his lips meet mine. "Hell yes."

I somehow have the wherewithal to make sure we stay clothed. Tommy and Rollo might roll in at any minute. Besides, in the midst of our strange reunion, my husband and my sons loom large in my mind.

My waning enthusiasm eventually betrays me, and Peace runs his fingers over my forehead.

"I'm losing you," he says.

"No. You're not. But I..."

"Shhh. You don't have to explain." He pulls me close.

Tears run down my face until his wet shirt sticks to my cheeks. I'm crying in a man's arms for the second time in two weeks, and it's a different man. What does that say about me, a thirty-five-year old mother of three who's hopped from one set of arms to another?

"Clay told me to do what I needed to do to figure out what I want."

"Is that what this is?"

"Sort of." I cry harder. "I'm sorry. This is so hard."

"Don't apologize. I'm just glad you're here." He clears his throat. "I love you, LeeLee."

I stiffen in his arms. His words fill me with joy and dread and every shade of emotion in between.

"You don't have to say it back. Not now. Not yet."

"Okay," I say. "But... thank you—for saying it."

"You're welcome. Now, you need to get back home."

So here I am a few hours later, *back home*, if the FROG counts as such. I stare at the ceiling fan spinning over the bed. My emotions whirl with it.

I didn't go into the house because I was afraid to see Clay. Free pass or not, I still feel awful. If Clay sees me with my blotchy eyes and my lips raw from Peace's five-o'clock shadow, he'll know something happened.

Instead, I crept like an amateur burglar onto my property, went up into the FROG, and changed into my nightshirt. I washed my face. The bathroom smelled like Clay's aftershave, the bed like his deodorant. Comforting, familiar scents—welcome scents. Yet, when I lay down and closed my eyes, I saw only Peace's face looking down at me as his fingers grazed my forehead.

I will find no easy answer, no solution that doesn't involve hurting people I love and possibly breaking my heart into a million sharp pieces. The tide has come in. I have no choice but to tread water until it retreats and my feet touch bottom.

Chapter 16

Ginny, 2013

It's hard to believe it's 2013 and even harder to believe we've been in Myrtle Beach for five years. Given our food-and-bev jobs, Peace and I are rarely off on the same days. Opportunities to have fun together are few and far between, so on a warm March evening, I beg him to come to Wahoo's Fish House in Murrells Inlet to watch me sing. Peace avoids bars on his nights off, but it isn't tourist season. By the party-hardy standards of the Murrells Inlet MarshWalk, the stretch of waterfront bars and restaurants fifteen miles south of Myrtle, things are pretty quiet. He finally agrees when I remind him I'll be safer if he defends me from my audience—those pushy creeps who think the singer is literally up for grabs.

Wahoo's has a nice setup—a screened-in outdoor bar with a lovely view of the bustling MarshWalk, the marina, and Garden City Beach on the other side of the peaceful inlet. White lights crisscross the ceiling, and multicolored liquor bottles are arranged in the center of the rectangular bar like church organ pipes.

The manager hooked me up with an older guitarist who plays these gigs because he enjoys them, not because he needs the money. He agrees to my playlist and contentedly strums away in the background. I don't have to yodel over him or kill time while he channels his inner Jimi Hendrix.

Peace sits alone in the far corner of the bar, near the parking lot entrance, away from the more crowded waterfront. He doesn't speak to anyone except the two bartenders who roll around the serving area like hamsters on a wheel. I finish my early set before nine, and now, I'm ready to really start my evening. As I bebop through the high-top tables toward Peace, Chad Dooley and his cute brunette girlfriend open the screen door. Peace occasionally buys weed and oxy from Chad, and we ran into him and his girlfriend once at a gas station. I can't remember her name, but she seems nice.

Before that chance meeting at the Exxon, I hadn't seen Chad Dooley in over ten years. I was surprised to discover that he turned out to be decent-looking. He's still as skinny as a rail, but he hasn't gone bald. Without his crawly mustache and wannabe gangster rapper routine, he's a reasonably cute country boy. I wave to him and what's-her-name as I sidle up to Peace.

"Hey, baby." I kiss Peace's cheek. "You look positively antisocial."

"Sorry." He squeezes my waist. "Just tired. You were great."

"Let's see if Chad and his girl want to have a drink."

He stares into his glass of beer like some exotic fish might be swimming around in there. "I'd rather not."

"You don't want to hang out with my old boyfriend?"

"Ha. It's not that."

"I'm kidding," I say, but his lack of jealousy is kind of annoying.

"You know I've never liked him. Besides, I'm paid up with him right now. If I so much as think about Chad Dooley, I owe him money."

"Some things never change. Dooley still has the best weed around." I grin, but Peace doesn't reciprocate.

"I'm tired, Gin. Fishing boats yesterday. Early shift at the bar today. My Adderall wore off hours ago."

Can't we go home? Damn it, Ginny, my head is killing me? Xanax... Xanax... Xanax...

My smile freezes, but I step onto the tightrope between our pact of telling him when I read his thoughts and staying silent to get him to do what I want. If I say something now, his bad mood will get worse. His tolerance for my readings has dwindled even as they grow more frequent. Sometimes, I pick up multiple people's thoughts at once, like staticky radio stations fading in and out.

"We'll go home soon," I say. "I promise."

"Hey, y'all," Chad says over my shoulder. "Up for an Asheburg reunion?"

"Hey! Long time, no see," I say.

I hug Chad, and he shakes Peace's hand. His girlfriend and I exchange cheek kisses.

I point at her expensive-looking knee-high boots. "Love your kicks."

"Don't tell anyone, but her daddy is rich. My little trust-fund baby." Chad pats her rear end.

I wish he would say her name so I don't have to ask again.

"We're not *that* rich." Girlfriend tosses her hair over her shoulder. She has a natural look, unlike the hardened women we usually see in these places. "My family owns a couple of furniture stores between Myrtle and Pawleys Island."

"She's a nurse at Tidewater Medical," Chad says. "Helping me with the oxy hookups."

Girlfriend scowls. "Hush up, Chad. You want to get me fired? And get yourself in trouble too?"

"Relax, sugar."

"People could be listening." Girlfriend's eyes dart over the patrons' faces. "You need to be more careful."

"Stop nagging, now. You sound like my mama."

"How's your mother? And what about Reesie?" I ask. "They still live off Mercury Road?"

Chad shakes his head. "Nah. Hate to bring up sad stuff, but my mama and Reesie both passed about four years ago."

"Damn," Peace says. "What happened?"

"The old trailer caught fire while they were both asleep inside."

"How *terrible*," I say.

"That's why I don't talk about it," Chad says. "You need anything, Peace?"

"No. I'm good with my Rx for another week or so."

"Let me know when you're out, brother."

Peace grunts and sips his beer. He watches Girlfriend over his glass. *Damn, she's good-looking... tall too... those legs... reminds me of LeeLee...*

A low blow, but I keep smiling. If I react, Peace will know I read him. I wave at the bartender and rest my boobs on the bar. Faster than I could say kamikaze or mind eraser, we have four shots on the house. I knock mine back then grab Peace's full pint glass for a chaser. Beer sloshes into his lap. I can't say it's an accident.

"Damn it." He looks down at his wet crotch.

"Sorry, baby," I say, but I hope he'll cool off.

Dance tunes play over the speaker system while the next band sets up. The driving beat of some Pitbull song reverberates through the wooden floorboards.

I take Girlfriend's arm. "You wanna dance?"

"Uh... I'm not much of a dancer," she says.

"No way! Me and my best friends, Jess and Palmer and LeeLee, love to dance. P., remember how we used to cut the rug? We were the Spice Girls of Bull Street." I do a little booty grind on Peace's knee.

Chad laughs, and even Peace chuckles.

"Guess we're not going home yet," Peace says. "Might as well take you up on one of those pills if you got one."

As Chad digs around in his pocket for a plastic bag of pills, I tug Girlfriend's arm.

"Come on, girlie. I'll show you some moves."

"I bet men fall in love watching Ginny dance," Chad says. "She's like one of those girls who seduce sailors. That's one of the few things

I remember from Ms. Mullins's history class, Viking myths or some shit."

"Greek myths," Peace says. "Sirens."

"That's it. Freaked me out when I went offshore. If anyone would get seduced by a sea witch, it'd be me."

"Boys, tonight y'all are partying with a couple of MarshWalk sirens!" I call. "Clear the way to the dance floor. *Wee-ah-weee-ah-weee-ah!*"

The crowd parts like I'm a patrol car. I drag Girlfriend along with me. If she looks the fool with her two left feet, Peace will stop thinking about her hotness and remember mine.

Within no time, my gyrations have the attention of every man in the place. Girlfriend sways in place while sucking rum and pineapple juice through a straw. She drains it by the time Kesha starts yowling about brushing her teeth with a bottle of Jack.

"Need 'nother drink," Girlfriend says. "'Nother. Want 'nother shot? I'm buying."

"You're a girl after my heart. Thanks, ah... ummm..." I can't keep talking to her and not know her name. "I'm so sorry, but I can't remember. What's your name?"

"Don't worry about it. I can't remember anything. Dating Chad will totally fry your brain." Her glassy eyes blink-blink-blink. "It's Meredith. If you want to find me on Facebook—"

"I'm not on Facebook," I say. "I don't need people knowing my business."

"If you ever are, it's Meredith Preston."

AFTER THAT LAST SHOT, pretty Miss Meredith Preston forgets she can't dance. She makes an ass of herself in a very Caucasian way, waving her arms and accidentally smacking the next band's backup singer. I intervene before the singer beats Meredith's ass, and

Chad half carries her out of the bar at last call. She professes her undying sisterly love and declares that Peace and I are her new favorite couple.

Peace looks in the mirror when we get into his truck. "*Ughhh.* So bloodshot. Like I got a red squid in each eye. I shouldn't be driving. Another DUI and I'm screwed." He slaps his cheek.

"It's only fifteen miles. I'll drive." As I say it, the truck's cab spins like the teacups at the Family Kingdom Amusement Park down the road.

"*Only* fifteen miles? No." Peace cranks the engine. "Your license is suspended. You don't need to be driving at all."

"Okay, *Dad*."

He glances at me as he puts the truck in drive. "You don't have to be nasty about it."

"Who's being nasty?"

He doesn't reply as he pulls out of the parking lot, and we drive in silence for a block or two. I try to read him, but I get nothing.

"I said *who's being nasty*? I'm not."

"Not tonight, Ginny."

"*What* is your *problem*?"

He doesn't say anything.

"The silent treatment." The bowstring tenses behind the arrow of my temper. "Why are you being a dick?"

"I'm not talking because I don't want to fight." He has one hand on the wheel and the other on the gear shift, as if he's holding the truck together. "I'm exhausted. We're both drunk. Let's go home and go to sleep."

"I don't want to sleep." I touch his thigh then creep toward his crotch. His jeans are still damp from me "accidentally" spilling beer on him.

He pushes my hand away. "Stop it. I'm trying to drive, and I'm not in the mood."

"Not in the mood, huh? What if it were Fancy-Boots Meredith in the car with you? Would you be in the mood then?"

"What?"

"I *saw* you looking at her."

"I was not looking at her any more than I was looking at Chad Dooley."

"Oh, *please*. Little Miss Thang with her sexy boots and her tight-ass jeans. She was a hot mess on the dance floor. She looked like a lame giraffe."

The seat belt notification dings a warning.

"She didn't want to dance," Peace says. "You made her."

How dare he side with Meredith! The thought slams through my brain as my hand slams the seat belt into the buckle. "Now it's *my fault* you were staring at her?"

"Ginny. *Come on*. You make no sense." He's begging me to think like he thinks. It reminds me of LeeLee in my parents' yard on that hot June day, eleven years ago.

I didn't cave then, and I won't now. "No, *you* make no sense! I'm supposed to be your girlfriend, and you're making eyes at Chad's girlfriend. You wonder why I can't trust you working at a damn strip club?"

"Here we go with the strip club. I need that job because it pays well, and you keep getting fired—"

"This isn't about money! You work with naked women—"

"They're my coworkers! I don't want to *talk* about this again!"

My temper's arrow lets fly, propelled by suspicion and jealousy so intense I want to kick the windshield. I'm *sure* Peace has slept with multiple women from the club—not just the strippers but the waitresses, probably the fifty-year-old assistant manager, and the cleaning crew too. "You don't want to talk about it because it's true! Let's go there now. They're still open. Go, go, go!"

"No fucking way." His laughter is almost shrill, nothing like his usual deep chuckle. "You've *lost* it."

I try to rip open Peace's mind. I demand that his memories and thoughts give up a name, a face, a hair color, anything. Nothing's there. It enrages me more, because I *know* he's lying to me. I *know* he's figured out how to hide from my powers. There has to be a way to get it out of him.

I reach over and slap him upside his head. I hit him once, twice, three times.

"What the—" He swats my hand, and the steering wheel jerks. He rounds on me. "What the *hell* is wrong with you?"

I look up to a red light. "Stop!" I scream instinctively.

Peace slams on the brakes, and we skid to a stop. By some miracle, no one else is crossing the intersection. No other cars occupy the road around us. If they did, any sober driver would call the cops.

Peace's chest heaves. As he blinks at the streetlights, my mind clears. Mortification and guilt rip away the Band-Aid of wrath and distrust. Peace has told me a hundred times that he would never cheat on me, yet when I was done up on coke, I stormed into MacDaddy's. I questioned every woman in the place, much to Peace's chagrin and his general manager's annoyance. I read the manager's thoughts as he kicked me out. *Poor dude... dealing with this crazy, paranoid bitch.*

Then and there, in that empty intersection, I promise to let it go. He admired Meredith's looks, but I observed that Chad Dooley had aged pretty well. We're human beings. We have eyes, and we see each other.

"I'm sorry," I whisper.

"Don't. *Please.* Just don't."

My eyes fill with tears. "What's wrong with me?"

"I just want to get home. It's only a few more miles."

"I don't know what happened. My mind does something when I'm like that, Peace. I can't control—"

"Not now, Ginny. Not. *Now.*"

I shut up. We drive back to our rental in silence. I don't get an acceptance of my apology, but Peace doesn't get a DUI either.

Chapter 17

LeeLee, 2015

On Friday night, Clay gets home early enough to read the boys bedtime stories, so I stay out of his way. I retreat to the second-floor piazza with my laptop and try to work on a client affidavit—my client's personal statement about her ongoing custody dispute. From my client's perspective, she left her ex, and he's still bitter. He makes up problems to make her look bad. In his warped version of events, she parties too much; she exposes the children to her many boyfriends; she doesn't monitor their schoolwork.

I've written hundreds of affidavits—diary entries of dysfunctional relationships crossed with therapeutic confessions—but this one hits close to home. I can't imagine Clay resorting to such tactics, but I've never been on that side of such conflicts. No one can know for certain how our post-divorce story might read.

A crash from inside the house startles me. I stand, but when I detect some twittering laughter, I sink back onto the wicker sofa.

Thirty minutes later, Clay sticks his head out the door. "Everyone is asleep. Bowman knocked some books off his shelf, but we cleaned it up."

"I appreciate the help. I'm trying to work on this affidavit."

He flips on the overhead light. "You're gonna go blind. You need some bug spray? The mosquitos are starting to wake up."

"No, thanks. Do you have everything you need in the FROG? Fresh towels? Shampoo, soap?" I hate questioning him like this, as if he's a distant cousin visiting from out of town.

"Yeah. Thanks. Well, good night."

I try to swallow the lump in my throat, an ice cube of sadness that will stay stuck unless I find the internal warmth to melt it. "Good night."

My phone dings as he disappears inside the house. It's Peace. Confusingly, my heart flutters, even as its wings are still heavy watching Clay withdraw to the FROG. I swipe over to Peace's text, a photo of us four girls on the boat at Saltmarsh's dock.

My light-blue tie-dyed bikini, plastic daisy choker, and jingly ankle bracelet identify it as a high-school photo. Jess has her hair in two short braids, and Palmer sports one of her ridiculous wide straw hats. In the nineties era of baby doll dresses and butterfly clips, no other teenager would have been caught dead in such a matronly chapeau outside the pomp and circumstance of the Carolina Cup. She sits between Jess and me. My tan legs drape over their laps, and Jess rests her elbow on my toes.

Ginny the navigator sits behind us, arms wide like a mermaid carved into the bow of a Viking warship. Her waist is tiny, but her bikini is tinier, two yellow triangles covering perky breasts that would never nurse a child. Though she was the fairest of us, she never wore a hat or sunglasses. She faced the sun head-on, like everything else.

Peace added a message underneath. *I remember taking this photo and thinking y'all were the prettiest girls in the world.*

Me: *So sweet. I looked at old photos the other day. And cried. My usual MO lately, ha ha.*

He doesn't answer right away, so I type a message to Big Lou in Dirty Myrtle. I ask him to see what he can find about Chad Dooley. Chad isn't on Facebook, and FindMe.com returned even less about him than about Ginny or Peace. The lucky bastard somehow kept one step ahead of the po-po. It would be up to Lou to do the research—or as Palmer had posited, leave a horse head in someone's bed.

After hitting Send, I check my inbox for something from LoveGinnyB525, but there's still no reply to my email. I reopen the original message and read it for the hundredth time.

Out at Saltmarsh, I wondered if Drew Smith was behind LoveGinnyB, but now, I have a new suspect. If the author had shown any complex thought, I would have to dismiss the idea, but the simplicity means Chad Dooley could have sent it. If Chad did something awful to Ginny, he might frame Peace.

On the other hand, we still have no *proof* anything bad happened to her. According to Palmer, who gets intel through the Blankenship family gossip line, Cheryl drove to Myrtle Beach and banged on the police department's door. Despite Cheryl's hollering, the police don't consider Ginny a missing person. She's a grown woman with drug problems who doesn't want anything to do with her family or friends.

That means the dog is still asleep, so why would Chad kick it?

I open a new email and start typing.

To whoever you are:

It's terrible to scare us about Ginny then go silent. You claim to want justice for her, but you're not telling us why we should be afraid for her safety in the first place.

If you are who I think you are, you were always bad news, and I can't imagine that's changed. If you hurt her yourself, I hope you'll have some decency and confess. I can't see why else you would reach out to us other than a guilty conscience.

None of us believe you about Peace. He has his own problems, but he's always been a good person. So either tell us what you know, or leave us alone.

LeeLee Moretz

I reread it a couple of times. The message feels indignant enough to provoke a response but not so accusatory as to scare the writer away or, God forbid, make him go into self-defense mode. I have three children and don't want to goad some whack-a-doo. I take a deep breath and hit Send.

"Mama?"

I jump in place. Trey stands in the doorframe, rubbing his eyes.

"Hey, buddy," I say. "You okay?"

"I fell asleep, but I woke up."

"You need a drink of water?"

"Yeah." Trey blinks and looks around the piazza. "Where's Dad? He's not in bed."

"Oh, he... he had to run back to the office."

"Wow. It's late."

I look at my phone. "It's only ten. Sometimes, he goes back there after y'all are asleep." Clay occasionally returns to the office after the boys' bedtime during intense trial prep, so it isn't a total fib. "How about I get you some water and I lie down with you?"

Trey yawns and nods. Three minutes later, I lie beside my oldest boy on his skinny twin bed. He snuggles next to me, and I run my fingers over his hair.

"Love you, buddy," I whisper.

"Love you too. Thanks for lying with me." *I'm too big for Mama to snuggle with me.*

"I'll lie with you no matter how big you are."

"I was just thinking I'm too big for that."

"That's funny. Must be my mom radar." I wonder how long that explanation will work. Surely, fifteen-year-old Trey won't believe in mom radar.

"Will you tell Dad I said good night again too?"

"Sure thing." I mean to follow through on that promise, but I fall asleep. A couple of hours later, I wake up and creep out of Trey's room. I peek in on Bowman and Malachy and stumble through the dark hallway to my bedroom. I check my phone. Five messages from Peace.

I found some other pics if you want to look at them next time we get together. Which will be?

*I can't wait, whenever it is *smiley face**

Sorry, did I say something wrong?

Hey, you there?

Ummmmm. Now I'm sort of worried. Hope everything is okay. Good night.

I shade my eyes from the phone's glare. Of course Peace wouldn't predict one of my kids needed me and he also expects a prompt response. Between kids and work, Clay and I sometimes take hours to get back to each other. Neither of us worries about it—it's part of our busy lives. I don't blame Peace for not getting it. He doesn't have kids or a job that follows him home.

Me: *Trey woke up, so I lay down with him and fell asleep. All is well. Let's talk in the morning. *smiley face**

Next, I send Clay a message. *T woke up, and I lay down with him and passed out, but he asked me to tell you good night again. So, good night from T.*

I go into the bathroom, brush my teeth, and wash away sticky vestiges of workday mascara. Out of habit, I look at my phone a final time when I climb into bed. To my surprise, I have a text from Clay.

Clay: *Thanks. I'll give him an extra kiss in the morning.*

Me: *Sorry. Didn't mean to wake you.*

Clay: *I'm awake. Can't sleep. Went down a Wikipedia wormhole.*

Clay and I have a long history of wasting hours on Wikipedia.

Me: *Topic?*

Clay: *Started out with Napoleon. Ended up with mass extinction of large mammals of North America.*

Me: *Wow. There are a lot of points on the graph between that A and Z.*

Clay: *Yeah. But it helps me not think about other stuff.*

Me: *I understand.*

Clay: *Gonna try to close my eyes. Night again.*

Me: *Night.*

I roll over, but sleep eludes me, so I concentrate on Clay's convoluted path from French dictators to saber-toothed tigers. *Napoleon, Waterloo, British Empire, colonialism, United States, Native Americans, bison, woolly mammoths...*

Mercifully, I get to the Ice Age and fall asleep.

A COUPLE OF DAYS LATER, another visitor from my past arrives at my place of employment. Cheryl Blankenship never makes a quiet entrance. Her asking for "my sweetheart LeeLee Lightstone" carries through the walls. Britt once again pokes her head into my office.

"Are you expecting someone? She said her name is—"

"Cheryl Blankenship."

"Do you want to see her?" Britt looks like she won't blame me if I ask her to tell Cheryl I'm busy.

"Yes. I asked her to come by this week. Besides, if you tell her to leave, she might decide to sleep on the sofa in the waiting room." I wave at the chair across from my desk. "Bring her in."

The door swings open, and Cheryl appears as if she's materialized out of thin air. "'Scuse me, sweetheart!" she chirps.

Britt retreats with raised eyebrows.

Cheryl rests one hand on the doorframe and one on her hip like an actress about to make her Broadway debut. She wears jean shorts, sneakers, and a fuchsia Sweetie Pie's T-shirt covered in white cat hair. Her smeary red lipstick clashes horribly with her shirt and her brassy boxed-blond dye job. She's as skinny as a blue heron on a vegan diet—not a healthy look on a woman her age, but when she smiles, I see the pretty woman she was. Clumpy mascara lines her sharp blue eyes. She closes the door behind her and holds out her arms.

"Oh my word. My *sweetheart*, LeeLee."

I stand and hug her. "Cheryl. So good to see you."

She squeezes me. A couple of tears sneak over her spidery lashes. "*Honey.* You're as lovely as ever. You look like a teenager."

"I sure don't feel like it." I wave at the chair across from my desk. "Sit down."

She sits and crosses one leg over the other. A pack of cigarettes rolls out of her purse when she sets it on the desk. "Oops. Damn cheap pocketbook. Don't tell Doctor Burke. He says I'm fixing to show signs of emphysema."

"Haven't seen Doctor Burke since I was about twenty, so your secret is safe with me. Jess said she's been trying to catch up with you—"

"I love my sweetheart Jessalyn, but I wanted to see *you*. In person." Despite the closed door, her voice drops to a whisper. "Hopefully, we can *see something interesting*. You know what I mean?"

"Uh. Yeah. I think so." It's been years since I've spoken about my powers. "I'm embarrassed that it's been so long since we've talked."

Cheryl clucks like a broody hen. "No, no! You're busy with your family and your fancy career, missy! Now... last time I saw you, at Burt's funeral service, you were pregnant—"

"Yup. Another little guy. Malachy. He's almost three."

"You noticed anything *interesting* about your kids?"

I shake my head vehemently. I always watch for signs my boys might be storytellers—or navigators, in Cheryl's language. So far, nothing.

"It still might show," she says. "Especially in the little one. Plenty of time for his talents to make themselves known."

"We'll see. What have Jess and Palmer told you?"

"My sweetheart Palmer filled her aunt Cheryl in on the latest. Private investigator. Anonymous email tips. You figured out who sent the emails yet?"

"I have some suspicions," I say.

"Dr. Drew was all puckered up about Peace at my last appointment. He agrees that Peace probably did something to her. His *own brother*." She shrugs. "There's certainly no love lost between those boys."

"Family stuff. They're arguing about their father."

"Be that as it may, maybe *Drew* wrote those emails."

"I thought about that." Cheryl's suggestion makes me consider revisiting the Drew angle. "But Peace—"

"Peace let my baby *disappear* and didn't have the courtesy to pick up the phone and call me." Cheryl's mouth sets in a stubborn red line, looking like an irritated wound.

"He definitely should have called. But Ginny wasn't exactly in touch herself, was she?"

"She always called me once a year. Or... sometimes every two years. She has a problem. You know that."

"Peace has the same problems," I say.

"That may be true, but don't you watch any of those shows on Netflix? The crime shows? If a woman goes missing, her man is the first suspect! Palmer said you saw Peace. Have you *read anything* when you talked to him?"

Her eyes bore into me, and I reach into my desk for a legal pad to hide my embarrassment. None of my recent, romantically charged readings from Peace had anything to do with Ginny's whereabouts. But that was because he didn't have anything to do with her disappearance.

I scrawl Ginny's name and the date across the top of the legal pad. "Nothing about Ginny." I lean on my elbows like I do when talking to a distraught client. "When you spoke to him, did he say anything about Chad Dooley?"

Her mouth contracts from a long, jagged gash into a round hematoma of disgust. "That white-trash boy who used to sniff around Ginny? *Ugh.* No."

"He's not a boy anymore. He's full-grown trash now." I give her a summary of everything Peace told me about Chad Dooley. "It was Peace who encouraged her to ditch him years ago, when he first showed signs of abusive behavior. I can't imagine he mellowed with age. I see plenty such men in my line of work. They're like sour milk. Time makes them worse, not better."

Cheryl stares out the window at the art gallery across the street. A giant painting of a cow looks back at her, as if waiting for her to call bullshit. "I know y'all think I'm a little cuckoo. Cat-lady widow out in the boonies, living off snooder-dooders and Diet Coke, watching too many missing-persons shows. But I only want the truth about what happened to her."

"We all do."

"I've known Peace Smith since he was in kindergarten. He was a sweet child and a polite teenager, but to me, these days, he's simply the most likely subject. And we have to start somewhere. As far as the police in Myrtle are concerned, Ginny wandered off like a lost house cat and I'm a hysterical backwoods loony. But I won't let the police forget about her. If I scream loud enough, they'll *have* to listen to me!" She smacks the desk with one hand. "They don't know my daughter like I do. Do you honestly believe Peace and Ginny split up with a snap of her fingers and never spoke again? Ginny's not one to—what's the saying? Quietly tiptoe into the twilight?"

"Something like that." I have a hunch she's unwittingly referencing the poet Dylan Thomas. Appropriate, since I can't imagine Ginny going gently into anything, day or night. She was born raging, raging.

"Right. As much as I want her to be as fine and dandy as a seersucker suit, it doesn't seem likely."

"Ginny could also be flaky. Remember when she bailed on our Charleston apartment? Maybe she pulled the biggest flake-out in Asheburg history—worse than Tommy's mama leaving his daddy for their accountant, marrying the guy, then buying a house three doors down."

"You heard about that scandal? It was before your time."

"Stories are the fine wine of small Southern towns," I say. "Unlike abusive men, they get better with age."

"Ginny believed you were a gifted storyteller, in more ways than one."

"The last time we spoke, she told me I was a *shitty* storyteller."

"Jealousy often flashes its green eyes from behind a mask of annoyance. A pack of feral hogs couldn't root it out of her, but the truth is Ginny envied you for reading people's thoughts." She shrugs. "Maybe she envied you for other reasons too."

"I can't imagine Ginny being envious of anyone. If anything, I was jealous of her. She was always the star of the show."

"The brightest star can get jealous of another's twinkle." A sad smile. "Even a straight-up sparkler like my crazy Ginny."

"Everyone always said, 'Oh, Ginny's so crazy,' but by the time she left Peace, he was legitimately questioning her sanity, like, severe mental health problems, psych-ward stuff."

Cheryl grabs a tissue from the box on my desk. I keep them handy because my clients shed a lot of tears in my office. "She did sound awful the last time I spoke to her." Cheryl swabs her eyes. "But she wasn't *sad* awful. More like *manic* awful. She'd been reading the past and future left and right. She figured out how to read thoughts, like you. Before we hung up, she told me her father would die in an accident. Not six months later, he got liquored up to high heaven and drove his truck into a tree on Toogoodoo Road. Burt Blankenship wasn't father of the year, but he was still her daddy. Seems she should have been sad about it... or worried... not *giddy*."

"Hmmm. So she figured out how to open the supernatural floodgates."

"That's exactly how she described it. She said she felt like the marsh at high tide, when it's saturated and creeping toward the road. Powerful enough to stop traffic." She reaches across the desk for my hands. Mascara-tear tracks streak her face. "LeeLee, Ginny learned how to do things—readings—she couldn't do at all when she was young. You can open yourself up to the otherworldly if you want to. You're our best hope of finding out what happened to her!"

"I'm not." Like any good lawyer, I cling to the procedural. "Our best hope is through the private investigator and talking to people who may know something, people like Chad Dooley. And I have children. I can't screw around with the supernatural."

"Look here. If Ginny was a swollen marsh at high tide, you're an exposed mudflat drying in the sun. Damned if y'all don't need to find a happy medium."

I rub my eyes. "Mean low water." I snicker.

"Mean low what?"

"Nothing. Talking to myself." I look up. "Confession. I *tried* to read Peace's guilty thoughts or catch one of his memories. I got nothing about Ginny."

She puts a hand over her heart. "But will you *keep* trying?"

"I'd rather focus on hard reality. But if it will make you feel better, yes. I don't know how to do it, but I'll try."

Cheryl blows her nose. "It's all I can ask. Ginny figured out how to let the tide flow free, but you figured out how to block it in the first place. Open the floodgates slowly, and you'll be fine."

CLAY SPENDS MOST OF the weekend prepping for a hearing. I often manage the children on my own, but his absence is still a reality check. If we get divorced, every weekend with my kids will be a grueling marathon of sports, lessons, birthday parties, and playdates, with no Clay to take over at dinnertime. No one to share afternoon beers or encourage me to order pizza instead of cooking something healthy.

Peace's steady stream of texts and our phone chats after the boys fall asleep provide some comfort. We rehash old jokes and create new ones. We lovingly gossip about Jess and Landon's IVF drama and Palmer and Tommy's unresolved love affair. He shows genuine interest in my photos of the kids and descriptions of our weekend plans—a baseball game, lacrosse practice, a birthday party, and Mal's swimming lessons. He even gets a kick out of our misadventures. On Saturday morning, Trey and Bowman get into fisticuffs over a baseball glove. Their scuffle results in Trey nearly smothering Bowman with the disputed glove. I drag my cherubic children apart at great peril to my personal safety then deliver an admirably patient-yet-no-bullshit shakedown.

They glower at each other from opposite ends of the sofa as I check my phone. I guffaw when I read Peace's latest text. *Hope you're having a peaceful morning!!* The perfect chance to share an admittedly hyperbolic anecdote about the dangers of parenting small, testosterone-fueled people. Peace and Drew regularly tried to kill each other back in the day, so he commiserates with appropriate lightheartedness—unlike Clay, whose three sisters rarely beat him up. The boys' constant brawling drives him mad.

By Monday, Clay is begging for some time with the kids, and I need a break. Jess's meeting at the medical university presents us with a rare chance to meet up after work. When I tell Peace our plans to meet at the Vendue Inn's rooftop bar, he immediately asks to join us, so I text her.

Me: *You mind if P. meets up with us too?*

Jess: *I thought you might ask that. Am I y'all's chaperone now?*

Me: *You are his cousin and my best friend. You don't come into town very often to see me. You haven't seen him in a million years.*

Jess: *M'kay.*

Me: *That a yes?*

Jess: *Yup. I'd like to see that fool. And Peace too. Ha ha.*

The Vendue's rooftop bar overlooks the pineapple fountain in Waterfront Park, the mouth of the Cooper River, and the space-age span of the Ravenel Bridge. When I arrive, I scan the crowd and find Jess and Peace at a high-top table near the railing. Peace looks like he stepped out of the Matrix in his crisp dark-blue button-down shirt, dark jeans, and aviator sunglasses. As usual, Jess wears scrubs. I stick out like a pelican in a flock of sparrows, wearing my white blouse, black skirt, and black pumps that put my height at over six feet tall. Chattering patrons observe me through squinting eyes as I self-consciously cross the space between the bar and the tables. I scoot past the requisite shaggy-haired guy playing an acoustic guitar and slide onto a stool beside my friends.

"Y'all look so professional." Peace sings along with the Jimmy Buffet cover. "*Health care to my left, legal to my right.*"

Jess's eyebrow pokes up past her oversized pink shades. "You certainly aren't the only boy in town. LeeLee strutting her stuff made all the tongues wag. A bunch of dirty dogs on the prowl in this joint."

"Thanks for defending my honor." I hang my purse on the back of my stool. "But those dudes make eyes at everyone, including you. *Especially* you. Nurse fantasies are a thing, right? I've never heard of a lawyer fetish."

Jess turns to Peace. "Not one word about whatever lawyer fantasies you're harboring."

"I didn't say anything." Peace slides his glasses down his nose and winks at me while Jess gives her drink order to the server. I get a Mich Ultra, and Peace gets his Coke, then we order a bunch of appetizers. We chitchat for a while about Jess and Peace's expansive extended family.

"I can never keep up with how many cousins y'all have," I say.

"Neither can I," Peace says. "Our moms have four other siblings, and they all have at least two kids. I can't remember some of my first cousins, let alone all these once- or twice-removed people. What does that even mean?"

"It means they're a level removed from our immediate craziness," Jess says.

"I always wanted cousins. Or any family, really," I say. "I don't know any of my father's relatives. My mom and I were both only children. Her parents died when I was little. We didn't have *anybody*. The Smith-Conway-Monroe family holidays were a dream come true."

"It was so fun when you and Mama Donna came to Saltmarsh for Thanksgiving and Christmas," Jess says in reference to the holidays we spent with Peace's family while he and I were an item.

"We were so happy to be with y'all. Definitely my favorite holidays until..." I trail off. I was about to say something about Clay's equally boisterous family, but with Peace looking at me, it doesn't seem right. "Anyway, it was fun."

"I still can't believe your mom is gone," Peace says. "I bet seeing you get through law school was a highlight of her life."

"I hope so. She passed not long after I was sworn in to the bar at the state supreme court. At least she got to think of me as a real lawyer for a couple of weeks, even if I wasn't practicing yet."

"She never met your kids, but she knew Clay, right?" he asks.

I squirm in my seat.

Jess speaks over the singer's surprisingly catchy version of "Lodi" by CCR. "Yeah. She loved Clay, didn't she?"

I nod. "She wanted us to move home so we'd be close to her."

"Oh Lord, stuck in Asheburg again," Jess says. "We live there, and it's great for us, but I cannot picture the Moretz family in the Burg. Not with Smith, Smith, Smith, Smith, Smith— "

"Point made, Jess," Peace says.

"And Smith owning all the legal biz in town."

"Sometimes, I wish we had," I say. "I didn't see her enough before she died. Then there was how she died..."

"How could you have known when, or how, she would die?" Jess asks.

"I don't know." If I hadn't smothered my readings for years, I might have known something. Enough to warn her or be there to comfort her.

"It's not like she had cancer and you could sit beside her hospital bed for months." Jess puts a hand over her mouth. "Eek. Open mouth. Insert stinky foot. Sorry, P."

"I got plenty to be guilty about," he says. "But she's right about you, Lee. Try not to feel bad. Mama Donna was always so proud of you. Any parent would have been proud of a kid like you."

"I just never wanted to be another thing for her to worry about. She had enough on her plate. I *still* can't go into a Walmart after all the years she had to work there. The smell of Lysol, rotten fruit, and cheap polyester nauseates me."

"You and Ginny dealt with family stuff the rest of us couldn't imagine," Jess says. "You had it even worse than she did, and you powered through it like a champ."

"I don't know who had it worse, me with my absentee, deadbeat alcoholic father or Ginny with her alcoholic father she had to deal with every day."

"I'm trying to say you had plenty of reasons to take a high dive into the deep end. You did the opposite."

"I bet Mama Donna is watching you right now," Peace says. "That sun on your back? It's her watching over you."

I rarely speak of my childhood struggles. But for his omnipresent anger, I hardly remember my father, though I hate bourbon because it reminds me of his Wild Turkey and Diet Pepsi cocktails. Like the scent of cheap spirits, my memory refuses to purge itself of other everyday heartbreaks from long ago—how my mother whispered numbers as she sat at the table, writing checks, or stared out the kitchen window with a dishrag in one hand and a dented pot in the other. At some point, I understood she muttered calculations as she balanced her lean budget in her head.

Though she never said so, I was the most expensive part of her equation—our two-bedroom house instead of a one-bedroom apartment, clothes I constantly outgrew, toys, dance lessons, doctor's bills when I got sick. Floof, the stray dog I begged her to adopt, had terrible teeth that required constant veterinary intervention.

Beyond making perfect grades so she would have a reason to smile, I refused to add to her burden by showing my anger or loneliness, my sadness or frustrations. I never dreamed of letting her know I was a freak of nature on top of the typical childhood angst. I wouldn't saddle my mother with my storytelling any more than I would saddle her with an unplanned pregnancy.

All I wanted was to be a source of joy and security in her uncaring world. I never got the chance to fully ease her load by purchasing her house so she could retire from Wally World. She never got to spend long, boring days gardening, collecting knickknacks, and knitting baby blankets for my boys. Damn life for taking her away from me too soon, but bless Jess and Peace for forcing me to think about her.

"Thanks, y'all. Maybe I wasn't a total failure as a daughter." I dab my eyes under my sunglasses with a cocktail napkin. "But enough about me. What were you saying about Cousin Ronnie?"

"It's *Uncle* Ronnie. Mama says he's going senile. He'd leave his own nose in the Family Dollar if it weren't attached to his face."

I let Jess ramble while we pick at our nachos and crab dip. I watch Peace through my sunglasses and guess he's watching me too. Bright sunshine hides the longing in our eyes, and Jess's motor mouth keeps us from delving into discussions of our increasingly complicated emotional tug-of-war.

"And Uncle Ronnie showed up on Mama's porch! Three miles from his house on Azalea Street. We have no idea how he got there. Unless he was abducted by aliens, he's got Alzheimer's..."

Poor Uncle Ronnie. His impending mortality trivializes my problems. At least I still have my memories. The good, the bad, the ugly, and even some that don't belong to me.

It's nice to just be with my old friends, sip a beer, and let the sun bake the back of my neck. It does, indeed, feel a little like my mama's warm hands.

OUR HAPPY HOUR WINDS down, and we get the check. Nature calls as we get up from the table.

"I'll meet y'all at the elevator," I say. "I have to potty."

"I got to go, girlie. Driving back to the Burg, not down the street to the Battery." Jess hugs us both.

"Loved seeing you." I back toward the bathroom.

"Y'all *be good*," Jess says.

"Always," Peace says.

"Hmph." Jess shakes her head and beckons to Peace.

He leans down, and she whispers to him in her ferocious way, giving Peace a Jessalyn Conway Walters lecture.

"I'll wait for you, Lee," Peace says as I turn.

A couple of minutes later, I'm washing my hands when a singsong voice calls my name.

"LeeLee! Hey-hey!"

I look over my reflection's shoulder. It's Claire Something-or-Other, another mom from Pinegrounds School, the private school Trey attends. Claire is pretty with curly blond hair and a noticeable boob job. She's divorced and, according to the Pinegrounds gossip mill, a regular on the bar scene and the dating apps. Tommy connected with her on Bumble or Tinder and met her for a drink. He said she was nice but overly interested in his income and liked her wine more than the average Mount Pleasant mom. Tommy is neither a slouch in the bank account department nor a wilting flower about booze consumption, but it was a one-and-done date for him.

"Hey, Claire," I say. "You got out for the night too?"

"My kids are with their dad. We have an every-other-week schedule. You know... I thought about calling you recently. I'd love to get more child support from him. I'm *so* not ready to go back to work. I can't even deal with part-time." She brushes a blond curl off her forehead. "My kids *need* me, you know?"

If I recall correctly, her daughter in Trey's class is the younger of her two children by several years, which means her kids are in school full-time. I try not to judge, but I've dealt with her kind before. She's blaming her kids for her own lackluster work ethic.

I take one of my cards from my purse and hand it to her. "It's really not that simple, but you can call the office and schedule a consult."

"Great! You want to have a glass of wine with me, Mary Kate Young, and Nicole Oppenheim?"

Mary Kate Young and Nicole Oppenheim are other divorced Pinegrounds moms. We represented Mary Kate in her divorce. Unlike Claire, she's an all-around badass. A successful financial planner, she makes her own money and is, by all accounts, a great mom. I don't know Nicole Oppenheim, but I've heard she works as an interior designer and has a healthy relationship with her ex-husband. They even spend holidays and vacations together. I consider telling

Peace I'll stick around to pick Mary Kate and Nicole's divorcee brains—even goofy Claire's if she, indeed, has a fifty-fifty custody arrangement.

"Umm... let me think for a sec—"

"By the way, who's that guy with you and your friend?" she asks. "He's hotter than a five-gallon jug of Texas Pete."

"Oh. He's... he's an old friend from Asheburg, my hometown. They both are—my friend Jessalyn, and Peace is her cousin."

"Pete?"

"No," I say. "*Peace.*"

"Sexy! Is he single? He isn't wearing a ring."

She must have an eagle eye to absorb such detail, since I didn't even notice her on the rooftop. "Yeah. He is."

"*Girlfriend.* Hook me up."

"Whoa, ah. I don't know—"

"You're married!" She grins at me with artificially whitened, marshmallow teeth. "You have to help us single ladies out. Plus you've known him forever, right? You can vouch for him being a good guy. *Is* he a good guy? Does he have kids? Ex-wife drama? What does he do for a living?"

My phone buzzes—a text from Peace. *You get lost in the potty, Mama?*

"Listen, he's, like... not really dating. It's complicated." I almost mention he's a recovering addict and only employed part-time, but that seems both childish and inappropriate. "If I hear he's on the market, I'll let you know. Gotta run home to the kids. Maybe we can get a drink another night?"

"Sure! Would love to. I'll call you about that consult. There has to be some way to make Rob pay more. He's such a cheap asshole. He deserves to feel some pressure."

My head spins as I walk out of the bathroom. Claire's aggressiveness reminds me that Peace is very single. He isn't rich enough for

Claire, but he's handsome enough to spark curiosity in any straight woman. In a relatively small town like Charleston, anyone new on the dating scene, male or female, causes a stir. Claire would be one of many sharks circling his diving bell.

What about Claire herself? She might be mildly disturbing, but I feel sorry for her. Ugh, what a life. For every post-divorce independent badass like Mary Kate and well-adjusted co-parent like Nicole, there's a Claire endlessly trying to get money out of her ex and trolling for men. The sun is sinking, so several men on the rooftop have removed their sunglasses. I make uncomfortable eye contact with no fewer than five leering dudes as I walk to the elevator.

Is that what I'm in for? Trying to give off Mary Kate and Nicole vibes while picking through a bunch of creepers? The idea that my future might involve roaming bars and scoping out single men while Clay cuddles the boys with a bedtime story makes me ill.

Peace removes his own sunglasses, and his blue eyes draw me in like a tractor beam. I almost run to him. I don't want to be like Claire. If Peace is still single if and when I figure out what the hell I'm doing, I won't have to be.

"Get me out of here." I press the elevator button.

"Why? Sick of Jimmy Buffet?"

"Let's just go." I shift on my feet and scan the crowd for Claire's table. I find the three of them in the corner.

Nicole is looking over her shoulder at us. Claire must have told her friends to check out the hottie with LeeLee Moretz. The elevator dings. Peace and I step into the relative darkness. The door shuts out prying eyes, and I exhale.

"Thank goodness. I ran into this woman—"

He pulls me into his arms. My sunglasses fall off the top of my head and hit the floor. He reaches behind him and hits the stop button. He kisses me, and I forget about circling sharks, weird leering men, and Claire What's-Her-Name. How can I think about her, or any of the uncomfortable truths her presence raised, when I'm the one kissing him?

THE DAYS TICK PAST, and Clay and I settle into an uncomfortable but functional routine. On Saturday, I take the little guys to Hazel Parker Playground on East Bay Street while Clay takes Trey to Folly Beach to practice surfing. We eat dinner together Sunday night, and Bowman talks so much about his new LEGO set that no one else says much. We don't fight in front of the kids, but while Bowman and Mal are too little to notice anything but their own wants and needs, Trey seems to sense something is off. I catch him watching me and Clay as if analyzing a swirling hurricane tracker on the Weather Channel.

Clay keeps his smile and laughs when the children expect it, but stress amplifies his negative emotions and throws his thoughts into the air like dark confetti at a funeral. Saturday evening, we shoot baskets with the boys at our stubby driveway basketball hoop. When he lifts Malachy for a slam dunk, his reflections are confusing subtitles in a poorly written scene. *Should I push for fifty-fifty time with the kids? My hours are ridiculous. How will I do it? But I'll miss them so much. Ugh, nightmare...*

Sunday dinner on the piazza, he slices into his pork chops. *Sitting with my beautiful family on my porch, yet everything is falling apart... Nice job, Moretz. You ruined your life.*

On Monday, he stands over my shoulder at bath time. *Family court retainers are highway robbery. No wonder Darlene is rolling in it.*

On Wednesday morning, I sneak out for my early spin class before the boys wake up. Clay comes inside to shower and get ready for work, and he leaves as soon as I walk in the door after class. He says a curt good morning as he passes me in the foyer, but his gruff thoughts stop me in my tracks. *Is she seeing Peace Smith? Should I get a PI to follow her? Alimony... alimony... alimony...*

I stew as I jump into the shower to prepare for work myself. Here is proof Clay might fight fire with fire in the courtroom.

Predictably, given South Carolina's conservative tilt, the state does not look fondly on divorce or any behaviors that might instigate it. Rigid, narrowly defined rules written into the state's code of laws are meant to both deter and punish a cheater. If a spouse commits adultery prior to the filing of a final settlement agreement or the issuance of a judge's final ruling at trial, that spouse is barred from receiving alimony. Though some men are alimony candidates these days, the laws generally have far harsher ramifications for women. Ironically, the supporting spouse—the person who pays out—doesn't have to pay more just for cheating. The *supported* spouse who cheats, however, is immediately shit out of luck. Darlene calls it the Hester Prynne Statute for a reason.

Even in my situation—with us as two working attorneys—Clay makes a lot more than I do. I'm an associate in a small shop and carry the majority of the responsibility for our children. He's a partner in his father's statewide firm. His salary is easily three times mine. I like to think I'll be independent of Clay if we separate, but I've worked on enough client financials to know it might not be so cut-and-dried. Either he'll pay me something to balance our lives—what alimony is supposed to do—or I'll have to up my professional game, maybe hang out my shingle. I'll be paying a full-time nanny and piling on additional stress.

I *know* all this, even if I've been in denial about what might happen if things get contentious. As soon as Clay's frazzled brain tells me he has visions of private investigators dancing through his head, I have to get serious about my defense mechanisms.

I have one ace up my sleeve. Clay told me to do what I needed to do to figure things out. I can argue that if any behavior of mine smacks of adultery, he's condoned it, but I have no proof he told me to do my thing other than his words. If he gets mad enough, he might deny it.

I fester over my options as I get dressed, wake the boys, get them ready for school, and hustle them out the door. I drop Bowman and Mal at their preschool across the James Island Connector then backtrack to Pinegrounds, Trey's school on the Ashley River. I head back over the river, down Lockwood Boulevard, past the Charleston County Courthouse—where I might or might not be getting a divorce—left onto State Street, rattle down cobblestone Chalmers Street for a block, and turn into our parking lot. As I put the car in park, I vow to start taking my own advice. I always advise my clients to act at all times as if a private investigator is hot on their trail.

That means I have to distance myself from Peace. Between the tension in the Taco Boy parking lot, the open-curtain make-out session in Tommy's house, and the kiss in the elevator, I've been far too careless already. It's Clay's Wednesday overnight in the main house with the kids. Peace and I are supposed to meet at Tommy's, but I need to make a mandatory change of plans. We have to keep our meetings public and platonic and our emotions under control.

I punch the code into the lockbox on the back door of the narrow gray row house that contains our little firm, open the squeaky door, and walk up the crooked steps to my office on the third floor. I drop my purse and briefcase on the worn Turkish rug and flop into my chair. After typing up a text to Peace explaining the new protocol, I hit Send and hope for the best. I sigh in relief as I read his reply.

Peace: *Of course I understand. How about we meet at the Griffon tonight instead of T's? Possibly the least romantic place in Charleston.*

Me: *You're the best.*

Peace: *I have my moments *smiley face* see you there.*

BY HALF PAST EIGHT that evening, my kids are asleep and Clay is settled into the master bedroom. Peace and I sit at the bar in the Griffon, a classic English pub across from the Vendue Inn and the Waterfront Park splash fountain. The band America's classic folk-rock homage to an anonymous steed moodily wafts from the dinged-up speakers behind the bar. The happy hour crowd has thinned. Only a few diehards drown their sorrows in the musty Griffon on a balmy evening when they could be whooping it up on Shem Creek.

Dollar bills cover every available inch of wall space—under the bar, between the rafters, on the support pillars. They commemorate bachelor parties, college football games, fraternity and sorority letters, and wedding anniversaries.

"This place has not changed one iota," Peace says as he orders a Coke. "A dollar bill up there probably still says 'Peace plus LeeLee.'"

"It's possible. Remember when we came here for Palmer's twenty-first?"

"Palmer got up and sang 'You've Lost That Loving Feeling' to Tommy because she was pissed at him for something. What was it?"

"He bought her red roses," I say.

"Everybody *knows* Palmer only does pink roses."

"Right, but then she decided she wasn't that mad after she had a few shots." I smile. "She ran up there and pushed that fat guy with the guitar out of the way—"

"His face." Peace's eyes bug out, and his mouth hangs open.

"Yes, yes! She grabbed the mic and yelled—she yelled—" I double over, and my hair falls across my face. I'm laughing too hard to finish.

"I believe she demanded that he take her to bed *immediately* or lose her forever."

"Good Lord, yes. We watched *Top Gun* so many times. Then we all called him Goose for the rest of the summer. Jess still had a fake

ID, remember? But it said she was, like, five foot nine. The tension every time she presented it!"

"Like on a game show, waiting for the wheel to stop spinning." He grits his teeth. "Will Jessalyn get to see what's behind Door Number One, or will she get sent back into the audience?"

"So funny." I tuck my hair behind my ears, as if restrained hair will make me appear more emotionally sedate. "Anything new with your dad?"

"Nope, but the come-to-Jesus with Drew is coming soon."

"P., I hate to suggest this about your brother, but do you think Drew sent those emails?"

"Hell, I don't know," he says. "It crossed my mind. I didn't mention it because it's depressing to think my brother hates me that much."

"I'm sure he doesn't. Forget it. A silly idea." I reach up to rub his shoulder, but as soon as my hand touches his shirt, I remember. I run my fingers through my hair instead, as if I've waved at someone who hasn't waved back. "I'm sorry we have to come here, but I can't risk anything that seems inappropriate."

"Like the other night on the sofa? Or the elevator?"

One corner of his mouth turns up, and it's all I can do to keep from planting my lips on that sensual curve.

"Hush, silly," I say. "Here I am trying to keep the butterflies in my stomach cocooned, and you're reminding them it's springtime. For now, we gotta douse those butterflies in romantic pesticide."

"Gotcha." He chuckles. "All good. I can be patient for a few weeks."

"It will be longer than that." My tummy butterflies freeze mid-flutter. "I mean... if I were to... follow through with... you know..."

"Leaving Clay?"

"Yes. It will be more than a few weeks until we get everything settled."

He frowns. "How long do you mean?"

"We'd have to reach a settlement or go to trial within three hundred sixty-five days from the date of filing—"

"Whoa. That's lawyer talk... but are you saying a year?"

"I hope we could reach an agreement quickly, but it will be complicated, especially related to the kids, then there's the financial stuff—"

"But a year?" he repeats. "A whole year?"

It's kind of annoying. We're talking about my whole life and my *kids'* lives. "It's possible. I have three children, a mortgage, and retirement accounts, plus Clay won't want to pay alimony—"

"Okay, sorry. I'm just surprised."

Peace always says he gets it, but it's in his nature to be accepting and agreeable. Does he *really* get it? Can he? It's one thing to enjoy my chaotic-mom-life stories but another thing to live with everything that comes with that.

Talking about it suddenly makes me nervous. It feels rushed. "Besides, I haven't made up my mind yet."

He chews on ice cubes and flags down the bartender for another Coke. "Right. Sorry if I'm pressuring you."

"You're not. Maybe I'm pressuring myself." As is the case too often lately, tears tickle my eyes. "I'm so happy sitting here with you. I want to be with you every night when I go to sleep. But I'm terrified of *everything else*."

"Nothing has ever mattered to me like your family matters to you. But I empathize, and I want to understand. I want *everything else*. That includes your kids." His smile widens as he talks. "I'd love to meet them! Get to know them. Maybe I'm destined for a ready-made family."

His proclamation takes me aback. "I—thank you. I mean... I always thought you'd be great with kids—"

"Three boys! I can play sports with them—"

"They have a *dad*, Peace."

"I know. But he can't toss a football like I can."

"Clay is a great dad," I say, because it's true. "It's not only about the boys. It's about Clay too. He's my kids' father and my husband. I thought I'd grow old with him until..." I start to say *until last year when he cheated*, but the correct answer is more like *until Peace Smith showed up in my office*.

My ears start ringing, and as Ginny used to say, my brain gets to tingling. I remember something else Ginny said when a reading came on. My scalp has centipede legs that crawl all over my skull. Readings pepper the air around me like a stream of unimportant social media updates. I have no idea who they belong to—the bartenders, the servers, or the patrons.

I've been drinking too much this week. I'll cut back after the weekend...

What was that blond girl's name again...

Damn drawers riding up my behind...

Bill wouldn't know a decent tip if it bit him in the ass...

If Maria dies, I won't be able to stand it. Please, God, please...

Then, from Peace, loud and clear, *I'll wait forever for you, LeeLee.*

My head throbs. "I'm gonna be sick."

"Whoa, Lee." He leans in, and I retract, lest I barf on his lap. He pulls me to my feet. "You're as green as a pile of collards. Come on. I'll help you to the bathroom."

We plow toward the restrooms. God forbid I have a PI on me. I look like a Wednesday-night drunk who's had too many Fireball shots.

I step into the tiny women's room, shut the door in Peace's anxious face, and clench the back of the toilet. I spit into the cracked bowl. A reading descends on me, with the dark clarity of an unpleasant memory.

I would know Ginny's voice anywhere. I heard it through my mom's landline a million times. She said the same thing every time she called. "Hey, Lee, that you?" Her shrillness always increased with excitement or anger. She whooped with girlish glee when her favorite song played on the radio. She shrieked in nonsensical rage when we confronted her about drugs in our Bull Street apartment.

This time, she's screeching at Peace. His voice fires back at her in rare fury. I see only their agonized faces—hers contorted by anger and his tortured eyes staring up at a ceiling covered in water stains. Their words ram around my head like bumper cars driven by poltergeists.

> *"I know you screwed her!" Ginny shouts. "If you deny it one more time, I'll jump out that window. I swear I will. I'm done with your cheating and lying. You ruined everything! You always do!"*
>
> *"You sound like my father," Peace says.*
>
> *"This time I'm going. I swear to God!"*
>
> *"Then leave. Go! Please!" Peace shouts. "Jump out the window for all I care."*
>
> *"Ha! I knew it. You want to be rid of me so you can go after Miss Fancy Boots. You've always wanted to leave me!"*
>
> *"Ow, damn it—get off me, you psycho!" Peace says.*
>
> *"Admit it!" Ginny screams. "Admit it, asshole!"*
>
> *"I promised you I'd never leave you alone, and I haven't. But that's not enough for you. Nothing ever is! So get out of my life, Ginny. Sweet Jesus, I just want some goddamn peace."*

I gag and throw up. The reading blinks off before I can hear anything else.

Peace bangs on the door. "LeeLee? Are you all right? Can I help?"

"I'm okay." I gasp, and hot tears shoot from my eyes. "Really. But I have to go home."

"Whatever you need." His gentle voice through the door makes my gorge rise again. I desperately wish I'd held it together long enough to learn whether Ginny left or if Peace said—or did—anything else.

I owe it to Ginny to find out what happened. I owe it to Peace—and to Cheryl. In that moment, I understand I owe it to my boys and Clay and even myself. The trajectories of all our lives hang in the balance.

Chapter 18
Ginny, 2013

I don't remember how I got to Chad Dooley's little house a few miles inland in one of Myrtle's many tract-housing neighborhoods. Peace and I only drove here once to get late-night weed, and I didn't realize I even knew the address. Somehow, on a June afternoon, I hauled my drunk ass across Dirty Myrtle like a bloodhound on the trail of a smelly sock. Now, here I am, on Chad's cement-slab patio.

I ring the doorbell four times. Johnny Cash music floats onto the front stoop when Chad opens the door. The man in black hears the train coming, but he hasn't seen sunshine since who knows when.

"Same, Johnny. Same." I peer around Chad's shoulder. "Where is she?"

"Hello to you too," Chad says, "but you ain't no June Carter. You look like my ornery grandma after too many gin and tonics."

"Shut up, Chad." I add an eye roll for good measure. "Where's Fancy Boots?"

"Meredith? She's not here. She's got her own place down in Garden City."

I push past him into the house.

"Come on in, Ginny Carter Cash." He shuts the door behind him. "What's chapping your ass, anyway?"

"That slut—Meredith—she had lunch with Peace!"

Chad lights a cigarette and takes a long drag.

"Don't you even *care*?" My eyes bug out more with each word. I probably resemble an irate frog.

"Eh. Meredith's a drag, always bitchin' about something."

"She bitched to *my* boyfriend about *you*! She told him you pushed her around. She wants Redneck Prince Charming to wheel up in his white Ford Ranger and rescue her."

"If I pushed her around, she deserved it."

His words barely register. I storm around the living room. "Peace does love to play the hero. Always trying to save somebody." I laugh. "He's been with my ass for ten years."

"His other girlfriend had her shit together. Wound so tight, I doubt she ever took a dump. She was one of them women's-lib chicks, right? You know the one. What was her name?"

I stop my agitated spiraling. "LeeLee. Freakin' *LeeLee*, my former best friend."

"Now *that's* messed up. Your man and your best friend."

"That was a long time ago. I'm pissed right *now* because Peace screwed *your* girl. You might not care, but I do!"

He approaches me with his hands raised, like I might bite him. Given my current mood, it isn't out of the question. "I don't give a damn what dipshit Meredith Preston does," Chad says. "If Peace wants her, he can have her."

"No, he can't!" I shake my head so hard that my ponytail hits my cheeks. "Or *she* can't. He's mine! She's been after him ever since we saw y'all at Wahoo's. Bitch!"

"Now, Ginny." He rests a hand on my shoulder.

I'm so fired up, I'm surprised he doesn't get burned.

He squeezes. "What the hell is Peace doing for you after all these years? Y'all ain't married—"

"I don't believe in marriage," I say with a dismissive sniff.

"Does he?"

"I don't know."

Peace and I never discussed tying the knot, and I often made a point to announce my disdain for marriage. I adopted that viewpoint after Peace and I turned twenty-six in Florida and he didn't bring it up. If I claim I don't believe in marriage, then I don't have to be hurt when he never asks me.

"I'm not the marrying type, so who cares if he believes in marriage?"

"I'm just sayin', he's dead weight."

"I'm not exactly a feather pillow myself." No matter how pissed I am, Chad dismissing Peace makes me defensive of him.

"And now he's cheating on you. You said so yourself. Screwing you over, like he did when he shacked up with LuLu."

"*LeeLee.* And yeah. He's cheating. I know he is. I've known for months. Years. I'm *sure* Meredith isn't the first one." Anger and jealousy swamp me again. I can't breathe for the weight of those muddy, boggy, flat-out slimy emotions. I close my eyes and will my supernatural powers to tell me the truth. Every fiber of my being screams that Peace is a liar and a cheater, but I need proof. If I tilt the compass the right way, it has to show me true north.

But my powers have never shown me any such thing. No matter how I call out for evidence, the only thoughts and visions in my head are my obsessions. They carry no sense of time flowing through the Déjà Vu River, just my paranoia, what I tell myself when I need an explanation for my suspicions.

"Hey," Chad says. "Snap out of it."

I grind my teeth. If I rub them together like flint on a stone, perhaps they'll spark a reading.

"Ginny, wake up!"

A sting on my cheek opens my eyes. "You smacked me."

"You were holding your breath. I don't need you passing out in my damn house." He points at a fat bag of gray-green weed on his cheap coffee table. "I can't have an amber-lance over here."

"Ambulance, you idiot." I sink onto the edge of his beat-up leather sofa and speak through snuffling sobs. "I *think* he's cheating. Sometimes, I'm sure of it. Sometimes, it doesn't make sense. But Meredith is younger and pretty and—"

"You're lucky I feel sorry for you—you telling me to shut up, calling me an idiot, and boo-hooing all over my furniture. Normally, I ain't got much patience for that kind of disrespect—or drama." Chad sits beside me. He pinches my cheek between one thumb and forefinger. "Look at me, Ginny. Get it together. You listening?"

I nod. His fingers dig into my face. I think of an old game we used to play as kids. We squeezed each other's cheeks. *Hi, my name is Chubby. My mama's chubby. My daddy's chubby. Even my dog's chubby.* Hysterical laughter builds in the back of my throat, but I can't smile with Chad's fingers jabbing into my face like meat tenderizers into a T-bone.

"Meredith *is* a slut," Chad says. "If she has the chance, she'll stick onto Peace like lint on a roller. You're right about them. I'm sure of it."

I crave hearing someone parrot my insecurities after years of Peace denying them. I jerk away from his fingers. "You think so?"

"Damn straight. And I always thought he was too nice to be real. All that Mr. America shit."

"Yeah. *Yeah.* I guess he is. I—" The room spins. "I need a drink."

"You can have a drink, but I got something better." He gets up, and I lean back on the sofa. I still don't know how I got here, as if I appeared on Chad Dooley's doorstep in the middle of a dream—or one of my readings. My heavy eyelids droop. For once, I'm too tired to think about navigating through the past or future, but a pleasant dream sounds appealing.

Chad claps twice, just below my chin, jerking me awake. This isn't a reading, but it isn't a dream either. It's more like a nightmare, my dismal reality where I accept that Peace is a cheating shithead and

I'm wasted on Chad's sofa. The compass whirls without stopping, as if both poles have simply disappeared.

"Wake up, chick." Chad hands me a plastic cup full of pale-orange liquid. "Nothing like a screwdriver, right? Use it to wash this down." Two pink pills rest in his palms. Each one has a rabbit on it.

"Leftover Easter candy?" I ask.

"Ecstasy. There's never been a better-named drug."

"I did X a few times in Florida."

"Then you know it's the bomb." He swallows one pill and gives me the other. "Be a good girl now, and take your medicine."

My brain defends my breaking heart by spewing hatred into my veins. Chad offers me relief from those awful feelings in tablet form. Some people might call me a total chickenshit, but if happiness appears under their noses when they feel that terrible, those same somebodies might not be so high and mighty.

I stick the pill in my mouth, chase it with his vodka-OJ stew, and gag. "Ugh. Too strong."

"Why don't you stay with me?" He thumbs my chin. "I always had a soft spot for you, Ginny. You're not like any girl I ever met. You're like lightning in a bottle."

My head wilts onto his shoulder. That's me, lightning trapped in a bottle—a beer, vodka, tequila bottle, a box of wine. "You can't rough me up like you did with Meredith. You tried that shit with me back in the day. But I'm grown, and I won't stand for it."

He puts his arm around me. "Never. I'll take care of you. I told you years ago. I had what you needed back then, and I still got it. Didn't I just show you that?" He shakes his pill bag in front of my face.

"Sure. I'll stay. Got nowhere else to go." I wave one hand around his living room and the kitchen beyond it. "You finally got a place with a foundation."

"That I did. I even got me some Corian countertops. *High-end.* I do what I say I'm gonna do." He trails his fingers over my arm, and it feels good—no, beyond good, like ecstasy.

Chad Dooley kisses me, and everything blurs—vodka seeping into orange juice.

I UNCURL FROM THE FETAL position and look down my body and over my boobs to my chipped pink toenail polish. I'm wearing a Jason Aldean concert T-shirt and a pair of unfamiliar striped boxer shorts. I focus on the bong on the dresser across the room and remember where I am, Chad Dooley's house. The lamp on the bedside table is on, but the darkness around the drawn shades tells me it's nighttime.

The room spins when I sit up, but overindulgence hasn't nauseated me in a long time. Years of my brain proving that puking was no deterrent made my stomach give up that line of defense. Still, I'm terribly thirsty, and every muscle in my body hurts. I catch my reflection in the mirror above the bong. Dark circles hang beneath my eyes—a combination of smeared mascara and fatigue. My hair hasn't seen a brush since I left Helping Hands, the shelter where Peace and I had been staying while we looked for a new place. That bird's nest is a mess of bleached tangles and split ends, but I haven't dyed it in a while. The top of my head is still reddish gold.

I vow to stop coloring my hair, forever. It sure doesn't make me look younger. I've just turned thirty-three, but even with my upturned nose and a splattering of freckles, hard living has engraved several lifetimes on my cheeks and across my forehead. As my father used to say after a particularly hard night, my face would make a freight train take a dirt road.

My phone is dead. I find a charger behind the bedside table and plug it in. My unsteady feet hit the floor, and I stand. It takes me a moment to remember the house's layout, but as I make my way to the bathroom, my clearing mind shines a light into my blackout.

I remember dancing, but I don't remember the songs. I smoked but couldn't tell you where the cigarettes ended and the weed began. I took pills in different colors, pharmaceutical jelly beans. We watched a television show about a middle-aged bald guy who makes meth. Chad professed great admiration for the main character.

I sit to pee and shiver, but it isn't the cold toilet seat against my butt that gives me the chills. Had I slept with Chad Dooley? We did a lot of making out, but I can't be sure.

Suddenly, it comes back to me. Things were hot and heavy, then Chad abruptly claimed exhaustion, got up, and passed out on the couch. No further explanation but no tent in his basketball shorts either. Despite my surroundings, I giggle. A quick peek in the medicine cabinet confirms my suspicion—a bottle of Viagra hidden behind some hair gel and expired Tylenol.

I splash water on my face and return to the bedroom. My phone has come back to life. I look at the time and date. I arrived sometime Wednesday afternoon. It's going on ten o'clock on Thursday night. I've been here for over thirty hours.

"What the hell, Ginny?" I admonish myself as I open my texts.

Peace's name is at the top of the list.

Chad's liquor drinks didn't nauseate me, but what I see when I open those messages turns my stomach. The barely intelligible words and images are a different kind of screwdriver in my gut. First, my texts to him. Line after line of hateful oblong blue bubbles.

Youl never see me again you dick is over and I so gllad

I cant beleve I stayed with yo.ur line cheatn ass for so longsds

I always know youd due me like this new Id figure it out

I hope Mererdithh gives you herps

Youll get you deserve in th.is lifes like every one who lied an defended you

Not kidding you better watchyur backkj !!!!!!!

Im donee wit you forrrrrever but to can play this game so hahhahahhhah asshole

The photos are even worse. All selfies.

Me sitting on Chad's lap with his nose in my cleavage.

Me behind Chad with my arms around him, kissing his neck.

Then, the pièce de résistance, as LeeLee would have said—me and Chad making out. The cherry on that mud pie is Chad's squirmy tongue.

"Oh. My. *Lord*," I whisper. "No. No. *No*."

I scroll to the end. The last message was sent around five in the morning. Almost seventeen hours ago.

No replies from Peace.

My fingers touch the screen to start typing something to make up for this hateful performance I barely remember. Before I can type the letter *I* to begin *I'm completely, truly, utterly sorry and incredibly embarrassed*, my brain gets to tingling. I press my hands into the sides of my vibrating head. Agony tops the headache growing in the base of my skull like a bramble patch.

I don't want the damn reading, but I don't know how to block it. I've welcomed them for too long. Any attempt to stop it will be like tossing a shrimp net over a whale. A fiercely, cruelly detailed reading is coming on whether I like it or not. I brace myself.

> *Peace sits in his truck and reads Ginny's messages. He couldn't sleep all night, and now it's just past dawn, and he's about to crank the engine. But where to go? He could drive to Chad Dooley's house and beat his ass. Sadly, though he's been with Ginny for over ten years, he doesn't want to fight Chad. All he cares about is the fact that he won't be listening to Ginny accuse him of cheating when he's never done anything but be loyal to her—stupidly loyal, according to the*

few people he considers friends these days, people like Meredith Preston. He'd texted her since she was the other side of the Chad-and-Ginny quadrilateral. She asked him to come over and talk. She wasn't upset about Chad's extracurricular activities. To the contrary, she seemed glad to have an excuse to invite Peace to her condo. She even said something about needing a new roommate if he was looking for a place to stay. He rubs his eyes. The last thing he wants is to get involved with someone else. He needs time to breathe after inhaling Ginny's toxicity for years.

He reopens the text messages. Ginny's big blue eyes stare up at him. Even with Chad's leering face beside hers, Peace feels a flash of remorse for leaving her with Chad. Relief and desperation to get away from Helping Hands and a lot of terrible memories quickly subsume his guilt. She's given him a reason to move on. He taps on the last photo. Chad Dooley's tongue is, as LeeLee used to say and Ginny picked up from her, the pièce de résistance. He opens Meredith's messages and clicks on her address. The pleasant female voice in his phone starts directing him to her place. Nice to hear a woman talking who isn't screaming at him or accusing him of being the biggest lying man whore in South Carolina. Ginny warned him to watch his back, and that means he should keep moving, get beyond her reach. He puts the truck in drive and leaves Helping Hands, and Ginny, behind.

That's it. I wipe at the tears that stream down my face as Peace drives away from Helping Hands. Drives away from *us*.

The open text box waits for my apology, but I finally know the truth. The *real* truth has nothing to do with my paranoia about Peace cheating. The reading has just told me that isn't reality.

Reality is as bad, if not worse. He doesn't want me to apologize. He's done, moving on down the road. As I so eloquently said in my text message, he's watching his "backkj !!!!!!!"

The thought of him staying with me out of obligation is worse than the thought of him running from me. I have some pride left.

I return to Chad's bedroom. Most of the bedding is crumpled in a lumpy ball on the floor. Orange dots stain the gray sheets. *Cheetos, maybe?* An old Tori Amos song pops into my head, the one about searching for redemption in the dirty streets. Here I am, looking for a savior in a pile of twisted bedding.

I clean up as best I can and wait for Chad to get home. I'll go back to Helping Hands tomorrow. If Peace is playing house with someone else, so can I.

Chapter 19
LeeLee, 2015

After yacking up my guts at the Griffon, I wake in the FROG to the sound of my alarm dinging gently on the bedside table. Luckily, I overslept by only twenty minutes. My body must have needed extra restoration after the intensity of the previous night's supernatural reaction. If I hadn't set an alarm, I would still be drooling on my pillow.

I have texts from Clay and Peace.

Clay: *I got the boys up, and we're getting ready for school. Can you confirm you got home okay? Your car is outside but no movement from you yet.*

Me: *Hey, sorry. I'll be inside in thirty minutes max. Overslept.*

I read Peace's messages next.

Peace: *You doing okay? I was really worried last night.*

Me: *Yes. Maybe something I ate. We had sandwiches at mediation yesterday. They sat out too long, ick.*

I wiggle my stiff jaw. I must have been grinding my teeth in my sleep. Pain shoots up to my ears and joins the headache wrapped around my skull like the tentacles of an angry octopus.

My phone dings twice.

First, Clay. *Oversleeping isn't like you.*

Me: *Just under a lot of stress. As I know you are. Jumping in the shower.*

I turn to Peace's messages.

Peace: *Drew and I had our come-to-Jesus via FaceTime when I got home last night. I'm heading to Asheburg today to visit Dad. Staying at Saltmarsh for a few days. Going to move the wood I collected at job sites into the Saltmarsh pole barn. Excited to bust into it and build some stuff.*

I chew on my pinky nail. Physical distance will force us to be careful. Besides, after my reaction to last night's profession of dedication, I need to think.

Me: *Great! I hope it all goes well with both Old P. and Drew, and I can't wait to see what you create.*

Peace: *I'm pretty rusty. Ha ha, carpentry joke. But I'm looking forward to swinging a hammer in a creative fashion. And seeing Dad and being home.*

Me: *I'll miss you, but I'm glad you're going. That's what you came back for, right?*

Peace: *Among other things, as I've come to realize.*

Me: *Keep me in the loop. I'll be thinking about y'all.*

Good Lord. More thinking. Think, think, think. Me and Winnie the Pooh, but my shit is a lot more complicated than where I left my honey pot.

Peace: *Thanks *smiley face* I'll be thinking about you. I'll text you later.*

As I get up and turn on the shower in the tiny bathroom, I wonder how much good all this perseverating is doing me. I asked Clay for space to think. Now I need space from Peace, too, and not only because of hired stalkers. What exactly am I trying to achieve? Perfect clarity about the most important decision I'll ever make? A reading of the future to give me direction? An overheard thought that will give me a reason to shift one way or another?

I'm sitting on a rickety fence with pointy posts. I can't stay here forever with proverbial wood jabbing me in my hypothetical rear end. The whole structure might collapse. I have to decide.

No great revelation comes to me as I drive the boys to school, walk into my office, or sit at my desk. Framed family photos watch me with nervous smiles from my bookshelves. I identify with the foxhounds in the stuffy painting above my desk. I can almost hear them baying restlessly as their vulpine quarry disappears behind the edge of the ornate wooden frame.

I stare at my dark computer screen until a tap on the door behind me makes me jump.

Darlene stands in the doorway in a pair of white jeans, a voluminous pink-paisley top, and a heavy turquoise necklace. "That computer can't help you until you turn it on."

"I know. I'm distracted."

Darlene walks into the office and sits in the chair across from me. She crosses one leg over the other and bounces a tiny foot encased in pink Chanel ballet flats. "You're distracted a lot these days."

"I'm sorry. Stuff going on at home. Have I missed anything? Messed something up?"

"No. You're as meticulous as always with your work, even if you either look like you're about to cry or you're grinning like a fool every time I walk by this office." Her bouncing foot goes still. "You thinking about divorcing Clay?"

"How did you know?" Darlene and I have a great relationship, but I haven't talked to her about my marital problems.

She shakes her head. "Honey, what have I been doing for the last thirty years?"

"Duh. I guess you know the signs."

"If Clay makes you feel like crying, who's making you smile?"

I rub my hands down my face to wipe away any expression that reveals the unpleasant details of my conundrum.

"Is it that man who came in here a few weeks ago?" she asks. "What was his name?"

"Peace. Peace Smith."

"He could only have sprung from one family, bless his heart. The lawyer Makepeace Smith's son?"

I nod.

"I met his father once at the bar convention," she says. "What a piece of work. If ever there was a stereotypical South Carolina lawyer, it was Makepeace Smith. Bow ties, bluster, good looks, and enough charm to entice rain out of a wispy cloud on a sunny day. The good ol' boy network incarnated."

I nod again at her sage analysis of Old Peace. "When we were teenagers, Old Peace intimidated the hell out of all of us—except my friend Ginny. No one intimidated her."

"That's the woman you hired Lou to look for. Your Young Peace is connected to her disappearing?"

"Yes—well, no," I say. "I'm trying to prove he wasn't involved."

"I'm sure you want to find your friend, but you also want this man exonerated for your own reasons."

Tears, *again*. "Yes. I admit it. But there's so much more to it—"

"LeeLee. You're a fabulous lawyer and a great employee. A little... aloof—"

"You think I'm aloof?"

Darlene raises one penciled-on eyebrow. "You've never gotten that before?"

I consider her question. Before I moved to Asheburg, my peers labeled me a snob. I accepted it because I was afraid to join in. I didn't want anyone to discover I was different. It took Ginny's whirlwind persona, our strange commonality, and an intensely close-knit group of friends to pull me out of my shell. I don't think anyone would classify me as a shy adult, but in so many words, my husband called me out for being aloof. "I understand what you mean."

"I don't need to know the details, but I can give you some insight after three decades of watching people get divorced—if you want it."

I take a deep breath in anticipation of the gut punch her words are sure to deliver. "Throw it at me."

"Most people who come into this office are at a point where divorce is the right thing, whether they can't stand each other or they're indifferent. The opposite of love is indifference, not hate. If you hate someone, you still have an emotional investment." She leans forward, elbows on her knees, and looks into my face like she's cross-examining me. "You get me?"

"Yes. I don't hate my husband. And I don't *not hate* him, either, not like you're saying."

"Regardless of what gets them in here, the majority end up happier once they move on. Still, during every consultation, I look for the answer to one question. There are lots of ways to ask it. You sit in on consults. You know what it is?"

A leading question. *Objection!* I think, but I respond with uneasy vagueness. "Uh... I'm drawing a blank."

"You're drawing a blank on purpose because I'm about to ask you the same thing." She points at me. "Are you leaving your husband for this other man or for yourself?"

"I'm not even sure I'm leaving him."

"I'm not going to lecture you. You know there are no guarantees, good or bad. You've seen people who co-parent brilliantly and people who file custody actions against each other a decade later. You've seen clients marry affair partners and end up back in this office within a couple of years."

"Not *all* of them."

"The general rules always have exceptions," she says. "But before you make this choice, understand what you're truly searching for."

Before I can reply, she stands. "I have a call with Clark Middleton about the McCallister case in five." She pats my shoulder. "You think about what I said."

"All I do lately is think. It's driving me nuts." My stacks of old law school textbooks and bar publications taunt me. *Marital Litigation in South Carolina, South Carolina Rules of Family Court, South Carolina Family Lawyer's Toolkit.* I tap one finger on my battered copy of *Family Law: Theoretical, Comparative, and Social Science Perspectives, Volume III*. "I've applied all these perspectives to my personal life. I don't feel one inch closer to a reasonable analysis or a sound conclusion."

"That's not nuts. It's the opposite of nuts. Some people in your shoes don't think at all." She smiles. "Your trial briefs always seal the deal, LeeLee. You're a natural ponderer. Take advantage of it."

TUESDAY EVENING IS my catch-up night, since the three boys don't get home from karate until almost seven. I usually give Kylie Chick-fil-A money, and when they burst through the front door in their white karate uniforms, there's no time for much beyond bath and bedtime. Sometimes, I work late, but after Darlene's pep talk, I take advantage of my free hour and go for a run. Ponder while pounding the pavement, so to speak.

My loop takes me along waterfront Murray Boulevard, where the harbor breeze's gentle push encourages me on and the slanting sidewalks drive me into the road to save my ankles. Oversized flagstones on the hollow, raised walkway vibrate under my feet as I turn onto East Battery. The famous mansions lining White Point Garden are lords and ladies lined up to politely applaud as I navigate a jogger's jousting tournament. I dodge meandering tourists, young men selling sweetgrass roses, and antebellum mounting blocks. Pressure from tree roots below creates miniature tectonic shifts in the sidewalks, so I jump uneven fault lines and climb cement mountains. I go up and down the cobblestone wharf streets and through Waterfront Park then a hard sprint back down Tradd Street.

I slow to a walk and turn onto my favorite street, Legare Street, where most houses are all but hidden behind twelve-foot brick-and-stucco walls. Oak branches reach over property lines like the limbs of a kraken. A few overzealous magnolias give the oaks a run for their money. I never tire of pausing to peek through gates into fairy-tale gardens, where stone cherubs caper atop gurgling fountains and ornate iron benches patiently wait to reveal inspiration to melancholy poets.

As my breathing slows and sweat cools my neck, I long for my inspiration. Darlene told me to take advantage of my pondering, and I promised Cheryl I would try to put my powers to good use in our search for Ginny. I feel no closer to a resolution to my conundrums, and given my unexpected regurgitation at the Griffon, I still have limited control over my supernatural ability. On the all-or-nothing continuum, I've been holding fast at a little more than nothing for years—just past nada. Abruptly throwing up in the Griffon while Ginny and Peace screamed at each other in my head was much closer to all, and all scares me to death.

I have no idea how to find my happy medium, my supernatural MLW.

If only I could consult with Ginny, but if Ginny were walking beside me, I wouldn't need to figure it out in the first place. As I already observed, in her absence, she's once again dragged me into the middle of the bridge. She's forcing me to jump, but this time, she isn't holding my hand. I remember how I squeezed her fingers and she didn't even wince. She didn't rip her hand away from mine. She squeezed back, just as hard. I miss her and her maddening fearlessness.

My ears ring. At first, I think it's lightheadedness brought on from pushing too hard on my final sprint. I stop and lean against an ivy-covered wall. Yellow lights flash before my eyes, and for a frightening second, I think I'll faint. Then my narrator speaks.

The navigator uses a compass to find her way, but sometimes, the compass will find the navigator.

"You need some water, miss?" The unfamiliar voice jerks me out of the reading.

I blink, and an elderly man with a shock of white hair peers at me from between the bars of an ornate iron gate.

Ivy branches scratch my bare arms when I straighten. To my horror, my mouth hangs open. I shut it like a baby trying to avoid a spoonful of pureed spinach. "Oh gosh," I say. "No, sir. Thank you. I just felt a little woozy."

The man doesn't look convinced. "You sure you're okay?" He points at the sidewalk. "I reckon that cement is right hard if your head were to hit it."

"I promise. I live right around the corner on Council."

"All right, then." He adds a grandfatherly admonishment. "Now, you promise me you'll go straight home?"

"Yes, sir," I say. "Right away. You have a nice evening." I turn around before he calls EMS to take me to the emergency room—or the loony bin. As I power walk back to my house, I recite that simple reading over and over in my head. *The compass will find the navigator.*

Frustratingly vague, even for the future, but at least it's something—something between all and nothing.

A FEW DAYS AND MANY hours of ruminations later, I walk down Broad Street to meet Palmer at Miller's All Day, a popular brunchy restaurant near the corner of King and Broad. As I turn onto King Street, I pass Berlin's, an old-school men's clothing store. Mannequins in seersucker suits, pastel blazers, and brightly colored bow ties look down on me like varying iterations of Old Peace preparing to intimidate a skeptical jury.

I walk into Miller's and scan the crowded community tables. Palmer sits in a booth with gray-and-white-plaid cushions under a shelf filled with retro album covers. She holds one of her beachy books in hand.

"Why are they always staring into the distance?" I ask.

She looks up and smiles her lovely Palmer smile. She has on expensive workout clothes, but her hair and makeup are perfect, as always. "Maybe an air of mystery? Why don't you write a book and find out?"

"I don't have the energy for imaginary people's drama." I slide into the booth across from her. "I have enough issues in my life."

"Does this mean we're going to talk about Clay? You've been avoiding the topic, which makes me think it's getting worse."

The server, a cute shaggy-haired College of Charleston student, comes to our table and takes our order. He suggests a libation from the extensive menu of mimosas and bloody Marys, but it's the middle of the week and we have eight kids between us.

"Guess it's time to come clean," I say as the server strolls on to the next table. "We've talked about splitting up."

"Oh, shit." She wiggles in her seat, as if settling in for the long haul. "How serious?"

"Serious enough that we're splitting time in the FROG." I still have a grip on the menu, as if I might find some salvation among the side items—bacon, grits, home fries, major life decisions.

She takes my hand across the table. "I don't mean to pry but—"

"Yes. Peace has something to do with it."

"Girl..." Her thoughts come clearer than the menu in front of me.

Should I tell her what I think? She might get pissed.

"I know you think it's a bad idea," I say. "It's written all over your face."

"Lee, I love Peace, but leaving Clay for him seems extreme."

"You almost left Dean for Tommy."

"Look how well that went." She holds up her book. "In these books, the old flame always turns up, right? Our heroine returns to her hometown. Maybe she inherits a bed-and-breakfast or leaves her big-city job and decides to open a coffee shop. Her first love is back in Possum Valley, waiting for her—still handsome, rich, surprisingly single, conveniently childless, and ready to commit."

"I know," I say. "You keep bugging me about writing a book, but I can't write something like that. Not taking anything away from those who do. I know how popular they are, and the good Lord knows I understand the appeal of a fairy-tale ending. I love reading them myself when I have the time, but I just can't write one. It feels too unrealistic."

"Exactly. We're living that reality. Tommy has a bitter, vindictive ex-wife and two kids who will have emotional problems from their parents' endless fighting. I have five kids—*five*!" Palmer raises a hand, palm toward me, and splays fingers tipped with shapely pale-pink nails. "I don't have a glamourous career. I don't have a grandma to die and leave me a bookshop. I'd be dependent on Dean. And you—"

"I only have three children, and I have a career," I say, "but I'd have to manage the kids and work on my own. Clay would have to do the same, all while paying me alimony. Then there's the house. I can't afford it. Clay can't, either, if he's paying me. Realistically, we'll all have to move."

"All true. We don't need to get started on Peace's issues. I'm glad he's sober, but he's definitely not"—she turns her book over—"'Brock Masterson, investment banker with a summer home on Nantucket.'"

"I wouldn't want anything financially from Peace."

"Good. Because he doesn't have anything, bless his heart."

"I'll have enough to deal with from Clay—financially, emotionally, all of it."

"How do you think Peace will adjust to the sedentary second-husband life?" she asks. "If he'd gotten it together back in the day, he could have been an amazing husband and dad, and y'all would be living at Saltmarsh and continuing the Smith legacy. But that's not what happened."

"These are the issues I'm wrestling with. But when I'm with him—when it's just us—"

"It feels amazing. I know. Exciting but safe. Different but familiar."

"Yes. I feel like I can forget about everything else." Her understanding is a relief until she douses me with the hard truth.

"Marriage is about every day, Lee. With Tommy, I realized I can't marry my escape. That makes no sense. Then he's not an escape anymore. If you're going to be with Peace, he'll have to mesh with *your* every day. I just hope he's up to the challenge."

"He says he is, and I want to believe him." I chuckle. "When did you get so wise?"

Her expression collapses into a frown, as if she's so sad and exhausted, even her Botox can't hold up her face. "The past two years have taken it out of me, girl. I'm barely getting by. I *can't* keep doing... *this*... with Dean. One of the reasons I wanted to meet up today."

"Ah. I see." I lower my voice. "You want to make an appointment with Darlene?"

She nods. "Yeah. But please don't say anything to Jess yet. Or Peace. *Please* don't tell Tommy—"

"As soon as you meet with me in that capacity, everything you say is privileged. Though as your friend, I wouldn't say anything anyway. I'll look at D.'s calendar when I get back to the office."

"Thanks. I know it's the right thing." She wipes her eyes. "But it's still so hard. I'm scared shitless."

I reach into my purse. I've been carrying tissues with me everywhere as of late. I hand her one. "A wise woman once told me, if you're going to do this, you need to do it for yourself."

"That's what I'm trying to do. But I've spent the last twelve years putting my kids first. That's why I stuck it out this long. I don't know how to do things for *me*."

"The hope is that everyone involved is eventually better off, right?"

The server appears with our yogurt parfaits before Palmer can answer.

I check my phone. "Emails are piling up. I'll have to eat and run."

"All good. There's one other thing," she says. "I'm not yet sold on 2015 LeeLee and Peace, but I still want him to be vindicated. I also want to find our G-Love. So I... um... I went sort of Instagram stalker."

"What do you mean?"

"I DMed Meredith Preston."

"Oh, hell no! I never would have had the nerve."

"I'm an old friend, not a former girlfriend, a level down on the stalker meter." She hands me her phone. "I screenshotted the relevant parts. Flip through. You'll get it."

I tap on the photos and slurp my yogurt while I read.

Meredith: *I was devastated when we broke up! I thought I'd found THE ONE. I hoped getting sober together would seal the deal. But looking back, I was one long rebound. I think he always loved Ginny, even though she was seriously insane. Sorry, I know she's your friend.*

Palmer: *We all know Ginny is a piece of work.*

Meredith: *And there was some other girl he talked about a lot named LeeLee. He was definitely still hung up on her too. I can handle competing with one old girlfriend but not two.*

Palmer: *Aren't you mad at him?*

Meredith: *I was at first, but he was so nice about it when we broke up. He was as sad as me, just because he hurt my feelings. He was always so good to me. He never cheated. I've been in some shitty relationships. It didn't work out, but it was still the best one I've ever had.*

Palmer: *I take it you don't think he did anything bad to Ginny.*

Meredith: *No way! We started dating like a month after he moved in with me and then we moved to Boone. We never saw her, and he never communicated with her.*

Palmer: *Devil's advocate. He could have been involved with her and you didn't know.*

Meredith: *I guess. What about Chad? Y'all looked into him? He's the opposite of Peace. Mean, a liar, a cheater. Once, he slammed a door on my hand. Fractured my finger. He claimed it was an accident later, but I knew better. I'd been with a few of his kind before.*

The next photo is of Palmer's kids.

"That's it?" I ask.

"Yeah. The rest was her asking questions about Peace. I felt bad for her. She's clearly still in love with him."

"He does stick with you." I sip my water. "Some women might get mad, reading what she said about him being hung up on me *and* Ginny."

"But to one of us, it totally makes sense."

"I'm glad she's sort of an alibi for him. Though it's true—he could have been in contact with Ginny and Meredith didn't know it." I look at my phone again. "I really have to go. I'll follow up with Big Lou about Chad. He's still the prime suspect in my book."

We sign our checks and walk out to the sidewalk.

"Thanks for listening to all my drama," I say as we hug.

"You nursed me through my Tommy debacle. I'm always here."

We say our goodbyes, and I backtrack down Broad Street toward my office. My choices seem starkly delineated, like the bright, multicolored stripes on a few old-fashioned awnings that hang over the uneven sidewalk. I could leave for me, or stay for the kids. It's difficult to objectively weigh the pros and cons between two such emotionally charged negatives. As I turn onto State Street, I find myself looking for Peace's shades of gray. Something between selfishness and martyrdom.

THAT NIGHT, PEACE TEXTS me as I sit on the second-floor piazza with a glass of sweet tea. The kids are asleep, but I'm not working. I'm doing what I promised everyone I would do—thinking about my life. My phone dings, and I read his message.

Peace: *I have a plan. But promise me you won't say no right away.*

Me: *This defeats the purpose of you asking me to promise, but tell me the plan first.*

Peace: *Such a lawyer *smiley face* I know it's been rough on you and Jess and Palmer. Worrying about Ginny. She's on all our minds. I've been wishing we could go back in time and hang out at Edisto. Ginny's birthday is next week. What if we went out there and celebrated her?*

I start typing, but Peace sends another message first. *I figure you and Palmer will feel weird if everyone stays in the same place. So I asked Dad if we could use our house and Rollo if we can use one of his rental properties. Guys' and girls' weekend. We can get together on the beach, for dinner, etc. Plus, the boys can go fishing, and Jess can't give Landon shit about it.*

Me: *You predicted exactly what I would say. The question for the parents is, who's going to keep all our kids?*

Peace: *Tommy doesn't have his kids this weekend. Ms. Walters is obsessed with Baby Mia and keeps her half the time, even when Jess and Lands are home. It's up to you and Palm.*

Me: *I love the idea, but I have to run it by Clay. Dean doesn't help Palmer very much.*

Speak of the devil, and she shall appear. A text pops up from Palmer on our girls' group chat.

Palmer: *Peace texted me about his Tribute to Ginny Reunion Weekend. Jess, he said y'all are in. Lee, what do you think?*

Me: *If we're in separate houses, I think I'm down. It will be nice to spend some time with y'all.*

Jess: *The idea of a weekend at Edisto with my besties sounds like heaven to me. I don't care if we see the boys or not. I see Landon every day, bless his heart. So it's about what y'all are comfortable with.*

I haven't told Jess as much as I told Palmer about my growing entanglement with Peace. Either he mentioned something to her, or she sensed enough on the Vendue rooftop to recognize the inevitable.

Palmer: *We do owe it to Ginny to celebrate her birthday. We've missed the past fifteen or so.*

Jess: *Can you get coverage, Palm?*

Palmer: *My nanny owes me hours. Lee, will Clay want you so close to Peace?*

Me: *I guess I'll find out.*

I return to my messages from Peace. *I'll talk with Clay as soon as I can and get back to you.*

Peace: *All I can ask. Miss you.*

Me: *Miss you too.*

I sit back in my rocking chair and sip my tea. The glass has been on the end table for an hour, and the ice has melted. It's gone from crisp chestnut brown to a sickish yellow. I remember what Peace said a couple of weeks ago about being older and wiser—black-and-white and shades of gray. The in-between might be a place of wisdom, but my tea went down a lot easier before melting ice diffused it. Now, it isn't sweet enough, but it isn't the crisp satisfaction of pure cold water either. Still, I have nothing but watered-down tea in my glass. If I'm thirsty, I have to drink up.

My phone dings again, and I seriously consider chucking it over the porch railing. I've more than maxed my communication quota for the day, but I can't ignore the phone's electronic gravity. Parenthood and professionalism won't allow it. I vow to silence it after one last text.

It's Darlene. *We don't have anything on the calendar tomorrow. Why don't you take a mental health day?*

Me: *Is it that obvious I need one?*

Darlene: *No comment, but I caught you staring into the black abyss of your computer monitor again.*

Me: *Okay. I will. Thanks. See you Friday.*

The door to the piazza opens, and Clay appears in his SpongeBob pants. "Sorry. Have to get some new razors out of the bathroom."

"No problem," I say. "Darlene gave me the day off tomorrow. We're kind of in a holding pattern with all our cases, so I will, in turn, give Kylie the day off."

"That's great. It's kind of dead around my office too."

"Springtime. Who wants to worry about their legal problems with this weather, right?"

"It's been really nice out this week," he says.

My heart sinks into my stomach like a stone descending through murky water as I think of our wedding song, "Into the Mystic." Once upon a time, we intended to float there, together. Whatever that actually means, it resonated in our young, idealistic hearts. This man once rocked my gypsy soul. How have we been reduced to chatting about the weather?

I wonder if Clay feels the same way, but his milquetoast response and expressionless face reveal nothing.

"Well," he says. "Okay. Good night."

"Night."

He disappears into the house. I peruse my work emails one last time and force myself to silence the phone. The piazza door creaks again.

"Hey again," Clay says. "I had a thought. Maybe I could take the day off, too, and we could take the boat out after the boys go to school."

A wholly unexpected proposition. "Um... maybe."

"It's just an idea," he says almost apologetically. "We'd be back in plenty of time for carpool pickup. I know you have a lot on your mind, and you do your best thinking on the water."

"True. Darlene *did* couch this as a mental health day."

He smiles. "I could use one too. If I can't relax on the boat, then I'm one mental health day away from the funny farm."

The idea of a boat day with Clay feels oddly intimate for the emotional place we're in, but he's right. There's no more relaxing way to pass the time. Maybe if I inhale some salt, I'll finally exhale a little tension. The clean air will lend clarity to my thoughts.

"Okay." I smile back. "Sure. I can meet you at the marina after I drop off the boys."

"It'll be quiet. Good to get an early start. Not like the old days."

"Nope. I'll stick with coffee over morning beers."

"I'll stop by Starbucks on the way."

We say good night again, and he reappears in the yard a minute later. He waves as he walks up the steps to the FROG. I wave back. He isn't twenty yards away, but it feels like the Saint Helena Sound separates us.

This is definitely not LeeLee and Clay circa the old days, the days before we had kids, when we spent every weekend on the boat with other couples but had no reason to get on the water before noon. Jess and Landon joined us on multiple occasions. While Clay wasn't *one of us*, Lands paid him the ultimate compliment of saying he could at least "keep up with us."

I've been experiencing constant reminders of the good old days lately, all along the olden-times spectrum—ten years, fifteen years, twenty years. Were any of them better than the others? What about *these* days? Could I possibly look back on them in the future and think of them as good, in addition to old?

I stand, pick up my watery tea, and retreat to my bed. Those questions are too heavy for a hard rocking chair and the piazza's still night air. They require sunshine, squishy boat cushions, and water whipped up by a humming outboard motor.

I LIKE TO THINK OLD Peace Smith would appreciate the name Clay and I have bestowed upon our beloved boat, a center-console Regulator with a pale-blue hull. *Stare decisis*, the Latin phrase meaning "stand by things decided," is the legal theory by which courts follow the principles, rules, or standards of previous decisions. On a beautiful moonlight cruise in the olden days, before children, I half-jokingly suggested we christen our brand-new vessel *Starry Decisis*.

Clay, being Clay, ran with it. Within a couple of weeks, he hired a graphic design company to tattoo the boat's new moniker across the hull. He even added twinkling stars to dot the *i*'s. Back then, the name was simply a fun legal pun, but as I drive to meet Clay at the bustling Charleston City Marina after dropping the boys off at school, it has bigger implications. I'm contemplating whether to stand by decisions I made long ago.

Clay steers *Starry* past the fuel dock and a long line of boat slips as we leave the marina. Boats of every size and shape fill the slips and line up on the visitors' docks, from waterborne jalopies to sleek mega-yachts straight out of a James Bond movie. We maneuver around moored sailboats dotting the Ashley River like giant sleeping geese.

Clay puts on his sunglasses, flips his baseball cap backward, and adjusts his neck gaiter. "Where do you want to go?"

I look to my right at the Ashley River Bridge and the Citadel then to my left into the Charleston Harbor. We often cruise toward the harbor, past the historic homes on Murray Boulevard and the Battery. From there, we head toward Shem Creek and the entrance to the Intracoastal Waterway at the south end of Sullivan's Island. The Intracoastal takes us past Sullivan's and the Isle of Palms, all the way to secluded Dewees and Capers Islands.

"Capers?" I ask.

"Hmm. The Intracoastal is always busy. What about the Wappoo Cut then toward Kiawah? I bet nobody's out there this time of day."

The idea of having the water to ourselves sells it for me. "Onward, Jack Sparrow."

As predicted, no other boats disturb the glassy water. I sit on the bench seat at the bow and stretch my legs. My old C of C hoodie and hot coffee ward off the morning chill. We cut across the Ashley and under the James Island Connector into Wappoo Creek. The houses in the creek-side neighborhoods are mostly older, sprawling ranches where meemaws and poppops hold court and spoil their grandchildren. Some of those fine upstanding citizens are perfecting their putts on the waterfront Charleston Country Club's emerald greens. Others are on their docks, tinkering with their boats or reading the paper. We catch the attention of a few dock dogs. Their barking warnings dare us to venture onto their elevated wooden territory.

The sprawling campus of Trey's school, Pinegrounds, sits behind the tree-lined marsh like a reclining grand dame discreetly sunbathing. Childish yells and giggles float across the creek from the marsh-side playground. I thank the good Lord and my in-laws for giving my boys such an amazing educational opportunity. It awes me that Trey is learning to read and write amidst those towering oaks and Bowman and Malachy will follow him. When they're grown men, the scent of pluff mud will remind them of recess and PE.

Vehicle traffic clatters and clanks over our heads as we pass under the Wappoo Creek drawbridge. During the eighteenth century, enslaved people from the local plantations deepened the creek, also known as the Wappoo Cut, to ease commerce and transportation between the Ashley and Stono Rivers. Their bare hands dug out the deepest, narrowest part of the cut, a perilous endeavor for which they bore all the danger and saw none of the benefits.

On a busy Saturday, heavy boat traffic and a ripping current turn the cut into roiling white water. Houses along the skinny channel sit on high retaining walls, as if trying to avoid the spray. Only a few have tiny docks built into the walls, since neither pilings nor boats can handle the battering. On this early morning, the cut is as peaceful as it ever gets. No other boats pass dangerously close to us. Once we leave the rattling drawbridge in our wake, we hear nothing but our motor and the hull slicing through the water.

The boat relaxes us because it gives everyone an excuse to shut up and enjoy the scenery, but Clay turns on the stereo anyway. One of our favorite songs, "Southern Cross" by Crosby, Stills & Nash, floats through the speaker beside me. Perhaps he wants to recapture the old-days LeeLee and Clay, but as we gun it into the Stono River and cross under the bridge connecting James and Johns Islands, the lyrics make me self-conscious. Lately, it seems like cheating, lying, and testing really are the path of least resistance.

Stephen Stills soothingly advises me that I will survive—or Peace will, or Clay. It all depends on the listener's point of view. He promises somebody amazing will come along to help us all forget our heartbreaks.

A hopeful, poetic sentiment, but as Stephen himself sings in the chorus, some loves cannot be forgotten. I sink into my hood and yank the drawstring until only my nose sticks out into the wind, but the song refuses to be silent. The playlist finally has mercy on me and switches to one of Zac Brown's beachy Southern ditties about scarfing down fried chicken with his rear end plopped in the sand.

We zip down the wide, empty expanse of the winding Stono River, past the Johns Island farm the kids called the Pig Palace. A herd of feral hogs mingles with the cows and goats congregating on the beach in front of the ramshackle house. To our left, under clouds that tower over us like skyscrapers, James Island ends and Folly Island begins. The shabby, famously raucous town of Folly Beach thumbs its nose at genteel, exclusive Kiawah Island across the broad junction of the Stono and Kiawah Rivers.

The sky touches both islands and the never-ending ocean in front of us. People talk about the big skies out west. I'm sure they're lovely, but I'll pit our horizon-to-horizon low-country skies against Montana or Wyoming any day.

We pull up to the deserted beach at the end of Kiawah. On the weekends, dozens of boats tie up offshore, but only the gulls and sandpipers stroll the sand on an early Thursday morning. We pull into the mouth of a small creek, and Clay throws out the anchor.

Once it catches, he smiles almost shyly. "Want a muffin? Or a bagel? I got some at Starbucks. Figured we needed some sustenance for our voyage."

I haven't had much of an appetite, but he looks so earnest, I can't refuse. "You got a chocolate chip muffin?"

He opens a brown paper bag and hands me a muffin topped with powdered sugar and chocolate chips. It looks surprisingly good. I nibble as he sits on the seat across from me with his bagel.

He wears sunglasses, so I can't fully read his expression, but his abrupt transition from baked goods to life decisions speaks for itself. "Do you know what you want to do, Lee? I don't want to rush you, but—" His voice catches. "I don't know how much longer I can be in this limbo."

"I know. I'm sorry. I just don't want to make a mistake."

"Then *don't.* Don't make a mistake. Don't give up on us after everything we've been through and we've built. I swear what happened last winter will never, ever happen again—"

"I believe you. Really."

"Then what is it? I don't understand."

I pause before answering. I genuinely believe Clay won't cheat again. *Then what is it?* he asked, and I don't know. "I don't fully understand either. That's the problem," I say before gently turning the tables. "What about *you*, though? What about how you said I never let you in?" I swallow. "What if I'm not capable of being close enough to you?"

"Who are you close to if not me? Except maybe your high-school friends. I know this has something to do with Peace Smith coming back into your life. I already told you that."

I set my muffin on the seat beside me.

"You're not denying it," he says. "Will you be honest with me? Are you...? Did you...?"

"I haven't slept with him."

"But you've... been with him in some way."

It's too hard to acknowledge it, so I don't reply. I lift my sunglasses and rub my eyes, but Clay's thoughts still make their way into the darkness. I imagine them in all caps.

OH GOD... I CHEATED FIRST... I TOLD HER TO FIGURE IT OUT...KEEP IT TOGETHER, MORETZ...

"O... kay. I won't ask for specifics," he says. "I don't want to hear them. Look, I know I can't be one of your old crew. But we've been together every day for thirteen years. Doesn't that count? Doesn't that actually make us closer?"

"It's not a competition. I *know* I seem like a crazy person. Getting caught up with my first love, who is a recovering addict and might have killed my best friend. I have a beautiful home in the city and three kids that I love and a husband who *wants* to make things work and can actually admit he screwed up." The more I talk, the crazier it all seems. "I see a lot of people in post-cheating situations. The way you handled it puts you in the category of those who should be forgiven. So I don't know why—"

"Lee, *listen* to yourself. We could be one of those couples that comes out stronger for all this. When you've seen someone at their worst—know everything about them and still want to be with them—how can that not be the person you're closest to in the world?"

Please, LeeLee, you know me better than anyone. I don't want to start over with anyone else. I love you. Please forgive me.

Like at the Griffon, my head starts ringing.

Peace Smith doesn't know you. You're my wife, the mother of my children. Please let me in...

My stomach churns, and the crystal-clear silence of a reading drowns out Clay's torrid thoughts. The type of allegorical story prologue that will bring me no clarity about the future but doesn't hold the detailed pain of the past.

My narrator is trying to tell me something but won't give it to me in black and white. It will be shades of gray or nothing.

> *Whether with Clay, with Peace, or on her own, LeeLee will never be okay until she stops hiding.*

I lean over the railing and heave up the bites of muffin I just swallowed. Somehow, my sunglasses stay on my face. I press them into the bridge of my nose. Bile stings the back of my throat.

"What in the hell?" Clay holds my arm as I retch into the ocean—or one of the rivers, whatever body of water it is. "Are you sick? What—"

I spit a couple of times and sink back onto the boat cushions. "You don't know me, Clay."

He's half sitting, half standing. His butt hovers over the seat. "What do you mean?"

"You do... but you don't know *everything*. No one does. No one except Ginny. She's the only one who truly knows me."

He plops onto the cushions. "I don't understand." *Wait, is she telling me she's gay?*

Despite myself, I snort a laugh. "No, good Lord, I'm not gay."

His eyes widen. "How did you know—"

"Because I read you."

"What?"

I can't believe the words coming out of my mouth. "I *read you*, your thoughts. You heard me say only Ginny knows me. The first thing that came to your mind was that I would confess to being a lesbian."

He stares at me with his mouth open.

I keep talking in time to my erratic heartbeat. "Before that, you were thinking about how you know me better than anyone, better than Peace, and I know you better than anyone. You don't want to start over with anyone else—"

"Holy shit."

The look of terror on his face makes me burst into tears. As I always expected, he fears me. He's repelled by this weirdo who can invade his private thoughts. He gently pulls my fluttering hands away from my face.

"No. No. No," I say. "Forget it. Leave me—"

"Lee. Baby. Stop."

I peek at him through my fingers. My sunglasses are blotchy with tears, so I remove them and set them in my lap.

"Can you please explain what just happened?" he asks. "Are you okay?"

His gentle concern makes me cry harder. He wraps his arms around me.

"You *hate* me," I say.

"Who hates you? Not me." He looks down at me. "But I want to know what's going on. Hold on. Let me get you some water."

I pull my knees toward my chest and rock back and forth. I expect him to jump into the water and swim away from the wacko he married. Instead, he retrieves a cold water bottle from the cooler. He gives it to me and sits beside me again.

"You ready to talk?" He hands a towel to me, and I wipe my face.

"I don't know if I'll ever be ready. I haven't been ready in thirty-five years."

"I'm listening if you are ready."

Something in his voice makes me start talking, and it all comes out, the first time I remember having a vision of the past or reading anyone's thoughts—on the day my father left our family—how the readings work—to the best of my ability to explain it—how Ginny and her mom are the only ones who ever knew but Ginny is the only one who understood.

"I've talked about Ginny, but you've never met her. There's no one like her," I say. "No one who can drive you insane yet make you want to be around her all the time. At least, that's how she was until the last year or so before she left town."

"When the drugs and booze took over?"

"Yes, but we were always going in different directions. The velocity of us moving apart sped up over the years. I always tried to fight this—this *thing*. I thought of it as being a storyteller, but I only tell stories to myself. Maybe that's why I can't write a book. I got so used to telling stories in my mind, I can't get them on paper, no matter how hard I try."

"You can, Lee," he says. "Someday, when the kids are older and work isn't so crazy—"

"That's not the point. Ginny and her mom called her a navigator—out in the deepest waters between the past and the future." I point around us. "Water like this, all mixed and jumbled until we don't know where it came from or where it's going. She made a path for herself despite the current. She faced this weird power we share with her sails open and full of wind. But I've fought against it every day of my life. I battened down the hatches and pressed it deep inside me."

"Dealing with it alone until you met Ginny must have been hard—and alone again once she left town."

"You really believe me?" I can't believe that he *can* believe, not when I've been so certain no one ever could.

"LeeLee. First of all, you just told me exactly what I was thinking. Second of all, some things sort of make sense now. Like how you knew I cheated. Did you, like... see it?"

"No. I saw you sitting in your truck outside the house. Being sad."

He looks down at his hands, clenched into one solid fist in his lap. "That was one of the worst hours of my life."

"I also read a few things—just stuff. You feeling guilty and worrying and—" Guilt overwhelms me. "Clay, I'm so sorry. I wasn't trying to. It was so strong, I couldn't block it out—"

"I'm sorry you had to see any of it, but maybe it was a good thing. You asking me what was wrong made me confess faster." His fingers uncurl. He removes his baseball cap, swipes his hair back, and slaps the hat on again. A typical Southern male stress reaction. "I might have gone nuts if I held that in."

"So, if we're talking about going nuts—that's what I was about to say about Ginny. I tried to squash it. She always pushed the limits in everything in her life, and this wasn't any different. She went from not being able to read thoughts at all to, according to Peace, showing symptoms of schizophrenia."

"Are you afraid of that? In addition to being afraid of people not wanting to be around you if they knew?"

I nod.

"You've been holding all this inside and keeping it to yourself?"

I nod again.

His big hands engulf mine. "I'm so sorry I made you feel like you couldn't tell me."

I suck in a small breath. The wind picks up, as if it's equally surprised by his reaction.

"No wonder something stood between us." He gently squeezes my fingers between his. "This is a huge part of who you are. You've been facing it alone for years."

I start crying again. This time, he doesn't ask me to stop, as if he knows the tears need to come.

"Ginny said I was a chickenshit for hiding it," I say through my hiccups. "For t-trying to sque-elch it."

"Your reasons make sense to me. But I also think... how can I say this? I think you need to find a middle ground."

"You sound like Cheryl. But Ginny—"

"You just said y'all are as different as a porterhouse and a veggie burger. You have no reason to end up like her. She paid the price for too much of this—what did you call it?"

More little gasps on my part. "Being a stor-storyteller. Or in Ginny-speak, a n-navigator."

"I like them both. I don't see why you can't be a storyteller and a navigator. Right now, you're paying your price for not really being either."

"I can't believe we're t-talking about this. Clay, seriously. If it's too much for you—"

"It's not too much for me." He lets go of my hands and sits back against the cushions. "It's a lot to think about, but... I'm an attorney. It's my job to interpret the rules human beings make to bring order to the world around them, statutes, laws, supreme court decisions. They're nothing but made-up rules. If I can treat statutes like they're as solid as the theory of relativity, I can believe in your kind of rules."

I ball up the towel and throw it into our beach bag. "What about the boys? It's not so bad now, but it'll be hard enough to maintain an open relationship with them when they're teenagers. If they know I can read their thoughts—"

"We have plenty of time to figure all that out. If one of the boys turns out like you, I'll need to understand. I'm glad you told me, no matter what happens with you and me."

I have only one reply to that last sentence. "So, what happens with you and me?"

"I told you a hundred times, that's up to you."

"You still don't want to get divorced?"

"Nope. But I've also accepted it m-might happen." His turn to inhale and exhale in a series of sputters that leak into his words. "No matter what my frantic thoughts m-might be telling you."

I reach out and remove his sunglasses so I can look him in the eye. "A bunch of us are supposed to go out to Edisto and celebrate Ginny's birthday," I say. "This weekend."

"I see. So you want me to keep the kids?"

"Do you mind if I go?"

"I assume Peace will be there." He clenches the edges of the seat cushions.

"Yes. I'm staying with Palm and Jess in a condo. But he'll be at his dad's house with the other guys."

He stands, but his fingers have left indentations in the cushions. "What can I say, Lee? I told you to figure it out."

"*Thank you* for listening to me. And for understanding. It's more than I could have expected of anyone." I hope I sound sincere because I *feel* sincere, but given what I'm asking of him, I can't be sure how he's receiving it.

"Just please promise me I'll know something after this weekend. You gotta put me out of my misery." He fidgets with his hat again.

"Or deeper into it. You ready to head back? I have some work I can do from home."

"I guess so."

"I gotta check my email. Give me a minute."

He fiddles with his phone. Clay always retreats into work when other things overwhelm him. But who am I to judge? We all have our coping mechanisms. I check my phone as he pulls up the anchor.

Peace: *I really, really miss you.*

I pause before replying. I've just confessed my biggest secret for only the second time in my life. Maybe Clay will decide he doesn't even believe me, but at least he didn't run away screaming. And he's right. While Trey hasn't shown any signs of being a storyteller or a navigator or whatever I want to call it, I was the same age as Bowman when I recognized my oddities. Mal isn't yet three. Clay would need to know how to help them.

Given his kind response and his simple belief that I'm telling the truth, that should be enough, shouldn't it? Why do I still want to run to Peace?

I answer Peace truthfully. *I really miss you too. But I'm very confused. BTW, I'll be there this weekend.*

Peace: *That's great. I know you're confused. We'll be together soon, and things will make more sense.*

Me: *Okay. I'll text you later.*

I set down my phone. In two days, I'll be at Edisto Beach with my oldest friends. A total escape. But like Palmer said, an escape is only an escape if it remains as such. I want Peace to be right about things making more sense when we're together, but given the current state of affairs, I doubt it.

As we motor away from Kiawah, I check my emails too. To my annoyance, still nothing from LoveGinnyB. What kind of perverse general riles up the troops and then goes silent as to any further battle strategy?

At least I have an email from Lou, the Sherlock Holmes of the Grand Strand. I click on his email. My heart sinks as I start reading.

Ms. Moretz,

Unfortunately, Chad Dooley passed away from a drug overdose about a year and a half ago. His body was found in his house over a week after he passed away. He has no living family, so he was cremated. The police report made no mention of any roommates or a girlfriend being around when the police found him. Please advise if you'd like me to look into it further.

I rub my eyes then start typing. *Thanks, Lou. Let me think about it, and I'll get back to you.*

In the span of a week, Chad Dooley has gone from a prime source of information and potential foul-play suspect to major dead end. Chasing that broken kite string can't provide anything of value.

Starry Decisis picks up speed, and I put away my phone. I came out here to relax, to try thinking clearly. Maybe I'm not succeeding at either, but I can drink in the sunshine and be silent. I pick out a tiny wave in front of us and keep my eyes locked on it until it disappears behind *Starry*. An old habit from my first days on the boat in Asheburg, when I learned being *on the boat* was a state of mind, like being on vacation. Like being *at the beach* meant Edisto, we always went *on the boat*—not a boat, not Rollo's boat or Peace's boat or Landon's boat, *the* boat. Most of the time, the girls didn't know which boat it would be until we got to the dock and there it was. The boat. The dock. The creek. The river. The beach. The ocean. The waves.

Back then, in the quiet hours at the end of the day, when the buzz wore off and no one said much, my eyes would latch onto a specific wave. To turn *the* waves into *that* wave, an individual entity among thousands. After the boat passed it, my chosen wave would keep marching toward the sea. It didn't matter that I couldn't see it anymore. For some reason, the thought always brought me comfort. As my husband and I head home to pick up our children, it still does.

Chapter 20
Ginny, 2013

The clock on the microwave reads 3:37 a.m. Once again, I don't know how I got to this place. I know where I am but not why. Even who feels out of reach. I don't feel like a real person, just a toppled statue on Chad Dooley's cold kitchen floor. A busted lip and a welt rising like a volcanic island on the side of my head. My left pinky finger is possibly broken. He stepped on it when I fell, after he smacked me and shoved me against the wall.

I've been on this floor with my back against the cabinets for so long, my ass has fallen asleep. A palmetto bug skitters across my sock, and my toes don't even twitch. For the first time in weeks, I start sobering up—in more ways than one.

Over four months have passed since I turned up on Chad's porch after Peace and I broke up. Early on, with the vague idea that I should set some boundaries, I tried to sneak Chad into Helping Hands. I got busted twice, and the social workers kicked me out, so I moved in with him. Despite his promise not to do me like he did Fancy Boots Meredith, he started pushing me around as soon as I had nowhere else to go. He was true to his word about one thing—he fed my cravings, and they became ferocious. Summer has crested and collapsed into fall, and most days, I'm too blasted to feel much pain.

As the microwave clock ticks toward four in the morning, my shallow breathing finally defogs a cloudy mirror. I have to face myself, acknowledge I've gone too far. This isn't Ginny the free spirit thumbing her nose at society's expectations. It isn't even Ginny the face-saver running from her pain and her problems. This is Ginny the hot mess. The drunk blob staring at her reflection in the glass on the oven door while her fingers throb like an old-school hip-hop bass line, one of those slow jams we listened to on late-night drives heading home from Rollo's land. "Regulate" by Warren G, maybe. If I get up and look out the kitchen window, I'll see a cool black night and a clear white moon. Ginny B. and Warren G, out there in those streets, consuming all kinds of shit. I giggle as I hold in a sob.

I've been consuming way too much. Peace is the one who outruns his oxy prescription. Alcohol and weed are my usual substances of choice, but the past couple of months, I zoomed through my oxy Rx. I resorted to begging Chad for a few pills to tide me over. Chad has become quite the salesman since that day his disgusting, muddy tea put me off mushrooms forever. He perfected the art of luring in his clients. His strategy centers on providing a lot of free merchandise up front.

As I sit there with my hands jittering and teeth chattering, I realize I'm on my way to becoming one of the true junkies I've always disdained—people who shoot poison directly into their arms instead of swallowing it or smoking it like civilized human beings.

I grab the ratty dishrag hanging from the oven door and hold it to my bleeding mouth. The coppery taste makes me shiver. As my mind emerges from the mist, it quickly gets to tingling. My compass steers me into a small patch of calm water amidst the riptide swirling around me. It's a simple reading of the future, vague yet painfully clear.

If Ginny doesn't get out of here tonight, she will never get out alive. Chad will kill her one way or another, be it through his poisons or his fists.

I stand on shaky legs. The room spins. My finger yowls like a stomped cat as I grip the countertop. Chad is sleeping on the couch in the TV room. His *Scarface* DVD returned to the main menu after he passed out. In addition to watching episodes of *Breaking Bad* on repeat from his box set, he's subjected me to every drug-dealer movie in history. All three *Godfathers*, *Goodfellas*, *Casino*, even silly ones like *Dazed and Confused*, the teenage weed-fest I thought of on the day of the mushroom incident.

Chad Dooley and I have both gotten older. Maybe he still loves the eternally youthful innocence of high-school girls, but I lost that naïveté long ago. I swear I'll never watch another television show or movie about gangsters or idiotic potheads. The only drugs in my life will be the ones I buy and pay for myself. I'm done purchasing my high with my blood and my pride.

I stand there swaying and inhaling the smell of stale weed. The scent is permanently seared into my nostrils, the carpets, and the upholstery. Chad once dreamed of having his own house with a firm foundation, and he's put his imprint on this place. I often wonder how he managed to buy it. He doesn't make enough money selling his wares to own this place mortgage free, as he likes to brag. He drives a ten-year-old Toyota Tacoma with a hundred eighty thousand miles on it.

Chad gasps and sucks in a snore. I jump and look over my shoulder, as if expecting to be confronted by a wild boar. He rolls onto his stomach, but he doesn't wake. I walk toward him. He's sprawled on his imitation leather sofa like a discarded scarecrow. He wears a white undershirt and a pair of cargo shorts. A couple of pill bottles sit on the coffee table, oxy and something else—maybe Xanax. A bag of weed and a disgusting plastic cup of warm orange juice and vodka round out the panorama, *Still Life with Narcotics*.

By some small blessing and his own faulty piping, Chad Dooley no longer has much of a libido. He likes to keep women under his thumb, sure, but he doesn't have much use for women underneath him in the more literal sense. So he usually sleeps on the sofa.

I remember what he said—and thought—as he loomed over me after he backhanded me across the mouth and I hit the floor.

"Damn it, Ginny, you keep running your mouth, and I'll shove your tongue down your throat." *Mouthy bitch, but she's still hot. I'll keep her around for a while. She turns me on...*

I pointed up into his shorts at the broken machinery in question. "A car battery couldn't turn you on."

That was when he stepped on my finger. I cried out as he pressed down with his New Balance running shoes, that man who never exercised beyond pushing remote-control buttons.

"You *ever* say some shit like that again, and I'll kill you. Got it?"

He retreated to the sofa, lit a joint, popped some pills, and drank a fifth of vodka mixed with a half gallon of OJ.

Four hours later, a urine smell hits me as I approach him. A dark crotch stain on his cargo shorts. He's wet himself. Disgust washes over me, as if he's peed on me too.

My head starts tingling again, and I stop in my tracks. It isn't the most opportune time for the past to pay a visit, but I'm too tired to fight it.

Chad creeps around his mama's trailer with a can of gasoline. This dump will go up easy, then Chad plans to never set foot inside a trailer again. Mama's life insurance money will be the big payload, but Reesie has a small policy, since she started working at the hospital scrubbing bedpans. He sloshes the gas around the base of the trailer and backs away. Mama and Reesie are both passed out drunk. Like mother, like daughter. Too bad it has to be like this, but Chad added mercy roofies to their final glasses of cheap wine. The smoke will kill them before the fire, and they'll never know what happened. He lights a match and tosses it into the darkness. As firelight turns the dry brown dirt of the backyard to an unnatural orange, Chad Dooley turns and walks into the woods.

That's how he paid for his house. He drugged his poor mother and sister, burned down his childhood home with them in it, and collected their life insurance money. If he did that to his family, the good Lord only knows what he'll do to the likes of me.

Something cold and calculated settles in my brain. For the first time in months, I see everything clearly, every hair on Chad's bony legs. He's too lazy to sit up to drink, so dried OJ stains the pillow. The remote control sticks out from under his stomach.

I pick up a ratty Walmart blanket and drape it over his back. I calmly study the angle of his neck. His face is sort of smushed into the corner and surrounded by cushions. Even better, his arms are above his head and under his pillow.

It's as if the universe set it up for me, sent me that warning reading, and provided me a way out. Sometimes, the simplest messages are the plainest, and I won't get this chance again.

I don't weigh much, but I've sobered up, and Chad Dooley's scrawny ass is comatose drunk. I pick up a pillow. My heart beats out of my chest. The bass line has picked up. No more chill vibes, it's something with a staccato tempo and a fierce message to deliver—less Warren G, more Eminem, LeeLee's old favorite. I have only this single shot. I can't miss it.

I sit on Chad's back and press the pillow onto his head with all my strength. My pinky finger shrieks, but I ignore it. No going back now. Better a broken finger than a broken neck. At first, he doesn't move. He's *that* hammered. His oxygen-starved brain finally calls out to his body, and he starts thrashing. I hold on for dear life—to keep mine going and to extinguish his.

His befuddled thoughts flicker in front of me. *What...? Who...? Help help help! Ginny, help! I'll have the money soon, Larry. I'll pay you back, I swear... Heeelp! Help...*

The thoughts fade as his limbs still. I sit on his back for at least ten minutes. If I let go, he might rear up like an ornery mule and donkey-kick me from one end of the house to the other.

Eventually, I lift the pillow and stand. He remains still, so I roll him onto his back. A small scream escapes me. He stares at me with dull blue eyes. I close them. Mercifully, like they do in movies, they stay closed.

I have to leave but can't simply walk out the door. I have to erase any evidence of Ginny B. from this place. I go into the bedroom and pack my one duffel bag of clothes. I shove my few toiletries—shampoo, bodywash, a hairbrush, deodorant, and a zippered bag of crusty makeup—into the duffel. I scour under the bed and all around the house for any further signs of myself, but fortunately, I travel light these days.

I consider my options as I remove a Coke from the refrigerator and a box of Cheez-Its from the pantry. I haven't seen the neighbors much over the past few months, and I have no car in the driveway. Chad didn't like me to go anywhere or talk to anyone, and he hasn't allowed any customers into the house since I started staying here. He didn't want me to know anyone's identity if the police started sniffing around. At the time, I was sort of bummed because I was still with it enough to be lonely.

Loneliness turns out to be a blessing in disguise. No one knows I've been living here.

My sugary, cheesy late-night snack also goes into my duffel. As I sling the bag over my shoulder, Chad's wallet on the counter inspires me. He paid for everything with Visa gift cards, since he didn't like leaving a trail. I grab five two-hundred-dollar cards. I open the apps on my phone and stop sharing my location with him, but I need to do something about *his* phone. I've looked over his shoulder many times, so I pick it up and enter the security code, 0420. I delete our text messages and my contact information. I almost take the phone with me, but I want it to look as if he simply ingested too much of his product, fell asleep, and never woke up. His phone should be lying around.

I wipe the phone on my shirt and set it on the floor beside the sofa. I think about fingerprints around the house, but the MBPD is familiar with Chad. He might have avoided jail time, but he's a known user. I hope the police will accept his death at face value, since no one will be crying over his loss and demanding an investigation—not his dearly departed mother and sister, God rest their troubled souls.

I take one last look at Chad Dooley. He appears to be sleeping peacefully. It makes me feel a little better. I never planned to commit murder, though my heart tells me Chad got what he deserved. I was supposed to be a famous singer, not a cold-blooded killer.

I shove my phone into my purse, then I walk through the door. For a moment, I stand on the stoop, unsure of my next move. No one is looking for me either. I have no place to go.

When there are truly no options left, the only place to go is home.

Chapter 21

LeeLee, 2015

My driver's-ed teacher at Ashepoo High School spent an entire session on the treachery of railroad crossings. In my teenage nightmares, Mama Donna's Camry stalled on the tracks, in the direct path of a fearsome metal leviathan. The door jammed, or my seat belt pinned me to the driver's seat. A train whistle shrieked a warning that came too late as a singular light bore down on me. I used to wake with a jolt in my bed on Carnation Street and stare into blessedly quiet darkness.

In my everyday life in downtown Charleston and its suburbs, my Volvo faces no danger of crapping out on any railroad ties. Modern overpasses carry me above all the crossings. Not so on the country roads leading to Edisto Beach. When I turn onto Route 174 and approach the railroad crossing sign, adrenaline leaks into my veins. I look over my shoulder down an endless iron roadway and step on the gas.

Once I make it over the tracks, familiar surroundings soothe me, just as the stillness of my bedroom quieted my adolescent terror. The well-known skinny corridor of Route 174 is a heavily trod passageway to my past, an asphalt arrow pointing toward my youth. Spotty sunlight dissipates through the same canopy of intertwining tree branches. The trees' expansive root systems are regularly sawed off to prevent them from reaching into the road and tripping up passing cars. The oaks are tougher than the most souped-up pickup truck.

As a reminder of the trees' immovable fortitude and human mortality, county sheriffs hammered yellow-and-black reflectors into their gnarly trunks.

Estates hide behind shrouds of Spanish moss, tucked at the ends of long driveways that slip under ornate gates like wily asphalt snakes. Some of the modest roadside homes are mobile, and some are stationary. Some are meticulously kept, and some are abandoned and collapsing in on themselves. I wonder how Edisto's population supports the myriad of tiny churches. Presbyterian, Baptist, AME, Pentecostal, Methodist, Holy-Ghost-Tabernacle-of-Christ's-Living-Word-Praise-Center-for-All-God's-Chosen, et cetera, et cetera. A large roadside sign forcefully reminds me that "Jesus is Lord of Edisto Island," so maybe that's my answer.

The woods open to impossibly grand swaths of marsh only to draw the curtains again as if the view is a secret that must be kept. A flash of misplaced color in the marsh catches my eye. For years, locals have adorned the Edisto Mystery Tree—an unimpressive dead tree in the marsh alongside the road—with seasonal decor. This time of year, the Mystery Tree wears a combination of leftover dangling Easter eggs and red-white-and-blue Memorial Day regalia.

I drive into the town of Edisto Beach, turn right onto Jungle Road, then take another right. Dockside Bar and Grill, where I first confessed to Ginny that Peace and I were in love, still sits between Dock Site Road and Big Bay Creek like a giant cinderblock beer keg. I pull into the gated parking lot beside Edisto's one high-rise condominium. A few spaces over, Palmer is getting out of her Range Rover.

Jess picked up the rental key from Blanchard Realty. By the time Palmer and I walk into our condo unit, she sits on the balcony overlooking Big Bay Creek, sipping a Corona Light and watching the parade of boats.

She yells through the screen door as we put our suitcases in the bedrooms and unpack our coolers and snacks. "Y'all! I want another kid so bad, but I forgot how nice it is when no one is relying on you to keep them alive."

"Doesn't Landon rely on you to keep him alive too?" Palmer asks.

"Yeah. But I can't do much for him when he's offshore," Jess says. "Hey, look. I see Old Peace's latest boat."

I walk onto the balcony. The Edisto Beach Marina spreads out below us.

"Where?" I ask. "How do you know? There are a hundred boats out there."

She points at one of the slips, where a gleaming sport-fishing boat that looks to be forty feet long sits. "See the name? The *Caseload II*. I bet Drew takes full advantage of that perk."

"Old Peace's boats got too big for the shrimp docks at Dockside over the years."

"Yeah, and last time I was in there, the floating dock wasn't attached to the restaurant anymore. It's just sitting out there, disconnected from everything."

The idea of the old dock being unhinged, rising and falling with the tide for no reason, gives me the creeps.

"Y'all want to go to Coot's for drinks and fried delicacies?" Jess asks.

"I brought salad mix." Palmer holds up a bag of spinach.

Jess and I burst out laughing.

"Oh, Palm," Jess says. "I love you, but I'll be damned if I'm letting you make me feel guilty for my fried shrimp basket."

"Seriously, girlie," I say to Palmer. "I've been living on Goldfish, carrot sticks, and Bagel Bites. Oh, and Clay and I survived a highly uncomfortable taco night, but it's hard to enjoy Old El Paso when you're staring across the table, trying to decide if you want to stay married to the person on the other side."

"You *do* look kind of skinny, Lee," Jess says with a hint of jealousy.

"Exactly, and not in a good way. My boobs are deflating like tires with a slow leak. My butt's getting flatter than expired tonic water. All this stress has killed my appetite."

"Is it as dead as Chad Dooley?" Jess asks.

"You did *not* go there, Jessalyn Conway Walters," I say.

"I did." Jess sniffs. "And I'm not apologizing. Chad Dooley did nothing for this world but use up oxygen."

Palmer shakes her head. "Talk ill of the dead, and you'll regret it."

"You think Chad Dooley will haunt me?"

"Maybe he'll possess you," I say. "If you start puking tonight, we'll know it's not liquor shots. It's the malignant spirit of Chad Dooley going all *Exorcist* on your ass."

"I'm serious, y'all," Palmer says. "Chad may have been an evil bastard, but I'm not trying to be haunted or possessed. That would be so tacky."

I put an arm around Palmer and squeeze her. "If there is an afterlife, Chad Dooley is roasting away in the fires of hell. Now, let's go. I need some hush puppies."

Palmer grips her spinach like an airplane floatation cushion. "I guess they have salad at Coot's these days—"

Jess snatches the salad and sticks it in the fridge. "If white lettuce doused in ranch dressing with fried chicken topping makes you feel healthy, have at it."

We spend the evening at Coot's Bar and Grill, the beachfront restaurant on the Edisto Beach Pier where the servers wear T-shirts emblazoned with a knobby bird's foot and the joint's unofficial motto, "Eat More Coot." The only way to describe the smell in Coots is *old*—old, damp wood, old pleather barstools, old alcohol, old memories. As if to prove the place is in a time warp, our bar seats face a Jägermeister tap. I crane my neck to see around the buxom bartenders, past their comprehensive selection of bourbons, and through a row of dingy windows. Over a mile down the jetty-striped beach, the wooden crown of the Smiths' third-story deck lords over lesser outdoor entertainment spaces.

"We'll be there soon enough." Jess pats my knee then orders her fried shrimp basket and a margarita.

She generously rambles about her fertility challenges so Palmer and I don't have to talk about our own jacked-up personal lives. Still, the specters of Peace and Tommy hang over the conversation, as if someone has placed cardboard cutouts of them at the table behind us. When Landon texts Jess that the guys are waiting for us to come by for sunset drinks, she finally broaches the topic we've all been avoiding.

"Sooooo..." she says as we get the check. "Y'all..."

"Right," I say.

"Yeah," Palmer says.

"This gonna be the weirdest night ever?" Jess asks.

"It's about Ginny," I say.

"Exactly," Palmer says.

Jess shrugs and sucks down the last of her margarita. "'Kay. If y'all say so."

That's the thing about a friendship as old as ours. We can say not much at all and still say a hell of a lot.

WHEN WE WERE TEENAGERS, the Defense Rests had bright-yellow siding. These days, the house is a dignified gray brown, as if to blend in with the dunes. Miss Lucy's pink tea roses beseech us through the slats of the wooden staircase as we climb the two flights to the main floor.

Jess opens the sliding screen door and yells, "The party's here!"

The house still smells like the Arm & Hammer carpet-cleaning powder Miss Lucy used to soak up the mustiness. The wooden paneling has gone from tastefully modern to painfully outdated to painted white and hip once again. The same faded hand-painted sign hangs over the kitchen entryway, inviting visitors to Sit Long, Talk Much.

The panoramic view embraces us when we reach the rooftop deck. I walk straight to the railing and open my mouth to gulp the breeze. My eyes just as greedily eat up the scenery—the skinny beach slashed by jetties to prevent erosion, the multicolored umbrellas like mismatched buttons, the mouth of the South Edisto River meeting the St. Helena Sound and blending into the deceptively calm ocean. That's the place where Ginny believes the future and the past mix until only a skilled navigator can tell them apart.

Jess taps my shoulder. "We're getting old, but this view never does."

"True, true." I wipe my eyes. "The wind."

"Sure. The wind." She winks. "Let's get a beer."

Tommy set up a Bose stereo. The Allman Brothers croon about Sweet Melissa and transient crossroads. The boys grill corn on the cob and the tuna they caught. Landon and Rollo picked up a keg, so Palmer, Jess, and I sit on stools around a covered tiki bar with red Solo cups of foamy Miller Lite. Peace stands beside the keg with his ubiquitous Coke.

Once again, I admire his willpower. I also admire the way his five-o'clock shadow emphasizes the strong line of his jaw. His baby-blue T-shirt brings out the color of his eyes, especially after a day on the water darkened his skin.

Jess elbows me. "You're drooling."

"I'm not looking at him," I say. "I'm... admiring the ocean, or... the clouds..."

She laughs. "Girl, you busted yourself! Maybe I was talking about the tuna."

Peace smiles at me.

My stomach flips like a well-done pancake. "I admit it. Maybe I am a little... spittle-y."

"You might be the writer among us, but that is *not* a word, Lee," Jess says.

Palmer takes one of my hands and one of Jess's. She watches Tommy as she speaks. "Y'all. *Please* don't let me do anything stupid."

"Me either," I say. "I have to go back to the condo tonight. A PI could be lurking in the trees with his binoculars trained on this porch. If ever there was a time for you to be full-on, wide-open, no-filter Jess, this is it. We're relying on you."

"You got to regulate our confused, hormonal asses," Palmer says.

Jess is up to the challenge. "I'll drag y'all out of here by your ovaries if I have to."

Peace appears at my shoulder as if drawn by the sound of our laughter. "What's so funny, ladies?"

"I have been tasked with keeping everyone here in line." Jess squints up at him.

"Isn't that usually LeeLee's job?" he asks.

"Not since you showed up again," Jess says. "Remember, you'll get my foot straight up your ass if you try to seduce her."

"Okay, okay." I giggle. "Thanks, Jess. I got it."

"Listen to you! Already trying to tone me down. You're doomed." Jess scowls. "Don't mess with her, Peace. Unless you want to marry her and make up for her lost alimony."

"Maybe I do," he says.

I put a hand on each of their arms. "Okay, y'all. Seriously—"

"Then you gotta get a *damn job* first." Jess tips her cup at Peace and slides off her stool.

"Ouch, cousin. I'm working on it," he says, but he's grinning.

Only Jess can say something so insulting and still be endearing.

"Landon Walters, you big stud!" She sashays across the deck and calls out to her husband.

Landon reclines in a lounge chair. "Baby, it ain't time for me to take you to bed yet..."

"Sorry," I say to Peace.

"We did get her riled up," Palmer says. "Shake up that Coke can, and you'll get the spray."

"Let's get back to the reason we're here," I say. "This is supposed to be about Ginny, right?"

"It is." Peace calls over his shoulder, "Hey, y'all! Everybody! Get chairs, stools, whatever."

We drag seating toward the center of the deck. I perch on my stool. Jess and Palmer boot Landon out of his lounge chair, so he sits on the edge of the keg. Rollo and Tommy sit in beach chairs. Peace stands in the center of the circle. Everyone waits for his cues, like we always have. His gravity still pulls us in.

"I'm glad we're all here," Peace says. "I've been... MIA... for a long time. But I thought about y'all. A lot." He looks around the deck at us—Rollo, Landon, Tommy, Jess, Palmer, and last and longest, me. "We both missed you. Ginny and me. We're here to celebrate her tonight, even if she's not with us."

"Here, here," Landon says. "Ginny B.!"

"G-Love!" Tommy says.

"My girl! Since Miss McCray's first-grade class," Jess says. "She read chapter books when the rest of us were trying to manage *Hop on Pop*. Miss McCray used to have her read for the class. She couldn't say her *R*s..." Her eyes widen, and she purses her lips. She puts one hand on her hip and imitates Ginny reading *One Fish, Two Fish, Red Fish, Blue Fish*.

Schools of *wed* and *bwuu* fishies dart around my mind. I didn't know six-year-old Ginny, but I can see her. Her bright hair, round blue eyes, russet freckles, and a nose that must have been less than a stub.

"I was in that class," Rollo says. "I remember."

"That's what I want us to do tonight," Peace says. "Remember. Let's tell Ginny stories. Come on. We all have favorites. I'll go next."

He clasps his hands before him like a preacher preparing to deliver a sermon. "I present to you 'The Tale of the Freshman-Year Homecoming Princess.'"

Palmer and Jess laugh out loud, and I smile. The story was before my time, but I've heard it. Our class elected Ginny to the homecoming court, but she skipped school and went to the beach the Friday of the homecoming game. She barely made it back in time to be presented to the crowd. The other princesses waited with their football escorts in their pretty dresses and high heels, their hair in French twists and their makeup just so. When Ginny finally showed up, Peace walked her onto the field, Peace in his football uniform, Ginny's sparkly homecoming princess sash over her tie-dyed beach cover-up. She wore flip-flops, and her hair was in a messy, salty ponytail. She sported sand up and down her legs and some on her face.

"The best part," Peace says, "was when Mr. Coleman asked her if she had anything to say, like he asked the other princesses. Everyone else thanked their classmates for voting for them and said it was such an honor to represent Ashepoo High School like it was the GD Miss America pageant. Then he got to Ginny. She looked him right in the eye—the damn principal—and said into the microphone, 'The whole freshman class must be batshit crazy, voting for me,' then—"

"'Coleman, you got a smoke?'" Everyone yells it out at once, including me, and I wasn't even there. It's a famous Ginny-ism, like so many others.

We trade Ginny-isms as the sun sinks toward the horizon. It seems to me like that golden orb itself lingers longer than usual, as if it doesn't want to miss a favorite story. Darkness falls as I finish "That Story about Ginny Almost Burning down My House."

"She was determined to teach me how to bake snooder-dooders," I say, "but y'all know I can't bake. I can ruin a tube of Pillsbury cookie dough. My cakes are too floury, and my brownies are always uncooked in the middle. Betty Crocker and Sara Lee and Mister Duncan Hines himself weep in their graves every time I crack an egg."

"Amen!" Landon says.

"But Ginny..." I get to my feet. "Ginny wouldn't give up on me. She was going to be my sugar salvation."

Palmer eggs me on. "So y'all put the snooder-dooders in the oven—"

"Then we started drinking vodka from my mom's stash mixed with Hi-C fruit punch!"

"Gag!" Jess mimes ralphing into her beer cup.

"We flat-out forgot about them," I say. "Went out on the porch and shot the shit. An hour later, we go back inside to watch *Reality Bites* on my VHS player, and it was like entering the seventh circle of hell."

Everyone cracks up as I wave my arms around and gag on smoky memories. "So I grabbed the fire extinguisher, and she grabbed the phone and dials 911. She's screaming into the poor 911 operator's ear—'*Snooder-dooders! Snooder-dooders!*'"

Tommy rocks back in his lounge chair. "The 911 operator probably thought she was Swedish—"

"Okay, y'all! I'm *done*." Rollo stands and throws up his hands.

Everyone stops mid-chortle. I drop my imaginary fire extinguisher. Rollo throws his Solo cup into the trash.

"Dude," Landon says. "What's your problem?"

"I said I'm done. I don't want to listen to this shit anymore."

"What shit, Ro?" Peace asks, as if inquiring about the time.

"This shit! We're supposed to be remembering Ginny—"

"That's what we're doing, man," Tommy says.

"Y'all are making a damn joke of her," Rollo says.

Silence descends on the deck, as if the encroaching darkness can dampen sound as well as light.

Rollo hadn't contributed one word to any of the stories. He hadn't laughed, either—odd for someone who speaks sarcasm like a second language.

Jess can't stay quiet for long. "Rollo, in case you forgot, Ginny loves to joke and make a scene and rile everyone up. It's her MO. She loves nothing more than to be the center of attention with everyone cheering her on like a female NASCAR driver crossed with Blanche from *The Golden Girls*."

"Maybe so. But she's a hell of a lot more than that. She's smart and beautiful. She's an amazing singer—and a damn good friend. You and Palmer used to fight over sleepovers with her when we were kids, Jess." Rollo points at me. "Don't get me started about what she did for you. Would LeeLee be here if Ginny hadn't taken her under her wing when she moved to Asheburg?"

"That doesn't matter," Palmer says. "Ginny was LeeLee's first friend in town, but we've all loved her for years. Ginny just opened the door."

"She always opened doors." He glares around the circle. "Y'all can't talk about any of that, can you? Nope. Just Ginny goofin' off. Ginny gettin' drunk or high."

"She was drunk and high through most of high school and college," Peace says. "Same over the last decade or so I knew her."

Rollo rounds on Peace. "You shut your damn mouth. You're the one who left her high and dry in the first place."

A collective gasp. No one ever speaks to Peace that way.

Peace looks like Rollo threw keg beer in his face. "Not fair, dude. You have no idea what it was like all those years living with her."

"I know I'd never leave a friend alone like you left her."

Peace and Rollo stare at each other over an expanse of weathered wooden planks that suddenly seem as wide as the Ashepoo River. Rollo's nostrils flare—in, out, in, out, like a spooked horse's.

He snatches a stranded beer cup and chucks it over the railing. It lands in Miss Lucy's hydrangea bush. The red cup clashes horribly with the blue flowers. It's all wrong, like Rollo raging at Peace.

"Screw this. I'm going to bed." Rollo blasts past Peace. His shoulder whacks Peace's arm. *You left her with Chad Dooley, you piece of shit. Chad goddamn Dooley...* Rollo stomps down the stairs. His thoughts leave impressions before my eyes, as if I've been staring at the words for hours. *Chad goddamn Dooley...*

The night is fully dark and quiet except for the neighbor's overactive bug zapper and some kids yelling over a game of flashlight tag.

I tentatively tap an ice pick on the uncomfortable silence. "That went from zero to sixty faster than Landon's old Mustang."

Nervous laughter peppers the deck.

"Sometimes, I think Ricky-Roll Blanchard is losing it," Tommy says.

"That's what happens when you smoke weed every day for twenty-plus years," Jess says.

"Maybe he's lonely," Palmer says. "Never been married. No kids. Must be hard, right? Sorry, Peace. But it is unusual at our age."

"It's not what I would have chosen if I'd been in my right mind," Peace says.

Palmer hugs herself, though it's still warm. "I feel sorry for him."

"You feel sorry for everyone, Palm," Jess says.

"And you don't feel sorry for anyone."

"No. I do. I feel sorry for Ginny." Jess wipes her eyes and lifts her cup. "I wish she were here. Happy birthday, G-Love. Wherever you are."

Everyone salutes Ginny, but I can tell the party will wind down. No one feels like cutting up after Rollo's meltdown. Jess empties her cup over the railing. Those poor hydrangeas are having a hell of an evening.

"Y'all ready to go?" Jess asks me and Palm.

"Yeah," I say. "Let me talk to Peace."

Jess grimaces. "LeeeeLeeeeeee—"

"Only talking. And only for a minute."

Peace picks up beer cups and paper plates. "That was a real buzzkill," he says as I approach. "Even for those of us with no buzz."

"No doubt. I was... uh... wondering, did you say anything to Rollo about Ginny's reunion with Chad Dooley?"

"No. Since he didn't want to talk about Ginny at Saltwater Cowboys, I haven't brought her up. Didn't want to make him feel worse. He'd *definitely* feel worse if he knew Dooley was involved." Peace rubs my shoulder. "Why?"

"Just wondering." I point around the deck. "Can we help clean up the mess?"

"I'll make these clowns help me. T-Dog, Lands, get off your asses, boys."

Tommy and Landon complain, but they stand and retrieve trash bags.

Peace's hand stays on my shoulder. "Wish you didn't have to go."

I give him a wan smile. I kind of wish it, too, but not as vehemently as I have over the past few weeks. The first surge of longing I felt when I saw him tonight has faded. I look into his earnest face, which is as handsome as ever. Maybe it's all the talk about Ginny coupled with Rollo's outburst—forcing me to acknowledge she's gone, no matter how much we want to believe she's safe. I feel the sharp edges of the twenty-year triangle among Ginny, Peace, and me, reminding me that Peace was the last of us to see her. I don't feel excited or randy. My emotions are along the banal spectrum of tired and heartsore.

"I know," I say, because it can be interpreted many ways.

"Right. PI might be watching."

"Beach tomorrow? It's a safe public venue."

"Yeah. Get some sleep."

"I hope I will." I join Palmer and Jess at the top of the stairs.

As we descend the spiral staircase, I think about Rollo's venting—not only the rant everyone heard but the part to which only I had been privy. Chad Dooley had been printed all over his thoughts like a busy pattern on a cheap shirt, but he hadn't gotten that information from Peace.

We walk down another flight of stairs, through the living room, and out the front door. We decide to leave my car and walk, since we've had a few drinks. At ground level, the nighttime air is stickier. We'll be sweaty by the time we reach the condo. Still, I don't mind wading through the dark early-summer stew with my girls. We've walked this stretch many a night. Shockingly, no one has ever been run over, fallen into the creek, or gotten eaten by a gator.

"Weird about Rollo, huh?" I ask them.

"Sort of. But not really," Jess says.

"I'm convinced Rollo has been in love with Ginny since Miss McCray's class," Palmer says. "Not surprising he'd take her going missing so hard."

I squint so I can see both their faces. "Did either of y'all mention 2013 Chad and Ginny to him?"

"Nope," Jess says. "Before tonight, I hadn't talked to him in months. Got some secondhand info from Landon. That's it."

"Did you tell Landon?" I ask.

"Not that I recall."

"What about you, Palm? Did you mention it to Rollo? Or maybe Tommy?"

"Nope," Palmer replies. "Y'all know I gave up Tommy talk like a Lenten resolution. I haven't talked to Rollo in an age either. Why?"

"Uh... I don't know. Peace thought Rollo would feel worse about Ginny if he knew she was hanging out with Chad. But Peace didn't tell him."

"Then I don't see how he can know," Palmer said.

I don't see how he can know either.

Chapter 22
Ginny, 2013

Rollo picks me up at the bus station in Walterboro. I refuse to go anywhere I might be recognized, which rules out every public venue in Asheburg, from the First Baptist Church to the Waffle House. Our only viable option—the firepit on his dad's land.

We don't say much on the fifty-minute drive out there. He sucks on Tootsie Rolls, and I rest my head on the window and watch soybean fields and pine forests go by, one-story houses and trailers, boarded-up country stores and junky used-car lots, roadside produce stands and pastures dotted with grazing horses. Hardly the walls of ancient Rome or the Arc de Triomphe, but they're familiar monuments nonetheless. I welcome them like a soldier on a long march home.

Rollo keeps the music low. James Taylor and I both have Carolina on our minds. I hum along until James moves on to fire and rain and the agony of losing someone he thought would be around forever.

"You want some water?" Rollo asks.

I nod and hold out my hand. My trembling fingers close around a chilled water bottle. I sip, and water dribbles down my chin. I badly want a *real* drink.

We drive past the Welcome to Asheburg sign. Our old high-school mascot, Al E. Gator, grins at me as if he knows all my secrets.

I close my eyes to block out the gator's leer, and before we drive past Redemption Corner, I doze off.

When I wake up, Rollo has parked, and he has a fire going. He sits on what I think of as the Ladies' Log, where I always sat with LeeLee, Jess, and Palm. He stares at the fire with a beer dangling between his knees.

The skinny, towheaded boy I remember has turned into a wiry man of medium height. He still has white-blond hair, but like a weak economy, it's inching toward recession. Though it's late October, he spends so much time on the water that he still has white circles around his eyes. He wears shorts and a long-sleeved fishing-tournament T-shirt. A tattooed egret stretches its long neck up his calf.

I gingerly open the door, ease out of the truck, and creep across the muddy clearing. "Hi there."

Rollo looks up. "Hey, sleepyhead." His greenish eyes glowing in the firelight remind me of an animated wolf glaring out of the forest, like in a Disney movie, when Snow White or Sleeping Beauty are lost in the woods.

"Or *Beauty and the Beast*," I whisper.

"What's that?"

"Nothing. I got used to talking to myself. A lot of time alone."

He cracks a beer and hands it to me. I chug half of it in a couple of swallows. "You got anything stronger?"

"Got some tequila in the truck. You want to smoke a bowl?"

I nod. After a few nips of tequila and some quality inhalation, my hands stop shaking. I wonder where he gets his weed these days. Certainly not from Chad Dooley.

"Surprising to get a message from the long-lost G-Love via my work email," he says.

"I found it on your dad's website. You're slinging real estate now?"

"When the urge hits me."

"Peace and I broke up," I say.

"I figured." He reaches into his plastic bag of weed and repacks the bowl. "When?"

"About five months ago."

"Damn." He lights up again. "Y'all been together this whole time? What's it been?"

"Over ten years."

A long puff then release. "Y'all ever get married?"

"No." I inhale some of his exhaled smoke. It's strong stuff. The kind that sort of smells like a dead mouse stuck in a wall.

"At least y'all don't have to get divorced."

"Fair point. I need something to be simple in my life. How about you?"

"Nope. Almost. In the end, I couldn't do it." He looks down at the bowl in his hands, turns it over a few times, then looks back at me. "Never felt right enough."

"You have any kids?"

"Any baby-mama drama? Nope. I might be a damn fool about most things, but I know to put on protective gear before going into battle." He grins. "Or at least retreat at the right time."

I push him. "Gross."

"Why you back now? And damn paranoid about seeing anyone. Do that leftover bruise on your face and the cut on your lip have anything to do with it?"

I lean toward the fire. My cheeks warm with a soothing, healing kind of heat. When it gets too intense, I turn to him. "I killed someone, Ro."

"Huh," he says with no obvious surprise. "Figured it might be something bad but not that bad. Who'd you take out?"

"Chad Dooley."

"What?" *Now* he's surprised. He leans back until he has a double chin, even as skinny as he is. "*Asheburg* Dooley?"

I nod, and the whole story tumbles out—how Peace and I hung out a few times with Chad and his Fancy Boots girlfriend, how I was sure Peace slept with her but I also *wasn't* sure. I'd lost my shit on him and run to Dooley, then everything went to hell in a handbasket faster than I could say "dysfunctional relationship with my abusive dealer." "Then, on that last night, I knew—the way I know things. If I didn't leave right away, I'd never get away from him."

"You smothered him while he was hammered." He picks up the tequila bottle and takes a long swig then reaches into his pocket for a Tootsie Roll. "Holy hell, Ginny." He unwraps it and pops it into his mouth. Tootsie Rolls and tequila must be a gross combination, but Rollo is a connoisseur of both. "Then you skipped out? When did this all go down?"

"A couple of weeks ago. I hope it looks like an OD. Happens all the time in Myrtle. Lots of messed-up people there."

"Lots of messed-up people everywhere." He stands and paces before the fire. "So, you need a place to stay?"

"Yeah. I have to figure out what to do next."

"If you stick around here, people will realize you're back. What about your mom?" He kneels in front of me. "You know your dad died, right?"

"I knew before it happened. I called Mama every couple of years—to check in. Last time we spoke, I told her about Daddy. She emailed me after it happened." I swallow a lump in my throat. Odd, since I didn't cry when I read my mother's email about my father's death. It was like reading the obituary of someone I didn't really know but who was rumored to be an asshole.

"You haven't talked to her since this—this issue—came up?"

"I'm not ready to see her."

"Why did you come to me? Why not LeeLee or Palmer or Jess?"

"Because they have their own lives. Mama made sure I knew LeeLee and Palm have a bunch of kids. To make me feel guilty for her lack of grandchildren. Last time I talked to Mama, Jess didn't have any kids yet—"

"Now they do. A little girl. A couple of months ago."

"Awww. Bet she's a cutie."

He shrugs. "I think so, but babies all kinda look the same to me."

"I can't bust up into their happy families. Crazy Aunt Ginny, who happens to be a murderer. Besides, you're the only one who won't judge me."

He wipes my wet cheek with his thumb. Then he smiles. "I'm judging the hell out of you, you wacko."

I laugh, and it feels good.

"But we'll figure something out," he says. "Let me think. My dad has an empty furnished rental on Mercury Road. Maybe you can stay there for a while. Lie low."

"Jesus *wept*. That would be amazing."

"You'll be just outside the Burg, though. Someone might see you at the Piggly Wiggly."

"If I go out, I'll go all paparazzi." I pull the hood of my sweatshirt up over my face "Scarf. Shades. The works."

"You need money?"

"I have a little. I have to get a job. And a car. Then I'll—then I can—" A barking sob, and I reach for the tequila bottle.

He sits beside me and puts his arm around my shoulders. "Hey. Baby steps. Ginny, it's okay. You're home now."

My crying eventually tapers off, and I ask him, "You heard anything about Peace?"

He stiffens. "No. No one has heard from him in years. Not even his dad or Drew."

"We haven't talked since we broke up, but... I still wonder if he would forgive me—"

"Ginny, *come on*."

How many people have said that to me over the years, trying to make me see straight or act right? I've never listened, but I can't ignore Rollo now.

"Peace left you with Chad Dooley," he says. "He's probably run off with that girl—what did you call her?"

"Meredith," I whisper.

"Isn't that what you thought he was doing? Screwing her?"

"Yes, but... No. I don't know. I had a reading—"

"I know your readings are real. But sometimes, you have to look at what's right in front of your damn face. Peace knew you were with Dooley, who used to push you around and supposedly did the same to this Meredith chick. Peace went radio silent. What do you think he's trying to tell you?"

"Maybe he's upset I sent him those photos of me and Chad—"

"Or maybe he was looking for a way out and you gave it to him."

My eyes fill again. Rollo is telling me exactly what I've already figured out.

He stands and paces before the fire again. "You've cried over Peace too many times."

"I know. But... I feel like my mind is clearer since... that last night at Chad's. It's hard for me to sort out what *really* happened from what I *thought* happened, but even if Peace did cheat on me with Meredith, I was..." It's time to admit it. "I was an absolute *nightmare* for years. Peace lived in a war zone. The war was in my head, but I dropped most of my bombs on him."

"That gives him an excuse to abandon you?"

"I don't know. But I'd like to talk to him—try to work something out—"

"You still want him?" He stops and stares down at me.

"I've always wanted him. Even when I didn't know it."

He sits beside me again. "Ginny, I... What if...? I've always..." *Should I tell her? Should I finally say it after all these years?*

I have to save him from saying it. It will change everything. I put my finger against his lips. "Thank you for picking me up. And for listening. And offering to help me."

His voice shakes. "I missed you, Gin."

"I missed you too. You were my best friend."

"What about the girls?"

"They were too. There's a lot of me to go around. I needed four best friends."

"You sure about all this?" He touches the fading bruise on my cheek. "All of it?"

I nod.

"Okay, then." He stands.

"Ro." I get up too fast and sway on my feet. "You know I love you—"

"No. No. No." He holds up his hands. *But you don't love me like I love you.*

"I mean that—"

"Forget it!" He walks to the truck. "Look at this! Pop-up tent. It covers the truck bed. I got a couple of sleeping bags from hunting. We can sleep in here if you want to. I won't touch you. I promise. Tomorrow I'll talk to Dad, and we'll go to the rental."

"You sure you want to... like... sleep in there, together? After... whatever we just *didn't* talk about?" It makes no sense, but it does.

"Yeah. Come on. It's been a decade, right? Let's smoke up and drink up. Get all Bruce Springsteen on this shit. Tell stories about the glory days."

I smile at him, but the light in his eyes suddenly bothers me. Now he looks less like a Disney-movie wolf and more like the real thing.

I'M TOO TIRED TO PULL the all-nighter Rollo has in mind. By midnight, I'm drunk and high—not in a fun way but in the way that makes me want to pass out. Peace must have felt like this on those nights I demanded he party with me—the nights when he popped extra Adderall and drank vodka mixed with Red Bull.

Rollo tucks me into a sleeping bag in the truck bed and says he'll stay awake until the fire dies down. I fall asleep immediately with the sound of cicadas ringing in my ears like buzzing electricity.

In the darkest part of the night, when even the bugs have given up and gone to sleep, I open my eyes. Rollo sleeps beside me. He lies on his side with one hand under his cheek. I don't have a brother, but I couldn't ask for a better stand-in.

I roll onto my back. Deep down, I always knew he wanted more than I did. I feel guilty, as if I've taken advantage of his dedication.

I have to pee, so I slowly unzip my sleeping bag and slide my toes into my flip-flops. Before falling asleep, I climbed into the truck's cab and scrambled into some old pajamas, a plaid button-down sleep shirt a few sizes too big. I chose the least sexy thing I owned for obvious reasons, and as a bonus, the shirt provides easy outdoor potty access.

The embers from our fire provide just enough light. I creep into the borderland where the glow meets the darkness, close enough to pee in private but not far enough to get eaten by a monster. I squat and let it flow. I don't feel drunk, but I don't feel sober either. I straighten, and my head starts ringing. I think the cicadas woke up, but when I get to feeling like some of them are crawling over my hair, I know it's a reading.

Peace is far away, but like the moon, his pull is strong despite the distance. The tide comes in, and the tide goes out, and with each rotation of encroaching water comes a brief reprieve and another deluge.

I press my fingers against my temples, and there's more.

> *LeeLee sits on a second-story piazza in a rocking chair. The house is in downtown Charleston. Her kids are inside, sleeping. A handsome man sits in the chair beside her. He's wearing SpongeBob SquarePants sweatpants. He loves her, and he's terribly sad. He stands and walks into the house then out the back door, up some stairs, and into a room above a garage. LeeLee has a choice to make. She misses Ginny. She wishes she could talk to her old friend about things only the two of them understand.*

It's the future. Not sure when, but I want to be with her when it happens, to sit on that rocker beside her and listen to her and help her make her decision. She's my friend, like Rollo, like Peace was, even when he was a lot more than that. I'm done taking my friends for granted.

As I stand there in the darkness, I understand something with absolute certainty. It has nothing to do with being a navigator, telling stories, or having readings. It's a plain old observation of how life works. I can't be the kind of friend my friends deserve until I get my shit together.

To be ready to help LeeLee when the future rolls around, I have to get sober.

I'M SITTING ON THE Ladies' Log with a blanket draped over my shoulders when Rollo wakes just after dawn. I sip a Sprite from his cooler. Sweetness and carbonation make my tongue tingle—not unlike the tonic I mix with vodka or gin. I clear my throat as if to hack up that thought and spit it out. I'm *done* with all that stuff.

Rollo emerges from the truck bed. He slept in his clothes from last night. He hops into his flip-flops and slaps a visor over his hair. He smacks his lips together as he walks across the clearing.

"You catching any worms, early bird?" he asks.

"Nope," I say. "Just this Sprite and a few peanut butter crackers I found in the glove box."

"My mouth tastes like cow shit."

"How do you know what that tastes like?"

"All the mushrooms I ate back in the day." He stretches his arms over his head. "You want to smoke a bowl? Wake and bake."

Everything in my body yells *yes, yes, yes*. But I speak the opposite. "Nope. Nope. Nope."

"One *no* is enough. We'll save it for later."

"I don't want to save it for later."

He purses his lips and raises one pale eyebrow. "So... you want to smoke it now?"

"No. I don't want to smoke anymore."

"Okay. You want to day drink?"

"I don't want to do that either."

"I'm not following you."

"I want to stop," I say. "Booze. Weed. Pills. Everything. I want to get clean."

"Where did that come from?" He props one foot on the other end of the Ladies' Log. "Last night, you were begging me for tequila."

I almost tell him about the readings, but he won't understand their power. "I was awake a lot last night. Thinking. About people I love."

He looks up at the trees. A few crows stare boldly back at him.

"Like Peace," he says.

"Yes. Like Peace. But also you, my mom, all our friends, LeeLee especially."

"Why LeeLee?"

Again, it's something I can't fully explain, not if I want to keep her secret, like I always promised I would. It's one of the only promises I've ever kept. "The last time I saw her, I said some awful things. I'd like to apologize to her. I want to apologize to my mom for running off on her. And to Peace. And you."

"You don't need to apologize to me for anything."

"I do." I shift in his direction so we're facing each other head-on. "I never fully appreciated you. Even now. You dropped everything to pick me up and brought me out here to the woods. You're straight up with me when I don't want to hear it."

"Jess was too."

"Everyone tried." I smile. "You were always the best at it."

He looks up at the crows again. One of them flies off, as if offended by his nosiness.

"So, you really want to get sober?" he asks.

"I can't make amends until I do."

"I'll help in any way I can. But don't expect me to join you."

"I won't. The world would be a boring place with you and me both on the wagon."

"Damn skippy." He returns to the truck. My guess is he wants a beer from the cooler, but out of respect for my new resolve, he returns with a Sprite.

"How do we do this?" I ask. "I need to be in a place away from all temptation. The house on Mercury Road will be a good start."

"The place has a lockbox. Let's head there. I'll call my dad on the way. You can take a shower there." He gestures around the clearing. "I'll pack up."

"I'll help—"

"Nah. Sit. You need to rest. Going cold turkey won't be easy. You'll feel like shit. You need to keep your strength up."

"I guess you're right." I already feel jittery. My head hurts, and I'm a bit nauseated.

He bustles around the clearing, picking up beer cans and food wrappers. He rolls the sleeping bags and folds the pop-up tent. After thirty minutes, only a thin stream of smoke in the ashes provides evidence we've been here.

He retrieves his sunglasses from the cab and approaches me. "I got an idea." He covers his eyes.

"Does it involve caffeine and cigarettes? 'Cause I still need those for now."

"I'll run into the Refuel. They got decent coffee." He shoves his hands in his pockets. "What about Boot Island? Dad wants me to go out there and make some repairs. You want a place away from everything, where you'll have no temptations. Boot is about as remote as we can get."

"Hmmm." Sunlight seeps through the tree branches, so I shield my eyes when I squint up at him. "How will we get food and stuff?"

"Same way we always do when we go out there. I'll take the boat back and forth. I have about a week's worth of work to do. That should get you through the worst of it. We bought this new compost toilet thing." He smiles. "High tech, girl. All the comforts of home."

The more I think about it, the better it sounds—that peaceful island. No running water, but it's a balmy time of year. I can make do with gallon jugs and swimming in the sound for a few days. I can even deal with a compost toilet, whatever that is.

I smile back. "Actually, that sounds great. What about you? You said you weren't joining me on this endeavor."

"Nope. But I can come ashore and get what I need."

"It's the best chance I have of actually doing this. You know me damn well."

He tousles my hair. "I always have."

Chapter 23
LeeLee, 2015

The next morning, I get up before Palmer and Jess and go for a run up and down the asphalt and dirt roads of Edisto Beach. I jog past the Defense Rests and retrieve my car. The house is quiet, as if the altercation between Peace and Rollo made it uncomfortable too. When I return to the condo, I bustle around the kitchen loudly enough to wake my friends then get in the shower. A couple of hours later, we return to the Defense Rests to start our beach day, but only Rollo and Peace are awake when we arrive.

Jess and Palmer take the golf cart to get doughnuts. I stay at the house and FaceTime my kids. The boys bounce in and out of the frame. They show me their pancake breakfast and update me on the weekend's victories and failures.

Trey made the pancake mix by himself—"I used the measuring cups, Mama."

Bowman asks for the thousandth time if we can keep the fat orange cat that sunbathes in our driveway—"I know he's the neighbor's kitty, but he's my best favorite friend!"

Malachy had a pee-pee accident yesterday after school, but in a dramatic turn of events, he made it through the night without wetting his Pull-Ups. He wants to keep it like a potty training trophy—"Here 'tis, Mama! See? All dry!"

Clay appears in the frame a few times as he cleans up the breakfast dishes, but he never moves into position to peer over my shoulder and look for Peace.

As the boys lose interest, I call out to him. "Hey, Clay, I'll let y'all go, okay?"

He responds from somewhere in the kitchen. "Sounds good, Lee. We'll talk to you later."

The boys and I trade endearments, then the call ends. I'm perversely glad I have something pressing to take my mind off my family's wholesome Saturday morning without me. I walk downstairs to the garage under the house, where the Smiths store their beach gear. Peace and Rollo are talking down there. I stop at the end of the staircase, out of sight.

"You wanted me to fix the damn golf cart, right? Forget about last night," Rollo says.

"No, man. You lost your shit."

"I was drunk."

"Normally, when you're drunk, you're the one telling the stories and making jokes," Peace says. "Don't act like last night's performance was your standard routine. It wasn't stand-up comedy. It was a tragic monologue."

"You sound like LeeLee, all book nerdy. You sleeping with her yet?"

"I love you, dude, but that's *none* of your business. You being pissed at me is our business."

"Fine. I *was* mad. I was lit from the shots we took on the boat. I started thinking about you leaving Ginny alone. You *know* how she hates to be alone."

"I know. But I also know I couldn't live with her anymore—"

"With Dooley, dude. With Chad fuckin' Dooley."

"How do you know she was with Dooley?" Peace asks.

I peer around the corner. Rollo stands beside a golf cart with a screwdriver in his hand.

"Uh. Her mom told me. She called Cheryl and told her." Rollo's thoughts say otherwise. *Damn it, keep my mouth shut. Shouldn't have smoked as soon as I got up...*

"Oh. Okay." Peace leans on the garage wall. "Listen, Ro. I wish I had called Cheryl myself. I know it was messed up, but—"

"It's done, okay? I said my piece, Peace."

"Don't shut me down. We need to sort this out. You gotta understand—"

Rollo jams the screwdriver into the golf cart's open battery compartment. "I'll never understand what was between you and Ginny. Maybe I don't want to."

"I know you always had a thing for her—"

"A *thing*?" Rollo chuckles. "You make it sound like we're still in high school."

"You know what I mean."

"Doesn't matter, since she never had a *thing* for me."

"That's my fault?"

"It's nobody's fault." Rollo wiggles the screwdriver, and the golf cart's lights flash. "It is what it is."

It's a lot of emotionally charged talk between two country boys, and they seem to have hit a testosterone wall. I close my eyes, but somehow, I still squint. I strain to find their thoughts, half-hidden in a darkness saturated by self-reproach and anxiety.

Peace: *I didn't know you had it that bad for her. Now I feel guilty. How did I not know?*

Rollo: *I wish this conversation would end. I wish I hadn't come this weekend. What was I thinking?*

"I'm *sorry*, man," Peace says.

I peek around the corner at Rollo again.

Tell him what he wants to hear... Rollo grins like a panting possum. "It's all good. Maybe I needed to get it off my chest. I feel better now. Seriously."

"You sure? I hate for this to ruin the weekend."

"I'm sure. Let me finish this, or someone will be walking to the beach."

"Cool. I'll head up and see if Tommy and Lands are awake."

Peace's flip-flops crunch on gravel as he walks toward the staircase. I flee upstairs with my heart pumping and blood zooming through my veins like the cars on Trey's electric racetrack. Rollo knows something. I'm sure of it.

Peace opens the garage door and smiles when he sees me in the kitchen. "Hey, you. Good morning."

"Hey." I wave him toward me. "Come out here—on the porch."

"Everything okay with the kids? Did Clay—"

I grab his arm, drag him onto the porch, and shut the sliding glass door. "Rollo knows something."

He looks at me blankly. "About what?"

"About Ginny! He knew about Chad, and none of us told him—"

"He said Cheryl told him."

"That was a lie. Cheryl visited me at my office, and she didn't know anything about Dooley. Besides, I just *know* he knows. I can't explain it. You have to trust me. We have to figure out *how* he knows. Look through his stuff, maybe—"

"Lee. You're not making sense."

The need for Peace to believe me tugs on my deeply entrenched secrecy, like the other boys trying to wrench him out of the pluff mud all those years ago. I can't ignore Rollo's thoughts—not with Ginny missing and Chad dead and no other leads on what happened to her. After twenty years, it's time to tell Peace. Clay took it well. Peace knows Ginny has this kind of power, so he'll know it's possible. He was relieved to escape from Ginny's abilities, but I'm not Ginny, and he said he loves me. One last yank, and my secret finally dislodges from the viscous muck of fear and insecurity.

"I *am* making sense, P.," I say, "because I read Rollo's thoughts."

Peace pales under yesterday's sunburn. "What do you mean?"

"I'm like Ginny."

"No."

"*Yes.* I am. I can read thoughts. I have readings." I choose Ginny's name for it. It feels more powerful. "I'm a navigator—like her."

"LeeLee. *Please* be serious."

"I'm as serious as the good Lord on Judgment Day." I rummage in my memory for something to prove it. I think about everyone talking about their fears at my first firepit. Then I remember something better. "That first time I went to Boot with y'all. Remember how I jumped off your back?"

"Of course. 'The Time LeeLee Stranded Peace up to His Butt Crack in Pluff Mud.'"

"Exactly. I never told you why I jumped."

"I figured you were afraid to fall in the mud—"

"I jumped because I read your thoughts. 'It feels so good to be close to her.' Over and over. I was having the same kind of thoughts. The guilt was too much with Ginny waving and smiling. I had to break the connection, so I jumped."

"Okay. Okay. Okay." He keeps saying it, as if trying to convince himself of the okay-ness of it all and failing completely. He sits on the wicker sofa in a heap. "Now you're saying you heard Rollo thinking about Ginny—"

"Last night, he was thinking about *Dooley*. That's why I asked if you told him. You said no. I asked the girls. They hadn't said anything to anyone either. I was on the stairs, and I heard y'all talking. Rollo was thinking he shouldn't have said Cheryl told him about Dooley because it's a lie. He wants to leave and thinks he made a stupid decision coming here this weekend."

"So you're saying—"

"I think Ginny told him about Dooley, which means he's talked to her sometime in the last few years."

Peace runs a hand through his hair. "Okay... but wait. You're like Ginny, and you never told me?"

"I never told you because I *hate* being this way," I say. "I've always tried to stop it. Ginny and her mom are the only people who know—well, Clay knows. But I just told him too."

"I *cannot* believe this." He leans back against the cheerful floral cushions with his legs splayed out before him. "What are the chances the two women I've loved most in my life would both have this bizarre ability?"

"So now I'm *bizarre*?" I twirl my finger beside my temple.

"No! But—after everything I went through with Ginny—"

"I'm *not* Ginny! I told you. I've fought it my whole life. She embraced it, welcomed it, wanted it."

"But can you control it?"

"I can block it most of the time if I want to. But lately... I don't know. Maybe I'm tired of keeping it a secret. It's a huge part of who I am, whether I want it or not. I have to accept it." I swallow. "I need the people in my life to accept it too. It's part of my baggage."

"Lee. This isn't *normal baggage*. It's complicated—"

"Like a drug addiction in remission isn't complicated?" I scowl.

"You're right." He stands and takes a step toward me. "I don't know what I'm saying. I need to process this—"

I back away. "Right now, what *we* need to do is understand what Rollo knows about Ginny. Screw you and me and our baggage for the moment."

He looks at me with anguished eyes, but he nods. "What do you want me to do?"

I turn in a circle with my hands on my hips. "When y'all go to the beach, I'll stay here. I'll go through his room."

"What are you looking for?"

"I don't know yet. It might be something real. It might be—"

"A reading?"

I nod. "Yup. That's what I'm hoping for. And if you don't like it, too bad."

"If it will help us find Ginny, do what you have to do."

AN HOUR LATER, I STAND in the first-floor guest room. I unzip Rollo's messy weekend bag and start fishing around. The old clock on the wall tick-tick-ticks in time with my heartbeat. *How did Rollo sleep in here with that thing rattling away?* My hands close on a bulging bag of marijuana. Bingo. Weed can be as effective as Ambien.

With every tick-tock, I imagine the sound of creaking stairs, the door opening behind me, Rollo asking me what the hell I'm doing with my hands on his underwear.

By the time I get to the bottom of the bag, it seems I'm fondling his boxer briefs for nothing. I haven't run across anything likely to spark a reading. Neither his electric razor nor his travel toothbrush gives off any supernatural vibes. I scowl down into the bag like I'm leaning over a stinky diaper pail. Governor's Cup Fishing Tournament T-shirt. *Nothing.* Bathing suit with pink flowers all over it. *Nope.* Pipe with a spiky green weed leaf decal on the bowl. *Not very subtle, Ro.* But still, nada. Zip. Zilch.

"Ginny, damn it," I whisper as I rearrange everything into Rollo's version of man tidy. "You're the navigator. Show me the way!"

I feel something. A tingle spreads from my forehead to the base of my skull, like warm water running over my head at a salon shampoo bowl. Ginny isn't with me, but her thoughts are. I've never read someone's thoughts from a distance—a distance that could include time as well as space—but maybe our talent connects us in ways we still don't understand. I hear her voice in my mind, see her bubbly handwriting.

The pocket, LeeLee... the pocket inside the pocket inside the pocket...

I already went through the bag's pockets, but I try again. Nothing. I reach into the large panel on the inside then unzip the interior pocket in that. I run my fingers along the lining and find another seam.

I poke one finger into it and touch a plastic bag.

My mouth hangs open as I pull it out and hold the bag before my eyes. It contains a lock of red-gold hair covered in reddish brown dust. I open the green Ziploc seam.

Cinnamon wafts from the bag—Cheryl's snooder-dooders, comfort, understanding, laughter.

The reading comes on like an unexpected tsunami. The colors of an early-summer morning inundate my mind. It could be yesterday, or it could be years ago.

> *The marsh. Woods behind it. A skinny beach morphs into a mudflat covered in oyster shells. Low tide. If LeeLee were really here—wherever here is or was—she'd be standing in the water herself. As it is, she can't take a step forward or back because the water is dark and she's not wearing shoes. Oyster shells wait in the murky darkness to rip holes in LeeLee's feet.*
>
> *Ginny wears a white T-shirt and jean shorts. She's barefoot in the dry sand. Her back is to LeeLee, like one of the women on Palmer's books, but LeeLee would know that hair anywhere. Ginny turns, shades her eyes, and looks over the horizon. LeeLee waves, but then she remembers Ginny can't see her. Ginny turns toward the woods and walks away. In*

LeeLee's dream at Jess's house, she left Ginny in the incoming tide, but this time, Ginny leaves Lee in the mud.

The reading fades like old print on a worn page. I frantically look around for a landmark.

To LeeLee's right, nothing. To her left, however, there's an old fishing boat. LeeLee hasn't been to Boot Island in fifteen years, and the writing has weathered since then, but she makes out the vestiges of its name in red paint, Good Times.

Chapter 24

Ginny, 2013

My detox week fully delivers—I mean like the UPS man drops an overnight package of agony on my entire being—headaches, backaches, muscle aches, chills, sweats, nausea, vertigo, tremors, stiffness. In a stubbly salute to the term *cold turkey*, goose bumps appear over my whole body. Worst of all, the brand-new compost toilet becomes my new best friend. I forbid Rollo from going into the little water closet and make him relieve himself outside. It's too embarrassing for someone else to be in there after my entire digestive system turns itself inside out. If I had the chance, I would swallow ten oxy and wash them down with grain alcohol. I beg Rollo to take me back to the mainland and get me something to make it all go away.

"No can do, Gin," he says. "That's how people OD for real."

"I give up. I can't do this. Can people die from alcohol withdrawal?"

"I researched it online before we came out here. It's possible but rare. You'd have to have DTs."

"Delirium tremens?" My teeth chatter. "I bet that's what's happening right now. Please, let's go back. I need to go to the hospital. Please, Rollo—"

"Nope. If you had DTs, you'd be hallucinating, feel confused. Either of those happening?"

"No, but hallucinations are the norm for me—"

"I'm not talking about your readings. I'm talking about straight psychedelic shit. You don't seem confused either. You're as bossy as ever. You know where you are? Who you are? What year it is?"

"I'm Ginny Blankenship. It's October 2013, and I'm in hell on Boot Island."

"See? You're good. Withdrawing off the pills is making you feel worse—"

"That will definitely kill me." I yawn like a roaring lion. "What the hell is up with all this yawning?"

"Yawning is another symptom."

His calmly rational demeanor makes me want to scream. "You're an addictions counselor now, huh?"

"I told you. I did some research to make sure you'd be safe out here. Opioid withdrawal doesn't kill anyone. It only feels like it will. You're stronger than this, Ginny."

I rock back and forth. My head is splitting, as if I'm having a reading of the whole history of human civilization.

Rollo holds my shoulders and makes me be still. "If I sense you're in any danger, I'll slap you on that boat and haul ass across the water, call an ambulance on the way. You'll be at Ashepoo General within a couple of hours."

"You can't leave me."

"I'll be here. I promise." His thoughts make it through my pain. *I won't leave you. I'm not Peace.*

I sleep when I can, and the days tick by. Rollo tries to keep the sawing and hammering to a minimum as he works on the cabin. He messes with the generator, patches up the roof, fixes all the screens, puts some bars over the windows to keep the island's raccoon population at bay. He quietly goes about his work with his headphones on. I wake from fitful naps to find him sitting beside me, reading a fishing magazine.

I wonder how the hell I inspire such loyalty in him. Or in Peace, who tolerated my antics for years. What do they see in me? As I lie there on a skinny mattress, under a blanket, while simultaneously sweating and freezing my ass off, I surely don't know.

After several days, my symptoms ease up, then exhaustion catches up with me. I sleep away another few days. I lose an ungodly amount of weight, but the cabin doesn't have any mirrors. My reflection can't stare back at me like an animated corpse. When I feel alive enough, I tell Rollo I want to wash off in the old metal tub. He's lugged dozens of gallon jugs of water to Boot over the years. We have plenty to spare.

I sit on the edge of my cot in what passes for the cottage's living space. No matter how much bug spray we spritz or how many citronella candles we burn, the mosquitos of Boot Island never surrender, and I smell like sweat and OFF! Deep Woods.

"Don't get too close to me," I say to Rollo. "I'm toxic."

"No arguing with you there." He cuts off the tops of gallon jugs with a fishing knife and slowly fills the tub. "That looks about right. None of the boys use this tub. We dump water on our heads."

"Thanks for filling it up."

"Sure." He retrieves soap and shampoo from the cabinet, sets the bottles beside the tub, then hands me an old towel.

"Umm... I gotta—" I motion to my clothes, a pair of black exercise shorts and a green tank top.

"Oh, right. Sorry." He backs away. "I'll be outside."

I nod. "Thank you again."

He walks out and shuts the door behind him.

I strip down and climb into the cool water. I don't mind the chill. I do mind the sight of my jutting hip bones, but the water feels like heaven. I wash my hair and splash until suds fill the tub. "Wish I had a rubber duckie," I whisper as wobbly bubbles balance on my fingertips.

The cold eventually sets in, and I reach for the towel. I stand to the sounds of rustling and something banging on the front porch. I wonder if Rollo is spying on me. It feels disloyal to think that about him. He's been so good to me the past week. He's been my savior.

I wish I loved him like he loves me. There's no reason *not* to love him. I try to feel something for him as I squeeze my hair dry. Don't get me wrong. I *do* love Rollo, but when I picture myself kissing him, it's terribly, awfully wrong.

I guess I'm an idiot. That man adores me and will do anything for me. I don't want him.

I retrieve under-stuff, clean shorts, and a Myrtle Beach House of Blues T-shirt from my trusty duffel bag. I run a brush through my hair then open a small makeup compact from my toiletry bag. My eyes and the dark circles under them fill the little mirror.

"Hey, Gin?" Rollo's voice comes from outside the cabin. "Can I come in? The mosquitoes have about sucked me dry."

"Shoot! Of course." I turn toward the door as he enters the cabin. The room spins, and I sit on the bed. "Whoa."

"Take it easy. You hungry? I can heat up some chicken noodle soup."

For the first time in days, I want to eat. "That sounds amazing."

He heats soup on the little gas stovetop. We sit at the table beside the barred window and eat soup, Cheez-Its, and apples. I drink a Sprite.

I eat and slurp too quickly and clutch at my belly. "My stomach is the size of one of those apples."

"Then don't fill it too fast." He looks at the pile of groceries. "I should get more supplies."

"You think we need to? I feel a lot better. We can head back in a couple of days. Did you talk to your dad about the place on Mercury Road?"

"I forgot to tell you. He leased it."

My heart sinks. "Oh. Does he have anything else open? Maybe I can look for a job. Or now that my mind is clearer, I might stay with my mom—if she'll have me."

"I'm sure she will, but do you want to rush it? It's so nice out here. Quiet. No temptations. No complications."

I smile. "That bathtub was kind of complicated. And there's no phone service. That toilet is nice as port-a-potties go, but I'd love to sit my butt on a real porcelain throne. And of course, we're sitting on five acres of slowly eroding land in the middle of the Saint Helena Sound."

"I don't think you should risk it."

"I'll have to get used to temptation—"

"It's only been eight days," he says.

"Gosh. I thought it was more like six. Has it been that long?"

"Let's wait a bit, see how you feel. This is the first time you've managed to get up and get around." He points at the pile of books in the corner. "My dad brought those out here. Maybe pick up a few. Relax, Ginny."

"I guess a few more days won't hurt."

"I'll run back to the mainland tomorrow and go to the grocery store. I need to fatten you up. I'll get some steaks and put 'em on ice, some potatoes. Sound good?"

"Sounds yummy. Can you take some of my clothes back and wash them?"

"Sure. You need anything else?"

"No. Not if we're only going to be here for a few more days." I pause because I don't know how to fully express my gratitude. I go with simple. "Thank you. For caring so much."

"I've always cared this much." He takes my hand and smiles. "But you see it now. Don't you see it?"

"Yes. I do." I gently remove my hand from his.

His face falls, and suddenly, he looks old, not just perpetually tan but weathered by the wind and sea salt and hard living. "But you don't feel different."

"Ro. I told you. You're my best friend. I don't want to hurt you—"

"It's okay. I won't bring it up again." He stands and pats my shoulder.

THREE DAYS LATER, I wake to a chill on an early-November day. Withdrawal has nothing to do with those shivers—it's a natural cool brought on by the changing seasons. I've always loved fall in the Lowcountry. Bright-green marsh grass fades to gold and auburn, the color of hazel eyes in the sunlight—it's our version of fall foliage. In a place known for its blinding sunshine, the clearest days of the year are ahead of us. I have the urge to get outside and breathe fresh air through a marijuana-free nose, even if cigarette smoke still dulls my nostrils.

I spent the last ten years or so beside the Atlantic, in Panama City then in Myrtle Beach. I love the ocean, but without wide-open marsh and the endless creeks that wind through it, it isn't *right*.

"Lord, if you're up there in those clouds, thank you." I put my feet on the floor. "Ginny B. is home."

I stand and get a Coke from the ice-filled Yeti cooler. Rollo left a fresh pack of Marlboro Lights on the kitchen table. I pick at the cellophane wrapper. Caffeine and nicotine, the last soldiers of my addiction. As Rollo said, baby steps. My physical symptoms have eased, but the cravings are still there.

If I plan to reenter society, I'll need some support from people who have walked in my shoes. Peace dragged me to AA a couple of times, but I found the meetings embarrassing and the people self-righteous. I wasn't ready then, but I'm raring to go now. If I had phone service, I would look up a meeting in Asheburg so I could crash one as soon as possible.

I picture my hypothetical AA sponsor. She'll be a woman in her fifties with twenty years of sobriety. She'll wear longish jean shorts. Have no butt, big boobs, feathered hair. She'll tell stories about growing up in a trailer with no air-conditioning to show me what made for a truly hard life. She'll keep my ass in line. Her name will be Pam or maybe Tammy. Someday, I'll be a Pam or a Tammy to some younger woman myself.

The Coke tastes delicious. Maybe I'll never give up caffeine. It's perfectly respectable, but the cigarettes will have to go eventually. As I drop a cig into my hand and pick up my lighter, I notice an ashtray on the table. Odd, since Rollo doesn't like anyone smoking in the cabin.

"Hey, Ro, you up?" I call up to the loft where Rollo sleeps. "Ro?"

I climb the stairs and poke my head into the loft, but Rollo isn't there, and he's already made his bed. I go back downstairs. His boots aren't beside the door. He must have gone out to check on the boat. Or the generator. Something like that.

I balance my Coke and lighter in one hand and an apple and my unlit cigarette in the other. My Coke-can hand grabs for the doorknob. I reach around the can with fingers like tentacles, but the knob is stuck. I jiggle it and drop my lighter. "Damn it."

I deposit the Coke on the floor beside the lighter and turn the knob, but it doesn't budge.

"Huh." I twist it harder. Nothing.

I peer through the slat between the dead bolt and the door. It's locked too.

"What the hell. Rollo? Ro!"

No matter how I shake it, the door won't budge. I stand on tiptoe, but I'm not tall enough to see anything but trees through the door's one small window.

I spin and eyeball the cabin's single main room. Rollo has stocked up on groceries and supplies, including a Costco-sized bag of Tootsie Rolls. More than we need if we plan to be here for a few days. Then there's the brand-new ashtray—bought in case someone would *have* to smoke inside the cabin.

My feet carry me across the planked wood floors of their own accord. I yank at each of the four small windows. They open, but Rollo put bars on them. He wasn't necessarily trying to keep the raccoons out. Maybe he was equally interested in keeping me in.

I climb the rickety stairs again and step into the tidy loft. Rollo's small black duffel bag is gone. I yank the flimsy curtain back from the window. More bars.

My breath comes in panicky gasps as my brain dumps adrenaline into my still-delicate bloodstream. I haven't rushed in weeks, and my recovering body can't handle it. The floor seems to shift below my feet, as if the boards have rotted and given way. I sink onto the bed and gulp air like a fish pumping water through its gills.

Out of the blue, I remember that unfinished reading—in this damn cabin, almost twenty years ago. It wasn't about Rollo's great-great-grandpa murdering someone out here. My power tried to warn me about the future. *My future.* Now, I understand.

Catastrophically claustrophobic.

I clutch the blanket, and something crinkles in my hand—paper, not polyester, a sheet ripped from a spiral notebook. The blue ink is written in Rollo's cramped handwriting.

Ginny, you must have come up looking for me if you're reading this. If you've already checked the windows and doors, maybe you're confused. Don't be. You're not ready to leave yet. It's too much for you back in town. You'll be using again in an hour, even after all we've been through. I locked the doors because you shouldn't wander around the island alone. You could get bitten by a copperhead or something. You'll be safe inside. You have plenty of food and water. I got a bunch of those lady magazines for you, and you have Dad's books. I'll only be gone a couple of days. I do have to work sometimes!

Remember, it's for your safety and to help you get healthy like you said you want to be. You need time to ride this thing out. It's not forever. You got to trust me. Haven't I taken care of you so far?

Love, Rollo

PS: There's an ashtray on the table.

I reread the note several times before it sinks in. Rollo trapped me out here. He said it's for my safety, and I need to ride this thing out, but something tells me there is only one conclusion he wants me to reach. He hopes I'll decide I want to be with him. If that was never a possibility before, it's beyond all imagining once he makes me a prisoner.

It's not forever. Until it is.

Chapter 25
LeeLee, 2015

I leave Rollo's room and text Peace. *I found something. I can't explain it over text. When will y'all be back?*

Peace answers within minutes. *Not sure. Everyone seems to be having a good time, but Rollo is kind of quiet.*

Me: *Can you get him to come back here with you?*

Peace: *Why, what are you going to do?*

Me: *I don't know yet, but I have to confront him. Just get him back here, K?*

Peace: *Okay. I'll figure something out.*

For the next hour, I sit at the countertop in the kitchen and strategize. If I flat-out ask Rollo, he'll deny knowing anything about Ginny. If he wanted us to know he's talked to her, he would have told us. He might claim he's had that lock of hair for twenty years. Reading something from him—thoughts, memories—is my best chance, but I worry I won't have enough control.

The glass door opens, and Rollo and Peace walk in.

I force a smile. "Y'all are back!"

"Ro's gonna help me fill a second cooler," Peace says. "If we're gonna be down there all day, we need reinforcements."

Rollo twists his head from left to right. The sound of his neck cracking gives me the heebie-jeebies.

"I'll bring up ice from the garage freezer, P.," he says. "But I didn't sleep well last night, so I'm heading home soon."

"Don't leave yet!" I smile harder. "The party just started."

"We're going to Dockside tonight," Peace adds. "The Crab Pot Trio is playing."

"Can't believe those guys are still at it," Rollo says. "Y'all have fun. I got... some stuff I gotta take care of. But I'll get the ice." He disappears down the garage stairway.

"Damn it," I whisper to Peace. "He can't leave yet—"

"What the hell did you find?"

"A lock of Ginny's hair—"

His eyes bug from his head like ripe blueberries. "No *way*. You serious?"

"But I *saw* something. I saw Ginny. On Boot Island."

"Holy *shit*. When? Like back when we were kids?"

"No. I don't know when. But it wasn't teenage Ginny. She was a woman." My voice catches. "What if—what if Rollo took her out there and, like—"

Rollo's footsteps thud on the stairs. He appears with two twenty-pound bags of ice on his shoulders. "Hey, man. Is this enough—"

One of the bags splits. Half-melted ice cubes shoot all over the floor.

"Crap!" Rollo says. "Peace, hand me some towels."

Rollo strips off his T-shirt and swishes it over the ice cubes like an ineffective mop. Peace stares at me as he grabs a beach towel from the counter. His anxious face mirrors his thoughts. *What do we do now? What do we do...?*

I grip the edge of the tile countertop and try to calm my nerves. For Ginny, I have to open the floodgates. I asked for her help earlier, and I got something. I reach out to her across the river of space and time dividing us.

The dream from Jess's guest room comes back to me once again. Ginny had been lost in the water while I dillydallied in the pluff mud, and when I looked down, rivulets of water ran over my bare feet. The inward tide. Slow and steady, but there is no force like it on earth.

I know what to do. As I let go of the countertop, I gingerly loosen the psychological fist that has gripped my power for years. I release the pressure slowly, like easing the cork out of a champagne bottle.

My heartbeat slows, and my senses sharpen. The ice cubes clink against one another as Rollo tries to scoop them up. I stand and walk into the aroma of his aftershave or deodorant—a product in a black bottle with an absurdly manly name like Winter Ice or Fiery Mint or Testosterone Pine—with an undertone of banana-scented sunscreen. And something fishy, literally and figuratively.

Rollo's tanned and tattooed bare back is to me. My tunnel vision zeroes in on the artwork covering his spine and shoulder. His older tats have faded—a smiling hippie sun, a marlin, a Celtic cross, and some Chinese calligraphy that probably doesn't mean what he thinks it means. One small design sticks out from the rest. It's fresher, sharper, about the size of a silver dollar. A compass, pointing at the initials *V.E.B.*

Rollo's true north. *Sometimes, the compass finds the navigator.*

"Let me help you, Ro." I press the blue-and-green compass with my index finger. It's an elevator button leading to the upper floors of my consciousness.

Here goes my tingly head again. The reading comes on hard, like the one last night. As if Ginny herself sent it to me, it's as clear as the ice cubes Rollo spilled all over Old Peace's linoleum.

Ginny and Rollo stand on the skinny beach. Rollo's boat behind them, anchored offshore.

Ginny pacing. Screaming. "What am I? Your pet poodle?"

"I told you," Rollo says. "It's for your own good. Look how worked up you are. You can't handle the stress of going back."

"I'm worked up because you've kept me out here against my will for a month—or more. Hell, I don't even know anymore! I want to get on that boat and go home!"

"Where is that, exactly?" Rollo asks.

"I want my mother!" Ginny screams.

"You came to me, not your mother. Now, let's go back inside."

"No! I'm never going in that cabin again! You can't make me!" She storms toward the water as if to wade to the boat.

Rollo pulls something black and pointy from his pocket. He brandishes the gun at her. "We're walking back to the cabin."

"You wouldn't."

"Why wouldn't I?" he demands. "No one knows you're out here."

"You told me you loved me. Now you're threatening to kill me? You're insane."

"What do I have to lose?" Rollo asks. "Maybe I'll kill myself too. Not much left for me if you're gone. I haven't decided yet. But I have decided you're not leaving. So you listen to me, Virginia Emily. You walk your happy ass back to that cabin right now."

The reading fades, and I stare at my hand on Rollo's shoulder. He looks up at me. "What's up, Lee?"

Only the need to get information from him keeps me from throttling him right then and there. "That's what you're about to tell us."

ROLLO STRAIGHTENS AND smiles, but his grin stops below his eyes. His mouth moves, but his eyes stay blank except for a twitch here and there—like the Japanese-animation version of a South Carolina bubba.

I lean toward him until our noses about touch. "Where is she?"

"Who are you talking about, LeeLee." It should be a question, but it's not. It's a bland statement.

That tells me he knows exactly who I'm talking about.

"Don't give me that shit. *Ginny.* Is she still on Boot Island?"

His green cartoon eyes vibrate in their sockets. Peace walks into the kitchen with a dustbin in one hand.

"Ginny isn't on Boot Island." Still eerily monotone. Nothing like Rollo's usual singsong voice.

"She *was* there. You *took* her there. So if she's not there, then it's because *you* did something to her."

Rollo turns to Peace. "You hear this, P.? Your girl thinks Ginny is on Boot Island."

"Is she, Ro?" Peace asks, as if Ginny ran up to the gas station for a pack of smokes.

"If anyone knows where she is, it's *you*," Rollo says. "You were the last one to see her two years ago."

"I thought Chad Dooley was the last one to see her," Peace says. "That's what you're mad about, right? Me leaving her with Dooley."

"Well, yeah. Of course it was Dooley. But you were the last one to see her before him. Or... whatever." He clears his throat. "How do we know she was with Dooley at all?"

"You said she told Cheryl and Cheryl told you." Peace picks up his phone. "But I've talked to Cheryl a lot the past few weeks. She never mentioned anything about Dooley."

"When I saw Cheryl," I say, "she didn't know anything about Dooley at all."

"Maybe... I heard about Dooley from someone else. Reesie—his sister—"

"Reesie Dooley is dead," I say. "So is Chad's mother."

"Look at you, Lee. The Inspector Gadget of Asheburg." Rollo points at the widening puddle of water and ice cubes. "Sorry I don't have time to clean that up. I'm gonna get going—"

"You're not going anywhere. You're staying *right* goddamn here, friend." Peace's usual cool, calm, collected veneer cracks.

"I am leaving, *friend*," Rollo says. "I got shit to do, and none of it includes listening to LeeLee spout off some craziness about Ginny and Boot Island."

"Is she still out there or not?" My eyes narrow. "Did you do something terrible to her?"

"It's Peace who did something terrible to her. If anything happened to her, he did it! Everyone in town thinks so. Cheryl. Even his own damn brother." Rollo jabs a finger in my direction. "But *you* don't care. You're a shitty friend now, like you were back when you started screwing him."

"Don't turn this on me—"

"To hell with y'all! I'm leaving." He strides past us, but Peace grabs him by the nape and spins him around. He throws Rollo across the room. The sofa skids backward when he hits it.

"You're not leaving until you start making some sense," Peace says.

"Your girlfriend here—your *married* girlfriend—she's the one who isn't making sense!"

I'm no trial attorney. I hate the pressure of standing before a judge with everything depending on what I say. I prefer to write a compelling argument, where I control all the headings, subheadings, and sources of material—no matter. With Rollo sprawled on that blue-and-white nautical-striped sofa, oozing subterfuge and projections, I start firing questions at him like Atticus Finch.

"Did *you* send the email to me and Jess and Palmer blaming Peace for killing Ginny?"

"No. I never—"

"Why'd you do it? Did you kill her yourself?"

"No!" he says.

"You wanted to frame Peace, right? Because you're jealous she never loved you—"

"Shut up, LeeLee!"

"She always loved him and not you, and you can't stand it. So you dragged her out to Boot Island, and you wouldn't let her leave! You threatened to kill her, to shoot her and yourself. Right there on the beach! 'Get your happy ass back to that cabin, Virginia Emily—'"

"Holy shit." Rollo's eyes widen. "No. No! I'd never really hurt her. If I knew where she is—was—but I don't—"

"You killed her, didn't you? *Didn't you?*"

"I didn't!" He grabs the sides of his head. "How did you know? No one else was there..."

"You *actually* took Ginny out to Boot Island and trapped her there? You really did that?" An incredulous Peace needs clarification. "Have you lost your mind?"

Rollo stands. "Don't you say shit to me after *you* left her! She came to *me*. Asked *me* for help. I took her out there and helped her get sober. I was there for her when none of you assholes were. It was *me*! You never did shit for Ginny or anyone else in your miserable, pointless life!" Rollo snorts. "You ruined Ginny's life. Watch out, LeeLee. He'll ruin your life too."

"Shut. Your. *Mouth,*" Peace says.

"I don't give a shit if Ginny wants me or not anymore." Rollo's laugh sounds mildly insane. "I want to keep her safe from *you*. You sorry excuse for a—"

Peace charges Rollo like the D1 college football player he once was. This time, the sofa bangs against the wall when Rollo hits it. Peace punches him twice in the stomach then in the nose. Blood pours from Rollo's face. He covers his head with his arms, but Peace keeps pummeling him. He holds him down on the sofa with a knee in his stomach.

"Is she still on Boot? Did you hurt her?" He shakes Rollo. "Where is she?"

"Peace!" I wrap my arms around his waist.

Noise behind me. Landon's flummoxed voice. "Holy shit—what the hell?"

I yank, and Peace falls away from Rollo. We stumble, and he catches me. He turns back to Rollo, but Landon is between them. He and Tommy hold Peace's arms.

"Tell us where she is, you fucking lunatic!" Peace struggles against them like a bull working its way out of a rodeo shoot.

Jess and Palmer flutter beside me and pelt me with questions—"Are you okay?" "What happened?" "What are they fighting about?"

"Call the police," I say as I gulp air.

"About what?" Palmer asks. "Good God in heaven, what the hell is going on?"

"About Ginny," I say.

"Oh, no. Is she—does Rollo—"

"I don't know. But we need to go to Boot Island."

TOMMY AND LANDON TRAP Rollo on the sofa. Whenever he tries to stand, Landon shoves him down again. Jess retrieves a towel for his bloody face, but she makes sure to give him her opinion. "I'm not doing this for your sake, you murderer. It's for the furniture's sake."

"Is he a murderer?" Palmer whispers to me. She's been crying. Her bright-blue eyes are so bloodshot they're almost purple.

"He won't give us a straight answer. He wants a lawyer. And it's surely not me."

"I can't even... What if she's out there, but she's... she's...?"

I hug her. I know what she means, as old friends do. Neither of us has to finish her awful sentence.

Not much happens at Edisto Beach, so we don't wait long for the police. We all back away when two officers arrive to cart Rollo off to wherever the Edisto Beach PD houses the rare criminals who end up in their hands. We stand in a quiet semicircle around the living room, like summer campers about to play a cringy icebreaker game. Rollo doesn't struggle. He acknowledges the cops as they read him his rights and handcuff him, but otherwise, he says nothing other than a soft request to call his father.

"You gonna walk out of here quietly?" the officer asks.

"Yes, sir."

Rollo shuffles toward the sliding glass door, one officer in front of him and one behind, like they're leading the elephant in the room back to the circus. He stops before he steps across the threshold and looks back at us.

"Y'all judge me," he says. "Thinking you're Ginny's *true friends* and whatnot. But we'll see who stands by her. I'll be the one to keep her secret."

Palmer whispers to me again. "What's he talking about?"

"Who knows?" I say. "Only Ginny can answer that question. And she can only answer it if we find her alive."

THE POLICE LIEUTENANT, Kyle Somebody, graduated from Ashepoo High School with Peace's brother, Drew. It's against protocol, but who you know carries a lot of weight with a tiny police force. Officer Kyle allows Peace and me onto the boat to Boot Island. The water is unusually flat and calm, as if the Saint Helena Sound knows we're in a hurry.

"On a day like this, it should only take about thirty minutes to get out there," Peace says.

We cram onto the bench on the bow of EBPD's one patrol boat. He puts an arm around me, but nothing about it is romantic. We're two worried people seeking comfort from one another. My hair whips into his eyes, but I don't think he blinks once during the ride.

Peace stands as the island comes into view. He guides Kyle around to the channel on the north side, where the toe of the boot long since wore off.

There it is, the brownish beach. Stripy lines of sticks and shell bits mark the tide's daily comings and goings. Old dock pilings—worn to stubs over the years—pigheadedly poke from the water. The abandoned boat rests with *Good Times* barely legible on the side.

"Low tide. We have to hoof it." Kyle throws an anchor. He presents us with a pair of camouflage waders. "I got a couple of pairs, but none will fit you, Ms. Moretz."

"I'll carry you, Lee." Peace's eyes sweep the marsh behind the beach.

That's how I end up clinging to Peace's back again as he bears me over the muck like my knight in shining camo, twenty years after "The Time LeeLee Stranded Peace in the Pluff Mud up to His Butt Crack." No Ginny watches him pick his way through the oyster shells. I pray she's somewhere just out of sight.

I rest my chin on Peace's shoulder. The sound of his quiet breathing comforts me. He delivered me safely onto that beach before. Even during his darkest days, he kept Ginny alive for years. Without him, she would have run afoul of some tragedy long before Chad Dooley's reemergence or Rollo's descent into obsession-fueled lunacy.

We will find her together and convey her back across the wasteland of disintegrating vegetation. Peace won't have to walk so far on the return trip. Kyle will move the boat closer to shore when the tide comes in. Eventually, the tide always comes in.

This time, I let Peace get all the way to dry land. He sets me gently on my feet. We wait for Kyle and his colleague, a young Black guy who looks like he's been on the job for about a month. Kyle talks softly to him as they approach.

"Prepare for the worst, Marcus," he says. "This is one of the craziest things I've seen in my days on this force. If it's bad, you still got to keep calm."

"Will do." Marcus has a crowbar in one hand for prying open the doors or windows.

Kyle claps him on the shoulder and turns to us, his face grim. "Y'all sure you don't want us to go up to the cabin first?"

"I'm sure," Peace says. "I need to be there."

"Me too," I say.

"All right." Kyle gestures at the trees. "Y'all lead the way."

We walk along the sandy path toward the woods. Mosquitos swarm from the marsh grass. Kyle whips some bug spray from his fanny pack. I cough and wave away the harsh scent of OFF! Deep Woods.

"Sorry," Kyle says. "Natural stuff won't do the job with these vampires. We need chemical garlic."

Young Marcus jumps when a spooked heron silently takes off in front of us. The gangly bird glides over the dune and resettles itself at the edge of the beach. It stretches its long neck in our direction, as if to blow raspberries at us for disturbing its solitude.

We step out of the sand and onto a carpet of pine leaves. Our intrusion annoys a few crows. They're more vocal about it than the stately heron. They yell at us in their croaky grandpa voices from the branches above.

The cabin appears in front of us like the witch's house from "Hansel and Gretel." Kyle and Marcus ease in front of Peace and me. We stop about twenty feet from the porch stairs.

"Miss Blankenship!" Kyle yells. "Virginia Blankenship!"

Nothing but the crows.

"This is the Edisto Beach Police! If you're in there, can you call out to us?"

Still nothing.

Kyle and Marcus lead us closer. We walk up the stairs to the little porch. I grip the railing. Someone has replaced it recently. It isn't as weathered as the rest of the wood. Rollo lied to Peace and Tommy about the condition of the place. He's been keeping busy out here while holding Ginny hostage.

Kyle bangs on the door. "Anyone in there?"

Still nothing. I've never had a panic attack, but I learn a person can recognize one without personal experience. If I were attached to my spin-class heartbeat monitor, my pulse would be rocketing into cardiac arrest territory. My lungs are suddenly too small, while my stomach expands to a gaping hole in my midsection. I start babbling. "Peace. She's not answering—something happened to her. She's dead. I know it. Palmer knew it. Oh my lord. What do we do now?"

"LeeLee?" someone interjects in a soft voice between Kyle's bang-bang-bangs.

"Stop, stop!" I say.

"LeeLee?" There's that voice again.

Peace's eyes widen. "Did you hear that? It sounds like—"

"Peace? Lee?" The speaker is closer to the door now.

"Ginny!" I press my forehead to the door. "Ginny, is that you?"

"Gin! Can you hear us?" Peace hits the door with his fist.

It vibrates against my forehead.

"Lee! LeeLee!" More banging but from the other side of the door. "Peace!"

I shove Kyle and grab the doorknob. I yank and tug. The knocking on the other side continues.

Peace takes my arm. "Let them open it, Lee."

I step aside. Kyle and Marcus whack and jimmy the door for what seems like an hour but in reality is about two minutes. Finally, when Kyle yanks, it flies open.

Ginny stands in the doorway. Her eyes are huge, fragile blue robin's eggs in her thin face. Her hair hangs to the middle of her back. She wears cut-off sweatpants, and a gray sweatshirt clings to her bony shoulders.

My eyes meet hers, and my brain tingles with one of her memories, one of her most beloved recollections.

> *The doorway of Ms. Mullins's tenth-grade history class frames LeeLee. She looks like one of those paintings of the historic people who stare out at the class from the textbooks, unsmiling but knowing and significant.*

In that moment, that's what I think about her. She does not smile, but she knows everything, and she has such meaning in my life.

"Ginny," I say, "honey, you hear me?"

She nods and blinks as if she's trying to keep mosquitos out of her eyes. Her mouth twitches. "Y'all came out for some good times."

She sways on her feet. Peace crosses the threshold and catches her before she falls. I'm a step behind him. She braces against us. She breathes against my bare arm, quick and shallow, as if there isn't enough air in the cabin. We hold her up, the way we've all tried to hold one another up since we were kids, even if sometimes we don't succeed.

PEACE AND I SIT BESIDE Ginny's bed when Cheryl blasts into Ashepoo General Hospital like a mama cow busting through barbed wire to get to her baby.

She follows her own voice down the hall. "Where's my girl? Where is she?"

A frazzled nurse says, "Ma'am, she's asleep—"

"Show me her face! I haven't seen her face in—"

Peace walks to the bedroom door. He intercepts Cheryl, and whatever he says makes her shut up. She peeks around the doorframe. Her face crumples as she sees Ginny lying in the bed with an IV in her arm. She tiptoes into the room. Peace follows her. He squeezes her shoulder, and she turns to him and cries in his arms, as if she never accused him of murdering Ginny.

He pats her back. "She's gonna be fine, Cheryl."

"Are you sure? She looks so pale and thin..."

I stand. "From what they can tell, that's the worst of it. She's underweight, and she hasn't seen much sun. But she told us she hasn't had a drink or a pill or smoked anything but cigarettes since Rollo took her out there. She even quit the cigarettes, like, six months ago. So, weirdly, she's healthier than she was before this all started."

Cheryl wipes her face and nods. "You saw her, didn't you?" She holds a hand to my cheek. "Out there."

I nod. "I did."

She hugs me. "Thank you, sweet LeeLee. I knew you'd find her." She looks at Peace. "Son, I'm sorry for thinking—"

He holds up a hand. "It's forgiven. She's here now. Mystery solved."

"One mystery lingers," I say. "The identity of LoveGinnyB."

"That doesn't really matter now," Cheryl says.

"I'd still like to know," I say. "Maybe Rollo sent it himself. Maybe it *was* Drew."

"I asked Drew during our day of reckoning," Peace says. "He denied it."

"Ehhhh. Let's just let it go. Whoever wrote it just wanted justice for her," Cheryl says.

"I know, but—" I pause. "How do you know the email said that?"

Cheryl pales. "Ah... Palmer forwarded it to me—"

"Cheryl," I say as it all makes sense. "*Cheryl.* Seriously?"

"Okay, okay! I'm sorry. I wrote the damn emails."

"You said you thought it was Drew!"

"I know. So awful of me. Riding on the coattails of a family squabble." She grabs Peace's arm. "I'm so sorry, Peace. But no one would *listen* to me. Not the damn police or any newspaper reporters or anyone. Everyone said I was nuts. I had to call in reinforcements. If I got LeeLee riled up, I *knew* she'd figure out what happened to Ginny."

"I'm not sure what to say," Peace says.

The nurse sticks her head into the room. "Only two visitors allowed."

"We'll go," I say. "You need some time with her."

"I'm so sorry," Cheryl whispers. She sits, takes Ginny's hand, and speaks to her softly.

Ginny shifts in her sleep, but she doesn't wake. She looks so childlike yet so much older than my memories.

Peace steers me into the hallway. "Well, damn. Last mystery solved."

"I cannot believe Cheryl would do that to you," I say.

"It worked, didn't it? You and the other girls got all fired up. She got her daughter back."

"I suppose, but—"

"I'm not worried about Cheryl or her alter egos right now. You want to go somewhere and talk?" he asks. "My truck?"

"How many important conversations have we had in trucks over the years?"

"I guess it's time for another one."

WE WALK INTO THE PARKING lot. He opens the door for me, and I climb into the passenger seat. He sits behind the wheel and puts the key in the ignition then rolls down the windows. The breeze feels nice, even if it carries the smell of cooking grease from the Waffle House across the street.

"So, what now?" he asks.

"We've been asking that a lot the past month."

"Has it only been a month since I showed up unannounced at your office?"

"Yeah. It seems like you've been back forever," I say.

"When we've known each other as long as we have, it doesn't take much to pick up where we left off."

"I feel like we'll always pick right back up. Now, we have to decide where we go from here."

He leans back against the headrest. "I thought I knew. But maybe I don't."

"Me being a storyteller, a navigator, my readings, it changes things."

"I don't want it to, Lee. But I have to be honest. It does."

"I could see it in your face as soon as I told you. Can you explain why?" I prop my feet on the worn dashboard, like I used to when we drove around the Burg, and wait for his reply. It takes a while. I don't read anything from him, but I sense he's sorting through painful memories and complicated thoughts.

"I've spent my whole life doing what people wanted me to do," he finally says. "Or failing at what they wanted me to do then feeling guilty and ashamed about it. Thinking back, I loved Ginny, but her readings... they always freaked me out. I accepted them because they were part of her. But as time went on, I saw what it did to her. She was as addicted to the thrill she got from them as she was anything else."

"I'm not like—"

"You're not like her. I know. And I might be able to handle visions of the future. Even the past—though it's weird when someone knows your most personal memories. But the reading my thoughts... I don't think I can go there again. Ginny was all-consuming. She took over my life those last few years we were together. I couldn't breathe. She was literally inside my head."

"But you didn't leave her," I say.

"No. I wanted to leave for years, even if I still cared about her. But I wasn't strong enough to do it the right way because of the guilt. So I left her with Chad, when I should have ended it years before. I took the easy way out. Rollo was right about the shittiness of that play. I gotta live with how I handled it, but I also gotta look at why I got to that point in the first place."

I watch diners enter and leave the Waffle House, a simple place, where most people's thoughts are limited to smothered, covered, or diced. I turn back to Peace and our much more complicated ruminations. "You're saying you don't want to be with me because I'll hear your thoughts sometimes."

"You will, won't you?" he asks in that calm, gentle voice I know so well.

"Yes. Even when I tried to shut it down, it still happened sometimes."

"You don't want to shut it down anymore, right?"

"No. I have to be who I am."

"You *should* be who you are. I have no doubt you'll manage it much better than Ginny did. We always used to talk about Ginny being so tough. She is, in her way, but you're *strong*, Lee. There's a difference."

"You should be true to yourself and what you want too."

"I lost myself the past thirteen years. I don't want to lose myself in something else again." He gives me a weak smile. "Besides, you said Clay doesn't mind, right?"

"He took it really well, but he might change his mind."

"I don't think he will. You have children and a life together." His eyes shine. "If I hadn't ruined everything all those years ago—if I were in his shoes—I would have the same reaction."

A tear tracks down my face, but I smile back at him. "Another life, right?"

"Yeah. It would have been a good one. I'll always have regrets."

"I don't know if I do, honestly. I probably always wanted some closure after how things ended with you and me, but back then, it would have been forced. Closure comes in due time, of its own volition." I look out the window again. "It would have been a good life, but I have a good life now. It's the life I fantasized about all those years ago, my family and my career, my home in a city I love. I just have it with someone else."

I know my words sting, but he doesn't challenge them.

"I *do* love Clay." That quiet revelation soothes my heart. "I never stopped loving him—even after he cheated and even after you came back. I was hurt, and now I've hurt him. But maybe everything had to happen. Him cheating. You showing up again. Clay recognized all that. It's why he told me to do what I had to do to figure things out. So we could really look at what's wrong with us and try to fix it." I exhale. "A lot of it is on me. I should have told him years ago, but I was afraid. It's awful that I let things get so bad."

"Don't be so hard on yourself. Whatever happened between you and Clay, it's certainly not all your fault."

"But I don't feel like it's all his fault either."

"Shades of gray, remember? If enough time passes, sometimes, you're the good guy. Sometimes, you're the bad. It's like... Think about my parents' house. The mud is there all the time, right? Sometimes, it's exposed. Sometimes, it's covered up."

"'And the tide rises, and the tide falls.'"

"Is that Walt Whitman?"

"No. Longfellow," I say. "I feel sort of sad, but I also feel better than I have in months. So there are my shades of gray."

"You going to talk to Clay?"

"Yes. If he'll try, I'll try—and I mean really try. I was going through the motions before."

"I'm sure he'll be willing. You're amazing." He tucks my hair behind my ear, then he taps the end of my nose. The nose he's always loved, even though I hate it. "You always have been. He knows that. You deserve that life and all the happiness y'all can create together."

"You deserve happiness, too, P." I realize I desperately want that for him, no matter who he finds it with. "Now that things are tied up, I'm sure you'll be able to find it."

"That a reading?" This time his smile is real.

"Nope. Just a good old-fashioned hunch." I pat his arm like we're a couple of geriatrics heading out for a Sunday drive.

"Ginny had those hunches sometimes."

"Was she right?" I ask.

"Usually."

"I'll be right about this too."

THAT NIGHT, I ASK CLAY to meet me on the second-floor piazza after the kids go to bed. I'm already up there when he walks across the yard from the FROG in the moonlight. He's Romeo in SpongeBob pajamas; I'm Juliet in yoga pants. I text him, asking if he wants a glass of wine, but he refuses in favor of water. I sit on one rocking chair and leave the other for him. Two glasses of ice water sweat on the table between the rockers, as if they, too, feel the tension.

He sits beside me and starts rocking. I resist the urge to remind him that we repainted the floor and his exuberant rocking will carve streaks in the wooden planks.

His thoughts buzz around my head like no-see-ums. *Just get through this. She's gonna tell me it's over. Just get through it...*

As soon as I can catch his hand, I grab it. "Thank you for being patient with me—"

"Please say it, Lee. If you want me to move out—"

"No. I don't want a divorce."

"You don't?" His mouth behind his beard twists into a line of confusion.

"No."

"No, meaning yes?" Clay is such a lawyer. Always in a tizzy about semantics. "Or no meaning—"

"Clay. I want to stay married. I love you. We'll work it out, if you still want to."

"Oh, Jesus." He takes my face in both hands and kisses me.

At first, I'm too surprised to respond, but his hands are in my hair, and his mouth presses against mine. For the first time in over a year, I relax into his kiss. It feels good. Right. Wholly appropriate.

I remember what Palmer said—different but familiar, exciting but safe.

After everything I've been struggling with lately—confusion, sadness, guilt, nostalgia, fear—I finally let my husband welcome me back into the safety of his embrace. We have much work ahead, but it's a relief to simply kiss him with none of the complications that came with my other recent kissing partner.

He rests his forehead on mine. "Thank you, baby. For forgiving me."

"Do *you* forgive *me*? For the past few weeks?"

He looks me in the eye, and I'm shocked I ever forgot how handsome he is, his pale eyes and wavy hair the color of sand drying as the tide goes out, his close-cropped beard and the freckles across his nose. His shoulders are broad enough to block any monsters that might stand behind him, waiting to pounce on me.

"It was hard," he says. "I thought I would lose you. But I already told you. I believe in us, that we can walk through the mud and come out cleaner and shinier than ever."

"I told the truth about my readings, the future, the past, sometimes people's worst memories—even their thoughts." I search those powder-blue eyes. "You're okay with that?"

"Under one condition. You don't hide it from me or try to squash it on my account." He rubs his chin. "Hmmm... let me tell *you* a story, Miss Storyteller."

"Frankly, it's nice to listen to a story that originates in someone else's mouth and not via the narrator in my head."

"Once upon a time, there was a young man of twenty-two who went off to law school, intent on following in his dad's footsteps but also being a better husband and father. On the first day of Con Law, he met this ass-kicking, smart, compassionate, beautiful woman."

I bite my lip. "That's so sweet—"

"No, no. I'm not nearly done. He convinced her to marry him. They had three babies in four years and somehow survived the sleep deprivation. He followed in his dad's footsteps, all right—managing partner, long hours, some slipups in the husband department."

I push his hair back from his forehead and run a finger down his cheek.

"His wife is the real star of the show. She does it *all*, man—holds the hands of rich assholes through their divorces, helps domestic violence victims. She's the goddess of homework and potty training and signing up for soccer and managing ear infections. She gets up at the crack of dawn and works out! She helps her workaholic husband with his cases and pushes him to hit the gym. She told him she's making him get a colonoscopy when he turns forty-five."

I smile. "You're not dying on me if I can help it."

"And she's so sexy, he sometimes gets a hard-on watching her blow-dry her hair."

My smile becomes a grin. "Clay! You do not."

"I swear I do. But guess what else she is? She's a storyteller *and* a navigator. She takes it all in, and she doles it out, and she cuts her way through rough waters. She's literally got otherworldly talents. Who wouldn't want to be married to possibly the most special woman in the world?"

My lip trembles, but I manage to say, "Just about the best story I've ever heard."

"Promise me you won't hide your light."

"I won't. I wish I'd told you years ago. I *really* wish I hadn't hidden it from my mom."

"You were trying to protect her."

"I was, but now I can look at it objectively. I'd be upset if one of our kids kept something so important from me. It's not the child's job to protect the parent. Mama would have supported me, and I didn't give her the chance. On top of that, I sent myself down a long, lonely road."

"Aloofness Highway?"

I nod. I wish I didn't have to drag him along in my search for an exit off that highway. "On that note, you said you wanted to be close to me..."

"Can't get much closer than in my head." Clay taps his temple.

"I'll always tell you if I read something. I promise."

He squints, and his nose crinkles. "You hear anything now?"

"Nope. All quiet."

"What I'm thinking at this moment will remain a mystery. We gotta keep some things mysterious. Isn't that what they say?"

"I've had enough mysteries for a long time. No more convoluted plotlines for me."

"Then I'll get straight to the point. How about we get in bed and fall asleep with my arms around you?" He runs a gentle hand down my arm. "If you're ready for that. No pressure."

"That sounds nice, actually." On a whim, I take one of his hands and kiss it.

He looks at the back of his hand like I sprinkled fairy dust on it then smiles up at me. "Meet me between the sheets. I'll retrieve my toothbrush from the FROG."

I beat Clay to bed. Memories—regular recollections of my life—come to me as I wait for him. In that terrifying first Constitutional Law class, my classmates all seemed breezily confident, and many had attorney parents and grandparents. G. Clayton Moretz, Jr., sat beside me, courtesy of alphabetical order. He smiled and introduced himself as *just Clay*. His blue eyes and square chin mesmerized me.

Just Clay volunteered to stand and summarize the case we were assigned to read, *Marbury v. Madison*. Our professor eviscerated him, but he took it without blushing, mumbling, or getting defensive.

"She made some good points," he said as he sat beside me again and started taking notes—as if he weren't the first person in our law school class to speak and the first person to be taken down a notch.

He's always that way—brave, outspoken, and unflappable—whether in a mock trial, in a real courtroom, or at the

Thanksgiving dinner table, challenging his cocksure father's antiquated opinions about the infallibility of American justice.

He loves me for all the reasons I want to be loved. He loves my intensity and my opinions. He supports my obsession with words on paper, even when it leads to me venting frustration over my incomplete novels and lack of inspiration. He loves me on days when I'm giggling and adventurous and on days when my aloofness morphs into moodiness. Hell, he told me he initially loved me *for* my aloofness, though I understand why that trait eventually got old.

Clay loves me in the ways Peace tried to love me, but because of his own demons, he couldn't manage it. He loves me like I always *hoped* Peace would love me. The reality of Clay's love is much deeper than the fantasy of Peace's. I may never have completely released the fantasy if life hadn't splashed my face with the truth. The strengths and weaknesses of both men. The beauty and the ugliness that exists in us all.

As Clay said, he can be a workaholic, but I've always admired his powerful work ethic. His perfectionism is intense, but it drives his success. Sometimes, he talks my ear off when I'm exhausted and want to watch TV, but his curiosity and voracious need for information have taught me plenty, from Wikipedia to the latest updates from the South Carolina Supreme Court. He latches onto things and won't let them go, like his fixation with waterfront lots. It sometimes drives me batshit, but his tenacity makes him who he is. How could I resent him for the things I also love? Shades of gray, I suppose.

I hear him checking on the boys. Hands down, he's the loving, patient, playful father I never had. He makes the most of every minute with his children. His family means everything to him. Me, the boys, our home. He made mistakes, but so have I.

He tiptoes into our room and gently pulls back the sheets.

"I'm awake." I roll over to face him.

Before he can get comfortable in the typical big-spoon-little-spoon position, I wrap my arms around him and rest my head on his chest. His heart beats steadily below my ear.

He squeezes me. "I think I'll sleep tonight. No Wiki-wormhole for me."

"You sure? Still a lot to read about the mass extinctions of North America."

"Nah. I just want to fall asleep with my wife."

He falls asleep before me. His deep breathing steadies, in and out like the tides that have been front and center in my mind lately. I'm not far behind him. As I drift off, I think about Ginny, asleep in her old bed at Cheryl's house under the oak trees. I hope she sleeps peacefully, with no stories running through her mind—not the future, not the past, just right now in her mama's house with her own thoughts. I hope she dreams, where things make sense but cannot be explained. Sort of like our readings but then again, sort of like life itself.

Chapter 26
Ginny, 2015

The day after I return to my mama's house, Peace comes to check on me. We sit on the front-porch steps. Though he and I have sat here many times, I haven't associated the porch with him in years. It became the place where I drank myself into a stupor while trying to navigate through LeeLee's memories, where she and I screamed at each other before she left for law school, the summer heat, my lukewarm vodka, the blanket draped over my shoulders. I lost my mind that day, and it kept roaming farther and faster over the next decade or so.

Once again, a blanket covers my shoulders but only because I'm so thin and always cold. Peace is dressed more appropriately for a summer morning in the Lowcountry, athletic shorts and a T-shirt from the ACE of Spades. A Yeti tumbler dangles from one hand. Ice clinks inside it whenever he takes a sip.

"You fall off the wagon?" I ask him.

"No. Why?"

"You're wearing a shirt from the only bar in town, and you're drinking out of a Yeti tumbler with ice in it. Bourbon and Coke?"

"Nope. Just Coke. Had dinner with Drew at the ACE last night to talk about Dad. He's got a week or two left. I'm spending as much time with him as I can."

I wince. "Jeez. I'm so sorry. That must be hard."

"It is. He's so frail I can see through him. He was always larger than life, but he's gotten so small now that life is leaving him." He takes a shuddering breath and lets it out slowly, as if the words hurt his throat.

"What will you and Drew do?"

"We'll see when we read Dad's will. Drew is the executor. That's how it should be, since he's been here dealing with everything. He and I are on the same page for once in our lives." He swirls his Coke in his tumbler. "He wants to move into Saltmarsh with his family."

"And you're okay with that? He might not have sent the emails, but he seemed like he had it out for you anyway."

"Drew can be an ass, but I understand why he always resented me. Old Peace pitted his sons against each other, even if he couldn't see what he was doing. With Dad gone, Drew and I can at least *try* to be brothers, not rivals for his approval." A pause and a swig of Coke. "Back in the day, I thought I'd live at Saltmarsh, but that dream is long gone. Drew deserves it after holding down the fort all these years."

"But you'll get something." I clear my throat. "I mean, I don't want to make it about money, but—"

"I know some people think I came back because of the money." He sets down his Yeti. "But I've spent my whole life worrying about what everyone else thinks. I know what's in my heart, and I've made my peace with Dad. He even suggested I pursue my woodworking. Can you believe it?" He wiggles his fingers in front of his face. "He actually encouraged his son to be an artsy-fartsy weirdo."

I smile. "I bet he imagines you chopping down trees like Abe Lincoln."

"Right. Not scavenging wood from dilapidated docks and staining sliding barn doors for"—he puffs out his chest like his father always did—"*those Mount Pleasant yuppies*."

"I think it's a great idea. You have a gift, and it makes you happy. He knows that in his heart."

"I hope so. Anyway, I'll get something. For now, I'm processing a lifetime of loving my father but realizing I always sort of hated him too."

"I know how that feels," I say. "But it was easier for me. My father was the kind of screwed-up parent that's easy to explain. Your dad was in-the-closet dysfunctional."

"Speaking of closeted dysfunctional people, I talked to Kyle with the EBPD. He said the county solicitor will be reaching out to you. They intend to charge Rollo with kidnapping and a bunch of other stuff."

"Is he in jail now?"

"His father paid his bond. He's at his parents' place on house arrest. I feel for them. They don't deserve this crap, not after everything they've done for him his whole life." Peace scowls. "Except for you and LeeLee, we all had pretty cushy lives growing up, but Rollo's parents never stopped spoiling him rotten. That's why he thought he could have you when you didn't want him. No one has ever told him no."

"I don't know, P. I hope the law isn't too hard on him."

"Come on, Ginny. I'm the first to acknowledge no one is all good or all bad. But that doesn't mean Rollo shouldn't face the awful music he composed himself."

"Rollo is messed up. No doubt about it, but you weren't there when he was helping me go through withdrawal. In his weird way, he truly thought he was helping me by keeping me out there. At least early on. Later, it was more about his... obsession... with me."

"I'm all about giving people the benefit of the doubt after everything that's happened in my life. I've destroyed every relationship that meant anything to me. But if I saw Rollo right now, I might strangle him."

"You won't always feel that way," I say. "I don't have your resolve, or strength. That year and a half on Boot... just me, in a cabin, in the woods, on an island, in the sound. No opportunity to run up to the ACE and get a shot when the craving hit me or find a new Chad Dooley to supply me with everything else. It forced me to get it out of my system. Rollo *did* do me a favor."

"And he's *keeping your secret* so far, right? You ready to tell me what it is?"

I consider telling him, but I decide against it. I burdened Peace with my issues for long enough. "Some things you're better off not knowing."

He watches the squirrels arguing in the yard. "Thanks for making me question my rage against him."

"How about my mama? You enraged with her?"

"Nah. Cheryl loves you more than anything in the world. She did what she thought she had to do. No harm ultimately came of it, and here you are on her porch."

"She really is sorry. She'll be relieved you forgive her." My phone dings, and I check my texts. "LeeLee. Checking in on me."

"She'd be over here if she could. She had to get home to her family."

"Are y'all together?" I blurt it without thinking.

He'll probably think I'm accusing him of something shady. Given my past paranoia, it would be a reasonable assumption, but his reply is neither defensive nor annoyed. Instead, his jaw works, and he squeezes out a single syllable. "No."

"Oh. I thought you would be." For the first time ever, the idea doesn't make me feel like punching him.

"She's married," he says.

"This is 2015. People don't stay married."

"We started down that path. It's not going to work." His jaw works overtime. His voice turns guttural. "She told me... about her... *powers*. How she's... you know, like you."

"Really? *Wow.* She never wanted anyone to know."

"She changed her mind. She knows she needs to accept it. It hasn't been good for her to keep it in all these years."

"Wasn't good for me letting it out so much either. Cheryl always thought LeeLee and I needed to find a middle ground."

"Is that what you'll do?"

I nod. "When I was on Boot, I was so completely *alone*. My mind never had so much free space and never will again. I realized I didn't need the rush of having constant readings any more than I needed the rush of a high."

"Sounds like it wasn't so bad."

"Are you kidding? It was hell. No hot showers. Canned food. Nobody but my brain for company and occasionally Rollo, who might kill me. Believe me, I wanted out of there with all my heart. When I finally had a useful reading, I did something about it."

"What do you mean?"

"Rollo told me the posse was getting together a few days before y'all found me. I cried my eyes out thinking about y'all together without me. But then my mental compass went haywire. It wasn't super clear—something that hadn't happened yet. But I saw LeeLee picking through Rollo's black duffel bag. Then the idea hit me."

"You put the lock of hair in his bag?"

"Yes. He brought me some cinnamon because I missed the smell of my mama's cookies. He went out on the porch to smoke a cigarette, and I stuck the plastic bag in his duffel. I had to hide it where Rollo wouldn't notice it, but I knew LeeLee would find it if I told her where it was. So I thought so hard, I almost gave myself an aneurysm. *The pocket in the pocket in the pocket, LeeLee.*"

"That's crazy," he says. "It's like a supernatural chicken and egg. Which came first, you putting it there or her finding it?"

"I only care that it worked. Y'all came for me."

He looks at me with his big blue spaniel's eyes. "I told her I couldn't be with her because of her powers."

"What? *Why?*" A snorting little laugh escapes me. "It's not like you're not used to it."

"*That's* why. You know how hard it was for me when you read my thoughts. When I was a kid, it felt like Old Peace was inside my head. I couldn't escape him. For years, he controlled everything I did down to what I was supposed to think. Then you and me together for all those years, and it got worse and worse with you—" He stops. "I'm not blaming you for everything that went bad between us."

"You're being honest."

"I need my headspace, Gin, if I'm ever going to figure out who I am."

"I hear you. And I understand how toxic our relationship was—"

"Wow. Thanks." He chuckles.

"We were perfect as first loves who should have stayed friends. As adults in a relationship, we brought out the worst in each other. If I could go back in time, I'd tell myself that." After twenty years, I can admit it. "But you and LeeLee were different. Y'all were... *great*."

"We were, but that was then, and this is now. When I saw her again, I thought she must be the reason I came back. But no matter how right it was between me and LeeLee back then, it's not any righter between us now than it is with me and you."

"Have you told her that? You can't break her heart again, Peace." Look at me, encouraging the Peace-LeeLee thing. Wonders never cease.

"She realized it before me. She knows she belongs with her husband and her children. I don't know where I belong yet, but it's not as the stepfather to LeeLee's kids and being the reason her family broke up." He grind-grind-grinds that chiseled jaw. "And she loves Clay. I knew how much she loves him, even if she didn't. I gotta let her go, like I had to let you go."

We sit in silence for a while. A lifted pickup truck roars down the state road, and an Amazon Prime van follows behind it. The neighbor, Old Mrs. Green, clucks along with her chickens as she tosses grain into their coop.

Peace scuffs his flip-flops against the porch stairs. "I sort of understand the weird reading you had on the boat that night at Edisto—at least the part about me—the moon and all that hoodoo shit."

"I remember. Your gravity was strong, but we escaped it eventually."

"I'm sorry if I messed up your life," he says. "Or LeeLee's."

"LeeLee's life isn't nearly as messed up as our lives, and I messed up my life. You helped me along, but I'm the navigator, remember?"

"You are, Gin. But what about the other stuff? You and LeeLee and death and being reborn? That's what really freaked me out."

"I don't know yet," I say. "I've got some time to think, since I'm hanging out here with Mama and her cats. I'll let you know if I figure it out."

Silence stretches again, but it isn't uncomfortable. Peace and I have spent many quiet evenings together.

He looks at his phone. "I should head over to Saltmarsh. Dad's awake in the late morning."

"Okay. Thanks for stopping by."

"Sure. I'm glad you're home, Gin."

"Me too, P."

He stands and walks to his truck. I feel a rush of simple affection for him, just tenderness toward someone I've known my whole life, who saved me in many ways.

He pauses as he opens the door. "Hey, Gin? I had a thought while we were sitting there. I can't explain it right, but... that night on the boat—'We cannot be reborn unless we die.'"

"That was it. Morbid as hell."

"Maybe not. Death isn't always morbid. Maybe life is just a bunch of deaths and rebirths. Think about it."

"Sure, P." I whisper to myself as he backs down the driveway and dust swirls around the truck, "Now that I'm reborn, I will."

Chapter 27
LeeLee, 2016

The girls invite Ginny to every holiday or birthday celebration to make up for the ones she missed. She tells me we don't always have to include her, like she's worried we feel sorry for her. Kooky Aunt Ginny, who was kidnapped and stranded on a deserted island for over a year and now lives with her mama in Asheburg. A bless-her-heart scenario if I ever heard one. She doesn't realize how much we missed her. None of us did until she came home. Now that she's back, I sometimes wonder how I got along without her for so long.

We go out to Clay's parents' house on Wadmalaw for Malachy's fourth birthday. Palmer helped me pull it together. With five kids, she's the guru of birthday planning. She has the decorations for every party theme imaginable. Mal's poolside dinosaur fest includes giant *Tyrannosaurus* floats. Gelsie has a few inflatable flamingos too. The floats jostle around the pool, squeaking as they rub against one another, as if the flamingos are afraid the dinosaurs will eat them.

Thirty kids run around at the height of the action, but it clears out, and only the diehards linger. The remaining children watch a movie on the outside projector under the watchful eyes of a few dads who hover beside Clay's well-stocked Yeti coolers. The four of us retreat to the covered pierhead at the end of the dock for an hour of tranquility. Jess sprawls on the bench swing with her feet up. She peers at us from over her pregnant belly. "I'm so swollen, y'all. I forgot these last two months are pure misery."

"You were willing to pay about twenty grand for that misery." Ginny tightens her red-gold ponytail and happily munches potato chips straight from the bag. A year after her trauma, she's still catching up on her weight, but she's taking yoga classes at Asheburg's new yoga studio, Lowcountry Flow. She might be skinny, but my girl is getting strong again.

"Lucky me," Jess says, "getting knocked up au naturel. With all the money I saved, I can get a tummy tuck and a boob job to put my parts back where they're supposed to be."

"You should wait until you're sure you're done having kids. You don't want to do it twice." As always, Palmer holds one of her lady-staring-off-into-the-distance books. She raises it. "Abigail Willoughby would just tighten her corset."

"You getting in some extra reading when Dean has the kids?" Jess asks.

"Girl, I'm keeping Barnes & Noble in business right now. I can't go anywhere or do anything until we have a settlement."

"Dean still have a PI on you?" Ginny asks.

"He'll track me until the settlement ink is dry. He won't miss the chance to get out of alimony."

"Mediation's coming up this week," I say. "We'll settle it then. Then watch out, Charleston. Palmer Blankenship is out of the cage."

"You think we can settle it?" Palmer asks.

"Almost all our cases settle in mediation or before. But given the size of your estate and five kids, plan on a long day. Bring Abigail Willoughby and company for moral support."

Palmer grimaces. "I don't know how you do it. This process is agony. You deal with people in agony every single day."

"Mediations aren't *that* bad. Better than going to court. Y'all know that still gives me anxiety."

"I've said it a million times, Lee," Palm says. "Write a few bestsellers, and you can kiss mediations goodbye."

"I keep telling you, it's not that easy," I say. "Not many J. K. Rowlings out there. Many are called, but few are chosen."

"Uh-oh." Jess squints down the dock. "I know that shriek. It's Mia getting close to bedtime."

"I should wrap it up too," Palm says. "Though this spot is heavenly. I could sit here all day. It's so nice to be out here, where I don't have to worry about the damn PI following me."

"Hang in there." Ginny does a little shimmy, potato chip bag in one hand, Sprite in the other. "Soon you'll be a free woman! All the single men of Mount Pleasant and beyond better brace themselves."

Palmer laughs. "For what? A single mom with five kids and an angry ex-husband? Not sure I'll be in big demand."

"Have you looked in the mirror lately?" Jess stands. "I haven't, but with this belly, I've got an excuse."

"Tommy will be first in line, cousin," Ginny says with a salute.

"He'll have to get in line with everyone else," Jess adds.

"Y'all are too sweet. But I intend to ease into the dating hot tub. I don't want to burn my ass."

Ginny and I exchange glances. Palmer and Tommy talk sometimes, but Palm remains nonchalant about her feelings for him. We decided that's a good thing. Better for Palmer to see what's out there, and if she decides on Tommy after keeping her options open for a while, so be it. Two forever couples might come out of our old group, but Ginny, Peace, Rollo, and I will not be part of that equation.

Palmer and Jess stand and give kisses all around before walking down the dock. They pass Clay, who holds up his hands and maneuvers around Jess's belly. Jess mock punches him in the stomach.

"Hey, y'all," he says to me and Ginny. He sits beside me on the other bench. "You feeling okay?"

"A little tired," I say.

"LeeLee, tired from a children's event?" Ginny asks. "She's the queen of the bouncy castle. The princess of the piñata. The—"

"Usually." I rest my hand on my tummy, which is a little rounder than usual. "But I got a princess on the way, so I am wiped out this time."

"Whoa, what?" Ginny raises her eyebrows.

"You ready to tell?" Clay asks.

I nod. "Open the bag, and let out the kitty."

"Hot damn! A fourth Moretz?" Ginny jumps up and hugs me and Clay. She tousles his hair.

"Watch the do, Ginny Lou Who." He bestowed a new nickname on her—an original after a lifetime of Gin and G-Love.

"You're still pretty. Don't worry," she says. Ginny and Clay get along like peanut butter and jelly. "You haven't told Palm and Jess yet?"

"Wanted to tell you first," I say. "At thirty-six, I'm apparently a geriatric mother, so we had all the tests. It's definitely a girl."

"Oh, y'all. A sweet little LeeLee-and-Clay combination."

My eyes water. I wave my hands to encourage the words out of my mouth, but they stay stuck. So, instead, I think it. *We're naming her Virginia.*

"Are you serious, Lee?" Ginny asks. "You're naming her Virginia?"

Clay frowns. "How did you—oh. Duh."

I nod. I suck in a little sob, and she flat-out bursts into tears.

"Whoa!" Clay says. "Those are happy tears, I hope? We could name her Bertha after my great-aunt—"

"Happy!" she chokes out.

Clay smiles as he looks between us. "I'll go back up to the house and let y'all cry it out."

Ginny wipes her eyes on a palmetto flag towel that someone hung over the railing.

Clay kisses me and runs a hand over my hair. "Love you, baby." He points at my belly. "And you, too, baby-baby."

"We love you more," I say.

He walks back down the dock.

Ginny reaches across the space between us and squeezes my hand. "Y'all are the cutest family on the planet. Of course, I love Jess and Landon. Now that grumpy-ass Dean is out of the picture, Palmer's whole family has increased in cuteness, but you and Clay and your brood are something else."

"You should have seen us eighteen months ago. The boys were as cute as ever. Me and Clay, not so much."

"But y'all seem so rock-solid now."

"Funny. I think back on those days, when everything seemed so hopeless," I say. "It feels like another life."

"There are a lot of ways to die," Ginny says.

"Whoa. Morbid."

"Ha, *morbiiiiiid*. Rollo said that about you on your first day in Ms. Mullins's class when you quoted Anne Boleyn."

"'She is my death, and I am hers.'"

"Right. That day, I thought you might be talking about me and you. Were you?"

I think back to that first day at Ashepoo High School. I was so nervous, I thought I might pee my pants. I remember Ginny sitting beside me, staring at me from behind the curtain of her gorgeous red-gold hair. "I honestly can't believe I said anything, but it popped into my head and out of my mouth. Maybe I was talking about us, and I didn't know it yet. But we're both still alive and kickin'."

"That's what I mean about a lot of ways to die. We're both here, living a different life. And we both had something to do with each other's... like, resurrection."

"So I'm your death, and you're mine, but we're also part of each other's..."

"Rebirth," she says.

"Yes! Rebirth, girlie."

I hold up one hand, and we high-five. A silly way to salute one another's metaphorical reincarnations but appropriate for our friendship.

"So, how'd you and Clay get to this new and improved life?"

"It took a while. We had some fits and starts, as Cheryl would say. A lot of hard conversations with brutally honest answers. We both had to regain trust."

"You about him cheating at the bar conference and him about you and Peace."

These days, Ginny and I are finally comfortable talking about Peace.

"I think Clay understands that I'm past it," I say. "I don't know if we're ever truly *over* someone who means that much. Those relationships are part of who we are. But I'm *past* it."

"I got past him when I was on Boot," she says. "You heard anything from him?"

"No. I promised Clay I wouldn't be in touch with him. I thought about asking him to make the baby's crib, but I don't think Clay would be down for that."

Ginny nods. Peace's father passed away about two weeks after Ginny came home, and he decided to move back to Boone. He used his inheritance to buy a cottage and started a reclaimed-wood furniture business.

"You talked to him?" I ask.

"No. Weirdly, I don't have the urge to talk to him. Haven't since he left town again. But Jess said he's doing well with his business. Dating a nice local artist. Some vegan meditation chick. Yin and yang and all that whoo-ha."

We both pause, as if trying to determine if either of us is bothered by that news, then I say, "So someone who is the opposite of both my OCD ass and your high-strung ass."

Ginny laughs with me. "Just what he needs."

"What about you? What do you need?"

"Right now, I'm enjoying working on my yin and yang."

"How's it going?"

We've spent hours talking about ways to manage our supernatural powers in a manner that is neither Unhealthily Bottled-Up LeeLee nor Exploding Champagne-Bottle Ginny.

"I feel good these days," she says. "Only getting one set of thoughts at a time, so it's less confusing. A few readings a week. Mostly the past but not too traumatizing. You?"

"Same. Though I had a reading of the future where a little girl named Virginia became president of the United States."

"Seriously?"

"No," I say. "But with that name and her Aunt Ginny's influence, she won't be afraid to shoot for it."

"I'm so sorry I called you a coward all those years ago. You're one of the bravest people I've ever met."

"So are you! Surviving out there on that island alone."

"I wasn't a total wilderness woman. Rollo brought me food and cases of Sprite and Coke. And cigarettes, until I quit."

"You heard anything about him through the Burg-vine?" I ask.

"Not much. He's in jail, and for whatever reason, he's keeping my secret. That's the most important thing."

I know about Ginny's secret. A reading showed me Chad Dooley's death was no overdose. I told her what I saw, and she didn't deny it. We haven't spoken of it since. Ginny's right. Some details, I don't need to know.

"You think he'll keep it forever?"

"No one can say. In the meantime, I'll keep living. Out on Boot, I made my peace with *that* night. At first, I thought I was trapped out there because I did something terrible. But now, I believe karma ain't that cut-and-dried."

"As Peace said, shades of gray. The tide goes in, and the tide goes out."

"Speaking of tides." Ginny points out over the creek. "Has Clay laid off his minimum-five-foot-mean-low-water kick?"

"For now. With the baby coming, I might have to cut back on my work hours. We need to do the renovation at Council Street. He's accepted that coming out here to visit his parents is a good option."

"It's a great option." Her eyes scan the marsh. "Y'all are damn lucky."

"From Charleston to the Burg, we're all lucky to live in the Lowcountry."

"Amen." She chuckles. "Nothing like a decade or so in Panama City and Dirty Myrtle to drive that point home."

"You can come out here anytime you can get away from the bakery. Just bring Gelsie a pie."

"It's nice when your mom's the boss," she says. "It's so cliché. Small-town girl comes home after her dad dies. Her mom uses the life insurance money to buy the local bakery. Now she's working there, making snooder-dooders and decorating cakes."

"And developing quite the YouTube following." I wave my hands in a dramatic flourish. "Ginny B., internet singing sensation!"

"I only have, like, thirty thousand followers, Lee. That's small viral potatoes. But it's a start. And at least my voice is out there in the world."

"Maybe Mr. Right will fall in love with you via viral video. Or he might stroll through the bakery door tomorrow in search of the perfect coconut cake."

She guffaws. "Girl. You clearly haven't been on Tinder in Asheburg."

"Gross." I laugh along with her. "Chad Dooleys abound, I assume. You need a Brock Masterson."

"Who? I don't remember him."

"He's not real, silly. He's a character from one of Palmer's books. A handsome, conveniently single, childless investment banker with a house on Nantucket. Or in your case, at Edisto Beach."

"I'm more likely to get eaten by an alligator than run into a Brock Masterson. But I got enough on my plate. My Prince Charming will show up eventually. But you... talking about those books. Palmer is right. You should write one."

"I've told her a million times. I can't write a story about perfect endings—not the kind of perfect endings people expect, anyway."

"But that's the story, isn't it?"

"What do you mean?"

"Happy endings aren't always what they seem."

I think for a moment. "You don't know how deep the water is until the tide goes out."

"That's the story you should write."

My eyes close, and I inhale until my lungs press against my ribs, the same bones my daughter will soon be kicking. I diffuse life-giving oxygen into my growing child—and my memories, even as I suck up some of Ginny's. "She stands in the doorway of Ms. Mullins's tenth-grade history class..."

"Yup," Ginny says. "That's the one."

"You okay with me telling it?"

"Somebody should."

I nod and open my eyes. The creek beyond the dock has reached ebb tide, the place where everything is briefly in balance before the water decides which way to flow. I have finally found my story.

Acknowledgments

First, I must thank the readers who have followed me on my fantastical adventures. From fairytale kingdoms to haunted houses and from detailed nineteenth century memories to vague twenty-first century premonitions, the enthusiasm for my unique brand of speculative women's stories has allowed me to keep writing what I love without accepting the limitations of narrowly defined genres. I hope you will continue to join me, and I promise to always strive to bring you relatable yet magical novels.

Thank you to Lynn McNamee and everyone at Red Adept Publishing for their feedback and assistance in polishing and producing this book. Thank you to my endlessly supportive family and friends, especially wonderful author friends like the fabulous Kristin Ness, because no one else truly understands this literary passion and the unique heartaches and triumphs that come with it. A shout out to my old friends from Walterboro, South Carolina, whose quirky hometown and unique friendships, as well as their sense of humor and talent for storytelling, inspired the setting of and the relationships in *Mean Low Water*.

I must always mention by name my mother, Dianne Wicklein, as well as my three children, Eliza, Harper, and Cyrus (who aren't really children anymore), as sources of pride and inspiration to keep hammering away at these passion projects.

Finally, I could not do any of this without the love, support, and patience of my husband, Jeff Cluver, who makes my reality magical every day.

About the Author

Stephanie Alexander writes enchanting, fantastical book-club-friendly stories for thoughtful, modern women. Stephanie's work always features strong female protagonists, relatable emotional journeys, and a dash of magic.

Stephanie grew up in the suburbs of Washington, DC. Drawing, writing stories, and harassing her parents for a pony consumed much of her childhood. After earning degrees in Communications and Sociology, she spent several years working at the International Center for Research on Women (ICRW), a think-tank focused on women's health and economic advancement.

Stephanie embraced full-time motherhood after the birth of the first of her three children. Later, as a single working mother, she attended law school and earned her *juris doctor* with honors. Her personal experience rebuilding her life after divorce inspires both her legal work and her fiction.

She currently practices family law in South Carolina. Stephanie and her husband live in South Carolina with their blended family of five children and two miniature dachshunds, Trinket and Tipsy.

Read more at https://stephaniealexanderbooks.com/.

About the Publisher

Dear Reader,

We hope you enjoyed this book. Please consider leaving a review on your favorite book site.

Visit https://RedAdeptPublishing.com to see our entire catalogue.

Check out our app for short stories, articles, and interviews. You'll also be notified of future releases and special sales.

Made in USA - Kendallville, IN
59044_9781958231548
08.16.2024 1405